"See, I knew

His eyes were

but his eyes showed Yolanda that

Maxwell reached over and wiped the tears off her face.

"Please don't cry."

Yolanda grabbed his hand and held it to her cheek.

He looked at her for a long moment. He slowly pulled himself closer.

He's going to kiss me.

She moved in. He reached closer and closer and, right before their lips touched, he stopped.

Yolanda looked into his eyes. She could see the struggle; he didn't want to cross that line.

She closed her eyes. She whispered, "Please."

SIX O'CLOCK

KATRINA SPENCER

Genesis Press, Inc.

INDIGO

An imprint of Genesis Press, Inc.
Publishing Company

Genesis Press, Inc.
P.O. Box 101
Columbus, MS 39703

Copyright © 2009 by Katrina Spencer

ISBN: 13 DIGIT : 978-158571-285-4
ISBN: 10 DIGIT : 1-58571-285-X
Manufactured in the United States of America

First Edition 2009

Visit us at www.genesis-press.com
or call at 1-888-Indigo-1

DEDICATION

This book is dedicated to my wonderful husband, Ronald, and to my loving parents, Kenneth and Norma Lightfoot. You are my circle, my cheese, my everything.

ACKNOWLEDGMENTS

I am truly blessed to come from a family that knows the valuable lesson to show love every day. I want to thank Pop for giving me loads of encouragement to keep writing. (Or as he would say, "Go 'head on Monk."). I want to thank Mama, for listening to me through my tears, for giving me the courage to continue writing, for pushing me past my fears and teaching me that other people's opinions of me do not matter. Thanks Mama. I love you. Thanks Piggi for always listening to me whine, and helping to put steel in my spine. Thanks for reading my book (twice no less!) even though I know you hate to read. You keep my hair bouncy as a jackrabbit and it is always beautiful. You are generous and kind hearted and very much loved. Thanks to Kim for the insight into the writing world and for your support. Keep writing. Thanks to Niki Lightfoot for always being so full of hope, and always telling me that my dreams would come true. Kiss Jordan for me. Thanks to Kimberly Cruz for staying a part of the family. Our 'Little Man' is all grown up! Thank you Willliam Moore for showing us so much love during the rocky years we've shared. Every day will get better and better. Love you Trey, Trey! Thanks to Rhonda Warren for loving me just the way I am. I love you girl and always will. Thanks to Percy Rosemond Jr., for reading my book and giving me constructive criticism. Thanks to Joyce Jenkins for being a friend and for my first writing gig at Forward Times newspaper. You are so strong and just being around you I hope to absorb your strength and positive attitude. Let's keep sharing books! I love you. Thanks to the clients of Behave Hair Salon, but especially Wanda Lane, Tammie Ridges, Tracy Mouton, and Jessica LaBove. I love all of you and hated to leave you but when you gotta go, you gotta go. Thanks to Genesis Press and my editor Deborah Schumaker, who made my road a lot easier.

And now as Vanessa Williams sang once, to '*Save the Best for Last*', my loving husband Ronald and beautiful daughter Isabelle. Ronald, your patience knows no end. You are my best friend; you know me through and through and still stand with me. It is a privilege and blessing to have you as my husband. You are the cheese baby, our love transcends time. Isabelle, you are feisty, funny and fearless. Don't ever change. Mama loves you.

Happy Reading!
Katrina Spencer
Sixoclockbook.com

CHAPTER 1

I'm not gonna wear it today. I don't have any, so I shouldn't have to wear it.

Yolanda stood naked in her bedroom, looking with disgust at her bra. She opened her closet door and looked at her body in the full-length mirror. Nope, nothing had changed; she was as skinny as ever, and her breasts still looked like two angry mosquito bites. Running her hand down her flat stomach, she imagined her hips miraculously spreading, making her look more like a woman. She turned sideways, confirming once again how sad and pathetic her flat butt was. She grabbed it, trying to imagine that it was big and round. But there was precious little to grab—other than skin. Even though she had performed this ritual many times, she still experienced a sense of disappointment.

Sighing, she looked at her bra again. With its pink lace flowers set in white satin it was pretty, beautiful in fact. But she felt vaguely cheated as it didn't do the job it was designed for—lift, support, define. It did nothing but limply rest on her chest. Putting the bra on, Yolanda once again relived the cruel taunts of the boys in junior high, who would run their hands down the girls' backs feeling for a bra strap to snap. But when one of them ran his hands down her back, there was no strap. She was mortified when she learned she was the only girl in her class who wasn't wearing a bra. Yolanda remembered going home and begging her mother to buy her a bra. Her first bra was size 32AA, the same size now. She pulled her white cotton shirt over her head and slipped into her black slacks, cursing her ancestors for sleeping with white women, thus diluting what could have been a thick, curvy body.

"Hey, Precious, baby. You hungry?" Yolanda asked, picking up her cat and rubbing behind her ears until she heard her familiar purr. "Yeah, well I'm hungry. Let's go eat breakfast."

She carried Precious to the kitchen and sat her down gently on the beige laminate kitchen counter. It was a small kitchen, more like an aisle really, but it fit her cozy studio apartment perfectly.

"So what do you want to eat today?" Yolanda asked absently, looking through dozens of cans of cat food in her kitchen cabinet.

Precious stopped licking her paws long enough to look at Yolanda blankly.

"Okay, tuna it is," she said, opening the can. She dumped the food into a red bowl with *Precious* stenciled on the side. She got a fork from the dishwasher and separated the tuna. She slid the bowl to Precious and watched her eat for a minute. She was a prissy little thing: she wouldn't eat if you didn't separate her food, and would not deign to eat on the floor.

She then turned to getting her own breakfast. Everyone seemed to be on one of those low-carb diets and was losing weight. But at five feet, ten inches and 110 pounds, Yolanda was on a mission to gain weight by eating a high-carb diet. She buttered two buttermilk pancakes and placed them in the microwave. She then put two pieces of white bread in the toaster and poured a big bowl of Frosted Flakes and dug in, taking big spoons of it, until the microwave beeped.

She poured a generous amount of maple syrup on her pancakes and spread butter and jelly on her toast.

If I keep eating like this, soon all this food will go to my hips and thighs, maybe even my butt.

She always found it funny when she overheard other women's conversations about food.

"I can't eat that doughnut, girl, it'll go straight to my thighs."

"I know. If I eat another one, my butt is gonna need its own zip code."

Now, there's a problem I wish I had.

CHAPTER 2

"Dee Dee, this is ridiculous! I would never do such a thing!"

Dee Dee Townsend sat back in her leather chair and watched Sheila Hatch cry, her tears turning her honey-glazed skin a dark red. Her eyes were bloodshot and puffy; her nose was running. Dee Dee reached across her desk and slid her a box of Kleenex. *She's a good actress. If I were younger, she would have me fooled.*

"All the evidence before me, Sheila, points to you," Dee Dee said calmly. "Can you give me another reason $10,000 is missing from the account on the exact day and time that you said you used the business card?"

"I told you, Dee Dee, I was getting supplies . . ."

"Ten thousand dollars' worth? Sheila, you know the rules. Anything over $1,000 must be approved by me. Besides, the salon had already received its supplies for the month."

"I know, I know, but I swear I didn't . . ."

"Did you also go to lunch that day, Sheila?"

"Yes, but—"

"You spent over $250 at—" Dee Dee looked down at a brown file on her desk, "Ruth Cris Steakhouse?"

"Oh, that. I can explain that. I took Michael out to lunch to celebrate his promotion. I had left all my credit cards and had to use the business card. I was gonna tell you—"

"When?"

"It slipped my mind. We've been really busy working on our new product line; I forgot to mention it. You can take it out of my next paycheck—"

"That won't be necessary," Dee Dee interrupted, closing the file. "Because of your long service and dedication to Behave Hair Salon, I'm going to give you until 5:00 this evening to remove all your things from the premises."

"What!" Sheila shrieked.

"Everything in your office belongs to you, except the computer and furniture. As stated in your contract all business files must remain, as they are property of the salon. Do you understand, Sheila?"

"No, Dee Dee, I don't understand. What's going on here? Fifteen years! I've been working here fifteen years and you're just gonna fire me? You can't just fire me like this!" Sheila pleaded. "I know all this looks bad, but I didn't do this! I've counted out over $100,000 in your hand! Why would I steal from you? I love you like a mother. Why would I bite the hand that feeds me?"

"I love you, too," Dee Dee said. Her voice was flat and even, and her brown eyes became cold and hard. "That's why I'm not pressing charges. But if you're on this property one minute after 5:00, you're going to jail. Is that understood?"

Sheila shook her head.

"Who is gonna replace me?"

"Theresa will step in as creative director temporarily, until I can find a suitable replacement."

"Theresa? Theresa McArthur? Anybody but her! She's probably the one behind all this mess! She has wanted my job since day one! Dee Dee, please, just give me some time; I'll prove she set me up—"

"No, Sheila, my decision is final. I can't keep overlooking this. In November, $2,000 was missing; you said you didn't know what happened. In January, $4,600 was missing; you said you would look into it. Each time your card had been used. You're the only one in the salon whose card has an unlimited amount on it. As much as I love you, Sheila, I can't keep turning a blind eye to this; it has been happening too long. Sheila, if you needed money, why didn't you just ask me?"

"Because I didn't need any money! I told you—"

Dee Dee raised her hand, motioning for Sheila to stop.

"You have to leave."

Sheila stood up, fresh tears streaming down her face.

"I'm sorry I let you down, Dee Dee," she said, walking out of Dee Dee's office for the last time.

Dee Dee watched as Sheila closed her office door, finalizing the decision she had made.

I'm sorry, too.

CHAPTER 3

Yolanda locked the door to her apartment and felt Houston's June heat slap her in the face. She hated that about Houston: the heat and awful humidity. Working in the laundromat in a hot Southern prison couldn't possibly be hotter, she thought.

Some of her neighbors were walking around in typical Houston summer uniforms: shorts, tank tops, sundresses, anything that was cool and let in any whiff of wind. *I wouldn't be caught dead in any of that stuff.*

She pulled her Camry out of her complex and whizzed into Houston traffic, begging it to not be too congested. She saw a lady jogging in a tank top and bicycle shorts, her iPod no doubt distracting her enough to endure the unbearable heat. Yolanda suspected everyone thought she was crazy by not conforming to Houston's dress code in the summer, but she couldn't bear it. She always, always wore pants or jeans and long sleeves on the hottest of days. She would be seen wearing a sweater or tunic—anything to cover her nonexistent butt.

Yes, sometimes she would almost suffocate from the heat, but she pressed on, convincing everyone that she wasn't hot, that the sweat on her forehead came from overexerting herself in some way. One of her teachers in high school had speculated that someone in her family was physically abusing her, and that she was using her long sleeves to hide bruises.

"Yolanda, you know you can always talk to me if anything is happening at home? You don't always have to wear those clothes."

"What do you mean, Mrs. Henry?"

"Don't you think it's a little odd to be wearing a turtleneck in May, especially considering how warm it is outside? Now, according to our guidelines, I have to investigate any signs of abuse—"

"Abuse? You think someone has been—abusing me?"

"Yolanda, these things are never easy to discuss, but as long as I've been teaching at this school, I've never seen you dressed—how can I say this?—appropriately. Even your gym teacher says that you don't dress in front of the other girls, that you always request to go to a private restroom stall to change into your gym clothes. That definitely sounds like a girl who is afraid to show her body due to bruises." She lowered her head and looked around the room, although class was over and they were alone. "Now what we need to do—"

"We're not gonna do anything! This is crazy! I'm not getting abused!" Yolanda blurted, shoving up the sleeves to her sweater to prove it.

"You see? No bruises."

"I thought . . . I don't understand . . . Why do you dress like that if you aren't trying to hide something?"

"Oh, I am hiding, trying to hide this beanpole figure that I was cursed with. Oh, and I change my clothes in the stall because all the girls in gym love to tell me how much I resemble the crackheads in their neighborhoods. The nicknames go on and on, so it is just easier to not give them any ammunition, okay?"

A horn blasting in the distance roused Yolanda from her reverie. She made a quick right turn on Post Oak Boulevard and followed the traffic until she made another right into the driveway of Behave Hair Salon and Spa.

She couldn't believe how fortunate she was to be working at the most upscale and prestigious salon in Houston. The Galleria was the Rodeo Drive of Houston. It was where the rich stayed rich and where the poor watched the rich get richer. She followed the circular drive, glancing up at the three-story salon. It looked like a villa in the south of France, with its rose- and caramel-glazed walls and high arched windows that were so wide that traffic could see inside its walls. The grounds were filled with antique statues of beautiful women looking both graceful and superior, the essence of the image that Behave projected.

She passed the valet stand and parked on the first floor of the parking garage directly adjacent to the salon. You had to be one of two things to get valet parking: a client or a manager. Yolanda was neither; so she parked and walked to the walkway connecting the salon to the garage.

She entered a narrow hallway that led her directly to the styling area. Soft classical jazz tickled her ears and got her in the frame of mind to work. Forty styling stations were lined up neatly, all facing floor-length, gold-leafed mirrors. The Louis XIV-styled chairs were upholstered in soft ivory suede and had gold-inlaid bases. The reception area of the salon was just as luxurious with its wide club chairs upholstered in fine raw silk. Oriental rugs Dee Dee had personally chosen during her many travels covered the marble floors. Everything had been painstakingly designed to provide the ultimate in comfort for Behave clients. From the salon and spa on the first floor, to the café, daycare, and small gym on the second floor, all the pampering needs of the clients were met within these walls. The third floor housed the private offices of the management staff. Yolanda liked to come to work early sometimes and imagine herself up there in her own office. She walked to her styling station and was surprised to see her best friend, Natalie, setting up her station.

She never gets here before me.

"Girl, what are you doing here thirty-five minutes early?"

"I got dropped off. My dad was having car trouble and had to borrow my car. So here I am, missing out on some much-needed sleep, I might add," Natalie said, laughing.

This week, Natalie Morrison's jet-black, shoulder-length weave was styled in a bouncy, feathered flip. Natalie changed her hair every week, thanks to her vast collection of weaves and wigs. In a flash, her hair could be short and sassy, be swept up into an elegant updo, or be long and silky straight. Her black wrap shirt was typically Natalie and was fitted too tightly around her big frame. Everything about Natalie was big. Yolanda knew that she was well over 250 pounds, but the way she carried herself, her weight was never an issue. Everyone in her family was overweight; in her house, you got *extra* dessert just for cleaning your plate at dinner. Natalie's mother called her glamorous and beautiful every day, and now Natalie had the confidence of a supermodel.

"Girl, something is going on," Natalie said, her eyes wide with nervous excitement.

"What is it?" Yolanda asked, looking around the salon to see if she could see any changes. Other stylists were milling around and talking before the work-day started.

"Everything looks fine to me. It's probably just you."

"No, no, something is wrong; everyone is acting weird. I'm gonna go ask Karen to see if she knows what's up."

"Okay, wait for me. I want to put my purse up—"

"That can wait! I wanna know what's wrong," Natalie said, pulling on Yolanda's arm.

"Now let's play it cool. We don't want to act like we're being nosy. We have to be slick 'cause Karen ain't gonna tell us a thing if she suspects something."

"Why don't we wait for the other receptionist, Michelle, to get here? Everyone knows she can't hold water," Yolanda said.

"I know, but I can't wait, so we're gonna ask Karen."

They walked up to the massive horseshoe-shaped oak reception desk. A master carver had carved BEHAVE HAIR SALON into the front of the desk. The craftsmanship was excellent and reminded Yolanda of something one would see in a fine home. They waited patiently for

Karen to finish talking on the phone. Her bronze skin and thick, wavy hair spoke of her Puerto Rican heritage. Her hands flew across the keyboard as she typed in client information for an appointment.

"So your appointment, Pamela, will be with Misty at 1:00 Friday afternoon. Just give us a call if you need to reschedule or will be running late. Have a nice day and we'll see you Friday," Karen said.

Without looking up, she asked, "So, ladies, what can I help you with?"

"Well, um, Sheila left a note on my station that she wanted to see me this morning. I was wondering if you could give her a buzz and see if it was okay if I go into her office," Natalie said.

Karen looked up. "That's strange; she usually gives me her schedule so I'll know about any meetings, and I didn't see your name anywhere on it."

"Well, that's because it isn't actually a meeting," Natalie said, pausing for the right word.

"It's more like, um, a gathering!" Yolanda added, proud of herself for finding the right word. She hated lying and she had never been good at it, so most of the time she just told the truth.

"Is this 'gathering' for the both of you?" Karen asked suspiciously.

"Yes," Yolanda said.

"No," Natalie said at the same time.

Karen shook her head. "Nice try, ladies. Look, why don't you try talking to Sheila later today? She is usually not that busy Tuesday afternoons."

Natalie sighed. "Thanks, anyway, Karen." They walked away, defeated.

"I told you not to say anything! Every time you lie, you mess everything up. You weren't supposed to open your mouth," Natalie complained.

"I'm sorry," Yolanda said, following Natalie back to the styling area.

"I was just trying to help," she added, setting her purse and bag down on her styling chair.

"I know, I know. I just wanted the scoop before it got crowded in here. Anyway, girl, what did you do yesterday? I called you all day."

"I was at my parents' house. Gina was showing off pictures of the baby, and my dad made it mandatory that I be there."

"Girl, that sister of yours . . . How old is the baby now?"

"Eight months. And she is so *precious!*" Yolanda added in a syrupy baby voice.

"Your dad still picking on you?"

"Does a dog have fleas?"

Natalie laughed.

"Don't worry, girl. He'll slack up."

"When? When I get a man and get married? Which we both know will never happen."

"Girl, where is your rubber band? You need to pop that thing about twenty times with all that negative thinking."

Yolanda looked through her purse for her stash of multicolored rubber bands, and picked a yellow one, hoping the bright color would lift her sour mood. Natalie had been making her wear a rubber band on her wrist everyday. Each time she thought a negative thought, she would pop it, hoping the sting would change her thinking pattern. She had been wearing them for a week and hadn't noticed a difference.

"Hey, there goes Maxwell. Maybe he's trying to get information," Natalie said.

Yolanda turned her head, trying to get a quick look at him. Maxwell Alexander was chatting with Karen at the front of the styling area. He was easily over six feet, five inches with a muscular body that screamed of early mornings spent at the gym. His smooth chocolate skin stood out against his tailored white shirt, peeking from under his black uniform blazer. All the staff members wore blazers with Behave's logo embroidered in gold on the front pocket. She never knew a man who wore the same thing every day but still looked so fresh and different. Just then, he laughed about something Karen said, and his beautiful white teeth shone like brilliant pearls against dark velvet. His dark brown eyes twinkled with amusement as he looked up in Yolanda's direction.

Yolanda turned away, embarrassed for having stared too hard.

"You think upstairs is as good as everybody says it is?" Yolanda asked.

Because the offices were located upstairs and stylists weren't invited up there unless they were being reprimanded or promoted, the whole third floor was nicknamed *upstairs*. To the stylists everything was better if you could just get *upstairs*. Wearing that jacket with the logo on the pocket instantly made you *somebody*. You were hot stuff if you could handle being promoted upstairs.

"Better. Do you know what they get paid up there? It's probably double what we get paid."

Yolanda had dreamed of working at Behave since she graduated from high school with her cosmetology license. Back then, they were located a few miles away from their current location, but Yolanda still knew that this was the place she would work. *You belong there*, she would say as she drove by. And now, after six years of hard work, here she was—a master stylist, no less. But know she felt greedy for wanting more. After six years of styling hair, she was feeling bored and wanted to try her hand at the business side of the salon. Her chances of being promoted were slim to none at best. There were only two reasons people left *upstairs*—death, or getting fired. Dee Dee was a hard woman to work for but her retention level was extremely high, and everyone *upstairs* was heard to be extremely satisfied with their cushy jobs.

Yolanda looked at Maxwell again. *Most of the women down here gush over him like a bunch of baboons. If I ever do get the chance to be promoted it will be for me, just for me.*

Natalie caught her staring. "I know what you're thinking. Just say something to him," Natalie said, nudging Yolanda's arm.

"Girl, you must be crazy. Besides, I wasn't looking at him."

Natalie threw her a look. "Well, I was looking at him, but not about what you think," Yolanda added.

"Fine. If you won't go to him, I'll just bring him over to you," Natalie said, walking over toward Maxwell.

"Noooo! Don't!" Yolanda cried, grabbing Natalie's arm. Natalie wriggled her arm free and went up to the front where Maxwell was.

Okay what do I do? I could just go hide in the break room, or the chemical room . . .

She chanced a look over and saw Karen talking on the telephone. Natalie was talking to Maxwell and pointing in her direction.

He's looking! I can't hide; I'll look like an idiot. Just play it cool. If he walks up, just smile and try to sound smart.

Just then, Yolanda saw Sheila Hatch rush over to Maxwell, say something to him and then walk out the front entrance of the salon. Maxwell followed her, his steps quick and purposeful.

Natalie walked back to Yolanda, who could tell by her friend's expression that something was very wrong.

"What happened?" she asked.

"Sheila got fired!"

CHAPTER 4

"She got fired!" Yolanda screeched. "She's been working here *forever*! What happened?"

"I don't know. Man, fifteen years, ten of those being creative director. I wonder what she did to throw it all away."

"I know! She looked so happy here. It must have been something pretty bad for Dee Dee to fire her. She treated her like a daughter."

"Yeah, even better than her own daughter, Jackie. Let somebody give me a company car and a six-figure salary! Dee Dee could be talking about my mama and slapping me in the face every day at lunch, and I still would be the biggest brown-noser. I gotta find out what happened!" Natalie exclaimed.

"Find out girl! And then tell—"

"I know, I know. You'll be the first to know. Look, I gotta stop running my mouth. I see my 9:00 up there, and I have to get my mind together to deal with all her whining," Natalie said, heading to the rear of the salon.

"They didn't buzz you yet; you still have some time left." All the stylists had intercoms connected to their stations and in different areas of the salon and spa to let them know their client had arrived.

"No, we'll talk later."

"Hey, wait! Tell me what Maxwell said."

Natalie gave her a look. *Not now*, she mouthed.

"C'mon, tell me what he said! Did Maxwell tell you anything good?" Yolanda said loudly.

"I don't know. Why don't you ask me and I'll tell you if it was good or not," a deep voice said behind her.

Yolanda stiffened, and she saw Natalie laughing as she slipped behind the door to the supply room. Yolanda took a deep breath and turned around.

"Hi, Maxwell." *This is your chance, say something clever.*

"You look really . . ." *Handsome?* She noticed fine prickles of sweat on Maxwell's nose. "You look really moist." *Moist? What was I thinking?*

Maxwell quirked his eyebrows.

"Thank you, I think," he said, a smile creeping onto his full lips. He ran his finger along his chin and waited for Yolanda to say more.

"I don't exactly mean moist; I don't know why that word popped into my head. I was just thinking of something to say, and then I started looking at you, and your nose has those little sweat sprinkles on them, which I personally think is cute." *You're dying; just shut up already*— "So I just thought of moist. It's not like you have a booger or something in your nose." *Did I just say booger?*— "It's just slightly moist, you know, nothing to worry about. I mean everyone—"

"Yolanda," Maxwell interrupted, putting his hand on her shoulder, "breathe."

Houston, we have contact!

She looked at his hand on her shoulder. His fingers were long and wide, with short, clear nails buffed to a natural shine. Yolanda looked up at him. This was the second time in three years that Maxwell had touched her. Sure, the first one was probably an accident. She had dropped some change in the salon café and he had bent down and picked the coins up. When he dropped the cool pennies into her palm, his long fingers had grazed her hand. That was nothing compared to this. This was intentional. *So of course I now have to ruin it.*

"Natalie was just telling me some disturbing news about Sheila."

He removed his hand from her shoulder.

"Really?" he said again, raising his eyebrow. "What have you heard?"

"I heard that Sheila got fired."

Shaking his head, he looked down. "I forgot how fast news travels in this salon." Looking up, he added, "Look, Yolanda, I'm going to be perfectly honest with you. Sheila is thinking about leaving, but nothing is final. Can I trust you to treat this information with discretion?"

"Sure, Maxwell, I won't tell a soul."

"Yeah, you were right. Sheila got fired."

"What did I tell you? I knew it!" Natalie said smugly, looking for a pair of latex gloves to apply a relaxer.

"Oh, hush, you don't know anything."

The supply room was big, bright, and neatly organized. Large colorfully painted shelves lined the walls and were filled with clearly labeled supplies. A wide oyster grey marble counter ran the length of the room, and a deep stainless-steel sink was in one corner. Under the counter were large white cabinets filled with combs, brushes, plastic caps, rollers—everything a stylist needed to make her day go smoothly. The eggshell-colored walls were covered with posters for color formulations, chemical applications, conditioning treatments, etc. A wide archway led to a chemical room, where all chemical applications, including relaxers and highlights, were done. The salon was beautifully kept, and Dee Dee wanted to make sure it stayed that way. She didn't want any stains on her expensive floors or her custom-made styling chairs. The salon also provided its clients with an extra sense of security. Having chemical work done in a smaller room away from the hustle and bustle of the salon gave them the privacy that allowed them to lie to their husbands and friends about their *natural* color in a bottle.

"*No, girl, I don't color my hair.*"

"*Honey, I don't get relaxers; I have 'good hair'.*"

In a virtual trance, Yolanda leaned against one of the walls and looked up at the ceiling.

"Did you hear anything I said to you?" Natalie asked, irritated. "What's wrong with you? Why do you have that stupid look on your face?"

"He touched me."

"What! Where? When?"

"When we were talking. He touched me right here," Yolanda said, pointing to her shoulder.

"Oooh, somebody's in love! Maybe you—"

"Who in love?" Maria said, interrupting loudly.

Maria Espinoza, the cleaning lady, had a habit of coming in at the tail end of a conversation. Her shoes were soft as clouds, so you never heard her walk up. Nosy people always had a way of getting information.

"It must be you, Natalie," Maria said, her Spanish accent heavy like a bag of wet towels. "You always have new boyfriend. You so pretty and nice; I know you have no problem with the men."

Maria's dark brown eyes told the story of someone who had a hard life, yet smiled through it all. Her face was amazingly smooth for her age, and her dark, shiny hair was streaked with grey and pulled back in a tight bun. Her short frame carried an extra fifty pounds that might have looked odd on someone else, but on Maria it added softness to her round face and body.

"No, it's not me this time Maria," Natalie said, reaching for a black nylon apron, which was hanging on a nearby hook, to protect her clothes from any chemicals.

"Why don't you ask Yolanda? Maybe it's her this time," she added, as she walked out of the room to attend to her client.

"Oh, Miss Yolanda, is you who in love?" Maria asked.

"No, Maria, it's not me." *Not yet, anyway.*

"If you filled out more, here and here," Maria said, gesturing at Yolanda's breasts and hips, "you would have no problem finding husband. Just eat more, then you find true love."

Maria trotted off silently, leaving Yolanda alone and feeling a little hopeless in the supply room.

CHAPTER 5

"Cut it all off! It's too hot outside, and this hair is driving me crazy!" Yolanda's client whined.

Yolanda shook her head.

"I am not cutting your hair! It took a year for you to get it this long. I'm not gonna cut it just because you're getting impatient. Houston is hot every summer, Lisa. You knew that before you decided to grow it out."

"I know, I know," Lisa said. "But I have a new boyfriend now, and we went to see that new Halle Berry movie, and he kept saying how cute her hair was. So I was thinking that maybe you could cut it like that? You know, wild and funky, but something that will fit my face?" she said, pushing her hair up.

Yolanda knew that she was trying to imagine the haircut already.

She sighed. "All right girl, but if y'all break up next month don't come in here wanting a weave down your back like Naomi Campbell's."

"Oh, no, girl, that ain't gonna happen. Rick is different. I can tell this guy is the one," Lisa said, widening her eyes for emphasis.

"What's so different about him?"

"His bank account."

Yolanda laughed and gestured to her assistant, Megan, to take Lisa to get her hair shampooed.

"Megan, take her to the chemical room first and give her a spot relaxer on her nape area and around her sides. I want it to be really smooth so it doesn't stick up too much in the back. Oh, and use sensitive-scalp relaxer; she's probably been scratching, and I don't want her to get irritated."

Towering over her petite client, Megan nodded and led Lisa to the chemical room. It upset Yolanda to see that Megan was also tall and thin, yet she was told she could be a model, while she was often given second and third helpings of dinner to help her *fill out*.

"Say, you hear about Sheila?"

Yolanda heard the familiar pop of chewing gum and instantly knew who it was without turning around.

"Yeah, Tasha, I already heard."

Please don't be wearing that horrible red lipstick today. She turned around to check and see. *Yep, there it is, brighter than ever. And already on her teeth and her chin . . .*

"Word goin' around that she stole a wad of cash and split," Tasha said, followed by another loud smack.

"That doesn't make any sense. Sheila was making enough money; she had no reason to steal."

"Maybe she stole for her wedding. Heard it was gonna be the talk of the town."

"That's ridiculous. I don't think Sheila would do anything like that, especially for a man."

"You actin' like you really knew her. How well did any of us really know Sheila? Yeah, she worked here a long time, but anybody can pretend to be loyal. Why leave a job where you gettin' your stash from?"

"All I'm saying is that it don't make any sense."

"The only thing that don't make any sense is that she got caught. Must've got lazy."

"Who lazy?" Maria asked, holding a stack of clean white towels.

"Nobody, Maria," Yolanda said quickly.

"Miss Yolanda, you not lazy. It impossible for you to be that skinny and lazy."

"Thank you, Maria, but I wasn't asking you for any advice, okay?" Yolanda snapped, snatching a white towel from her hands.

Maria walked away, shaking her head and mumbling something in Spanish under her breath.

"What's wrong with you? Why were you so mean to her?" Tasha asked.

"I don't know, she just . . . she gets on my nerves sometimes."

"That's a sweet old lady. She didn't do nothin' . . ."

"Not to you, Tasha," Yolanda interrupted, "but she always has something to say to me."

"She don't mean no harm! Just blow her off. Just yesterday she tried to give me make-up tips. Like I need make-up tips from an old lady!" Tasha said, laughing and showing more lipstick on her teeth and putting more on her chin.

"Yeah, okay," Yolanda said.

CHAPTER 6

"Girl, I got juice!" Natalie screamed into the phone.

"Spill it!" Yolanda said, turning down the volume on her television. She was curled up on her couch watching *Entertainment Tonight*, but when Natalie had gossip it was always entertainment.

"I know why Sheila got fired!" Natalie sang out.

"Ooooh . . . Why?"

"She's a thief!"

"What? No . . ."

"Yep. Stole money from the salon account."

"No, she didn't! How much?"

"I don't know. Probably 'round twenty grand."

"Twenty-thousand dollars!"

"Yep."

"Girl, you lyin'."

"Nope."

"Why would Sheila steal? She's the most honest person I know. Remember when somebody was stealing all the combs and brushes from the supply room? It was Sheila's idea to put that video camera in there. She caught that girl . . . what was her name?"

"Debbie," Natalie answered.

"Yeah, Debbie. She caught that girl two days after it was installed. That doesn't sound like a thief to me."

"Humph. Takes a thief to catch a thief."

"Yeah, I guess you're right. Who's gonna replace her? That's a big job."

"Theresa's gonna fill in temporarily . . ."

"Theresa?"

"Yep. Everybody knows Theresa can't stand Sheila. She's been wanting that girl's job for years . . ."

"Well, she got it," Yolanda said.

"Not necessarily. You know Dee Dee's gonna promote Jackie to that position. Keep it in the family, right?"

"I guess. Jackie is Dee Dee's daughter, so that would make more sense. But wait a minute, if Theresa is filling in as creative director, who's gonna be assistant manager?"

"Girl, get this, she's gonna interview stylists from the salon with over five years of experience and over $2,000 in retail sales a month."

"Great, how do you get an interview?'

"Girl, upstairs has to invite you. You can't even apply. Word is they only interviewing five or six people."

"Really? They taking this serious, huh?"

"You would too if your best employee had just stolen $30,000 from you—"

"I thought you said it was $20,000?"

"I did? Well, I don't remember how much, but it was enough to get her butt fired, okay?"

"How much retail do you have?" Yolanda asked.

"I don't know. Last time I looked it was around a grand. What about you?"

Yolanda knew her sales were around three grand, maybe more. Every client left her chair with some kind of styling aid.

"I don't know; mine is probably right around the same as yours."

"Well, I guess they won't be asking either of us to go upstairs. That would've been cool, right? Wearing those cool jackets with the logo on the pocket. That's immediate respect right there."

"That's true. Man, Dee Dee works fast! The woman is good."

"That's why she's the boss. Look, I need to run; I've got plans tonight."

"What plans? You got a hot date or something?"

"Something like that," Natalie said, laughing.

"Well, girl, don't let me stop you from going out. Just one quick question, though."

"Shoot."

"Where did you get all this info?" Yolanda asked, suddenly curious.

"Maria."

"Really?"

"If you ever wanna find something out, she's the first person to go to. She knows everything. People forget she's standing there and they talk around her and she picks stuff up."

"That's more than just *stuff.*"

"Tell me about it. Now can I please get off this phone?"

"Sorry. Call me later."

CHAPTER 7

Natalie hung up and preheated her oven.

She had a date, all right.

A date with her stove.

Ever since she was a little girl, Natalie loved to cook. People always guessed that about her, but they were just judging by her weight that she could throw down in the kitchen. But Natalie had a gift, something special. It went beyond frying a chicken or making Southern-style gravy. Natalie actually knew the difference between chicken soup and bouillabaisse. She knew the difference between liver and onions and a good foie gras. She loved the taste of toasted brioche with gravlax on the side. Sure, she could just say she liked buttery bread with thin pieces of salmon on it, but that wasn't the point. The point was that she loved to cook. Loved it to the point where Food Network was her daily fix, and most weekends she went to Barnes and Noble to get new cookbooks.

But now what used to be a hobby, something Natalie did just for fun, was slowly turning into her passion. Cooking was something she felt compelled to do, something she needed to do. She had binders upon binders of original recipes that she'd worked on for years. Now her hand itched when she wasn't making some kind of culinary delight.

How did I ever get so caught up in doing hair that it became my job, my career?

She had never plotted her way to hairdressing. But that, too, she had a knack for. She was good at it; she made good money and, most importantly, she was comfortable. She could do a haircut blindfolded, could do a weave in her sleep. But when she thought about cooking, that's when her palms began to sweat and her chest pounded with excitement. That was her true love.

Natalie knew she couldn't keep this up. Cooking was her love, yes, but it was also affecting her job. She wasn't as focused as she used to be, didn't have the same drive. She knew she was going to have to put cooking where it belonged. On the back burner.

CHAPTER 8

Theresa McArthur turned the knobs on the shower and got in, the cold water shocking her skin and sending goose bumps all over her body.

She'd been stuck in meetings and forums all day for Dee Dee's new product line for the salon, and she was exhausted.

When the water began to warm, she turned the dial all the way to cold, shivering under the freezing water. After several minutes, she got out and toweled off. She applied a thick creamy lotion all over her body, ignoring the huge scar on her left shoulder. She only thought about it when she was naked, so she threw her robe on and quickly left the bathroom.

It felt good to be in New York again. Being here made her wonder why she ever left.

Maxwell. He was why, and it was time to get him back again.

She sighed and threw herself over an armchair in the living room of her hotel suite. The room was great, no doubt about that. It looked out over downtown Manhattan, and the sparkling lights of the city twinkled beneath the moonlit sky. She itched to go out, but didn't want to be alone; instead, she ordered dinner from room service.

She had been back at the salon for only a month, and already all the same old feelings for Maxwell were rushing back. She swore after what had happened between them that she'd never come back to Houston, but here she was accepting an offer of being assistant manager, working directly under Maxwell. Now with Sheila gone, she'd been asked to step in as creative director, a temporary position, she knew, but one she planned on filling well.

Being back in Houston also got her thinking about her past. She'd wanted to visit her father, let him know she was back in town, but she didn't want to see Carol. She hoped she never saw her again. She touched her scar. Her breath quickened, and she willed herself to calm down; she was safe. *I'm safe now, I'm safe now.* She repeated the affirmation until her heart slowed down and she was breathing like a normal person again.

CHAPTER 9

"You gonna pass that ball or what?"

"Sorry, sorry," Maxwell mumbled as he passed the ball to his best friend, Tony.

"Where's your mind at today?" Tony asked, giving him a friendly shove. "These dudes out here are whopping our butt. Get your head out of the clouds."

Maxwell nodded as he watched Tony run the court and try unsuccessfully to do a slam dunk. His five foot, seven inch frame barely got off the ground, and the ball bounced dismally off the backboard with the finality of their losing score: 20 to 12. Tony picked up the ball and threw it across the basketball court.

"Tony, I'm going to stop playin' with you if you don't stop with this sore loser mess," Maxwell warned.

"Man, shut up. It's your fault we lost."

"Nice game, man."

"See y'all later," their opponents said as they left the court.

"Yeah, good game, guys," Maxwell said, following Tony off the basketball court to the locker room.

"If you hadn't been daydreaming, we coulda' beat those dudes," Tony snapped as he opened his locker.

"So I made us lose? What was all this?" Maxwell asked, crouching down low, imitating Tony's horrible attempt at a slam dunk.

"Shut up," Tony said, grabbing his gym bag out of his locker.

Maxwell laughed.

"I always thought you were gonna grow out of being a sore loser. Remember when we were in the seventh grade and we lost that track meet?"

"Yeah."

"You got so mad you pulled that boy's shorts down. What was his name?"

"Fred? Fred . . . Fred something. Yeah, I remember. I got kicked off the team for that. I can't believe you remember all that stuff."

"It was pretty memorable."

Maxwell started laughing again.

"Why you laughing now?"

"Just remembering some of the crazy stuff we used to do," Maxwell replied, wondering how they'd remained friends after all these years.

People in their old neighborhood, South Park, used to call them the Shadow Brothers because, wherever one was, the other wasn't far behind. Going to a predominately black school made Tony's white skin stick out like a sore thumb, and the kids teased him relentlessly. One day Maxwell saw a group of boys jump him after school. Tony's nose was bloody, his pants were ripped, he was dirty, but every time one of the boys knocked him down, Tony got back up, ready to fight again. Maxwell stood back watching, wondering why he wouldn't just lie down and give up. Why wouldn't he just take the licks and let the bullies move on to some

other victim? He was stupid. Or maybe he was coura-
geous for standing up for himself, not letting anyone
punk him. Or maybe he was just plain crazy. He was
probably all three. Either way, Maxwell liked him
instantly. He broke up the fight and warned the boys
not to touch him again.

He walked Tony home after that, and they had been
friends ever since. Their race was never brought up;
Maxwell didn't even notice that Tony looked like an off-
brand Brad Pitt. His thick, blond hair always found its
way across his dark-blue eyes, and he was forever pushing
it back off his forehead. He was muscular, but not overly
so. His muscles were a nice surprise under his Hanes T-
shirt. Maxwell never cared what Tony looked like and
knew that Tony would have it hard growing up in a black
neighborhood. So they became brothers, through high
school, through college. Tony supported Maxwell when
his mother was diagnosed with cancer and he dropped
out of college, and Maxwell supported Tony through his
parents' ugly divorce. Through thick and thin, they were
there for each other.

"Hey, man, what happened to Andre? He was supposed to hang out with us this morning," Tony said,
pushing his blond hair out of his eyes.

"Right here, man. Sorry I'm late; it was hard to get
out of the house."

His long legs strode to them, and he gave each of
them a friendly pat on the back.

"What are you doing here? I thought you had to be
home with the kids," Maxwell asked.

Andre waved his hand dismissively. "Chicken pox? Brenda can handle that. She don't need me there with the boys." He sat his gym bag down on the wooden bench where Tony was sitting. "So, we playing or what?"

"Sorry, you missed it," Maxwell said.

"Missed it? Y'all finished playing already?"

"Yep." Tony said.

Andre sat down on the bench. "So what are we gonna get into now?"

"*We* are gonna take a shower and head to work," Maxwell said, stripping off his sweaty shirt.

"Oh yeah, that's right, y'all both work on Saturdays." He stood, grabbing his gym bag.

"You going home?"

"No. I'm gonna go work out. Maybe meet up with some of my co-workers and play a round of golf."

"In this heat? Man, you crazy." Maxwell said.

"Well, I'm not sitting around that house just to watch the kids itching and vomiting and stuff. I need a break."

"What about Brenda? I'm sure she would like to get out for a couple of hours—" Tony stopped talking when he saw Andre's stony look.

"Brenda is doing her job. She's a housewife. She don't get any breaks. Deuce," he said as she walked out of the locker room.

"There goes Mr. Fleming, always bringing a ray of sunshine in our dreary little lives," Tony said sarcastically.

Tony and Maxwell had met Andre Fleming their senior year in high school. His parents had just moved from Austin, and Maxwell could tell right away that his sandy brown hair, pecan skin, and light brown eyes could work to their advantage. His tall good looks could only add more girls to their roster, so he invited him to sit with them at lunch. Andre felt like the missing piece in Maxwell's and Tony's friendship, and he fit in like he had been hanging with them for years.

Maxwell was not surprised to learn that Andre's easy smile and warm personality won him the heart of many girls, but Andre only had his eyes on one: Rosslyn Hadley. Senior year you wouldn't see the one without the other. They were so close that Maxwell was shocked as any one to learn that she broke up with Andre two days before prom. Hurt and broken-hearted, Andre took Brenda Emerson, the one girl who had trailed after him the entire senior year. More shocking than ever was when he *married* the girl a month later, forgoing his dream of going to school to be a veterinarian.

Brenda's family came from money, so Andre leisurely worked at one of Brenda's father's furniture stores. Brenda's desperation reeked of bad cabbage, and her feelings for Andre bordered on worship. She would jump if he *thought* she should be jumping. She was an annoying little pest, and for the life of Maxwell he couldn't figure out why Andre would stoop so low in the looks department for a girl. Brenda was past ugly, she was what you called *OOOgly*. But she tried to be pretty, and that was her downfall. Her insane blonde hair weave against her shiny, acne-riddled ebony skin, her bright clownish make-up, and trendy clothes, did nothing to hide what God gave her. Instead, you laughed at her attempt to fight the ugly. *Just let it be,* Maxwell wanted to scream at her when he would visit their house. Her long red nails would circle around his beer bottle, and when Maxwell mumbled a thanks to her, her thick pink lips would open and you would glance at a mouth of yellow crooked teeth that could be mistaken for gold any day. She was sweet, though, Maxwell would give her that. And she loved Andre. That she did.

"You going to stand there all day, or are you going to hit the shower?" Tony asked.

"Yeah, I'm going in. Can't be late for work, I got a long day ahead of me."

"Yeah, me too. I gotta go over some menu stuff." Tony said.

"Oh yeah, how's the promotion coming?" Maxwell asked.

Last week, Tony was promoted to head chef at Hotel Bellagio, one of Houston's most prestigious hotels. He loved it, but Maxwell could see he was stressing from all the added responsibility.

"It's killing me, man. But I'm getting the hang of it. Thanks for meeting me up here; I needed something to take my mind off work."

"Anytime," Maxwell said, heading for the showers.

CHAPTER 10

"Hey, Mama! You home?" Yolanda yelled.

"Yeah, baby! I'm in the kitchen!"

Yolanda walked through her parents' house, glancing at the destruction her father had caused with his latest remodeling project. She shook her head as she looked at the living room; where once there were walls, now there were only exposed beams.

Her parents lived in Acres Homes, a black neighborhood in northwest Houston. It was the perfect blend of city and country. Roosters crowed in the mornings, and you were never surprised to see a horse beside your car. It was a poor neighborhood, but not poor on values or respect. It was the kind of neighborhood where everyone knew each other and their family history just by giving a street or name.

You Trisha Collins? Old Trisha on West Montgomery Street? Girl, I know you from way back. How's your mama?

She loved riding up and down the streets remembering how some of them used to be old dirt roads but were now paved, and had street lights and stop signs to boot.

Walking through her parents' house reminded her of how much things can change yet stay the same. The outside never changed; it was always painted white, with a dark forest green trim. Two massive trees stood close to the chain-link, steel fence that surrounded the house, and her father still hadn't fixed their cracked up, crooked concrete driveway. Her mother had been dreaming of a carport for years, but her father never got around to it, arguing that *in Acres Homes, nobody needs all that excess stuff.* But the inside of the house was totally different. Gone was the old brown carpet that she and her sister, Gina, would play on, but gave her mother sneezing fits because of her allergies. It was replaced with mahogany-stained hardwood floors that took her father months to restore. Gone were the space heaters and *Frosty,* the name Gina gave to their window-unit air conditioner. When her father got the roof replaced two years ago, he got her mother the best gift: central air and heat. Now she could cook all day without sweating her hair out from the heat.

"Hey, Mama," Yolanda said, walking in the kitchen and planting a kiss on her mother's round face. Her mother smiled warmly, tucking a wisp of thin brown hair behind her ear. Yolanda wished she could've been blessed with her mother's body. At her age, she was still short and curvy in all the right places. Instead, Gina took after her mother, leaving Yolanda with the beanpole figure that her father had cursed her with.

"Where's Daddy?"

"In his study," her mother replied, taking a fresh batch of cookies out of the oven. "Go speak."

"I don't feel like it."

"Girl, get yo behind in there and say hello! What's wrong with you?"

"Okay," Yolanda said, dragging herself to her father's study.

She knocked lightly on the door.

"Come in, baby girl!" he yelled through the thick oak door.

Yolanda walked in.

"Hey Daddy . . ."

"Oh, shoot. Thought you was Gina. She supposed to be bringin' the ham. What you want?"

"Nothing, Daddy, just speaking."

"Well, come over here and give me a cheek."

Yolanda walked over and pressed her cheek against her father's, a ritual he started because he thought it was inappropriate to give his daughters kisses. His cheek was rough and scraggly from not shaving.

"So, Six, what you been up to?"

I hate when you call me that.

Yolanda had been given the nickname Six O'Clock at thirteen, when her father had noticed she wasn't developing into a woman. So he called her Six O'clock, meaning that she was straight up and down like the hands on a watch at six o'clock. She never found it funny, and always told him to stop calling her that. He told her he would stop when she gained weight and filled out like a woman. Neither happened, so the nickname stuck.

"Nothing much, I guess. But at work—"

"Did your sister call you and tell you that the baby, Porsche, is trying to walk?"

"No, she didn't."

"That girl is eight months old and so smart. I tell you, Gina's doing something right. All her kids are gifted."

"Yeah they are smart." *Smart-mouthed.* "Anyway, at my job—"

"Mama, where are you?" Gina screamed in the background, interrupting Yolanda, as always, when she had something important to say.

"Gina, that you?" her father yelled, jumping up from his chair and turning the TV off. For Gina, he would cut the TV off; for Yolanda, he barely made eye contact during the commercials.

"Move out the way, Six," he said, gently pushing Yolanda aside, away from the door. "Gotta see baby girl."

Yolanda nodded and watched him walk out, wondering how he could talk about her when he was tall and skinny himself. *Well, except for his beer belly.* If you took all his features apart—his big ears, bulbous nose, the heavy moustache that hid a mole on his upper lip, and his thick, outdated bifocals, you would think he was unattractive. But he wasn't. All together, he made a good package and you could see how, back in the day, he was a very handsome man.

Yolanda walked back into the kitchen and watched her father give Gina a big hug. They exchanged cheeks.

"Where those babies?" he asked her, taking a huge pan covered with aluminum foil from Gina's hands and placing it on the counter.

"Trevor is staying with them. Anita and Devon were fighting again, so they're on punishment. I couldn't stay in that house another second; I had to break free."

"What? Your little angels fighting? I just don't believe it!" Yolanda said, with a dollop of sarcasm.

Her mother gave her the *don't start* look, so Yolanda added, "Seriously, are the kids okay?"

"They're fine, just missing their Aunt Yolanda," Gina said, walking over and giving Yolanda a hug.

Yolanda hugged her, feeling a roll of fat on Gina's stomach. *Good, she still hasn't lost all the baby weight.*

Gina's short hair, which was usually in tight curls, was laid down smoothly and had a sleek side part. Gina was much shorter than Yolanda, being only five feet, four inches tall. Her face was still round from the extra weight she gained during her pregnancy with Porsche, which was her third. For a little while Yolanda had the upper hand, until Gina lost the last ten pounds she needed to lose. Then she was back to the Coke-bottle figure she was known for. *Maybe if I popped out a few babies, my boobs would get bigger.*

"When are you gonna baby sit again? You know the kids love you."

Never. When pigs fly . . .

"Baby, why don't you take 'em this weekend? You could take 'em to the zoo like you been promising," her mother volunteered.

"They would love that!" Gina screeched.

"Yeah, Six, take 'em. You ain't got no man, so we all know you ain't got no plans."

"I can't this weekend," Yolanda answered, ignoring her father's comment.

"Why not?" he asked.

"I have something to do."

"You got a date or something?" Her father laughed for the longest time, as if Yolanda having a date was the funniest thing on the planet. "Well, is he at least black this time? That other one you brought home a couple of years ago . . ."

"Arthur, leave the girl alone!" her mother interjected. "You know she's sensitive about that."

"No, Mama, it's okay." Her heart seized just at the mention of her ex-boyfriend, Russell, but she played it off well, not wanting to rehash old memories.

"See, Cathy, she all right. I just wanna know what Six been up to, that's all. So come on, girl, spill it. Why can't you watch the kids this weekend?"

"Can this wait until dinner?"

"No, it can't . . ."

"Dad, don't worry about it. If she has plans . . ." Gina began.

"Don't you worry, baby girl, it must be a good reason your sister has for not watching those kids. So what is it, Six?"

"I got a job promotion," Yolanda blurted.

She wasn't sure why she lied, but she needed something to put her on even ground with Gina. She didn't have a man, so she should at least have a promising career.

"Really? To what?" her mother asked excitedly.

"Assistant manager," Yolanda mumbled.

"What?"

"Assistant manager."

"You don't say!" her father said, smiling. "Come give me another cheek, Six!"

Yolanda walked over and gave him another cheek.

"Congratulations, Yolanda! If I had known, I would have baked you a cake," Gina said.

"Baby girl you always did make the best desserts. Say, Cathy, remember in high school when Gina won that contest? Got a certificate and everything. I sure am proud of you, baby girl, you can bake your butt off! Can't she cook, Cathy?"

Her mother nodded and looked at Yolanda and mouthed, "I'm sorry."

"It's okay," Yolanda mouthed back.

CHAPTER 11

Yolanda gets to the playground first.

She's a little girl again, playing on the slides, the seesaw, the monkey bars.

She sees the swings and runs toward them.

She jumps on and swings herself higher and higher.

She feels so free.

Suddenly, she feels someone grab her arm and yank her off the swing.

She lands hard on the ground and feels a painful burning sensation in her arm. It might be broken.

A group of little girls, no more than ten years old, stand above her, looking down at her. She can't see their faces.

They begin to attack her, each taking turns hitting her face, kicking her in the back, and stomach.

She screams.

Yolanda woke up in a cold sweat. She looked up at her alarm clock. 6:00 A.M.

She turned on the light on her bedside table.

These dreams have to stop; they're driving me crazy.

She took a long sip from the glass of water by her bed.

Just then the phone rang and startled her, almost making her drop the glass.

Who could it be this early?

"Hello?" Yolanda said, her voice groggy from sleep.

"What's up, girl! Get your lazy butt out of bed! You have to get an early start, Miss Assistant Manager."

"Don't say that! I don't have the job yet."

Yolanda almost couldn't believe it herself. When Karen told her Maxwell wanted to talk to her upstairs, she just assumed it was something bad—just like they all did when they had to go upstairs. She could barely stop her knees from shaking as she walked out of the elevator onto the third floor. It looked like the lobby of a hotel Yolanda knew she couldn't afford. Huge sofas in the reception area sat under bright windows that reflected the shine of the hardwood floors. She went up to the desk, and gave her name to Victoria, the secretary, and soon was following her down the long hall to Maxwell's office.

His office was set in dark tones of mahogany, from the dark paneled walls to the rich brown leather furniture to the gleaming wood floors. It would be impossible to suggest that Maxwell's office belonged to anyone other than him.

"Thanks, Vicki. Have a seat, Yolanda," he said, his eyes never leaving his computer screen.

Vicki nodded, and with the click of the door, was gone. Yolanda sat in the brown leather chair in front of his desk.

He removed his glasses and studied her for a moment.

"Due to the departure of Sheila, we have a position available for assistant manager. We feel that after training, you would be qualified for this position, so we are inviting you to interview for it—if you think this is something you would be ready take on."

"I was born ready," Yolanda blurted. "I want the job."

Maxwell laughed.

"Well, your enthusiasm is hereby noted, but there will be two interviews, and then Dee Dee and I will make that decision. You do know that you will no longer have the creative outlet of styling hair? That you will have to change gears and think about the business side of the salon? Of course you'll be appropriately compensated, but it is something to consider. Everyone in management is pretty content, so having a position become open is pretty rare—"

"I know. I've waited a long time to have this opportunity, and I want to interview."

Maxwell put his glasses back on.

"Great. We'll set the interview up for next week."

"I still can't believe all that happened to you! I know you're nervous, but you have to be excited too, right?" Natalie asked, yanking Yolanda out of reliving her meeting with Maxwell.

"Yeah, there are a lot of people who want this job."

"Don't mess this up worrying about other people. You just worry about you and do the best you can. Now get up and get dressed. You know you move slow in the morning. Just remember the little people downstairs when you get the job."

"Girl, there is no way I could ever forget about you! Don't even start thinking like that."

"I'm just saying, that's all. Go, get ready and let me know the minute you know."

"I pretty much have to get it or my parents will know that I lied and that I'm a total loser."

"Girl, put your rubber band on and pop yourself a billion times for being so negative. That's no kind of attitude to take into a job interview."

"Okay."

"Now get your butt up and get that job!" Natalie said, and hung up.

She looked at her clock. 6:13.

She sighed and decided to follow Natalie's advice and get ready for work.

Yolanda scrutinized herself in the mirror.

Her soft brown hair was straight after thirty minutes with her ceramic flat-iron. She wanted to look professional, sophisticated. Her make-up was light, showing off the spray of freckles she had on her nose and cheeks.

After minutes of standing in front of her closet, she chose a simple black long-sleeve shirt with wide-leg pants. She left her shirt tucked out, and accented it with a thin, black belt at the waist.

"Always wear a belt," Yolanda remembered her mother saying. *"Since you don't have much of a shape, you have to build your body."*

She looked at herself in the full-length mirror. *You're not half bad.* She smiled and made herself not look at the rest of her body. *Okay, just a quick peek.* Sometimes it surprised her how skinny she was. She didn't have anything that truly identified her as a woman. It was one of the reasons she would never cut her hair.

She sighed, grabbed her purse, gave Precious a kiss, and locked the door to her apartment.

Maxwell took another sip of his coffee and checked who he was going to interview next.

Yolanda Peterson.

He smiled, and buzzed Vicki to bring her into his office.

He could tell by the way she carried herself that she had a crush on him, but he hoped that it wouldn't interfere with her work. He wasn't immune to the many women that threw themselves at him, and Yolanda was just one of many. He was beyond flattered by all the attention, but it bothered him that not one of the women had tried to really get to know him. Beyond mindless flirting, no one had really tried to get inside his head.

Except Theresa.

She let Maxwell know whenever possible that she was ready to renew their relationship. He still had strong feelings for Theresa . . . but not enough to overcome all the lies she'd told. She had been leading a double life, a life that he had no knowledge of. *How could you really love someone that you never really knew? That you might not ever know?* He shouldn't have been engaged to a woman without knowing what was in her past. *Did she think she could keep running away?*

He watched Yolanda walk into his office, thinking it was wrong to compare the two women, but Yolanda had nothing when it came to Theresa's beauty. Theresa's presence captivated you, demanded your attention. Yolanda was so skinny she made you shudder and want to look away. Everyone at work knew the girl could eat, so that blew his anorexia theory out of the water. No one ever heard any noises in the restroom that could possibly suggest bulimia, so everyone had put her weight issue aside, guessing that she had been born with a very high metabolism.

As she sat in front of his desk, he watched her twist several colorful rubber bands on her wrist, snapping them against her brown skin. Her feet tapped on the wood floor and she glanced around the room, refusing to give him eye contact. He smiled to ease her nerves and she smiled back, seeming to relax a little.

When she smiles, she is kinda pretty. Really pretty, in fact. Let's just say the girl has a pretty face.

"Yolanda, I won't be technically interviewing you. I'm just going to be filling you in on your duties if you're chosen to become assistant manager and asking you a few brief questions."

She exhaled, releasing some of the tension in her shoulders.

"How long have you thought about being assistant manager?"

"For a while now. I've been doing hair for eleven years, six of those at Behave, and I'm ready to take the next step and learn how a salon really operates."

"Well, Behave is a really big salon. If you get hired, you'll be part of the team with all the other assistant mangers. You know we have several?"

"Sure. You have Peter, who is in the spa, and Angela in the café—"

"Yes, and many more. The assistant manager for the stylists will have a full plate of duties. If you get chosen, you will have to be proficient in customer service and conflict resolution. How would you feel if you had to write someone up for bad language in the salon?"

"I don't think I would have a problem with that."

"Even if this person was someone you were close to?"

"No. If she was caught breaking the rules, she would have to understand that it's nothing personal. I have a job to do, just as the stylists do."

"Good. You would also be in charge of the stylist inventory. That includes retail and any products the stylists might need in the course of their day."

He watched her nodding as she took in all the information.

"You would also be responsible for doing all the scheduling for the stylists and the receptionists. Maid service, cleaning, and landscaping will all report to you for their duties as well."

"So basically, if something is not clean or not right—"

"Then it is your fault for not taking care of it."

"Well, this sounds like a lot of work, Maxwell, but let me assure you that I'm the woman for the job."

"Really?"

"I know you all already know my retail sales and customer service are excellent. You also know that in the six years that I've been here, I've never been written up. Never been late. Nothing. But that is not even the most important reason you should consider hiring me."

"And what would that be?"

"I'm the best. There's no beating around it, I'll do the best work for the job."

Maxwell leaned back in his chair. He wasn't impressed much, but Yolanda had passed with flying colors. She came in looking like a sheep, but came across like a lion.

"Very good, Yolanda. You've done well. We'll let you know if you receive a second interview."

CHAPTER 12

The mariachi band was in full swing as Yolanda took another sip of her margarita. Natalie was shaking her head to the beat as she tried to figure out what they should start with. Doneraki was near the job and had become one of Yolanda's favorite Mexican restaurants. It reminded her of being at a coastal bar in Mexico when she and—well, never mind; no sense in ruining the good mood she was in. Natalie had insisted that they go out and celebrate her having aced her first interview with Maxwell.

"I'll just have queso with fajita steak in it, to start. Oh, and another margarita," Natalie told the waitress.

"I'll have the same."

"So was Maxwell all business, or what?"

"Very serious. He barely cracked a smile the whole time was interviewing me. I doubt he allows any play-time at work. I mean, he's Dee Dee's right-hand man. He's in charge of all the managers, the creative director, everyone."

"So that means—"

Natalie stopped when she heard Yolanda's cellphone. Yolanda looked at her and picked up.

"Hello?"

"Miss Peterson?"

"Yes?"

"This is Beverly, Dee Dee's personal secretary. She has requested that you come for a second interview tomorrow morning at 9:00 sharp."

"Great. I'll be there."

"Thank you."

Yolanda hung up the phone and started beating the wood table. Her heart pounded from excitement.

"You got it?" Natalie asked.

"I got the second interview!" Yolanda squealed with delight.

"I knew you would!" Natalie said, her excitement matching Yolanda's. "That job is as good as yours."

"You know what? I'm starting to believe that myself."

CHAPTER 13

Today wasn't half bad. Maxwell pulled his black Hummer out of the parking garage and headed home. He still had not gotten used to Sheila not being there. *Why did Sheila need to steal?* She hadn't shown any signs that she needed money or was in any kind of trouble; if anything, she seemed happy and relaxed. Her boyfriend, Michael, had just proposed, and they were planning their wedding. Everything seemed fine. *Maybe she stole the money for her wedding reception.* She was having it at the Houstonian; that place was definitely expensive. But with what Dee Dee was paying her and Michael's new promotion at NASA, they should be able to afford a big wedding. It made no sense . . . *Why did Sheila take that money?*

He had to find out. Sheila had cleaned out her office but had left one box of files on Maxwell's desk. She was the only one Dee Dee entrusted with unlimited access on her business credit card. He'd looked through the files and had seen evidence of cash advances withdrawn on Sheila's card. But for the life of him, he couldn't figure out why she would need such large sums of money when she was getting paid so well. He owed it to her to find out what really happened. The last time they'd talked her voice had been so choked with tears that Michael had come to the phone and ended their conversation, explaining that she was getting too upset.

He pushed the thought out of his head and instead focused on the beautiful trees around him. He loved the fact that even though Houston was a big city, it was surrounded by nature. It was not unusual to see parking lots surrounded by pine trees, sidewalks filled with azalea bushes, and street medians overflowing with crape myrtles, their fragrant blooms a rainbow of pinks and purples.

Maxwell turned the radio on to his favorite jazz station. He had a ritual going; R&B and hip-hop in the morning to wake him up and smooth jazz in the evening to calm him down and help him unwind. Another lesson learned from his father, Ray.

He was in a pretty good mood, and since his father's restaurant wasn't too far from his loft apartment downtown, he decided to make a quick detour and get a drink. It was still early, he might even catch the happy hour crowd.

His father owned Ray's, one of the hippest Creole restaurants in Houston. It catered to Houston's elite: wealthy businessmen, rich, bored housewives, and young urban singles. What made his place stand out wasn't just the delicious food, it was the entertainment that he managed to get on most weekends. It wasn't unusual to see the latest R&B crooner on the small stage, making the Cajun blackened chicken breasts with homemade Cajun seasoning taste even more delicious than before. His father had a knack for charming people in the door, and for the past eight years the restaurant had seen huge success. *The Houston Chronicle* had called it "first class in food and entertainment." He loved the atmosphere at Ray's Place, from the ocean blue walls to the contemporary chairs. His father had been, and still was, involved in every detail of the place. He liked to call the décor jazzy, classy Las Vegas.

On his way, Maxwell passed the sleek new Metrorail, the first phase of a city planning initiative meant to meet the transit needs of Houston's growing population. When it expanded to other parts of the city the system was expected to make a major dent in Houston's traffic problem. During the initial phase, his father complained that all the construction would deter people from coming to the restaurant. But his patrons stood by, and he was busier than ever. Maxwell waited patiently for traffic to let up so he could start looking for a place to parallel park. He saw a prime spot right in front of the restaurant, but knew he could never swing his Hummer into such a small space. After several tries, he gave up and knew his lazy butt would just have to walk. He parked a block away and got out in the hot, heavy summer heat.

Walking quickly to avoid ruining his Egyptian cotton shirt with sweat, Maxwell prayed for a breeze. *Thank you,* he thought, as he felt a small, pitiful excuse for air sweep across his cheek. He finally reached the heavy oak doors to the restaurant and welcomed a burst of cool air.

"Hey, Debra," he said to the beautiful hostess.

"Hey, Maxwell," Debra responded in a friendly voice. A little too friendly. "You here to see yo daddy?"

"Yeah. He around?"

"Check in the back."

"Thanks."

"Wait, Maxwell, you want me to hang your suit jacket up for you?"

"No thanks, I'm fine."

She reached out and touched his shoulder. He stopped and looked down at her. "You sure?" she asked, a look of desperation in her eyes.

The desperate look in Debra's eyes disgusted him, as it did every time he saw her. He tried to be pleasant to her because he knew she had strong feelings for him, but at every opportunity he let her know he wasn't interested. "No thanks, Debra," Maxwell said firmly, walking to the back of the restaurant to find his father.

It was crowded, filled with people laughing, drinking and eating; the triple threat, his father used to say. "Son, if you feed people, make him laugh and give them a little alcohol, that money will slide right out of their hand." His theory seemed to be working as he maneuvered himself through the sea of white tableclothed tables, the smell of bacon-wrapped shrimp and chicken and sausage gumbo, making his mouth water. Maybe he'd stay and have a bite to eat . . . He reached his father's office and knocked.

"Yo, Pop, you in there?"

He put his ear against the mahogany door and heard a woman's laugh.

Not again.

He was about to knock again, but the door swung open and a beautiful woman walked out. Laughing, she looked Maxwell up and down and walked past him back into the restaurant. Maxwell slammed the door behind her.

"I'm tired of this, Pop. This has got to stop."

Smoothing his pinstripe Armani suit, Ray stood and glared at his son.

"I'm serious, Pop."

"Stop acting like that. You worse than some of these women. I ain't doing nothin' but being a man. If you don't like what you see then stay out of my restaurant. Last time I checked it said Ray's, not Maxwell's."

"I'm not tryin' to preach, Pop . . ."

"Sounds like what you doing."

"Look, I just want you to slow down."

"Maybe you need to speed up," Ray said. "What you doing here, anyway? I thought you'd still be at the sissy parlor. I mean, beauty parlor," Ray said, chuckling.

"Not funny, Pop," Maxwell said quietly.

"Come on now, boy. What respectable man would want to work at a beauty salon? Besides to get women? And you doing a poor job at that. When you gonna come be my partner at the restaurant? You know I could use your help."

"We're not having this discussion again. I'm well aware you hate my job, but I like it. I went from dumping trash for Dee Dee, to sweeping hair, to barber, then manager, then maybe one day partner. That's what I want."

"Oh, boy, wake up!" Ray said sharply. "You know Dee Dee ain't giving you no partnership, especially when her own daughter works there! She's gonna keep that salon in the family; I keep tellin' you that!"

"Yeah, Pop, you keep telling me that, but I don't wanna hear it right now! All this mess just to get a drink."

"Boy, man up! Stop being so sensitive," Ray said. "Come on, let's go to the bar and I'll get you that drink." They walked out together and Maxwell wondered why he came to see his father as often as he did.

"Who was she, anyway?" Maxwell asked.

"One of our new waitresses," Ray said, winking at him.

He burst out laughing. He couldn't help himself.

Walking behind his father, Maxwell watched as he worked his way through the restaurant, a king surveying his kingdom. He looked pretty good for his age, Maxwell thought. In fact, take away a few gray hairs and they could pass for brothers. Ray was tall, at least six feet, two inches; not as tall as his son, but still taller than the average man. They shared the same dark, smooth skin and both were physically fit.

Maxwell watched him flirt with a group of women half his age.

If mama were alive, he wouldn't give those women a second glance.

She had died of cancer only a few years ago, but Ray was acting as if everything was all right. He wondered if he would ever go back to the father who played golf with him and read his Bible for fifteen minutes every morning. He was afraid that the good part of his father had died with his mama.

He reached the bar and ordered a vodka on the rocks.

"Hey, Rick, get me a glass of merlot," Ray said, taking a stool next to his son.

"You was walking behind me; how you get here so fast?"

"I wasn't flirting."

"Watch it, boy," Ray said, smiling.

Maxwell smiled, too. Even he was not immune to his father's charm.

"Did you speak to Debra when you came in?" Ray asked.

Maxwell gave him a weird look, thanked Rick for his drink and took a sip, feeling the pleasantly familiar liquid burn his throat.

"Well?" his father said impatiently.

"Yeah, I spoke."

"What happened?"

"Nothin'."

"She likes you, son."

"I don't like her."

"Then who do you like?" Ray asked. "You haven't brought a woman around in a while. What you waiting for?"

Maxwell thought about it. What was he waiting for? What did he want? He knew he was tired. Tired of the playing around, tired of the games, the schemes women played. He was bored with the life he'd carved out for himself. He wanted a wife. Kids. He wanted more, and he was beginning to fear he would never find someone to share his life with. Especially after Theresa.

"I don't know, Pop."

"Well, you better find out. You ain't gettin' any younger."

Maxwell looked at the gray in his father's hairline. He was right; he didn't have much time at all.

CHAPTER 14

Dee Dee Townsend sat alone in her office early Friday morning. She was at her computer reviewing last week's income. She smoothed the hair at the nape of her neck, a habit she'd picked up after cutting her hair. She felt tired just thinking about the long day ahead of her. Her workload had tripled since Sheila's forced departure. Dee Dee was desperate for a replacement, but needed someone who came with experience.

These past five years have been really hard.

First, there were all the problems that came with the relocating to their salon's site, a beautiful, 35,000-square-foot beauty oasis in the prestigious Galleria area. She employed forty stylists, twelve barbers, twenty-five shampoo technicians, fifteen nail technicians, six massage therapists, and eight facialists. And that was not counting all the employees who ran the café, the in-house daycare, and the gym. Problems arose every second, but with Sheila by her side, Dee Dee was able to concentrate on bigger issues. With her gone, she was feeling overwhelmed.

Never in her wildest dreams had she thought she would go this far.

I wish Mama was still alive.

Dee Dee smiled, remembering when she was ten years old how she loved to run to her mother's salon, that was affectionately named after her, to help her. The smell of sulfur and hairspray made her stomach churn with excitement; she knew she was in a place where she belonged. Her mother would smile and give her a broom and Dee Dee would sweep any stray hair on the floor. When her mother was in a really good mood, she would let her towel dry the client's wet hair, taking extra care not to get anyone's shirt wet. Sometimes she would get a tip and would go next door to Mr. Bailey's corner store and buy a cherry popsicle and eat it on the steps, licking it fast so the hot sun wouldn't melt it. Dee Dee longed for those simple days again.

Her mother had died when she was nineteen years old. Her father hadn't shown up for the funeral; she mistakenly thought that he would show his face after all those years. All she had ever known was her mother, and she didn't know if she could go on without her. She remembered sitting in her mother's salon, crying at the thought of never seeing her again. She had worked beside her mother forever, how could she step inside her salon and not hear her laugh, or her witty comments to her clients? Dee Dee looked around the salon and saw all the work that her mother needed to do to renovate the place. She had never gotten around to it, complaining she didn't have enough money. The checkerboard black and white linoleum floor was worn and cracked, the styling stations were nothing more than wood planks drilled into the walls.

Her death could mean something. Her death could breathe new life into this place. Her death could resurrect this salon.

When she received her mother's life insurance check she knew she was doing the right thing when she gutted the entire salon, bringing everything up-to-date. Gone were the rickety old styling stations and worn black leather chairs that held more grey duct tape than leather; they were replaced with supple leather hydraulic chairs that spun with the flick of a wrist. She had updated the linoleum floors but kept the same checkerboard design. She thought long and hard about it but finally decided to change the name from Dee Dee's Hair Salon to Behave Hair Salon. It seemed more fitting, and more of a tribute to her mother, considering all the times that she had to sit down and *behave herself* in her mothers' salon.

She must have done something right in those old days because all six hairstylists stayed on after her mother died. In fact, those six tripled within a year, until she had to double the salon's square footage and decided to also add a spa. Every year her business continued to grow; new services would be added to meet the demands of current trends, which meant new stylists and staff to meet those demands. One day, Dee Dee realized that she'd taken the salon further than she, or her mother, ever imagined.

She looked at Michael's picture on her desk. He was smiling, his eyes squinting from the sun. She had bought a smaller frame after she cut her husband out of the picture. She had cut Jonathan out of almost all her pictures. *It was his fault. All of this mess was his fault—*

"Come in," she said, responding to a knock on the door.

Dee Dee watched Maxwell walk to her desk.

"The two young ladies are waiting for you in the hall."

"They're both early. That's a good sign. So what do you think about of our two candidates?"

"I think both of them would do well . . ."

"But?"

"But I really like Yolanda's spunk. She seems like she'll really put forth a lot of effort to get the job done. I think you should show extra attention to her."

It was not like Maxwell to give any employee extra attention just for having spunk, especially without noting any other qualifications. Dee Dee looked down at Yolanda's file. "Tell Beverly to send Yolanda in."

Yolanda could barely walk straight. Her knees kept knocking and she kept taking deep breaths to calm herself down. *Everything is fine. You're real close, just don't mess anything up.*

She was surprised to learn that Maxwell had interviewed eight stylists and only Yolanda and another stylist named Denise had made it to the second interview. The two waited patiently, neither sure if it was better to be called first or second. By the time Yolanda had decided second was better, she was following Beverly down the hall to Dee Dee's office. As Beverly knocked on the door she took another deep breath and said a quick prayer.

"Come in," a soft voice said.

Dee looked up and smiled when Yolanda walked in. Her office was cool and serene—like Dee Dee. With its pale green walls, spotless white furniture, and marine blue and silver accents, it reminded Yolanda of an expensive beachside retreat.

"Have a seat, Yolanda," she said, gesturing to a seat in front of her desk. "Thank you, Beverly."

Yolanda sat down.

"So how are you feeling this morning, Yolanda?"

"Well—"

"Excuse me, Dee Dee," Beverly said over the intercom, "you have a call on line three."

"Thanks, Beverly. Hold on just a minute," Dee Dee said, giving Yolanda a small apologetic smile.

Yolanda nodded and looked around Dee Dee's enormous office, trying to block out her phone conversation. *Some people have it all.*

Her office was beautiful, yet lacked any of the personal touches that she expected. Besides a picture of a teenage boy on her desk, nothing else gave an inkling into Dee Dee's personality. Yolanda felt she worked hard to keep a distance from her employees. It was working, because Yolanda felt awkward and out of place. Dee Dee's skin was unlined and smooth as glass. *How old was she? Forty? Forty-five?* Dee Dee laughed suddenly, low and throaty. *Even her laugh is sophisticated.*

She looked down at Dee Dee's desk and studied the intricate details of the aqua green marble top. Yolanda ran her hand over the top of it, feeling its cold hardness, and knowing she would never have anything in common with this woman.

"It's from Greece," Dee Dee said, noticing Yolanda openly admiring her desk. "My husband got it for me when we went there a couple of years ago."

"It's beautiful."

"Thank you. Sorry about the interruption."

"No problem."

"So you're interested in being one of our assistant managers?"

"Yes, ma'am."

"I'm not that old," Dee Dee said. "Please call me Dee Dee."

"Okay," Yolanda said, feeling the tension in her neck slowly easing.

"Maxwell really recommends you highly."

"Really?"

"Yes, we were quite impressed," Dee Dee said, looking through a brown file.

We? Does that mean Maxwell was impressed, too?

"When asked, 'Why should you be assistant manager?' you said simply, 'Because Behave needs me.' Would you care to elaborate?"

Yolanda's heart raced as she tried to remember what Natalie had told her right before the meeting: "If you pretend something long enough, soon it'll come true."

Yolanda pretended she had confidence.

"I think of this salon as a body. Separately, every body part plays an important role in making them all work well together. Without one part, the body can't function well. I'm that missing part," Yolanda said.

Dee Dee sat back and looked at her reflectively.

Yolanda looked back.

"I think I've found my new assistant manager," Dee Dee said.

"And this is your office," Maxwell said, holding the door open for Yolanda. She walked in.

"Dee Dee said you could change the wall colors to your liking, and can buy new stuff later . . ."

Yolanda wasn't listening. She was caught up in a dream. It wasn't the biggest room; in fact, it was quite the opposite, but it was hers, all hers. She looked at the dark cherry office furniture, the large window with a wide window seat overflowing with big fluffy white pillows flanked with dark cherry bookshelves. She walked over to the window, looked down at her view of the parking lot, and bounced up and down like a schoolgirl on her window seat. She was about to jump on top of the cushions a la Tom Cruise but stopped herself and stood up next to Maxwell.

"Are you listening to anything I'm saying?" Maxwell asked.

"No," Yolanda whispered. She cleared her throat and looked up at him with tears in her eyes.

"Have you ever wanted something so badly, and you work hard for it, thinking it will never come? And then one day it's in your face and you're like, I can't believe I just made my wish come true?"

He smiled.

Embarrassed, Yolanda looked down, knowing she had shared too much.

"I think that it's wonderful you made a dream come true. You're entitled to be proud of that accomplishment. Own it," he said.

Yolanda looked up, and they locked eyes.

"Knock, knock," a female voice said from the doorway. Maxwell quickly dropped his gaze to the floor.

Did we just have a moment? Or am I just crazy?

"Was I interrupting something?"

"Not at all, Jackie," Maxwell said, "come on in."

Jackie Townsend walked over to Yolanda and grabbed both her hands.

"My mother just told me the news of your promotion. Congratulations!"

"Yolanda, you know Dee Dee's daughter, Jackie. She made technical instructor a couple of years ago. I'm sure you've seen her around the salon," Maxwell said.

"Yes, of course," Yolanda said, smiling weakly.

She had seen Jackie around the salon hundreds of times, and even though Jackie was always extremely kind and polite, her friendliness somehow made Yolanda uncomfortable.

Jackie was the spitting image of her mother. Same short crop of dark hair, same heart-shaped face with delicate features. They were both tall and curvy and wore expensive designer clothes. After that, the similarities stopped. Dee Dee was cool, sometimes even cold, and very reserved. Her face had a hardness to it, like a soldier going to war. Jackie was overly friendly and sociable, her eyes usually beaming brightly.

"I just wanted to come in and say hello before our meeting Saturday. You must be really excited, huh?"

"Yeah, I'm really anxious to get started."

"I know! I remember my first day like it was yesterday. I was *sooo* nervous! Well, anyway I'm on my way to teach a class, but let's exchange numbers later on, okay?"

"Sure. No problem."

"All right then, see you guys later," Jackie said, leaving in a whir of sunshine and smiles.

"She seems nice," Yolanda said.

"She is."

"Is she always that cheerful?"

"Unfortunately, yes," Maxwell said, laughing. "Well, I guess you've just about met everyone. You remember Theresa McArthur, right?"

How could I forget? I remember when she clowned me in the salon cafe.

"Now, ladies, that is what I call a sunken chest!"

It was the oldest joke in the book, but for some reason it got everybody laughing.

I can't stand her.

"Yeah. Where is she?"

"She's out of town right now, but she'll be back for Saturday's staff meeting." The salon was closed on Monday, so Dee Dee held the weekly staff meeting on Saturday mornings.

Yolanda nodded and looked around her office.

"Where does that door over there lead?" she asked, pointing to a door in the corner.

"Oh, I almost forgot. That door leads to my office; our offices are connected. Dee Dee thinks managers and assistant managers should work hand in hand, so in a lot of ways you're my right-hand man."

"Woman," Yolanda corrected.

"What?"

"I'm your right-hand woman."

"Yeah, okay . . . Right-hand woman. Anyway, I'm usually in my office or walking around the salon, so call me if you need me. We're all connected with these ear-pieces," Maxwell said, pointing to his left ear. "Everyone on staff has a code, so you just dial the code on your keypad. It's all attached to your waistband. You'll receive yours tomorrow. Now come into my office. There are some things I need to brief you on—your duties, what's expected of you, things like that."

This day just keeps getting better and better. Yolanda beamed as she followed Maxwell into his office.

CHAPTER 15

"This box is heavy! I'm about to throw my back out carrying all this stuff for you," Maxwell complained, picking up a large cardboard box.

"Shut up, dude, that's the last one," Tony remarked, holding open the front door to his brand new home.

"Put it over there," Andre said, sitting in a chair in the foyer, drinking a Corona.

"Man, what are you doing?" Maxwell asked.

"Supervising," Andre said.

"Whatever. Say, Tony, what you got in here? Feels like some concrete blocks," Maxwell said, bending his knees to protect his back as he set the box down on the floor.

"Nothing much. Just all my Star Trek stuff."

"Star Trek?" Andre and Maxwell asked in unison.

"Why are you guys acting so surprised? You guys know I'm a Trekkie."

"Since when?" Andre asked.

"Since college."

"So all those conventions you go to—they're not cooking conventions?"

Maxwell and Andre looked at each other and burst out laughing.

"Forget you guys," Tony said, walking to the spacious, open living room and sitting on an old, beat-up leather chair.

"May the force be with you," Andre said.

"That's from Star Wars, idiot, not Star Trek," Tony said defensively.

"Star Trek, Star Wars, same thang," Andre said, sitting across from Tony on a plastic lawn chair.

"When are you getting your furniture?" Maxwell asked, taking a seat on a metal folding chair.

"Next week. New house, new furniture."

Maxwell could see the pride radiating from Tony's face. And he should be proud. He had saved for two years to get his house built. Building a new home seemed like the thing to do lately in Houston. With all the sprawling land available, it didn't make sense to build up— like New York or Chicago—it was better to build out. And out Tony did. All the way to Sugarland, a small suburb on the outskirts of Houston.

"This house is way too big for you," Maxwell remarked, as he looked around the Spanish-style interior.

"Right now, maybe. But I plan to fill this bad boy with a wife and a bunch of kids."

"What? A wife? Kids? Be careful what you ask for," Andre said.

"I know what I'm asking for. I want a family. I didn't build this house for nothing."

"Maxwell, you hear this man?"

"Yeah . . . So?"

"So? He wants a family!"

"And? There's nothing wrong with that. I want a family myself. Speaking of family, I'm surprised you're over here helping Tony out. Isn't today your anniversary?"

"Yeah."

"It is?" Tony said. "Why didn't you tell me that when I called you? You didn't have to—"

"I know I didn't have to, but I wanted to help you. Besides, Brenda will be okay. It ain't the first anniversary I'll miss, and it definitely won't be the last."

"How many years did you guys make?" Tony asked.

"Fourteen," Andre said flippantly, taking another swig of beer.

"Wow, fourteen years. Congrats, man. That's an accomplishment," Maxwell said, giving Andre a friendly pat on the back.

"How is getting married at eighteen an accomplishment?" Andre asked.

"It's not the *getting* married, it's the *staying* married. A lot of people don't make it that long, you should be proud," Maxwell said.

Andre nodded and left the room.

"What's eating him?" Tony asked.

"Who knows," Maxwell said.

"Hey, how's work going?" Tony asked, changing the subject.

"Good, good. We just hired a new assistant manager."

"Is it a woman?" Andre asked, handing Maxwell a Corona.

"Why does that matter?" Maxwell asked, twisting off his beer cap and taking a swig.

"It doesn't. I'm just curious," Andre said, sitting back down.

"Yes, it's a woman."

"Is she cute?"

"No!" Maxwell said too quickly. "Well, maybe. She's got an okay face."

"You said that a little too fast. What is she, fat or something?" Tony asked.

Maxwell burst out laughing.

"Far from it, man. She is so skinny she could hoola hoop through a Cheerio."

"That's original," Andre said dryly.

"Whatever. But you get my point. She's skinny."

"And ugly," Andre added.

"She's not ugly. She's just . . ."

"Average?" Tony offered.

"Yeah, she's average."

"So on a scale of one to ten she'd be what?"

"A three. No, I'll give her a five for her face and a three for her body."

"That's pretty low. She must be a dogface," Tony said, laughing.

"Hey, my wife is a dogface! No harm in finding you an ugly woman," Andre said. "Go marry her and then we both can be dodging anniversaries."

"In your dreams, Andre."

"Well, you need to stop dreaming and get you an ugly woman—"

"Stop calling your wife ugly!" Tony interjected. "Brenda has a kind personality, a warm heart, and, and, and . . ."

Andre and Maxwell exchanged glances and burst out laughing.

"Since we talking about your job, how are you doing with Theresa back working with you?" Andre asked.

"Is she hitting on you?" Tony asked.

"Actually, she's been keeping things pretty professional. I mean, she hints that she wants us to get back together—"

"Don't do it, man!" Andre said.

"Why not get back with her? Everyone deserves a second chance." Tony said. "Besides, Theresa is a beautiful woman . . ."

"Did you forget what that girl did to me? She's the biggest liar in history!" Maxwell said, draining his beer and setting the empty bottle on the terra cotta tiled floor.

"Exactly my point, pretty women can't be trusted. Stay away from her. Far away from her," Andre said.

"That's gonna be pretty hard to do considering we work together now."

"What were you thinkin' by saying it was okay for her to work there, anyway?" Andre asked. "That was stupid. You knew how hard it was for you to get over her. When Dee Dee asked you to re-hire her you should've told her no."

"I know. It's been years. I thought—I mean, I'm over her, so it's okay."

"Sounds like you trying to convince yourself," Andre said.

"I'm not. I'm over her. We're through."

Tony cocked an eyebrow.

"I'm serious, man. It's over."

"Whatever you say, Maxwell," Andre said, "whatever you say."

77

CHAPTER 16

"Girl, I still can't believe you got it! Who knew that my girl would be sittin' on staff. Must be nice, huh?" Natalie said.

"I'm not gonna lie, it feels pretty good," Yolanda said.

It was after a long day of work and Yolanda and Natalie were at another one of their favorite restaurants, Willie's Grill & Icehouse. It was small and conveyed the rustic feel of an old Texas icehouse, complete with outdoor seating, open garage doors at the entry, pool tables on the roof, and lively music.

"Ladies, are you ready to order?" their waiter asked. He was wearing a typical Willie's uniform: a blue T-shirt with blue jeans, and wore his hair in tight neat cornrows.

"Yes," Natalie said, opening her menu. "I'll have your hot buffalo wings for an appetizer, and your full rack of Texas barbecue ribs and a double order of onion rings—no, make that french fries," Natalie said, handing him the menu.

"And you, ma'am?" the waiter asked Yolanda, his voice soft and feminine.

"Um . . ." Yolanda said, scanning her menu. "I'll have what she's having," she said finally.

Giving her a weird look, he took her menu and left.

"People act like I can't eat or something."

"Why are you saying that?"

"Did you see the way he looked at me? Like I was crazy for ordering all that food. Just watch, I'm gonna tear that food up."

"I'm well aware of your appetite. Don't worry about him, he don't know you like I do."

"That's the thing, nobody really knows me. They just immediately start judging me and try to figure out which eating disorder I have."

Natalie reached across the table and yanked on a bright blue rubber-band on Yolanda's wrist, giving her a loud *smack*.

"Ouch! All right, I get the point," Yolanda said, rubbing her wrist.

"Now let's start celebrating your new job promotion and stop whining about things we can't change."

"Okay. Yesterday, Maxwell was showing me around my new office and I started crying and we locked eyes for a minute," Yolanda said.

"Oh no. Yolanda, not again," Natalie moaned.

"What? What are you talking about?"

"Please tell me you are not falling for your boss—"

"Technically he's not my boss."

"Girl, it was cool when you just thought he was cute, I mean everybody at work does. But I hope you are not seriously considering—"

"No! Girl, please . . ."

"Good. I was hoping you didn't try to get promoted for a man."

"Whatever. That's not true. I really did want to move up for me. I'm not like you; not every decision I make involves a man."

"What's that supposed to mean?"

"It means just what I said. This has nothing to do with Maxwell. Sure he's nice looking, but it's not going to interfere with my work."

"You don't have to get so defensive all the time," Natalie huffed.

"I'm not getting defensive, I just—"

"Look, everyone who knows you knows you fall really hard. I just don't want to see yourself doing the same thing you did with Russell."

Yolanda twirled the straw around in her margarita.

"He still bothers you, huh?"

"No, what bothers me is other people who think I'm not over him. Trust me, Russell is in the past. I don't give him a second thought."

She'd die before she told anyone how she saw him leaving Macy's a couple of weeks ago. He was with his mother and, when she saw him, she stopped dead in her tracks, not sure what to do. She didn't have to think long. He made the decision for her. He looked up, recognition flashing, and then he gave her a look that begged her not to come over and speak. His eyes begged her to just leave him alone, to let him enjoy this moment with his mother and to not ruin it. To forget him. To move on. She nodded and kept moving until she could get to a seat and bawled her eyes out in the shoe department, not caring if anyone saw her, not caring who saw her. *He doesn't love me anymore.* She was faced with the question that everyone woman with a broken heart had to ask: Did he ever really love me?

"Look, I wasn't trying to ruin the mood. We're here to celebrate, so let's celebrate! Girl, I'll be right back," Natalie said, standing up. "That beer is running straight through me."

Yolanda watched Natalie walk to the restroom, her big hips swinging with confidence. She wished she could feel as good at her size as Natalie felt at size 24.

"Excuse me, miss?"

The most famous words sung by legendary Luther Vandross was now being asked to her. "Can I Take You Out Tonight" was one of her favorite songs and now this gentleman was asking her the chorus of the song.

Yolanda turned around and saw a pair of the most beautiful dark eyes she had ever seen.

"Can I ask you a question?" he asked, his voice smooth and rich as honey. She knew this guy was gonna ask for her number. *Calm down. Smile at him.*

She looked up at this gorgeous man, gave him a smile, and answered in a low, throaty voice, "Sure, ask me anything." She could almost hear Luther singing, "Can I take you out tonight?"

"Does your friend have a man? She's beautiful."

Yolanda's smile vanished and her heart started beating fast, but for a different reason: the familiar sting of rejection and the stab of jealousy. But mostly she was hurt and embarrassed for thinking this guy, or any other man, would want her.

"Yeah, she has a husband." As soon as the words left her lips she felt bad for lying.

Disappointment washed over his face. "Are you sure?"

"Yeah, I'm sure! I'm her best friend, so I would know. Now step," Yolanda said angrily, cursing herself for being so upset and cursing him for not wanting her.

He stomped away, shaking his head. Yolanda pulled hard on another rubber band. The sting didn't help her stinging ego.

"Who was that fine man?" Natalie asked, sitting back down.

"Nobody," Yolanda said quickly.

"Well what did 'nobody' want? Was he trying to talk to you?"

"I can say for a fact he was not interested in me."

CHAPTER 17

"So what are you gonna wear?"

"I don't know, Mama."

"Why don't you wear that navy blue pantsuit?"

"I can't."

"Why not?"

"Because I have to wear my Behave jacket."

"Oh. Can you pick different pants and shirts?"

"You may wear different color shirts, but you always have to wear black slacks."

"Why?"

Yolanda sighed. Her mother loved to ask 'why' to everything she said. She never accepted information at face value.

"Baby, I know you're nervous about your first staff meeting tomorrow, but I think if you came in dressed to impress, you wouldn't be so nervous," her mother advised.

"Speak for yourself," Yolanda said under her breath.

"What was that, baby?"

"I said I need some more shelves."

"For the living room?"

"No, my bedroom," Yolanda added, rolling her eyes.

"Speaking of bedrooms, let me tell you about what your father did to my closet . . ."

Yolanda listened half-heartedly while eating tortilla chips and mentally going through her closet, trying to think of something to wear. *Daddy must be real bored. I wonder if he misses his job at the post office. He calls himself remodeling, but it looks more like demolishing.*

". . . so now I have to find a place to hang my clothes! Can you believe this man? I swear, Yolanda, everyday it's something."

"Well, Mama, just hold on. It'll be over soon," Yolanda said patiently, rubbing her eyes and hoping her voice did not reveal her exhaustion.

"I know, baby, but I feel like he's gonna send me into an early grave."

Please don't mention blood pressure, don't mention blood pressure . . .

"And it has my blood pressure all up!" her mother said.
Gimme a break.

"Okay, Mama, everything will be fine, but I have to go and iron my outfit for tomorrow."

"All right, baby. Listen, you coming over again this Sunday?"

Oh, great. Another Sunday of Daddy doting on Gina. Count me out.

"I don't know, Mama. Maybe."

"Well, good night, baby."

"Good night Mama. Tell Daddy I love him."

"Okay, sugar. Bye-bye."

"Bye." Yolanda said, relieved to hang up the phone. She had talked to her mother so long she didn't have time to do much of anything.

Yawning, she reached into her closet and took out her Behave jacket. She held it up to her chin and looked at herself in the full-length mirror, proud that she was finally getting to wear it.

Watch out, world, here I come.

They're beating her again.

She's trying to fight them off but they're getting stronger, meaner.

"Mama! Somebody! Help me!" she yells.

No one comes.

She can hear them laughing.

"No one's gonna save you," one of the girls says.

They yank on her pigtails.

They pull so hard that Yolanda feels her hair tearing out.

One of the girls stands over her and shows her the pigtail that she pulled out of her head.

"Lookey what I got!!" the girl says.

Yolanda cannot see the girl's face as she spits on her.

"So a bunch of little girls are whopping yo butt at a playground? You called me at 2:00 in the morning for this stuff?" Natalie shrieked into the phone.

"Listen, these dreams are steadily getting worse," Yolanda said, her voice rising with concern. "This time I woke up all hot and feverish . . ."

"Girl, relax. You know you get like this before an important day. It doesn't mean anything."

"But it was weird . . ."

"So? All dreams are weird."

"Yeah, I know, but this one felt real."

"I can't handle you calling me every time you get one of these crazy dreams," Natalie said, yawning.

"I'm sorry, but they're starting to freak me out. What do you think they mean?"

"Why don't you go talk to a doctor or something if they're bothering you that bad?"

"I can't."

"Why not?"

"Because black folks don't have shrinks."

"What? Girl, please . . ."

"Okay, name somebody," Yolanda challenged her.

"Look, Yolanda, I'm not gonna name somebody so your neurotic butt can be comforted, okay? Besides, who goes around talking about their psychiatrists, anyway?"

"That's because they don't have one."

"Good night, girl," Natalie said, hanging up.

CHAPTER 18

"Hello, passengers. This is the captain speaking. We'll be back in Houston in two hours. Thanks for flying United Airlines."

Theresa sat back in her first-class seat and closed her eyes. Dee Dee had her running around like a chicken with its head cut off, but she didn't mind. It felt good to be coming back from a week-long business management conference. Dee Dee was unable to attend because of problems with the manufacturer for Behave's new product line. Dee Dee didn't like the smell, the design of the shampoo bottles wasn't sleek enough, and on and on.

At least Sheila is not here.

Theresa burst out laughing, causing the other passengers to turn and look at her.

"What?" she said, daring anyone to say something.

I thought so. Y'all ain't stupid.

All those years, all the arguments they had, all the times Sheila said she was trying to sabotage her, to take her job. All that mess is over, *'cause ding-dong, the witch is gone!*

The good part was that it was all true. Sheila had been right all those years; she had been trying to take her job.

Well, I need it more than she does because she's got a man and I don't.

I'm out here on my own with no support system, so I need this job more than she does. Besides, it feels good to feel important like this. For a little while, anyway.

Dee Dee reminded her everyday that this was all temporary.

I know Jackie is gonna be creative director.

The thought made her sick to her stomach, but there was nothing she could do about it. *Blood is thicker than water.* Right now she would just have to ride the wave until it ended.

"Excuse me, attendant?" Theresa said, snapping her fingers.

The flight attendant ignored her, too busy smiling at one of the male passengers.

"Excuse me!"

"I'll be with you in a minute, ma'am," she said, her voice traced with irritation.

Isn't this first class? What's going on? Miss Thang think she's cute with all that long blonde hair.

Theresa looked at her and sneered. She was tall and crazy thin, like all those actresses lately. Carol would've looked at her and twisted Theresa's arm: *"See, why couldn't you look like that? That girl look decent and moral. You lookin' like some harlot with those big ol' breasts of yours. Ain't you got no dignity, no shame?"*

Theresa rubbed her arm, as if Carol were sitting right next to her and twisting her arm behind her back until she heard the familiar pop of a broken bone. Carol would have loved this attendant. This woman filled her standard of what beauty truly was. She and probably Yolanda, that girl from work.

Yolanda possessed no qualities that would distinguish her as a woman. Flat breasts, straight hips, and an even flatter butt. Oh, Carol would love Yolanda. Every time Theresa looked at Yolanda, pure, hot hatred filled her heart. Her whole life she had been told that having her voluptuous body made her look like a prostitute. Having a body type like Yolanda would've made Carol happier. "You see her?" Carol would say, pointing at a skinny woman in the street. "Now there's a woman with real class. A woman with real style. Why did I have to give birth to you? A little Jezebel hussy?"

Theresa knew she was wrong for hating Yolanda; she shouldn't have to pay for her painful past. But somebody did. And it felt good to be the one with the power for a change. The power to make somebody else hate herself and wish she had been born into a different body. So she made an effort to make Yolanda's life miserable, as miserable as her own life had been.

Theresa watched the attendant pass her for the second time, not acknowledging her waving hand.

When she walked past a third time, Theresa stuck out her foot slightly, causing her to trip and fall, hitting her chin hard on the armrest of a passenger's seat.

She sat up wailing, her mouth covered in blood, her front tooth chipped.

Looks like somebody won't be smiling for a while.

CHAPTER 19

Yolanda pulled into Behave's circular drive and got out, handing Marco, the valet, the keys.

"Morning, Yolanda. How's it going?"

"Great. Hot out here, huh?"

"Yeah, but I don't mind. I turn on the air conditioning when I park the cars," he said, speeding away and parking in Yolanda's new reserved parking spot in the garage.

Yolanda still couldn't believe how quickly everything had changed. Here she was getting valet parking on her first morning as salon assistant manager. She was on her way to her first staff meeting, and her mind was like a dry sponge, eager to get wet and thirsty to learn how to run a megasalon like Behave so efficiently.

She walked up the cobblestone driveway, her low heels clicking on the hot stone. She saw Jose, the handyman, tinkering with the fountain in front of the salon.

"Good morning, Jose."

Wiping the sweat off his forehead with the back of his hand, Jose looked up and nodded in her direction.

Well, I guess some things never change, Yolanda thought, walking up the steps to the front entrance of the salon. Since she started at Behave six years ago, Jose might have mumbled 'hello' twice.

She inhaled the scent of lavender and honeysuckle, intensified by Houston's heavy heat, from the potted topiaries lining the steps to the salon. She pulled open the heavy, intricately designed wrought-iron door and was instantly greeted by Karen, one of the receptionists.

"Good morning, Miss Peterson, did you have a good weekend?" Karen asked, smiling widely.

"Yeah, it was pretty good. And yours?"

"It was okay. Just tried to stay cool," Karen said, picking up the ringing phone.

Yolanda ran into Jackie at the elevators.

"Morning, Jackie."

"Morning, Yolanda. You on your way up?"

"Yes, first day, remember?"

"That's right," she said, as they stepped onto the elevator.

"How do you feel? Nervous?"

"Actually, I feel pretty good. Any advice?"

They stepped out of the elevator and went to the café. She had told Jackie she wasn't nervous, but her stomach kept doing flip-flops. She didn't want to ruin her first meeting by barfing on everyone, so she thought something light to eat would settle her nerves.

"You don't need any advice. You're going to do just fine. Don't ever be late, though; Dee Dee doesn't accept tardiness," Jackie said, her voice bright as a summer's day.

"Not for you though, right? You could probably miss a meeting and your mama wouldn't fuss."

"Excuse me? My mama? Don't get it twisted. I'm treated just the same in this salon as everyone else. I don't get any special treatment from Dee Dee. Never have, never will," Jackie said, her voice harder.

"I'm sorry, I was just—"

"Don't worry about it!" Jackie said, her smile returning. "What are you going to get?"

"Um, I don't know . . ."

"I'll just have a large black coffee," Jackie said, sliding her staff card through the electronic scanner. Everyone on staff had an extra perk by having member cards so they didn't have to pay a dime for food or anything they might need during the day. Stylists and other employees were given deep discounts, but nothing was free.

"And for you, ma'am?" the server asked, turning to Yolanda.

"I'll have two large bagels with cream cheese."

Smiling, he told her to 'have a nice day', and handed her a crisp white bag with the salon's logo, a beautiful woman cracking a whip over someone's hair to make it *Behave.*

"You eat? Man, looking at you I would have thought you skipped almost all your meals!"

Jackie laughed, but Yolanda didn't.

"You have a pretty fast metabolism, huh?"

"I guess."

"You want me to wait for you while you eat? We could go to the meeting together. I'll introduce you to everyone."

"Um, no thanks. I think I've met everyone. Besides, I have to clue my assistant, Megan, in on some last things about my clients."

"You mean her clients?"

"Yeah. I'm sorry, I mean her clients."

"It feels weird, doesn't it?" Jackie asked.

"What does?"

"Giving up one dream for another."

"Yeah, it does."

"Don't worry, everybody felt that way one time or another."

"Did you?" Yolanda questioned.

Jackie frowned. "Yes, even me," she said tightly. "Especially me," she added, walking away.

Yolanda walked into Dee Dee's office and immediately wanted to run out. Everyone was clustered in small groups together, and although she knew most of the people, there were still a few she wasn't quite familiar with. She regretted not accepting Jackie's offer to introduce her to everyone. Determined, she walked up to one of the receptionists, Michelle.

"Hey!" Michelle said, her Southern twang a comfort to Yolanda's ears. "Congrats on your promotion! I know you've wanted this for a long time."

"I know, I still can't believe I'm here."

"Have you met everyone?" Michelle asked.

"Um . . . I think so except . . . Is that Theresa talking to Maxwell in the corner?" Yolanda asked, instantly jealous.

"Yeah. She's been filling in for Sheila ever since she left."

"I thought she was out of town?"

"She came back yesterday."

She watched Maxwell and Theresa talking. Theresa was absolutely drop-dead gorgeous. Her Behave business suit hugged her curves. That wasn't a surprise; the girl could wear overalls and her body would curve its way through the denim. Yolanda knew all the squats in the world wouldn't give her a quarter of what Theresa had. She watched Theresa laugh at something Maxwell said and toss her long sandy-brown hair behind her ears. *Please let it be a weave. Let me have something over her.*

She watched Theresa run her fingers through it and saw golden-blonde highlights throughout, and knew from all her styling experience that it was all hers. Every strand of it. Her brown almond-shaped eyes sparkled behind long, sooty lashes. When she smiled Yolanda saw a perfect row of white teeth.

"Is something wrong?" Michelle asked.

"Why?"

"I don't know, you just had a funny look on your face."

"I was just wondering . . ." *Does Maxwell like that light-skinned beauty? Do I still have a chance?* ". . . wondering if this Theresa girl is gonna be the new creative director?"

"Girl, no," Michelle said, laughing. "Everyone knows it's gonna be Jackie."

"Why Jackie?" Yolanda asked.

"Well, for one, she's Dee Dee's daughter; for two, she's Dee Dee's daughter for three . . ."

"She's Dee Dee's daughter," Yolanda added.

"You're a quick one. Yeah, Jackie knows she's a shoe-in. Must be nice."

"Why?"

"As creative director you start off with six figures a year, you get a company car, a Benz no less, and an expense account. I mean the list goes on and on."

"The low six figures, right?" Yolanda asked.

"Try again, sista. Come on, you need to meet Theresa. It's about time y'all get formally introduced."

"Um . . . wait . . . maybe we should do it after . . ."

"After what? The meeting?"

"Yeah."

"Dee Dee's on the phone on a conference call. We have at least ten more minutes. Come on."

Michelle grabbed Yolanda's hand and dragged her to where Maxwell and Theresa were standing.

"Hey! Y'all met Yolanda yet? She's new to staff," Michelle said loudly.

Yolanda watched Theresa's light brown eyes give her the once-over.

"We've spoken on occasion," Theresa said, her voice hard and clipped.

Yolanda looked at Maxwell for an introduction. He looked at her and then looked down, suddenly interested in his expensive alligator shoes.

"Theresa, this is Yolanda Peterson, our new assistant manager," Michelle said, stepping in. "Yolanda, this is Theresa McArthur."

"Nice to meet you," Yolanda said, extending her hand.

Theresa hesitated, looking at Yolanda's outstretched hand. She gave her a weak handshake, then dropped it quickly, as if she might catch some horrible disease.

"Nice shirt, girl. Is it new?" Michelle asked, admiring Theresa's Versace shirt.

"Yeah, I got it last week."

"Where did you get it from?" Yolanda asked, trying to get in the conversation.

"Why?" Theresa asked.

"I don't know . . . I was just asking . . ."

"Listen, Yoranda . . ."

"It's Yolanda."

"Yolanda, Yoranda, whatever. I got this shirt at a place that designs for a woman's body."

"What's that supposed to mean?" Yolanda said, her voice rising from embarrassment.

"It means, boo, that you have the body of a teenage . . ."

"Don't, Theresa," Maxwell said, trying to cut her off.

". . . a teenage boy," Theresa said.

"That's enough," Maxwell said.

It was enough. Enough for Yolanda to feel the sting of hot tears behind her eyes. Theresa gave Yolanda a long, hard look and walked away. Maxwell followed close behind her.

"What was that all about?" Michelle asked.

"I don't know," Yolanda croaked, willing her tears not to fall.

"I thought you said you hadn't met her before?"

"We have, I just haven't talked to her. Not really, anyway."

"She has got it in for you."

"I don't know why."

"You better find out. Theresa can be . . ."

"A witch?"

"Well, at least you didn't cuss. You know how Dee Dee feels about cussin'. She won't tolerate any bad words, and you don't even want to know what she does if she ever catches you using one." Michelle paused and looked off into the distance. "Take it from me, you don't want to get on Theresa's bad side, especially this early in the game. She can make your life hard. Real hard." She coughed, and looked back at Yolanda. "Find out what's eating her and resolve it. And quick."

Yolanda nodded, well aware that she should take Michelle's advice very seriously.

"The meeting is about to start," Michelle said. "Come on."

She followed Michelle through a wide oak door leading to the conference room that joined the two spaces. The conference room was in sharp contrast to Dee Dee's office. Where her office was light and serene, this room was dark and impressive. A long, oval ebony table engulfed the center of the room. It could have easily seated twenty or more people, Yolanda guessed. The walls were in different tones of brown, a plastered effect that gave them a rich finish that no paint brush could duplicate.

She followed Michelle and took a seat next to her, then she noticed the disapproving glance Maxwell gave her, so she moved to the seat next to him.

"This was Theresa's old seat, now it's yours," he said.

After the run-in with Theresa she didn't like sitting in anything that had once belonged to her, even if it meant not sitting next to Maxwell.

"You okay?" he whispered, swallowing the last bit of the cinnamon mint he'd been sucking on.

"I'm fine."

"Sorry about all that. She's not usually like that."

"It's okay," Yolanda said, smiling and trying to pretend Theresa's words hadn't stung.

"It's just that——" Maxwell began, but was interrupted when Dee Dee appeared.

"Good morning ladies and gentlemen," Dee Dee said, walking over to her chair in a manner befitting a regal queen.

"Morning," everyone said in unison—like fifth graders responding to their teacher.

"I'm sorry about the delay; I had a very important business call. I trust everyone slept well?" Dee Dee said to no one in particular while scanning a black folder.

Everyone nodded or said yes.

"Good, good. Unfortunately, I'll have to cut this meeting short. I'm expecting another phone call in twenty minutes."

She went around the room asking questions relevant to this or that department: Were retail sales up? How was salon morale this week? Is our fall advertising campaign up to par? Was the new product line going to be ready by winter? And on and on it went until she came to Yolanda, who had been busy taking notes and trying to absorb everything.

"Okay, everyone, in case you didn't already know, we have a new assistant manager, Miss Yolanda Peterson," Dee Dee said, clapping.

Everyone clapped and gave her warm smiles. Everyone except Theresa. She yawned and looked at her flawless French manicure.

"Yolanda, why don't you stand and tell us a little bit about yourself and some of your objectives," Dee Dee said.

Was she for real? Oh, please don't tell me I have to do this high-school crap . . .

"You do know what your objectives are, don't you?" Dee Dee asked.

"Yes, of course," Yolanda said, standing and smoothing her suit jacket.

"Well, tell us. We're all dying to know," Theresa said, her voice heavy with sarcasm.

Yolanda ignored her and tried to think of something clever to say. "Um . . . Well, my name is Yolanda Peterson. I'm twenty-nine years old and one of my objectives is to . . ." . . . *kill Theresa, kill Theresa . . .* ". . . to make Maxwell's job easier by assisting him in every way possible," Yolanda said and sat down.

"Very good. Well, I'm afraid our time is up," Dee Dee said, standing. "Everyone have a wonderful day. Michelle, please follow me; there are a few things I need to discuss with you about our front-desk procedures."

And just like that, the meeting was over. Yolanda never felt so relieved. She organized her notes, trying to stay next to Maxwell a little while longer.

"So Maxwell," Theresa said, loud enough for everyone to hear, "we all still invited to Ray's tonight?"

"Yeah, but you don't need an invitation; everyone's welcome," Maxwell said.

"Well, I don't know about everyone," Theresa said, looking directly at Yolanda. "Your father doesn't take kindly to strange faces."

Hurt by Theresa's cruel remarks, Yolanda looked at Maxwell, desperately wanting him to invite her to his father's restaurant so she could show Theresa that she had every right to be there, that she belonged. But the invitation never came. And as the conversation swirled around her about how live the restaurant was on Saturday night and how much fun they were gonna have, she got up and left.

CHAPTER 20

Natalie filled out her registration form online.

Her hand shook as she moved her mouse to the send button.

Just do it. Quick and easy, like a Band-Aid.

She clicked her mouse and sent her form to one of the top culinary schools in Houston.

It was done. She had just pre-registered to start school next week.

Seeing Yolanda chase her dreams and succeed made Natalie realize that it was time for her to start her life. She had been hiding behind styling hair all these years and couldn't live her true self. But now she'd finally taken the first step toward regaining her life. It was going to be hard. She didn't know how she was going to juggle working and going to school at night, but she knew that, like most women, she had to get everything done. She sighed, already feeling exhausted from work that hadn't even begun.

I wonder how Yolanda will react when I tell her tomorrow.

She knew her friend would always have her back, but Natalie knew Yolanda would be disappointed that she wasn't staying in the same field. When Yolanda made management, she knew her promotion would take her as far as she wanted to go in this business. Natalie would just have to tell her that hair wasn't for her anymore and that she longed for the day when she could open up her own restaurant. She closed her eyes and saw her restaurant as clearly as she could see her own apartment.

The restaurant would be draped, top to bottom, in warm tones of honey and caramel, colors so sweet you couldn't wait to bite your mouth down on a rich osso buco, braised to perfection with the perfect blend of seasonings that brought out the flavor of the veal. She would serve it with creamy mashed potatoes and sautéed spinach with roasted pine nuts. She rubbed her stomach and pictured herself eating every savory, delicious morsel.

She woke up from her reverie feeling starved, and went into the kitchen to fix a quick snack.

CHAPTER 21

"So how has your training been going?" Jackie asked, taking a bite of her chicken salad sandwich.

"It's been going pretty well, actually. Maxwell has been very nice and patient," Yolanda said.

Actually, the training was kicking Yolanda's butt. She never knew this would be so hard. It was great working with Maxwell, but he was a perfectionist and didn't care how many times she had to do something over and over again, he wanted it just so. Trying to remember all the codes for the computer system and which days to order what for inventory had Yolanda's brain turning to mush. She didn't know if she could squeeze anything else in. She was tired, but she got energy from knowing that this is what she'd always wanted. Yolanda could feel the approval from her former workmates as she and Jackie ate their lunch in the salon café. *This is all worth it.* Finally, she was getting looks of envy, looks that she normally dished out to other women. She was getting full doses of it. It wasn't right by any means, but she savored the feeling, knowing it wouldn't last long.

Yolanda scanned the café, looking for Natalie. They always sat together for lunch, but lately she had been too busy to take a break and had to sit in her office to eat, quickly gulping down a sandwich while going over files.

There was a large mural on the wall behind them of black people eating and drinking outside. It could have been a picnic or a family reunion, but whatever the occasion, everyone looked happy. The café was filled with both staff and employees, all sitting in their own cliques enjoying a hot meal.

"When is your probationary period over?"

"In about six weeks," Yolanda said, taking a big bite out of her bacon cheeseburger.

"How can you eat all that junk and not gain weight?" Jackie asked.

Yolanda shrugged and inhaled a handful of fries.

"Okay, girl, watch out . . . that stuff is gonna go straight to your hips one day."

Let's hope so.

"Hey, girl!" Natalie said loudly, walking over to where Yolanda and Jackie were sitting. Her white shirt was unbuttoned, showing plenty of cleavage and stretch marks, and her tight black pants couldn't stretch another inch over her enormous hips and thighs.

"Where have you been hiding?" she asked, pulling out a chair.

"Excuse me," Jackie said sweetly.

Natalie turned around to look at Jackie.

"Yes?"

"We were having a staff discussion, and it really isn't appropriate for employees to listen in on this kind of stuff."

"First of all, we're all employees, and second of all, if it's that important, save it for a staff meeting. I'm trying to talk to my friend," Natalie said.

"Listen, um . . . ?"

"Natalie."

"Yeah, Natalie. I'm trying to be civil here, but we were having a private discussion. Sit somewhere else," Jackie said, smiling tightly, her eyes cold and hard.

"You stuck-up little—"

"Natalie!" Yolanda cut in. "Why don't I call you later on tonight, okay?"

Natalie turned and gave Yolanda a long look. Yolanda pleaded with her eyes for Natalie to just drop it. Natalie shoved the chair back hard and walked away, twisting her big hips as she went.

"First things first, don't associate with anyone at work unless they are on management," Jackie said.

"Why?"

"It'll cause problems. Trust me, just don't do it."

"But Natalie and I are friends. We've been friends for years; I can't just stop speaking to her," Yolanda said.

Jackie shrugged and finished eating her sandwich.

"See right there?" Maxwell asked. "Your numbers are all wrong, it should be up 22.6 percent, not 21.4 percent. Better check that out."

"Right."

Maxwell leaned closer to Yolanda, looking over her shoulder at her computer. She froze. *He has never been this close to me.*

"Check that one out, too," Maxwell said, tapping on Yolanda's computer.

"Okay," she said, looking up into his eyes. *Women would kill for those eyelashes. He could be in a mascara commercial.*

"What?"

Yolanda jumped slightly, not realizing that she had been openly staring at him.

"I was just looking at your eyes."

"What about them?" he asked.

"They're beautiful."

He frowned.

"Well, it seems like you have this under control," he said getting up. "I'll come and check your progress tomorrow." He turned and went into his office.

What did I say? Was I being too forward? I've really messed up now . . .

"Knock, knock."

"Come in," Yolanda said, wondering if she should apologize to Maxwell. She didn't mean to make him feel uncomfortable.

"Hey, you wanna go get some drinks tonight?" Jackie asked.

"Sure. When?"

"Now. That is, if you're finished."

"Yeah, I'm pretty much done here."

"Where did you want to go?"

"What about Ray's?" Yolanda asked. She was dying to go, and by the looks of it she wasn't gonna get invited anytime soon.

"Nah, we're supposed to be going there after Saturday's staff meeting. I'll wait until then. I was thinking more like Jax," Jackie said.

"Okay, sure," Yolanda said, trying to hide her disappointment. "We can go there. Just let me tell Maxwell I'm leaving."

"Sure. Meet you out front," Jackie said, beaming brightly.

She straightened her desk, trying to make enough noise to lure Maxwell out of his office.

He didn't.

She knocked on his door.

"Come in."

Yolanda opened the door slightly and poked her head through.

"I just wanted to let you know that I was leaving."

"Good-bye," he said without looking up.

She closed the door, upset with herself for making that stupid remark about his eyes. She grabbed her purse off her desk and took the elevator downstairs to meet Jackie.

"Hey, Miss Thang," Natalie said. When they were both stylists they would wait on each other in the reception area, then meet up for dinner. Yolanda had been so busy she had forgot about their routine.

"Hey, girl," Yolanda said, feeling awkward. "Look, I'm sorry about lunch."

"Water off a duck's back. That wasn't even the worst part of it. Let's go get something to eat and I'll tell you the rest. I'm starving."

"I can't."

"Why not?"

"I already promised Jackie that I would get drinks—"

"Enough said. Go have fun," Natalie said dismissively.

"Look, I'll make it up to you. Can I call you tonight?"

"You owe me big time. Saturday night, Doneraki. You better be there," Natalie said, reaching for a hug.

"You know I will," Yolanda said, thankful for having such an understanding friend. She gave her a warm hug and left. She didn't want to keep Jackie waiting.

Jackie watched Yolanda approach her car. *She was almost pretty.* Her long brown hair was in soft curls cascading down her back and her caramel skin was smooth and creamy. She was just too skinny. *Poor girl, she's gonna have to marry a white man. A black man wouldn't touch her with a ten-foot pole. He'd get tired of telling people that she wasn't a crackhead, that she was just naturally that skinny.*

It made Jackie uncomfortable giving her a hug, because she could feel all her bones. A gust of wind blew and Yolanda's clothes pulled against her and Jackie saw the outline of her body and shuddered. Her thighs were like toothpicks and her chest was flat as a pancake. *Poor, poor girl.*

"You sure you wanna ride together? I could just follow you," Yolanda said, getting into Jackie's Lexus.

"Nah. You live close to the salon, and your car will be fine. Besides, we can talk more. I want to learn more about you," Jackie said, pulling out of the parking lot.

"What do you want to know?" Yolanda asked, adjusting the vents so she could feel the air conditioner.

"Oh, I don't know . . . What made you want to be a hair stylist?"

"It's a funny story actually. I'm not a morning person, but when I was in high school, I would get up two hours earlier than necessary just to curl my hair."

"Really?"

"Yeah. So my mother saw all the fuss I was making over my hair, and she suggested I take cosmetology in high school. I guess the rest is history."

"That's good that your mother is so supportive of your career," Jackie said.

"I'm sure it's the same for you and your mama, right? Aren't you and Dee Dee close?"

Jackie paused, trying to think of something appropriate to say. She didn't know this girl well enough to say that the relationship was strained, to say the least.

"Yeah, we're close. As close as a mother and daughter could be, I guess." Jackie turned on the radio, and they and jammed on Keyshia Cole's urban poetry all the way to the bar.

Jax Grill was packed. Then again, the place never failed to draw a crowd, its down-home barbeque and upbeat music being the main attraction. Happy hour was in full swing, and Jackie had to circle the parking lot twice before finally cutting off another car and stealing a spot. The bar was located in a part of town that was unpretentious and casual, a nice change from the upscale atmosphere of the salon. It was clearly a come-as-you-are scene; everyone was dressed casually in T-shirts and jeans. Jackie and Yolanda could hear the zydeco music blaring through the speakers as they took off their jackets and threw them into Jackie's trunk.

The band was on a break when they got inside, which was probably the reason they found a small table near the rear of the bar. Yolanda had never gotten a seat inside, always having to melt outside on the bar's oversized patio.

"I can't believe we found a table!"

"I know, I'm surprised," Jackie said, pulling a platinum flask from her purse and taking a swig.

"You don't want to wait until we order?" Yolanda asked, surprised that Jackie couldn't wait until the waiter came.

"Girl, I'm just relaxing after work, that's all," she said, taking another swig. "You want some?"

"No thanks. But maybe you should put it away. This isn't BYOB."

Jackie shot Yolanda an icy look, and took another drink. Finally, she screwed the top back on, muttering "Party pooper" under her breath.

"It looks nice, though," Yolanda said, trying to dispel the tension in the air, nodding at Jackie's flask, which had rows of diamonds on the rim. "Where did you get it?"

"My mom gave it to me."

"It's beautiful."

"It's all right," Jackie said, tossing it into her large Louis Vuitton bag.

"Excuse me, but we were sitting here."

Yolanda turned and saw two tall Hispanic women looking down at her.

"Oh, I'm sorry, we didn't know," Yolanda said, grabbing her purse.

"We're not going anywhere," Jackie said, smiling as she looked up at the two women.

"Look, we just got up to get some drinks—"

"And? You move, you lose."

"Woman, give us our table back!" one woman demanded.

Jackie stood up.

She said something in Spanish to the women. She was smiling, but her voice was a low growl. The two women backed up.

"Sorry," one of them said. "Keep the table."

"*Gracias*," Jackie said, sitting down. Her nostrils were flaring and her face was red with anger. *Well, as red as black people can get.*

"What did you say to them?" Yolanda asked, curious.

"Nothin' really," Jackie said. "I told them I was packing, and if they didn't leave I would kill them."

"What? Are you serious?"

"Yep," Jackie said, her color returning to normal. "So, girl, what are you gonna drink?"

"Um, I don't know. Listen, are you okay?"

"Me? I'm fine," Jackie said, smiling brightly. "You wanna split some wings?"

"Thanks again, girl. I had a good time," Yolanda said, getting out of Jackie's car.

They had laughed and talked for hours. Yolanda was surprised by how much they had in common. She had felt a little uncomfortable right after Jackie had threatened those women, but as the evening wore on, she forgot all about it.

"I had a good time, too. Let's do it again soon, okay?" Jackie said.

"Sure," Yolanda said, closing Jackie's door. She walked to her car and sped off into the night.

CHAPTER 22

Theresa wasn't sure why Dee Dee wanted her to come to work early. She didn't even ask. The valet crew didn't come until 8:00, so she pulled her BMW into a parking spot near the front that was normally reserved for clients. She would have Marco move her car into the garage later. *If there was a later.*

Theresa loved her parking spot. It used to belong to Sheila, but now it was hers, all hers. She knew she was just a temporary fill-in for creative director until Dee Dee found an adequate replacement. She tried to keep to herself, to not become attached to this place. But Behave had a way of pulling you in, making you feel at home. And Theresa did feel at home, more at home than at any other salon she had ever worked. Behave was definitely unlike any other salon. Even though it was big—enormous, in fact—it had a tranquil quality to it. It could be teeming with clients, some eating and talking in the café, others chatting with their stylists, still others buying products to *tame that wild hair.* Even with all the hustle and bustle, the Behave experience could still soothe, ease, seduce, you into a trance-like state, making all your problems melt away. At least for the moment. Theresa did not want to leave, but she knew her time had come to an end.

Theresa got out of her car and started walking toward the entrance.

"Hello, Miss Theresa."

"Hello, Jose," Theresa said. Jose was at the front door holding it open for her. Every time Theresa walked by, Jose always stopped whatever he was doing and complimented her on everything from her clothes to her hair—even her body. This habit of his bothered most of the women at the salon, and he had been in two meetings with Maxwell about his unwelcome glances. One more complaint, and he was out.

"You lookin' really nice, Miss Theresa," Jose said, practically drooling.

"Thank you, Jose," Theresa said, walking past him and noting he smelled of grass and sweat. She kept walking, but turned at one point and saw that he was still watching her. Theresa had that effect on men. It both irritated and flattered her at the same time. She liked men to be attracted, but a small nagging sensation would creep up her spine and she would become uncomfortable with the attention. It was if Carol was standing next to her and she could feel her body stiffen, preparing herself for a blow to the head. *"What'cha been doing for them men to be lookin' at you like that?"* She could feel the pain in her head like Carol had just hit her. Her breathing quickened and her hands began to tremble violently. A cold sweat poured over her and she punched the floor number and scrambled in the elevator. Nausea washed over her and she took deep breaths, trying to steady her breathing. Her psychiatrist, Dr. Perry, told her to try to calm herself down before she reached for her medication. *Breathe, breathe . . .*

She could feel her heart beginning to slow down to a normal pace and her hands stopped trembling. Her panic attacks had become more frequent in these last months. Seeing Maxwell, memories of Carol—all set off panic attacks. She had been struggling with them ever since she had left high school, but she had only got diagnosed three years ago. All that time she never knew what was happening to her, but she felt like she was losing her mind. *Breathe, breathe* . . . She couldn't talk to Dee Dee in this condition—she would have to go to her office and freshen up.

"You wanted to see me, Dee Dee?" Theresa asked, standing in the doorway of Dee Dee's office.

"Yes, come in and have a seat," Dee Dee said, looking at something on her computer.

Theresa sat down.

Dee Dee took off her glasses and looked long and hard at Theresa. It was a look that would unsettle most people, make them fidget or glance away. But not Theresa. She looked back, mentally preparing herself for what Dee Dee was about to say.

"I think you know me well enough to know that I'm pretty straightforward. I'm incapable of small talk. That being said I want you to be my new creative director. I'm announcing it at today's staff meeting," Dee Dee said.

"Excuse me?"

"It goes in effect starting Monday. The office you're in now will be yours for a few days, then you'll move to the office next door to mine, Sheila's old office."

"Wait, wait . . . I don't understand. I thought I was just . . ."

"Temporary? Yes, I know, but I was just testing you to see if you fit. You're more than qualified, and I am confident you will do a wonderful job. I want you to look at this contract," Dee Dee said, handing Theresa a thick folder. "Read it carefully, and if there's anything in it you need to discuss, just tell me. You'll find it more than fair."

All my dreams are coming true. I told you, Carol, I told you I was gonna be somebody one day . . .

"Thank you so much for this opportunity, Dee Dee," Theresa said, trying to keep her composure. *I just wanna scream and shout and do cartwheels all over the place!*

Dee Dee grabbed Theresa's hand. "Thank yourself for being such a brilliant, talented black woman. You are my right hand, an extension of myself. I know you can make me proud and lead this salon into a bright future."

"Thank you, thank you so much. I don't know what to say."

"Don't *say* anything. Be a woman of action and *do* something," Dee Dee said.

Theresa stood up. She wanted to cry. She wouldn't in front of Dee Dee, not yet. *Why wasn't this woman my mother? Life would have been so much different . . .*

"I promise, Dee Dee. I won't let you down," Theresa said.

Dee Dee smiled.

Yolanda was the last person to arrive for the meeting in Dee Dee's conference room. Because she was so late, she was tense and jittery.

"Come in, Yolanda, we've been waiting for you," Dee Dee said.

Yolanda walked in, and saw a mask of disapproval on Maxwell's face. She knew he would talk to her about being late, and it set her more on edge. She sat down between him and Jackie and felt his body shift away from her. Jackie was smiling broadly at her. She smiled back, relieved to see a kind face. She scanned the room and was surprised to see Theresa sitting on the other side of Dee Dee. She had been hoping Dee Dee would have found Sheila's replacement by now so she wouldn't have to see her. After that last incident, Yolanda had studiously avoided Theresa, which wasn't hard to do. Their feelings for each other were mutual, so Theresa stayed away from Yolanda as well.

"You almost missed the best part," Jackie whispered.

"What?"

"She's about to announce me—I mean, who the creative director is."

"Really?"

"Yeah, listen," Jackie said. Yolanda said a little prayer for Jackie, although she knew she didn't need it. She knew it was gonna be Jackie. *Who didn't know that?*

". . . and after much careful deliberation, Behave Hair Salon's new creative director will be . . ."

Jackie Townsend, Jackie Townsend . . .

"Theresa McArthur!" Dee Dee said, clapping loudly.

Stunned silence fell over the room, and then everyone started clapping and offering their congratulations. Yolanda looked at Jackie. She was smiling and clapping loudly. Louder than anyone else, in fact. She seemed genuinely happy for Theresa, but Yolanda noticed her nostrils flaring. And her face was turning a dark red.

"Congratulations Theresa!" Jackie said, walking over to Theresa and giving her a hug. Soon everyone else followed suit, leaving Yolanda the last one to offer her congratulations.

"Congratulations Theresa," Yolanda said, reaching for a hug, too. Theresa paused for a nanosecond and then gave her a quick hug.

"Girl, you're so bony! I could break you in half!" Theresa said, laughing.

Why did I even hug this girl? I am so stupid . . .

"Okay, meeting adjourned. You guys have a great day. Theresa, come by my office in an hour," Dee Dee said, walking away.

"What are you doing tonight?" Jackie asked Theresa.

"I don't know. I didn't have anything planned."

"Let's go celebrate!" Jackie said.

"Why don't we go by my father's spot? They're having a Musiq Soulchild concert tonight," Maxwell said.

"I forgot about that! That's tonight?" Theresa asked.

"You can get us in? We don't have tickets . . ." Yolanda started to ask, then stopped when she saw the annoyed glances from everyone in the room.

"It's my father's restaurant, Yolanda. I don't think I'll have a problem getting in," Maxwell said, a smirk on his lips.

"Us in," Theresa said. She curled her lips at Yolanda. "I'm sure you have plans tonight, don't you Yolanda?"

"Not that I recall . . ." Yolanda said.

"I forgot. With that body, you look like you spend a lot of your Saturday nights alone."

A few people snickered.

"That's enough, Theresa," Jackie said, coming to Yolanda's defense. "Maxwell, you have enough tickets for all of us don't you?"

"Sure."

"So, Yolanda you coming?" Jackie asked.

"I wouldn't miss it for the world," Yolanda said, eyeing Theresa.

"So what seems to be the problem?"

"I don't know. I just feel so out of place. I don't think I belong here," Wanda, a new stylist, said, her eyes tearing up.

As assistant manager, it was Yolanda's job to monitor and maintain morale.

"Wanda, everyone has those days. You just need a couple of weeks to adjust."

Yolanda remembered her first month at Behave over six years ago. Seeing all the other stylists exhibiting their talents, styling prowess, and self-confidence, she had become convinced she would never measure up. Even the clients were intimidating: businesswomen, politicians, athletes and their wives, sometimes even celebrities. Once, Natalie said she saw Nia Long getting a haircut. But then again, she wasn't sure, because she really didn't see her face, just the back of her head as she left. They still argued about it.

Yes, Yolanda knew all too well what this young girl was talking about.

Her earpiece buzzed.

"Yolanda, this is Maxwell. I need to see you in my office ASAP."

"Okay, I'll be right up." She would have to make this quick.

"Like I was saying, this salon can seem a little scary at first . . ."

"A little scary?"

"Okay, terrifying, but you won't find another opportunity like this again. How long were you on the waiting list before you got hired?"

"Five months."

"You came all that way to quit now? I know you're stronger than that. There are people dying to have your job, but they're not here. You are. Now toughen up. You can handle it."

"All right," Wanda said, sniffling hard.

"Talk to me anytime, okay?" Yolanda said, walking away.

"Hey, where's the fire?" Natalie said, grabbing Yolanda's arm.

"Nowhere, girl. Maxwell just called me . . ."

"Yeah, yeah. Listen, what happened at this morning's meeting?"

"Um . . ." Yolanda hesitated. It was against Behave policy to pass on information to employees until the monthly salon meeting, and even then, not everything was discussed. "Nothing really."

"You're lyin'."

"No, I'm not."

"You're a horrible liar, so spill it."

Yolanda's earpiece buzzed again. It was Maxwell again.

"Look, I can't talk about it right now."

"We have a little bet going on down here, and I just wanna know who the new creative director is."

"I can't tell you until the meeting in two weeks . . ."

"Who is it? I know it's Jackie, I know it is. Just tell me," Natalie whined.

"Really, I can't . . ."

"Come on, I got $100 bucks riding on this. It's Jackie, isn't it?"

"No," Yolanda said, looking around. *I shouldn't be doing this.*

"It's Theresa," she whispered.

"Who?" Natalie said, getting closer.

"Theresa. Theresa McArthur."

"No way."

"Believe it."

"Theresa is the new creative director?" Natalie said loudly.

"Shut up!" Yolanda said, looking around to see if anyone had heard.

"I'm sorry, it took me by surprise."

"I gotta go."

"What about tonight? We still on for Doneraki?"

"Yeah, yeah, sure. I'll call you," Yolanda said, hurrying past the reception desk. *Maxwell's gonna kill me . . .*

"Miss Peterson?"

"Yes?"

"You have a call on line three," Karen said.

"Take a message," Yolanda said, still walking.

"I can't; they say it's an emergency."

"Can I use one of the phones up here?" Yolanda asked.

"Sure, knock yourself out."

"Hello?"

"Yolanda?"

"Mama, what is it? You said it was an emergency."

"Well, that was the only way they would let me talk to you. Anyway, how you doing, baby?"

"Mama, I need to call you back, I'm right in the middle of—"

"I know, but I was just thinking about you and decided to give you a holler."

Yolanda rolled her eyes.

"Mama, I love you but I have to hang up."

"Oh, baby, ain't you sweet! I love you, too, baby. Bye . . ."

She hung up.

"Thanks, Karen."

"While you're up here, I really need the new schedule. You were supposed to give it to me Tuesday."

"I'm sorry, I forgot . . ."

"I really need it. Clients are trying to make appointments and . . ."

"I know how important it is, Karen. I'll give it to you by 5:00. Is that okay?"

"No, but I guess I'll make it okay," Karen said, taking a call.

"Hey Yolanda!" Michelle called out. "I need you to look at yesterday's inventory order and sign it so I can give it to Maxwell."

"Can this wait?" Yolanda said, frustrated.

"No, I need you to sign this now so I can work on today's inventory."

"All right, all right," Yolanda said. She looked through the papers, made sure everything was in place and signed the order.

"When does this get logged into the computer?" Yolanda asked.

"After Maxwell approves it. You all right?" Michelle asked. "You look kinda stressed."

"I am. I'm always running around, sign this, do this. This promotion isn't as glamorous as I thought."

"Welcome to the real world," Michelle said, answering the phone in her Southern twang. "Thank you for calling Behave Hair Salon. This is Michelle. How can I help you today?"

Yolanda walked away and ran to the elevators, bolting through as soon as the doors opened. She knocked on Maxwell's door, out of breath.

"Come in," his deep voice boomed.

She walked in apologizing. "I'm sorry about not coming right away—"

She stopped when she saw Theresa sitting in a chair across from Maxwell's desk.

"Next time try to get here promptly, Yolanda," Maxwell said curtly.

I hate getting fronted like this, especially in front of Theresa.

Theresa didn't say a word, not even acknowledging her presence. She looked up at her and a wicked smile crept across her lips. Yolanda turned her head.

"This is a list of people I need you to talk to today. They all need to be given a written warning. They have to sign it. Have it back to me in an hour," he said firmly.

Yolanda looked at the list. It contained over twenty-five names, from stylists to café workers. The warnings were for lateness, dressing inappropriately, excess customer complaints, among other infractions.

I can't finish this in an hour!

"You want this in an hour?"

"Will that be a problem?"

"No, it's just that it's a lot of people. . .."

"Yolanda, it's not brain surgery. Can you handle it or not?"

Yolanda looked at Theresa. That smile was getting bigger. *I'm gonna slap that smile off your face.*

"You'll have it an hour."

"Good," Maxwell said, turning his attention back to Theresa.

"So back to what I was saying, if we just increased our—Yolanda?"

"Yes?" Yolanda said, still standing by his desk.

"Good-bye," he said.

Theresa burst out laughing.

Yolanda walked out, Theresa's laughter chasing her.

She went into the restroom down the hall and looked in the mirror.

"You are a fool."

CHAPTER 23

Yolanda walked outside. Her neck was stiff and tight, her shoulders ached, and she could feel the beginning of a headache behind her eyes. She was not surprised that the sun was long gone. She had stayed longer to catch up on some of her work. Mentally exhausted, she was at the point where she couldn't make one decision, didn't want to think. Dee Dee made it look so easy. *How did she do it?* Yolanda was gaining more respect for Dee Dee with each passing day. She had created something out of nothing and was running it so effortlessly. Well, not effortlessly; Dee Dee worked hard. She was the first to arrive and the last to leave. Behave was her ship, and Dee Dee was its captain.

At least I got my reserved parking spot. Right next to Jackie. She saw Jose and his wife, Maria, walking to his truck. They were such a weird couple. Him always flirting and looking at other women, her being so unaware she probably never noticed.

"Good night, Jose. Maria," Yolanda yelled across the parking lot. Jose turned around and nodded. Maria waved, and hoisted her short, heavy frame into the truck and they drove off.

Jose flirted with anything in a skirt, any woman that breathed, except Yolanda. It never bothered her, though.

All her co-workers would gather around and talk about the latest sexist joke he had told them, or some nasty compliment that he had given one of them. She hated it, and was glad he never came around her with none of his nonsense. *I mean, maybe I would tolerate it if he was good-looking, but Jose? Gimme a break.*

She got in her car and sped off, hoping for a good time at Ray's, happy she was finally invited.

"You want another drink, ma'am?"

"Um . . . yeah, another margarita would be great. Can you bring some more chips, too?"

Natalie picked up her cellphone and pressed redial.

"Hey, Yolanda, this is Natalie. I hope you didn't forget about me tonight. I'm sitting here like an idiot, waiting for you. Where are you?"

Natalie hung up and scanned the menu.

Ray's was crowded. The line to get in curved down the block and there was no place to park. Not for free, anyway. Yolanda drove to the parking lot across the street. Seven dollars to park, the sign read, in bright red letters.

Yolanda dug in her purse for the money and rolled down her window to give it to the attendant approaching her car.

"Ten bucks," he said, his long dreadlocks hitting Yolanda's car window.

"Excuse me?"

"Ten bucks. Ten bucks to park."

"But your sign says seven."

"That's the sign, I'm saying ten bucks. It goes up when they have concerts across the street," he said, his breath heavy and sweet from the peppermint he was sucking on.

"Rip-off," Yolanda mumbled under her breath, handing the man ten dollars. He then directed her to a parking space.

Earlier, she had gone home and changed into a bright red shirt, hoping it would bring everyone's attention up and away from her anorexic body. Even so, Yolanda heard the whispers from the mostly black crowd as she walked toward the end of the long line.

"She is sooo skinny!"

"She need to eat."

"Look at her legs! They look like toothpicks."

Yolanda hated walking past lines ever since high school, when she had to walk past the lunch line in the cafeteria. She hated high school. She always wore baggy pants and big T-shirts. And she never tucked her shirt in. She had no butt, so she took pains to hide that fact: a backpack, a jacket, anything to hide her nonexistent butt. But one day, she felt different. She was a sophomore in high school; she was getting older and it was time to be herself. *I don't have to hide behind anything. I'm just gonna be me.*

So she did the one thing she had never thought she would have the courage to do: She tucked her shirt in.

She didn't care who saw, or what anyone said, but she felt better that she wasn't trying to hide behind a piece of cloth. Emboldened by this newfound confidence, Yolanda went to school. No one said anything; nobody even noticed.

So far, so good.

That is, until she got to the cafeteria.

In high school, she had a huge crush on Derrick Wright. But who didn't have a crush on Derrick?

He was a bright, shining star in Yolanda's dark, lonely life. He was involved in everything: football, track, the debate team, national honor society. That is why Yolanda liked him so much. He wasn't just a dumb jock. Derrick was smart and going somewhere.

She passed him in the cafeteria, giving him a huge smile that screamed: notice-me-love-me-be-my-boyfriend. He smiled back, his teeth white and perfect, glowing against his light caramel skin. He grabbed Yolanda's hand. She stopped, not sure what to do.

"Hey, girl, what's going on?" he said, smiling. His friends were smiling, too.

This is good, real good. He's acknowledging you in front of his friends. Talk, say something.

"Hi."

"Where's it at, girl?" Derrick asked, smiling.

"Where's what at?" Yolanda replied, confused.

"Your butt! You ain't got no butt, girl! Where is it?" he screamed, laughing uproariously. His guffaws could be heard throughout the cafeteria.

"You the man, Derrick."

"Boy, you crazy," his friends said, slapping him on the back, laughing.

Yolanda ran out of the cafeteria and into the restroom, Derrick's mocking laughter trailing her long after she could no longer actually hear it. She untucked her shirt, and from then on wore her shirts out to hide her butt.

"Hey, Yolanda! Yolanda!" Jackie said, waving wildly near the middle of the line.

"Hey, girl!" Yolanda said, relieved to see a familiar face.

"Come on, you can skip," Jackie said, stepping back so Yolanda could get in front.

"Thanks. Everyone else inside?"

"Yeah, they're already in there."

"I hope we can get a table. It's crowded."

"Don't worry, Maxwell always reserves a table for us near the front."

The line moved quickly and they were soon inside.

"Hi, Jackie! You guys here for the concert?" the hostess asked. She was standing behind a whimsical stand shaped like an inverted triangle, painted in muted colors of purple and green.

"Yeah. Did Maxwell reserve us a table?"

"He sure did." She marked something on her book, smiled to both of them and told them to follow Sandra to their table. "Most of your party is already seated. Have a great time," she sang.

Yolanda followed Jackie through the eye-dazzling space, passing a sweeping staircase that led to the mezzanine floor. It must have given spectacular views of the entire restaurant, and Yolanda reminded herself that next time she came she would try to sit upstairs. The modern chairs were covered in an iridescent satin that would change from purple to green to blue, depending on how the light hit it. The booths were just as luxurious, with high backs and partitioned walls that ensured privacy. The walls were painted a subdued ocean blue, and seemed to twinkle in the romantic light. Long, modern light fixtures hung from the high ceilings. Yolanda had to remember not to stare, open-mouthed, at all the opulence.

Yolanda sat down at the end of the table next to Michelle, with an empty seat at the head of the table and another empty seat right next to her. Jackie sat directly across from her next to Lacy, one of the managers in the spa. Yolanda said her hellos to everyone else at the table; most of them were on staff, so she was acquainted with a few of them since her promotion. Their waiter came over with a chilled water carafé and poured water into their glasses.

"How's it going, Jackie?" the waiter asked, not spilling a drop of water on the pristine, white tablecloth.

"Pretty good, Bailey. Bailey, this is Yolanda," Jackie said, nodding in Yolanda's direction. "Yolanda just got promoted to management."

"That's great," he said, handing them their menus. "Hopefully I'll be seeing more of you. Our specials tonight are penne with rock shrimp and a spicy tomato cream sauce, pan blackened Ahi tuna filets, and a slow cooked Carolina pulled pork with a maple and Tabasco sauce.

What can I get for you to drink?" Bailey asked, his long arms behind his back, totally comfortable in his element.

"I'll have white wine," Jackie said giving Bailey her menu back. "You know I don't need this! I've got these dishes memorized, I come here so often! I'll start with—"

"A platter of chilled, steamed crawfish?"

"Yes, but make sure—"

"That it has the Remoulade dipping sauce? It wouldn't be complete without it," he said laughing. "And for you, ma'am?" Bailey asked, looking at Yolanda.

Yolanda glanced around the table to see the choices of the delectable appetizers everyone else was nibbling on. "I'll have that," she said, pointing to Michelle's plate.

"The Cajun Seafood Risotto? Excellent choice. And to drink?"

"White wine will be fine."

He nodded and left.

"This place is spectacular! I can't believe I've never been here."

"Yeah, it is pretty remarkable. Where's Maxwell?" Jackie asked, nudging Lacy.

"In the back talking with his father. I think the entertainment is running late."

"And Theresa?" Jackie asked.

"She's not here yet," Michelle interjected. "I'm sure she'll be here soon, though."

Yolanda assumed the two empty seats were for them, considering everyone else was already here. *There's no way I'm gonna make it all night sitting next to Theresa. I should have gotten here earlier.*

The waiter arrived with their drinks and Yolanda wanted to chug it down, but took a lady-like sip and scanned the menu.

"So, Jackie, are you going to venture out and try something different?" Bailey asked, his blue eyes twinkling with amusement. "Or are we having the usual?"

"Don't play, Bailey. The usual."

"What's the usual?" Yolanda asked.

"Thick-cut pork chops with a roasted garlic and bourbon barbecue sauce," Bailey said.

"That sounds yummy," Yolanda said, looking down at her menu. "But I think I'll have the pecan coated catfish with Creole mustard sauce and lemon? And the herbed dirty rice for a side."

"Very good ma'am," he said, taking her menu. "Your appetizers will be here shortly.

Yolanda caught Theresa walking in, catching glances from all the men in the restaurant, married or single. She wore a short, tight black dress with a simple V-neckline that hinted at her cleavage. Her long hair was in soft, loose waves and danced behind her back as she walked her way to their table. Yolanda looked down at her red shirt and felt tacky and overdone. Theresa slid in next to Yolanda and reached into her black clutch bag for a bottle of prescription pills. Her hands were trembling as she reached for Yolanda's water and took a long sip.

"You all right?" Jackie asked.

"Just fine," Theresa answered. "Just feel a migraine coming on. Thought I better catch it before it got too bad." She took another sip of Yolanda's water and then handed it back to Yolanda without saying a word.

Excuse you, Yolanda thought. She put her glass back on the table.

Bailey came and took Theresa's order and then she began a lively conversation with everyone on the new product line.

That is, with everyone except Yolanda. Every time she tried to add anything to the conversation, Theresa would ignore her comment as if she didn't exist. Soon she quit talking and dug into her creamy risotto with the zeal of a homeless person.

"Sorry everybody," Maxwell said, walking up. "Musiq's limo is running late, but he will be here shortly. Everybody, you guys remember my father?" he said, gesturing to the man standing next to him. "Pop, I want you to meet Yolanda. She's new to management."

"Pleasure to meet you," Ray said, extending his hand to Yolanda. They shook hands.

"How do you like the place?"

"It's great!" Yolanda said, her voice full of girlish enthusiasm.

Theresa rolled her eyes. *"It's great!"* she mimicked, in a low voice.

Yolanda dropped her voice a few octaves. "The place really is beautiful though—"

Ray put his hand up to answer his cell phone. "Outside? Okay I'll be there." He put his phone back inside his jacket, smoothing his Versace tie. "That's the entertainment. I have to go. Nice meeting you, Yolanda.

Especially nice seeing you again, Theresa." He leaned over and whispered something in her ear and she put her head back and laughed.

"I'm trying," she said, looking at Maxwell.

"Try harder," Ray said, walking away.

An uneasy feeling settled in the pit of Yolanda's stomach. Their entrées arrived, and silence filled the table as everyone dug into their food. Yolanda closed her eyes, savoring the succulent catfish. She opened them and saw Maxwell sitting at the head of the table, watching her.

"Looking at you makes me want to eat all over again," he said, his eyes searching her face.

Theresa groaned. "Looking at *her* would make *anybody* want to eat."

Yolanda saw Jackie fight back a laugh.

Yolanda slid her water glass next to Theresa. "Obviously your Lithium hasn't taken effect. Perhaps you need two more pills?"

Jackie burst out laughing, followed by additional laughter down the table.

"No you didn't, you little—"

"Hey, hey. Let's settle down, Musiq is taking the stage," Maxwell chimed in. "Good one," he whispered to Yolanda, before taking a sip of his drink.

The lights dimmed slightly, giving the restaurant a more romantic feel, and Ray introduced Musiq Soulchild to the small stage.

His smooth voice filled the restaurant and Yolanda rocked to the beat. She was so close to the stage she could see the frayed hem of his designer jeans as he crooned out his R&B tunes. The dance floor began to fill with couples dancing to his melodic songs. People were standing up and shouting, hands waving in the air, Soulchild's music moving them. When they played "B U D DY," Maxwell jumped up.

"That's my jam! I gotta dance to this one."

Maybe it was the wine, or being inspired by the live music, but Yolanda did something she never did. She took a chance.

"You wanna dance?" Yolanda asked, not breathing.

"Yeah," Maxwell said, pulling Yolanda's chair back. He reached for Yolanda's hand and she grabbed his tightly. They reached the dance floor and all of Yolanda's inhibitions melted away. If there was one gift that God gave her, this was it. Yolanda could dance her butt off. In fact, they both loved to dance and they moved easily together.

> . . .*Girl, I can't lie, it'll be fly*
> *If you were my B U D D Y*
> *Don't be shy, give it a try*
> *I could be yours if you could be mine . . .*

The song switched to Musiq's hit "Love." The song was slow and purposeful and they both paused, looking at each other. Yolanda started walking off the dance floor, but Maxwell took her hand.

"Can I cut in?"

"Sure, Theresa," Maxwell said, looking down at Yolanda. "You don't mind, do you?"

Of course, I mind.

"C'mon, girl, I'll give him right back," Theresa said, squeezing between Yolanda and Maxwell.

Yolanda watched Theresa, her arms linked around Maxwell's neck, looking up into his eyes. She then looked at Maxwell, searching for some indication of who he thought danced better, she or Theresa. Yolanda could see all over his face that he liked Theresa's dancing more. She watched, tormented, as Maxwell whispered something in Theresa's ear and she threw back her head and laughed, her long wavy hair swishing like a horse's mane at full gallop. They looked like they could be on a postcard. Yolanda walked back to the table, disgusted.

"You were looking real good out there!" Jackie said, smiling.

"Yeah, I know . . . until somebody had to spoil it," Yolanda said, sitting down.

"Who, Theresa?" Jackie asked, watching them dance. "Same ole Theresa. That girl will never change. She'll never let Maxwell go."

"What do you mean *let him go*? They used to go out?"

"Yeah," Jackie said talking, over the music. "A long time ago. They broke up, and she's been trying to get back with him ever since."

"Why did they break up?"

"Can't remember. But it was bad. Real bad. Took Maxwell a long time to get over her. I'm surprised they're friendly."

"Why?"

"They were engaged. Broke up a month before the wedding. Theresa was the love of his life. Never knew why it was over, just one day, the wedding was off."

When the song ended, Theresa and Maxwell walked off the dance floor laughing. They walked arm in arm to the bar and ordered drinks. Yolanda felt sick.

"I'm leaving," she said, grabbing her purse.

"What! Why? Musiq's not even finished yet!" Jackie said, surprised.

"Suddenly I don't feel so good. I'll call you later."

"All right, girl. Be careful."

Yolanda didn't hear her. As she walked through the crowd all she could think of was Maxwell. Maxwell and Theresa.

Yolanda thinks she's slick. Jackie chugged her wine down and waved at Bailey for a refill. Something a little stronger than wine.

It was so obvious that Yolanda wanted Maxwell. Everything she did revolved around him.

It won't hurt to keep her around. She could come in handy during my next step. Besides, I like Yolanda. She's a little weird, but I still need her.

Jackie watched Maxwell and Theresa laughing at the bar.

Having somebody hook up at work would give her the distraction she needed right now.

I'm gonna help you, Yolanda. I'm gonna help you get Maxwell.

CHAPTER 24

"What happened to you last night? I waited for you for over an hour!"

"I'm really sorry. Things have been crazy. I'll make it up to you . . ."

"That's what yesterday was for, remember? You were supposed to be making it up to me about frontin' me in front of Jackie. Now you telling me you gonna make it up to me for standing me up? What's going on with you, Yolanda? It feels like I haven't talked to you in months. You haven't showed me your office, you haven't called me. What's going on?"

"I know. Look, Natalie, can I call you back? I'm right in the middle of something," Yolanda said, looking through a stack of paperwork.

"They got you that busy you can't talk to your best friend? I really need to talk—"

"Natalie, I know, but can it wait? I'm getting buried under paperwork and I have a deadline to meet. I promise I'll . . ."

"Yeah, yeah, I know, you'll make it up to me. Fine," Natalie said, letting out a long exasperated breath, "I'll let you go."

"Thanks, girl. I'll call you later."

Natalie hung up, and put the cordless phone on the end table. It fell, and she kicked it hard under the couch. *Ever since Yolanda got this promotion she doesn't have any time for me anymore.* She kept hanging around Dee Dee's daughter, Jackie, a stuck-up brat. Natalie was glad she didn't get promoted to creative director, served her spoiled self right. *I hope Yolanda don't start acting like Jackie. Although she is starting to act funny. It's probably too late.*

Natalie walked back to her small pine breakfast table and started studying for her first quiz tomorrow night. She had been in school only a little over two weeks and already was overwhelmed by schoolwork. She had been late for work twice this week, something that rarely happened, but she was losing sleep by staying up and doing so much work. She really needed to talk to someone. She had hoped today would be the day she could tell Yolanda her great news. But it would probably wait. The more Natalie waited to tell Yolanda, the more she no longer wanted to tell her. She didn't think Yolanda deserved to know her good news.

"Okay, everyone listen up, I have some very exciting news," Dee Dee said.

"*Essence* magazine will start a new column on what's hot in select cities, and Houston will be spotlighted in their upcoming January issue. The editors feel that Behave Hair Salon is one of Houston's top salons so . . . we've been selected."

"All right!" Maxwell said, clapping and encouraging everybody else to do the same.

"This is going to take a lot of hard work from everyone," Dee Dee said, looking around the room. "This is August, and *Essence* has a four month lead time, so that doesn't give us much time to come up with a concept and execute it. Theresa, that will be your job. You need to think of a creative concept that will actually portray Behave. Since it will be in January, I'm thinking clean, sexy, fresh. I want this to be modern with a traditional slant. We'll use the same ideas for our spring ad campaign," Dee Dee continued. "Maxwell, I need you to pick the styling team. We need four of our best stylists and two nail technicians. Also talk to Andre from Forward Boutique and see if we can get clothes for the models. Tell him there will be a free plug in it for him.

"Yolanda, work closely with Maxwell. Since you just got off the salon floor, maybe you can suggest a few stylists. You're still fairly new, so watch and learn. All right, any questions?" Dee Dee asked, taking a deep breath.

She answered everyone's questions, occasionally glancing at her watch.

"Okay, you guys, get to work," Dee Dee said, standing. "Theresa, by the way, I want a daily report on everything, every evening."

"Yes, Dee Dee, that won't be a problem."

The briefing over, everyone left the conference room. Everyone except her daughter Jackie.

"I assume you want something?" Dee Dee asked, walking back to her office and sitting at her massive desk.

"Why do you always think I want something, Mama?"

"Dee Dee. At work, refer to me as Dee Dee just like everyone else."

"I'm not everybody else! I'm your daughter!"

"I'm well aware of that fact," Dee Dee said, turning her computer on.

"Could you pay attention to me for one minute?" Jackie said, beating an angry fist on Dee Dee's desk.

Dee Dee sat back in her chair and looked at her daughter.

"I'm listening," Dee Dee said, her voice cool and steady.

"Why didn't you have an assignment for me at the meeting?"

"I didn't feel you needed an assignment. But if you're feeling left out you can assist Theresa . . ."

"I don't want to assist Theresa! I want my own thing! I want to feel important, too!" Jackie yelled.

"Lower your voice," Dee Dee said icily.

Jackie took deep breaths, trying to get control of her emotions. "All I'm saying is that I would like to feel needed."

"You are needed. You teach and instruct all those shampoo technicians how to become Behave stylists. You are very important. What more do you need?"

"I want you to love me."

"I do love you!" Dee Dee said, frustrated.

"Not the way you loved Michael."

Hearing his name sent sad chills down Dee Dee's spine. Had it only been three years since Michael died? She looked at his picture on her desk and her heart twisted in pain. Her arms ached knowing she would never hold her son again.

Dee Dee sighed. "I don't know what else I can do to show you my love, Jacquilyn. You're just gonna have to believe me."

She looked up at her daughter and saw the pain in her dark eyes. *Did I cause that pain? I want to hug her, hold her so tight she can't breathe. But I can't move.*

"I have work to do," Dee Dee said finally, returning to her computer.

"Of course, you do," Jackie said, walking out of Dee Dee's office and letting the door softly click behind her.

Dee Dee sighed and rubbed her hand down the back of her head, missing the long strands that she would gather up in a high ponytail. She had been feeling like she was getting too old for all that hair and had cut it all off the day before Michael's funeral. *For goodness sake, I just turned fifty last year. Oprah says fifty is the new forty . . .*

A year after she and Jonathan were married she got pregnant with Jacquilyn. Nothing had come easy with her— not the birth, her childhood, her adolescence— nothing. They had spoiled her, and Jacquilyn grew up feeling entitled, feeling that everything that came her way was owed to her and she should not have to work for it. When she was a teenager, she would ask her to help at the salon, to sweep the floors and make herself useful. Every chore was met with resistance until Dee Dee stopped asking, giving them both less headache. After high school Dee Dee pushed college on her, saying that it was important for her to have a business background.

"You didn't go to school and look how well you turned out! There's no way I'm doing it, either."

Dee Dee relented and gave her a small position shampooing hair, believing that everyone should work themselves up the ladder, even if she owned the ladder. Jacquilyn balked, saying she shouldn't have such a menial position. After several jobs, she finally settled on being assistant technical instructor and then moved up to being head technical instructor.

But it wasn't enough. It seemed it was never enough. Jacquilyn wanted more, more, more. *She wants me to die. Then she thinks my empire will be hers.* She felt that was Jacquilyn's secret prayer, for her mother's death.

When Dee Dee saw that the salon was about to burst at the seams from so many people she made the decision to find a bigger salon. That's when everything came to a head, when Dee Dee saw all the hate that was bubbling just underneath the surface in her daughter's heart. Jacquilyn was ecstatic to learn they were expanding to a new salon location. She saw this as her opportunity to branch out on her own. Dee Dee played along, dangling the salon in front of Jacquilyn so she would cooperate with their move to their present location. She told her to wait a year, and she could do whatever she wanted with the old property. In that short time, she saw a transformation in her daughter. Jacquilyn became a hard worker and listened to her mother's every word. She was helpful and took the initiative on projects. Her motives were still in the wrong place; Jacquilyn was only helping because of what she thought she was getting out of it, but even still,

Dee Dee relished those short months. She really did intend to give it to her, but an offer came on the property that she couldn't pass up, so she sold it without telling Jacquilyn a word. She knew it was wrong, and promised herself she would tell her when the time was right, but that time never came up.

Six months into their new location, Jacquilyn stormed into her office and screamed at her that the old salon had been leveled and that someone was building a car wash there.

"What's going on? There's got to be some mistake—"

"There is no mistake, the owner can do whatever he wants to his property," Dee Dee said, keeping her voice even.

"The owner? I'm the owner! I never told anyone—"

Dee Dee looked at her. "I sold that property six months ago. You never owned it."

"What?"

"You never owned it."

"But you said—"

"I know what I said!" Dee Dee said, guilt making her voice go sharp. "You weren't ready—"

"You wouldn't have done this to Michael," Jackie said, her voice flat and even. Her hands were clenched, as if she would strike her.

Dee Dee gave her a steely gaze. *She wouldn't dare . . .*

"Michael has nothing to do with this."

"He has everything to do with it. Did he put you up to this?"

"Don't be ridiculous. He would never do such a thing."

"It's always about him! Everything is. Somehow he weaseled his way into my business deal—"

"It's not Michael! It's you! You are not ready. You can't cut it!"

Jackie flinched.

Dee Dee let out an exasperated sigh.

"What I meant to say is that I don't even know who you are anymore. You didn't want to go to business school—which your father and I agreed to. But then, you didn't want to learn anything around the salon—"

"What do you think I've been doing all this time! I've been here busting my butt for months—"

"That's just it, Jacquilyn. That isn't enough time to learn how to successfully run a salon. Now, Michael comes into my office—oh, baby, I'm sorry," Dee Dee said, when she saw tears falling from Jacquilyn's face.

"Not yet, but you will be," she said, storming out of Dee Dee's office. Things had not been the same between them ever since.

She looked at Michael's picture again, and couldn't believe that those two had came from the same womb; their personalities were like night and day. While Jacquilyn complained about doing every menial chore, Michael would insist on helping with everything. He rarely had to be told to do anything and took the initiative with chores around the house, as well as the salon. He would love to come into her office after school and listen to her tell him how the business was run, how to make something grow from nothing.

It's never easy for a mother to admit that she favors one child over another, but Dee Dee did. Michael was like Cool Whip on apple pie, he made everything just that much sweeter. Jacquilyn was lemonade that lacked enough sugar, you could see the potential, but needed to keep adding sweetener to get it there.

The phone rang and Dee Dee jumped. She picked it up on the second ring.

"Hello?"

"Hey, it's me."

"Oh, hello," Dee Dee said, irritated by the sound of her husband's voice.

"I was in the neighborhood and wanted to know if I could stop by? Maybe take you to lunch?"

"I'm busy."

"We don't have to go out. I could bring lunch to you."

"I told you I'm busy. I'll probably have to skip lunch altogether."

"Well, what about dinner?"

"I have to work late."

After a long pause, he said, "I'm really trying, Dee Dee."

She didn't respond. She looked at Michael's picture.

"You're not making this easy for me."

"Why should anything be easy for you?"

"I miss him, too."

"You're supposed to. You're the reason he's gone."

"You don't care, do you, Dee Dee? You don't care about me at all."

"No, Jonathan, I don't."

She hung up.

CHAPTER 25

Ever since I was a little girl she's done this. Always patronizing me . . .

Sipping on the bourbon she had hidden in a drawer in her desk, Jackie sat in her office in complete darkness. She took a long swig, and some of the intense liquid escaped her mouth and slid down her cheek. She swiped her mouth with the back of her hand. The familiar burning in her chest from the liquor was like an old friend coming back to visit.

Even though she had a drink just before the meeting.

And an hour before that.

And at breakfast . . .

So?

Who cares?

Nothing wrong with having a little drink now and then. . .

I got it under control.

It's her fault I'm like this. . ..

Why am I here if she doesn't give me anything to do?

She's watching me. . ..

Testing me . . .

I'm ready, Mama!

Ready to take over the world.

She laughed then, long and bitter.

It's not easy knowing you're not the favorite.

Jackie remembered growing up watching her mother
dote on her younger brother, Michael.

I was the oldest; I should have been the star.

She remembered coming home from high school,
excited because she made an "A" on her first cosmetology
exam. She rushed into the kitchen, breathless. Her
mother turned to look at her. And frowned.

The wind got kicked out of Jackie's sails as she listened to her mother criticize her about her hair not being
neat enough.

"I'm sorry, Mama . . . I was rushing."

"Jacquilyn, you could at least stop and take a comb to
your hair! I own a hair salon and my daughter goes
around like some kind of Raggedy Ann doll! Go to the
bathroom right now and fix it! I don't want to look at you
like that!"

"But, Mama—"

"Now!" her mother said, her eyes becoming hard slits.

Jackie walked to the bathroom down the hall, and
started combing her hair. She heard when her brother
raced in from the back door, his small feet sounding like
a brigade marching to battle.

"Michael!" her mother cried, reaching down and
giving him a warm hug.

"Hey, Mama!"

Jackie stepped out of the bathroom and watched
them. At first she thought Michael's shirt was covered in
shadows, that her eyes were deceiving her. But they
weren't. He had spilled what looked like chocolate milk
all over his white polo shirt.

How come he wasn't getting yelled at?

Angry, she stormed into the kitchen.

"Look at his shirt! He's got chocolate milk all over it! How come you're not yelling at him, Mama? Why you always yelling at me?"

"Oh, Jacquilyn, do we have to start this right now? I'm tired."

"No! You should yell at both of us or neither of us—"

"For heaven's sake, he's a child. They get dirty, okay? You're almost a grown woman—"

"That's not fair."

"Life's not fair! I am so sick and tired of you always comparing yourself to Michael. I'm trying to raise you to be self-sufficient—"

"No, Mama, you said it right at first. You're tired of me," Jackie said, walking away, ignoring her mother calling her name.

If there was one thing she got from her mother, that would be it—the last word.

I guess you taught me something after all. Jackie took another gulp of bourbon.

You'll see.

You'll see I'm just as good as everybody else.

Sheila, Theresa, everybody.

I'm gonna prove to you I'm somebody.

CHAPTER 26

"You are looking at one of the stylists for the *Essence* shoot, young lady," Tasha said, putting on a pair of latex gloves in the supply room.

"Congratulations. When did they post the list?" Natalie asked, taking off her apron. She had just finished her last morning client and had an hour break for lunch.

"Just now, in the technical room."

"I'll go in there and—"

"No need to rush. Your name is not on it."

Natalie sucked in her breath.

"Really?"

"Yep," Tasha said, smacking on her gum. "They going to pull us all together for a meeting later today. Jackie has already told me I have to tone down my look, whatever that means."

Natalie saw a hint of red lipstick on Tasha's chin and wondered how Yolanda could let this fool get an opportunity like this.

"I thought Yolanda was supposed to be looking out for you up there. What happened?"

"I don't know."

"Hey, well don't get too down. Maybe she got you doing something even better."

"Yeah, maybe," Natalie said, grasping at straws.

"See you later," Tasha said, leaving Natalie in the supply room. Maria was stacking thick white towels in the corner cabinet.

"Hey, um . . . Maria, have you heard anything about the *Essence* shoot? Maybe somebody talking about the stylists they were going to pick?"

"Miss Natalie, they say you too fat. Mess up pictures. In my 'pinion, you prettiest of all."

"Thanks, Maria. That means a lot," Natalie said, looking up at the fluorescent lighting so tears wouldn't stream down her face.

"Anytime, Miss Natalie."

Natalie stood in front of the list of stylists for the *Essence* shoot, her anger at a low boil.

How could she do this to me? How could she leave me out in the cold like this?

Natalie remembered when she first met Yolanda at the salon six years ago. She was having lunch in the café and everyone was talking about the new girl working there. No one talked about how talented she was, or how great her clientele was. They all talked about Yolanda's weight. Or lack of it. Natalie had to admit that when she first saw her, she had immediately thought of all those TV ads showing starving children in some Third World country. *For just a dollar a day you can help save a child's life.* Yeah, Yolanda was that skinny. But all Natalie's life she had been fat and hated being judged by it. She promised herself she would get to know Yolanda, and not judge her as so many others had judged her weight.

And now this. *If Maria knows why I haven't been picked, then Yolanda knows, too.*

And it wasn't the fact that her name wasn't on the list.

It was the fact that after all these years, after all the times Natalie had stuck up for Yolanda, and rooted for her, just this once when Natalie needed her to get behind her, Yolanda wasn't there.

She'd let this job go straight to her head.

Natalie knew there was a strict line between upstairs and downstairs. But she didn't know that Yolanda, her best friend, wouldn't cross it, that their friendship wasn't important enough for her to stand up to people and say, "Yes, that's my friend Natalie and we're gonna eat lunch together!"

But Natalie had other things on her plate. *I should actually be relieved that I won't have to take time away from school for more salon work. But Yolanda doesn't know about me going to school. She didn't think I was qualified to tackle the job. I'm her best friend! Was. Was her best friend.*

She was afraid, afraid she was losing her best friend.

CHAPTER 27

Theresa knocked twice on Maxwell's door and then pushed it open.

"Hey, baby, I was just . . ."

She stopped short when she saw Yolanda sitting at Maxwell's desk. He was leaning over her, apparently explaining something on the computer screen. The fact that Maxwell was so close to Yolanda was unnecessary and inappropriate. *He used to help me like that, always finding an excuse to get near me. Now he keeps his distance like he could catch a fatal disease just by touching me.*

She could almost hear Carol's words chanting; "*That Yolanda girl sure is pretty. Thin as a blade of grass, innocent as a newborn baby. Nothing like you, you café lookin' whore . . .*" Theresa's blood began to boil. Maxwell was hers. True, they were no longer engaged, but that would change soon. She had sensed his resistance breaking down. He wanted her back, and she *needed* him back. This time she would handle things differently. This time she would be honest about *everything*.

Theresa coughed discreetly.

Maxwell jumped back, his guilty expression making it appear that he had been caught red-handed doing something off limits.

"Was I disturbing you guys?"

"No, not at all," Maxwell said, clearing his throat. "Did you need something?"

"There are a lot of things we need to discuss, and I was hoping we could have a working lunch? I need to bounce a couple of ideas off you."

"I don't know; I'm kind of swamped here."

"It doesn't have to be right now. It could be a late lunch, maybe around two?"

She was begging and she knew it. It was out of character for her to ask any man for anything, but if this is what it took to get him back . . .

"That would be fine. I'll meet you downstairs at two."

"Great," Theresa said, looking at Yolanda. *Thin as a blade of grass, innocent as a newborn baby . . .* "Oh, Yolanda, I need to see you in my office before you leave today."

"For what?" Yolanda asked.

Theresa's left eye twitched. "Don't worry about what, just come to my office before you leave," Theresa said, her tone threatening.

"Look, Theresa, I wasn't trying to be rude . . ."

"Being rude would mean you would have to think, and we both know you have a problem in that area. Now, meet me in my office later today or I'll be forced to talk to Dee Dee about your attitude. That's something you don't want, right?"

Yolanda stared blankly at her.

"Right?" Theresa asked again, her voice rising.

"No."

"Good. Maxwell, see you at two," Theresa said, closing his door.

She walked into her office, her hands trembling violently. She grabbed a bottle of water on her desk and tried to open it, but her hands were shaking so badly that she threw the bottle down in disgust. Her plan to get Maxwell back wasn't going as well as she had hoped. She didn't mean to behave that way in front of him, but just looking at Yolanda made hot anger rise in her chest, and she felt she needed to take every opportunity to remind her how small she was. She wanted Yolanda to hate herself as she had hated herself all her life. She sat down behind her desk and tried to slow her breathing, but quick tears left her eyes and she knew this one was going to be a bad one. She reached in a side drawer on her desk for her pills, sweat pouring from her chin. The phone rang and made her almost jump out her skin.

"Hello?"

"You called me?"

That voice. *Her* voice. Theresa's heart began to beat out of her chest, and she gripped the receiver so tight her knuckles turned white.

"Yeah, but that was a couple of days ago."

"What did you want?"

"I wanted to speak to Daddy. Is he around?"

"He's around, but I ain't allowing him near the phone. That negro called himself talking back to me this week, so he won't be talking for a while."

Chills ran up Theresa's spine and her body quaked from fear. What damage had Carol done to her father this time? She tried to pity him, but she remembered all the beatings she had endured, crying out for her father's help and not getting it. He would close the door to his bedroom and pretend not to hear her screams. She couldn't pity him; he had created his own prison.

"Did you hear me, girl? What did you want?"

"Nothing. Just tell him—tell him I'll call him back later."

"You must be back in Houston. When'd you get back in town?"

"I've been here for awhile. Listen could you just tell Dad I'll call him—"

"You back working at that salon again?"

"Yes. In fact, I got promoted."

Silence.

"Carol, did you hear me? I got promoted."

"I heard you."

"So? Don't you have something to say?"

"No, not really. We both know what you did to get the job."

"What do you mean?"

"Who'd you sleep with this time, Theresa?"

"What? I can't believe you asked that." Theresa could believe it. There was nothing that her mother didn't think she could or would do for more money.

"Well, with your history, I can't put nothin' past you. You'll do anything for money."

"Carol, it's not like that! You always thought that I was up to no good. Why can't you just recognize that I didn't turn out to be what you thought I would."

"You just gettin' older. You probably just don't have the energy you used to have, sleeping with all those men."

"This is ridiculous! I don't sleep around, Carol! I never did—"

"Not in my house you didn't. Them hot showers would burn the hussy right out of you—"

"Hot showers?! You burned me with scalding hot water for starting my period!" Theresa screeched, rubbing her shoulder and feeling all over again the scalding water permanently marking her with a third-degree burn.

"What ten-year-old you know start her period at that age? In my day, girls didn't start to cycle until they were in junior high. You was sleeping around then, and some little boy popped you open and got you to bleeding too early. You was a liar then and you a liar now. Talking about getting a job promotion. Hah. You wasn't nothin' but a prostitute then, and you ain't nothin' but a prostitute now. You are a disgrace—"

Theresa slammed the phone down on Carol's vicious words.

Carol would never think anything else of her, would never recognize that having a curvy body and pretty face didn't necessarily mean she was a slut. Theresa couldn't help the way men looked at her, no more than any woman could. She wanted to relish the looks, but Carol's words would bounce around in her head and she would find herself terrified and shaking. Like now. She found her pills and popped two in her mouth, letting them dissolve into her bloodstream, changing her back into a sane thinking woman instead of the sniveling mess she was now.

I am a new woman now, I am a new woman now.

She repeated the words until the drugs took effect and she was calm. She was a new woman now, and soon Carol would see it and Maxwell would, too. He was her ticket home. He'd almost succeeded in making a decent woman out of her last time, she was determined that this time she would make sure he succeeded.

"You ready?"

"Sure," Theresa said, blowing her nose. "Just let me close this document."

"You okay?" Maxwell asked, walking closer to her desk. "You coming down with something?"

"No, no, I'm fine. Would it be all right if we left for a while, though? I'm not really in the mood for being around a lot of people at work."

Maxwell saw a faint trail of dried tears on her cheeks and decided not to press the issue. She obviously needed to talk, and he would oblige her this one time.

"Sure, I have some time. Where you want to go?"

"The usual?"

"No," he said quickly.

"Oh, come on, Max, do you think a little pizza is really going to rekindle our relationship? If it could, I would have asked you to eat there every day!"

She was teasing him, and he laughed, remembering the ease he used to feel in her presence. California Pizza Kitchen was walking distance from the salon, but in this heat they would be two puddles by the time they got there. Maxwell had the sense of history repeating itself as they left the salon with him driving.

They arrived in minutes, passing people on barstools facing floor-to-ceiling windows that looked out into Galleria traffic. The shiny, canary yellow floor tiles gave the place a sunny and fresh look that Maxwell knew would lift Theresa's mood. It's hard for a Texan to give credit to something called California, but Maxwell had to admit he loved the food and rarely had any complaints. He ordered his usual, Cajun pizza, and Theresa ordered hers: original BBQ chicken. They found a small table in the spacious dining room and dug in.

Maxwell laughed as he saw mozzarella cheese stretch like glue from her pizza to her mouth, finally landing on her chin.

"The more things change, the more things stay the same," he said, wiping her chin with a paper napkin.

"Thanks," she said, "I needed that."

"No problem."

"No, I mean, thanks for bringing me here. I really needed this."

"Like I said, no problem."

"I hate to ask this, but, Max, do you think you'll ever forgive me?"

The sun from the huge windows danced on her hair, making it sparkle. He remembered sitting here with her, running his hands through her hair and thinking he could do that forever.

"I forgive you, Theresa. I told you that."

"But do you understand why I did it?"

"Why you lied? No, I don't get that."

She sighed.

"You didn't grow up the way I did."

"Everyone has a tough upbringing, Theresa. You can't keep using that as an excuse."

"Who is using that as an excuse? I'm just trying to get you to understand why I felt I needed to lie—"

"See, that's exactly what I'm talking about. We loved each other. There was never supposed to be a reason for you to *need* to lie. How can I marry a woman who would never tell me the truth? Who based our relationship on a lie . . . no wait, *lies*? You were never honest with me—"

"That's not true . . ."

"Oh, yeah? Your last name is one. You couldn't even tell me that McArthur was your ex-husband's name, one of many names, in fact. Your real last name is—"

"Bryant." Theresa said.

She sighed wearily.

"If you were born with that name, you wouldn't ever want to keep it." She shook her head. "Let's just drop it, okay? I'm sorry I even brought it up."

"I'm sorry, too."

CHAPTER 28

"Hey, Natalie! What's going on?"

"Nothing."

"I know it's been a while since we've talked, but ever since we got that *Essence* assignment, things have been crazy. So what's been happening with you?"

"Nothing new," Natalie said, "especially since my name was nowhere on the list for stylists. You didn't have anything to do with that, did you?"

"No, I mean . . . I sent your name in. You didn't get it?"

"Stop actin' like you didn't already know, Yolanda! You're *upstairs* now, remember? You made it to the big leagues and left your friend down here still trying to make the majors."

"Natalie, I honestly sent your name in—"

"Oh, I believe you sent my name in, but what I can't believe is that you let them people up there dog me out. You are the last person on earth who I thought would've let me down like this. I could see if I couldn't style hair or something, but y'all didn't pick me because I'm fat!"

"What? Natalie, listen . . ."

"Then to top it all off, you pick Tasha over me! Red lipstick Tasha! I didn't think you of all people would discriminate against somebody because of her weight."

"Just hold on a minute, Natalie. So you weren't chosen for the *Essence* shoot and you think it's because of your weight? That's ridiculous . . ."

"Maria told me that's what happened."

"So anything that Maria says makes it true?"

"I told you that woman is like watching the five o'clock news. Everything out of her mouth is fact."

"You know what, I don't have time for this. I call you to tell you how my day went and you're blaming me for not making the *Essence* shoot? You are being so—"

"I'm being what? 'Cause the only thing I can think of is friend. I've been a friend to you this whole time, Yolanda, and you've been so self-involved with being in *love* with your boss . . ."

"I'm not in love with him!"

"Whatever. All I'm saying is that you're not around. You left me sitting alone at Doneraki—"

"I told you that was an accident!"

"Stop lying. You forgot, plain and simple. You going around with your new friend, Jackie—"

"So that's what this is all about?"

"What?"

"You're jealous."

Hot anger gripped Natalie's chest, almost making her choke.

"Excuse me?"

"I made something of myself, accomplished a goal and made it to management, and you are jealous of the fact that me and Jackie are being friends . . ."

"Friends? You're so stupid, Yolanda. The girl is using you, plain and simple. Do you actually think she likes you? Or anyone, for that matter? You really have lost your mind if you think I could ever be jealous of you. There is nothing you have that I want, or don't already have, okay?"

"Look, I really didn't call you to argue, Natalie. I just wanted a peaceful conversation about my day."

"See? There you go again. *Your day.* You're not the only person with stuff going on in her life. Wake up, the world doesn't revolve around you."

"Okay, okay, you're right. I'm sorry, all right?" Yolanda said.

"Natalie?"

"I'm here."

"I'm really sorry. I'll find out if what Maria said was true, and see who made the final decision on the stylists and see if I can beg somebody to let you on, okay?"

"Beg somebody? Ain't nobody got to *beg* anybody to do anything for me. But I believe you, Yolanda, I believe you're sorry. And I'm sorry too for thinking that you could have ever been a friend of mine."

"Natalie—"

The hum of the dial tone was Yolanda's response.

There are more girls this time.
Their blows are vicious and cruel.
Yolanda feels a warm liquid escape her nose and cries

out from the pain. She knew it was broken, the blood in her mouth tells her so.

"Cry again like that, and I'll give you something to cry for," a girl threatens.

Her voice is familiar.

The girl steps into the light, and through her swollen eyes Yolanda can see the girl's face.

She screams.

The face is hers.

Yolanda woke up with a start. Her bed sheets were drenched with perspiration. She felt both cold and feverish. She picked up her glass of water from the nightstand and drank it straight down.

I'm gonna have to do something about these dreams. They are destroying my sleep. Now I'm gonna be awake for the rest of the night. She found the remote control and turned on the TV.

CHAPTER 29

Maxwell arrived home mentally and physically spent. He went straight to the bar and poured himself a scotch on the rocks. Drink in hand, he plopped down on his living room sofa and tried to unwind. Normally, his spacious loft apartment was a welcome escape from the non-stop hustle of the salon. Tonight, however, his mind roamed to and fro—restlessly, anxiously. Dee Dee's demands. Theresa's expectations.

Dee Dee has got me running around making sure everything is going right with the upcoming magazine shoot.

And Theresa. *I don't know what to do with her. It's obvious that she wants me back, but I can't go back there, I can't open my heart again . . .*

He closed his eyes and thought about all the good times they'd had. They had been so happy. When she walked into Behave Hair Salon, to him, Theresa was like a breath of fresh air. They quickly fell in love, and after only six months of dating, he proposed to her; she had him that sprung.

Then he found out about her past.

The sad part was that Theresa's own mama told him. Told him about the real Theresa. All the stories she'd told him of her childhood—growing up an only child . . . her parents death . . . being raised by her loving grandparents. . .

Lies, lies, lies . . . all lies.

"Is this Maxwell Alexander?"

Of all the places to call, she had to call him at his job.

"Yes. Who may I ask is calling?"

"This is Carol, Theresa's mother."

"That's impossible. Her mother is dead."

"Humph. So that's what she's going around saying this time? Well, believe you me, I'm alive and kicking, baby."

Maxwell started coughing and reached for a glass of water.

"I'm sorry, ma'am, but I think you've got the wrong person."

"This is the Maxwell Alexander that's engaged to my only daughter, Theresa Bryant, isn't it?"

"No, ma'am, my fiancée's name is Theresa McArthur."

"I'm talking about her maiden name—Bryant, not her ex-husband's name."

"No, no, you've got the wrong man. Theresa has never been married."

She laughed then, long and raspy, almost like a cough.

"So you're saying that Theresa was not raised by her grandparents?"

"That lyin' hussy! She don't even know her grandparents. Listen, that's why I called you. I figured you needed to know the truth about who you really dealing with . . ."

And so she told him about Theresa's wild days as a teenager, her sexual escapades, her problems with drugs and alcohol. It was a list without end. Or so it seemed.

"Five?"

"You heard me boy, five miscarriages. And them just the ones I know about. Yeah, that hussy is dry as a bone. Doctors say she done messed her insides all up with all the drugs, so ain't a chance in the world that she can have a baby."

"You saying she can't have children?"

"Nope. That girl is barren as the Sahara desert. She can't never have no kids. What she do, lie and tell you that she want a big family?"

She started laughing hysterically.

"Boy, wait 'til I tell Harold that she done caught another one talking about that family mess again. He gonna laugh 'til his head fall off!"

"What do you mean, 'another one'?"

"Boy, you really think you special, don't you? You would probably be her *fourth* husband, and probably the tenth or eleventh person she's been engaged to. Ain't you been listenin' to anything I've been sayin'? She's a fraud, son, a fake, a phony. Ain't nothing real on her, except I am surprised that she kept her first name this time. Look, you tell her the jig is up, okay?"

Maxwell remembered his hands shaking from anger.

"Why are you telling me this?"

" 'Cause it ain't right what she be doing. I thought that maybe if you knew who she was, who she really was, it might help you decide whether or not you would want to spend the rest of your life with this girl. I mean, wouldn't you want to know who you was marryin'?"

"Yes," Maxwell said, his voice cracking. "Yes, I would like to know. Thank you, I guess."

"I ain't saying y'all got to break up; I'm just saying you should know the whole deal, that's all."

When the call ended, Maxwell didn't know what to think, much less how to process what he'd been told. All this time working together and then falling in love, and now this. Everything she ever said was a lie. She was a lie.

He later confronted Theresa about what her very alive mother had alleged, and fully expected her to scream and shout, "Lies!" He expected her to say, "They're all lies!"

Instead, she just sat down on the couch and cried soundlessly. She admitted everything and then some. Admitted things he didn't want or need to know.

"Do you still love me?" she asked, her face red and puffy.

"Theresa, how can I still love you when I don't even know who you are?"

She nodded, slid the three-carat engagement ring off her finger, and walked out of his apartment for the last time.

It broke his heart to see her leave, but there was no way he could be with someone whose life was a web of lies and deceit. And what about children? Not having kids was a big deal to him. A very big deal. If they had gotten married, how was she planning to get around that? With another lie? And yet another to keep her deception alive?

She never came back to work after that. Dee Dee simply said she had resigned due to personal problems.

Yeah, she had personal problems.

Over the next year or so, he heard reports of her moving around a lot—New York, Chicago, L.A. She wrote him from D.C. apologizing for everything she'd done and asking him to call her so they could start over. He kept the letter for a couple of weeks and then threw it away, angry at himself for actually considering it.

She resurfaced in Houston a couple of months ago, and was hired immediately as one of the assistant managers. Maxwell now regretted having complained to Dee Dee about his workload. If he hadn't, maybe they would have never seen each other again.

What was she doing? I thought I could handle being around her, thought that after all this time I was strong enough. But every day gets harder and harder. She even smells the same, like warm vanilla. He closed his eyes, trying to remember what it felt like to be with her.

He sat straight up. *I'm not going down that road again. I've been a fool once; I'm not gonna be a fool twice. I'm getting too old for this mess. I want to settle down, have some kids. I'm thirty-six years old, thirty-seven in a couple of months. I don't want to be a bachelor forever.*

Maxwell picked up the remote and clicked on the TV, effectively blocking Theresa from his mind. For now, anyway.

CHAPTER 30

"Maxwell, you have a minute?"

"You're not trying to weasel out of staying late to do inventory, are you?"

"No, no," Yolanda said, easing into one of the chairs in front of his desk. "I just need to ask you something."

"I was actually about to buzz you in here, anyway. Go ahead, shoot."

"Who picked the stylists for the *Essence* shoot?"

"Theresa. Dee Dee makes the final decision, but—"

"Theresa suggests who gets picked. I'm sure she just goes by looks alone."

"What do you mean?"

"Nothing. It's just that one of my friends wasn't chosen—"

"Maybe she wasn't qualified for the job. Look, if she has any complaints, she'll have to talk to you or Jackie. I don't have time to deal with somebody getting her feelings hurt over something like that. But I need you to talk to one of the stylists," Maxwell said, handing Yolanda a manila folder.

"What's the problem?"

"There has been a drastic change in her job performance. She's been late for work seven times in the last month, she has several client complaints, and even though she wears the standard black and white, her out-fits are too tight and too revealing," he said.

"So you want me to write her up?"

"Exactly. Let her know that this time is just a warning, but if her subpar performance continues she will be placed on probation for three months."

"Who is it?" Yolanda asked.

"It's on the file," he said.

Yolanda looked down at the file and her blood ran cold: Natalie Morrison.

I can't do this. I can't write her up. I have to think of a way out of it.

"Yolanda? Everything okay?" Maxwell asked.

"Yeah, um, Maxwell, I don't know if I'll be able to do this."

"And why not?"

"It's just that I'm swamped with work . . ."

"Listen, Yolanda, I know you're feeling nervous, but part of my job is to delegate responsibility. Now I know you can handle this; it's in your job description."

"All right," Yolanda said, rising.

"Oh, and Yolanda?" Maxwell said.

"Yes?" she said, hopefully.

"Make sure you call her into your office. Always handle situations like this in private. It leaves the other person with a little dignity."

"I understand."

"You have a nice office. Small but nice," Natalie said. "Who paid for the furniture?" she asked, running her hand along the edge of Yolanda's dark cherry desk.

"Behave paid for it. We're given a small stipend for office furniture. The amount is based on office size and length of employment."

"Nice, nice." Natalie said, her eyes darting around noticing the cream walls, dark office furniture and heavy silver accessories on the bookshelves. She finally sat down in the chair facing Yolanda.

"First, I want to apologize," Yolanda said. She figured the best way to break the news to Natalie was to soften her up, and to let her know she had a job to do.

"No, actually, I should apologize to you. I shouldn't have hung up the phone in your face. It's just that . . . well, things have been hard, to say the least. I really miss having you around the salon."

"Natalie, I miss you, too. I really want us to keep being friends . . ."

"Me, too! I know deep down that you aren't responsible for me not getting the *Essence* shoot. Things have been happening, and I haven't been on top of my game—"

"Well, that's kinda what I wanted to talk to you about."

"I know that's why you called me in here, Yolanda, but you don't even have to apologize to me anymore. I forgive you. Let's just put this whole thing behind us. I'm sure somebody else made all those fat comments. I know you wouldn't ever say such horrible things. So pretend you're in here writing me up or something and tell me all the juice up here!"

"Well, speaking of writing you up—"

"I mean, you should've seen how everybody was looking at me downstairs, like I really was up here getting in trouble. I had to put people in check, especially Tasha, and let them know that my girl would never do me like that."

"Listen, Natalie—"

"Look at me running my mouth!" Natalie said, laughing. "Go ahead, tell me your news first. I have something to tell you, too."

"Well, it seems like you have been having problems," Yolanda began.

"Yeah, everybody's got problems. That's what I've been trying to tell you—"

"Yes, I know, but your problems are starting to affect your job performance."

Natalie's eyes grew small as she stared at Yolanda.

"Like how?" she asked. Her voice, too, had changed. It was frosty, guarded, defensive.

"Well, for instance, you've been late several times."

"That's what I've been trying to tell you . . . I've been staying up late so I—"

"Maybe you need to start going to bed earlier and not party so much."

Stunned, Natalie slumped in her chair, her eyes now wide with disbelief.

"What else?"

"You have gotten several client complaints."

"I seem to remember when you were a stylist, way back when, you got a lot of complaints, too."

174

"This isn't about me right now," Yolanda said. "Also, there's the matter of . . . your clothes."

Natalie's eyes shrank to tiny slits.

"What about my clothes?"

"Well, we think—"

"Cut the *we* mess, Yolanda!" Natalie yelled. "What's wrong with my clothes?"

"They could be a little more conservative. Right now we, I mean, I, think they are too provocative for work."

"Provocative?"

"Yeah, um, maybe you should go up a few sizes so everything wouldn't be so tight and then—"

"You bony heifer," Natalie said icily.

"Excuse me?"

"You heard me," Natalie said, her voice thick with menace. "You get promoted and all of sudden you top stuff, huh?"

"Natalie, calm down—"

"No, you calm down!" Natalie yelled. "Who do you think got you this job, huh? You would be nothin' without me. You didn't even know about this position until *I* told you! I'm thinking you call me up here so we can talk, but instead you're trying to write me up!"

"Natalie, you know, I didn't want to do this . . ."

"Then don't! You know I'm trying to get promoted to senior stylist. If I get written up, they won't even consider me for another year!"

"I'm sorry, Natalie," Yolanda said, taking deep breaths. *I hate this. I hate confrontation, especially with somebody I love like a sister.*

"Yeah, I bet you're sorry. Give me the slip so I can get outta here."

Yolanda slid the white slip of paper across her desk.

Natalie snatched it and scribbled her signature across the bottom. She threw the form back at Yolanda and got up to leave.

"Natalie, please don't be like that. This is just business, nothing personal, okay?"

"Nothing personal? Nothing personal? You must be on something if you think that you could write me up and still think we could be cool? I don't know who you think you're dealing with, but *I am a person.* And my best friend writing me up I take *personal.* There is no other way I can take it. But I'll tell you one thing, since this is just *business,* to you, I'll keep you as just *business,* too. You don't mean anything to me from now on. Don't call me when all this Jackie and Maxwell stuff blows up in your face. And it will, Yolanda. You up here with the big dogs, but don't think they don't bite," Natalie said, walking out of Yolanda's office and slamming the door.

"You sure you don't want another slice of pizza? I'm gonna eat it all."

"No, no," Yolanda said. "You go ahead."

"Knock, knock," Dee Dee said, walking in. "I was just letting you guys know I'm leaving. I know this is inventory time, but don't stay too late. Enjoy the rest of your evening—what's left of it, anyway."

"Thanks a lot, Dee Dee. Good night," Maxwell said.

She nodded and left, her soft musk perfume wafting behind her.

"She's an incredible woman," Yolanda said.

"Yes, she is."

"You guys must be pretty close."

"We are, in a way. Dee Dee is very private, so you can get only so close to her."

Yolanda nodded and returned to her paperwork. She looked at her watch. 11:10. *I hope I'll be home by one.*

"So did everything go okay today?"

"What do you mean?" she asked.

"With Natalie. I've been so busy I never did ask you how that went."

"Oh."

"I assume it didn't go well?"

"No, it didn't go well at all," she said, remembering Natalie's furious reaction. It was as if there was a video recorder in her mind. She kept rewinding the scene over and over, sometimes in slow motion. Natalie was stubborn, and Yolanda knew she would never talk to her again. Slow, quiet tears ran down her face.

"Hey, hey," Maxwell said, walking around his desk and sitting in the chair beside Yolanda. He put his arm around her shoulder.

"Do you want to talk about it?"

She shook her head, tried to be strong, willing herself to stop crying. But the tears came, flowing like a dam unplugged, and the more Yolanda tried to stop them, the more they flowed.

He gave her a tissue.

She took it and blew on it, hard and noisily. The tissue broke and some of her snot flew onto her hand.

He handed her another tissue.

Embarrassed, she took it quickly and wiped her nose gently, more ladylike this time.

"I'm sorry," she said, looking down.

"Don't worry. A little snot never hurt nobody," he said.

She looked up and smiled.

"See, I knew I could make you smile."

His eyes were kind and warm. He hadn't said much, but his eyes showed Yolanda that he understood. Maxwell reached over and wiped the tears off her face.

"Please don't cry."

Yolanda grabbed his hand and held it to her cheek.

He looked at her for a long moment. He slowly pulled himself closer.

He's going to kiss me.

She moved in. He reached closer and closer, and right before their lips touched, he stopped.

Yolanda looked into his eyes. She could see the struggle; he didn't want to cross that line.

She closed her eyes. Faintly, she whispered, "Please."

It was the please that made Maxwell pull away. He couldn't do this. Her eyes were closed, her lips pursed as if she was in a movie. But this wasn't a movie, and he couldn't make a move on her like that, especially seeing that she wanted, no, *needed* more.

Yolanda opened her eyes.

"We should get finished here," Maxwell said. "It's getting late."

He watched her face crumple like a tissue as she backed away.

"I'm sorry," she said, her voice trembling. "I should never have—"

"It's not you, Yolanda, it's me."

He sighed. He was giving her the *it's not you, it's me* speech. Why was he giving her a speech at all? She wasn't his woman; he didn't owe her anything.

"Look, let's just get done," Maxwell said, his tone sharper than he intended. He kept his head down and pretended not to see Yolanda wiping away tears.

CHAPTER 31

"Chop the tomatoes concasse. If you've been reading your glossary, you'll know what that means."

Natalie chopped her tomatoes coarsely, proud that she'd stayed up and remembered what the term meant.

Her instructor passed by.

"Very good, Miss Morrison. But if you would hold your knife like this," he said, standing beside her and sliding the knife so fast and with so much skill that Natalie felt jealous. "Here, try again," he said, passing the knife back to her.

"Thanks."

Chopping was exactly what Natalie needed right now. She imagined the tomato was Yolanda and chopped to her heart's content.

She couldn't remember a time when she'd been so upset. It was sad, really, how their relationship had ended over . . .What had ended it?

Yolanda was being so selfish. She had really let this whole promotion change who she was as a person. *Or maybe she'd always been like this? Was I too blind to notice that I was more of a friend to her than she was to me?*

It didn't matter now. She had enough saved to last until the two-year course was completed, and her father had already offered to loan her money if she didn't find a job right away. But she was through. She hoped she never saw Yolanda's face again, and she probably wouldn't. From this day forward she was no longer an employee of Behave Hair Salon. She was on her own.

CHAPTER 32

"Mama, is it wrong to be in love with someone at work?" Yolanda asked, chopping up potatoes for her mother's famous potato salad.

"It depends."

"On what?"

"Oh, a lot of things. Stuff like that can get complicated. I like things as simple as I can get 'em."

"What if it's too late?"

"It's never too late to do the right thing," her mother said, putting more flour on the pie dough she was rolling out.

"I tried to kiss a guy at work yesterday."

Her mother kept rolling out dough, waiting for Yolanda to continue.

"Well, not just a guy. Technically . . . he's my boss."

"What? Yolanda . . ."

"I know, Mama, I know. But I couldn't help it! I've had this thing for him for ages and when the opportunity presented itself, I don't know, I just went after it."

Her mother stopped rolling the dough and looked at her.

"What? Oh, Mama, we didn't kiss, okay? He wasn't having it, and we didn't do anything."

"What you did was enough."

"Awww, Mama—"

"You fall in love way too fast. You never try to get to know the person first."

"I do know him! He's smart, sexy, kind, nice . . ."

"What's his middle name? His favorite food? His hobbies?"

Yolanda stood there dumbfounded.

"You take all the fun out of everything, Mama."

"All I'm saying is that I don't want you rushing into anything. I don't want you to get hurt like last time."

"You mean with Russell? It's okay, Mama, you can say his name."

"Yeah, with that Russell. It takes you so long to heal, Yolanda. I just don't want you getting your hopes up too fast. Just take things slow."

Her mother's cautionary words took Yolanda back to her first real boyfriend. Her first true love.

She had been twenty-three years old and had just started working at Behave. She had been on the waiting list for four years and, after several interviews, she had got her dream job. Or what she thought was her dream job. Her hair styling skills were subpar compared to all the cutting edge styles at the salon, and for the first time, Yolanda felt inadequate at her job. At her previous salon, she was a master stylist and often helped other co-workers who struggled with the latest styles. Now she was the fledgling stylist who couldn't comprehend the new techniques Behave used. On top of that, she had to fend off rumors of an eating disorder, despite the way she devoured huge lunches at the salon café. The only friendly face had been in Natalie Morrison, a fellow stylist who showed her the ropes around the salon and defended her against nasty and hurtful rumors about her weight. Her calendar was filled with hair classes where she had to learn up and coming haircuts, color and celebrity hairstyles that would expand her hair knowledge. Dee Dee also required each new stylist to take a technical exam upon arrival to her salon to make sure they were on the level where she deemed a cutting edge stylist should be. It was followed by a practical exam, to see if you had mastered the Behave way of styling hair. Both of Yolanda's exams were set for the next day, so she sat at the Starbuck's a block from the salon and studied her manual. She was on a lunch break, and didn't want to sit in the salon café and cloud her mind with comments about her weight. She had been studying so hard she didn't even hear him sit down next to her at the wrought-iron table.

"Looks like you need a refill," he said, handing her a Styrofoam cup emblazoned with the Starbuck's logo.

"Excuse me?"

"Tall, white chocolate mocha, right? Extra whipped cream," he said, sliding the cup across the table. His dark hair looked like spilled ink on his pale skin, and his blue eyes twinkled waiting for a response.

"How did you know—"

"Forgive me for sounded forward, but I've been watching you. You come here a lot and you always order the same thing."

"Really?"

"No, but that would be cool, huh? Having a secret admirer? Seriously, I was standing behind you in line and heard your order. I saw you had run out of coffee and thought you could use a refill."

"Well, that was, nice of you. I guess," Yolanda stammered.

"You work at that big salon down the block?"

"Yeah. How did you—"

"Your shirt," he said, pointing to her chest. "That's a dead give-away."

"Oh," Yolanda said looking down at her shirt. Since she was still in training was required to wear a black T-shirt with BEHAVE HAIR SALON written across the front in big white letters.

"So what do you think about my hair? Think I'm due for a haircut?" he said smiling, showcasing a perfect row of white teeth.

"Your hair? It looks fine. I mean, you could get a hair cut if you want, but you really don't need one."

His dark eyebrows furrowed. "You mean you wouldn't use the excuse of giving me a hair cut to get to know me better? Honestly, I'm shocked!"

Yolanda stifled a smile, enjoying the easy banter with this stranger. She looked at her watch and closed her books. Lunch was almost over and she needed to get back to work.

"What, leaving me already?"

"It's been nice, but I need to get back to work." Yolanda said, scooping up her books and coffee. "Thanks for the coffee," she said, leaving.

The next day, she walked up to the reception area to greet her next client and saw the same charming blue eyes looking up at her.

"Well, I must say it wasn't all that hard to find you. Your reputation precedes you."

She stiffened. "What have you heard?" She wondered how word could have spread so quickly about her mediocre styling skills.

"That you are the most beautiful stylist working here, of course." He pulled out a white rose from his dark suit jacket and handed it to her. "Name is Russell Steinfeld. Yolanda, are you ready to get started?"

She gushed over the effort he had taken to learn her name; that showed real initiative—something no man had ever showed her. She led him to the spacious shampoo area and got to work. Over the course of thirty minutes, she found out he worked near the salon at his father's law firm, Steinfeld and McGregor, and like her he was just starting out. He was twenty-six years old, no kids, never been married, and had just bought his first home. He made Yolanda feel at ease, and for the first time in her life she didn't think about her small boobs or flat butt—she was herself and centered her thoughts on his conversation.

"There," she said, whipping off a styling cape from his shoulders. "You're all done." She handed him a gold-leafed hand mirror so he could check the cut in the back. "What do you think?"

"What I think is that you did a remarkable job, Yolanda." He handed her back the mirror and slid a fifty dollar bill into the palm of her hand. "Thank you," he said, holding her hand longer than necessary.

Yolanda pulled her hand away. She looked down at the money in her hand. "You need to give this to

Michelle up front," she said, offering the money back to him.

He shook his head. "That's for you; your tip." He gave her a bright smile and walked up front to take care of his bill.

Natalie walked up. "I don't normally go for white dudes, but if you don't get him, I will."

Yolanda walked away, knowing she would never see Russell again.

On his third visit to the salon, he offered to take her out to dinner. She accepted.

Their love was new and fresh. They were like children eager to learn more about each other. He taught her how to use chopsticks, introduced her to sushi, and to helped her understand computers. She introduced him to her soul food. But more than that, she introduced him to her family her, her cat, her life.

She never had anyone, especially a man, make her feel so beautiful, so special, so loved. She imagined a three-carat engagement ring, a huge wedding, bi-racial children with blue eyes and honey skin, summers in the Hamptons, late nights of deep conversations.

What she got was a wake-up call.

"Yolanda, this past year has been wonderful. My father has been hinting that I'm on the fast track to becoming partner. But I need to settle down, get married, have kids. You know, all the things we talk about," Russell said, reaching for her hand across the table. They were at her favorite Italian restaurant, Maggiano's.

Her heart started racing.

He's gonna propose. He wants to marry me.

"So, I need to stop playing games and get serious in my life. I'm not getting any younger . . ."

This is it! I've been waiting for this all my life . . .

"So, I need to find a wife. It's been fun, Yolanda, really, it has. But in the grand scheme of things, you're not what I'm looking for in a wife. We need to part ways—"

"Part ways? Are you—"

"Breaking up with you? Yes." He squeezed her hand. "You didn't really expect for us to get married, did you?"

"Of course I did! I wasn't in it for fun! I thought we were, were something serious."

Russell dropped her hand and sat back. "Yolanda, sweetie, what drew you to that conclusion? You've never been to my job, you've never met my family, I've never hinted that this was more than what it is."

"And what is this?"

He shrugged. "Good fun, nothing more."

Her stomach lurched and she ran from the table to the restroom and vomited. Down the toilet went the three-carat ring that would have sparkled on her left hand, the wedding she never got to plan, the kids she never got to have. She vomited all her dreams away.

"But you said you loved me, Russell," Yolanda whined on the car ride home.

"I know, sweetheart. That's what makes this so difficult. I'm so sorry, Yolanda."

She stopped eating, she couldn't sleep. She lost much-needed weight, which made her look more pathetic.

Six months later she couldn't believe her eyes when she saw his photo in the *Houston Chronicle*. His engagement photo. That photograph sent her into a deep, dark spiral of depression that took her over a year to recover from.

If she ever recovered.

"You know his wife is pregnant again?"

"Really? What is this, their third child?"

"Fourth."

"How'd you find out?"

"Saw it in that Houston Society magazine."

Well, folks, Houston socialite Veronica Steinfeld is pregnant again! Guess her husband, hot-shot criminal defense attorney Russell Steinfeld, is keeping busy, but not in the courtroom!

Yolanda shook her head as if trying to erase the words from her memory.

"It's okay to feel sad, Yolanda. Just don't beat yourself up about it."

"I'm not sad! Who said anything about being sad?"

"Okay, maybe *sad* is the wrong word. You've got a fabulous life, Yolanda, with or without a man. Remember you're the meal; he's just the dessert."

"I know, Mama, I know. It's so easy for women with a man to say stuff like that."

"That's because women with a man would pay any kind of money to get rid of him."

"Yeah, right. Then how come I get all these women coming up to me telling me I need to get married, and how wonderful marriage is?"

"Liars. All of 'em. Misery loves company. They just see you have potential for happiness and they tryin' to ruin it. Any woman who tells you marriage is bliss got a cheatin', alcoholic loser at home. The women who tells you to take your time? Now those the ones who got some sense. Those the ones who are happily married."

"So what should I do? Should I talk to Maxwell or what?"

"I can't tell you what to do, but . . ."

"Aww, come on, Mama! What should I do?"

"Talk to him. But don't expect a relationship. You're only twenty-nine, Yolanda, always trying to rush your life away. Just take your time."

"So I guess you're happily married?"

"Bingo," her mother said, laughing.

CHAPTER 33

Theresa paced the small studio. She checked her watch: 9:07 A.M.

Where were they?

"Theresa, the photographer is getting anxious. You sure you told the models to be here for 7:00?" Maxwell asked, his voice low.

"Yes, I'm sure," she whispered. "I don't know what's going on, but they should have been here two hours ago."

"You're gonna have to say something to the photographer. He says if they don't arrive in five minutes, he's leaving."

"He can't do that!" she shrieked.

"Well, he will, unless you figure out something."

"I'll have to stall him."

Her first big assignment was quickly turning into a huge disaster. Everyone had worked so hard to make sure everything would run smoothly, and now unimaginable failure was looming. *Essence* had already sent photographers to take shots of the salon and staff, but they wanted some special shots of the trendy hairstyles Behave was known for. Dee Dee hand-selected the models, rented them a small studio, and then passed total control to Theresa. *I don't know what's going on. Everything went so smoothly at the last photo shoot. If these models don't show up, we might lose the chance to be in* Essence.

Theresa tried not to think about it as she approached the photographer, a short, stocky, bald white man in his early forties. He had picked up some of his equipment and had begun to pack up. *I have to do something. My job is on the line.*

"Excuse me, John, is it?" she said, her voice a silky purr.

"Yeah, I'm John."

"Can I talk to you for a minute? Alone?"

"I don't see why. I'm leaving," John said, signaling to his two assistants to begin packing up.

"Why? I thought we were just about to get started."

"Lady, we were supposed to start two hours ago. I don't know about you, but my time is precious."

"I assure you, John, my time is precious, too," Theresa said, keeping her voice low and seductive.

He looked at her for a moment, and then continued packing his equipment.

"Look, how much?" Theresa asked, her voice a low growl.

"What?"

"How much extra would it take for you to stay?"

He looked her up and down, a slow smile playing on his lips.

"Not me, jerk. How much money do you want?"

"You wouldn't have to pay me a dime, lady. A couple of minutes alone with you would be payment enough."

I can't believe this greasy fool honestly thinks I'm gonna sleep with him. I mean, look at me! I wouldn't touch him with a ten-foot pole.

"Look, I got two words for you, buster: sexual harassment. Don't ever again dare to talk to me in that manner. You were paid to do a job, and your short, pudgy butt better well do it. All right, pal? Or should I get on the phone with your wife and let her know that her husband is attracted to ethnic women? I'm sure this wouldn't be the first phone call she has gotten from another woman, would it, John?"

He looked down at his wedding ring and looked back at Theresa, his eyes turning cold and hard.

"Five thousand dollars. Or I walk."

"You must be crazy. You're not that good. Two thousand dollars, and I strongly suggest you take it."

He looked at her long and hard for a moment.

"Fine," he snarled.

"So he'll stay?"

Theresa nodded.

"Good, good," Maxwell said, relieved. "How'd you do it?"

She hesitated. "I paid him."

"Really? Dee Dee already paid him. You offered him more? How much?"

"Not much. It doesn't matter; he stayed, didn't he?"

Maxwell gave her a warning glance.

"She's not gonna like you going over budget, Theresa. She made it real clear about that . . ."

"I know . . ."

"Just be prepared, is all I'm saying. She's gonna chew your butt out."

"I know, okay? But what else could I do? Do you know how hard it would have been to get another photographer? Especially of his caliber? I didn't know what else to do, so lay off."

"Did the models come yet?" she asked.

"Yeah, they came a couple of minutes ago. They're getting changed."

"I'm gonna ask them what their problem is. They're over two hours late!"

"They said you called them and told them to get here at 10:00."

"What? I never told them that!"

"Well, somebody called them," Maxwell said, looking down at Theresa.

"Don't look at me like that!"

"Like what?"

"Like I'm lyin' or something. I told you I didn't call them. Why would I do that?"

"I don't know, Theresa. Look, let's just get through this."

"Fine," she said brusquely, walking away.

I am not going crazy. I called all those models personally and even sent them all an e-mail. Dee Dee is gonna kill me for all this crap going wrong.

CHAPTER 34

"Please, please everyone take a seat. Let's get today's meeting started," Dee Dee said, sitting down.

She took deep, long breaths, trying to mute her anger. *Control. Keep it under control.*

"The first issue I would like to bring to the table is our photo shoot last week with *Essence* magazine. As you know, the first session at the salon went smoothly, but the second session, in the studio, was a disaster," Dee Dee said, her eyes concentrating on Theresa. "Now I want to know why I received a call from the editor telling me how unprofessional and unorganized we were."

Dee Dee looked around the room at each staff member. She didn't mention how the editor threatened to remove them from the magazine altogether, and how she had to plead with the woman and guarantee that it would never happen again. No, she didn't tell them that. All they needed to know was that she was pissed, and wanted answers.

"So who wants to go first?"

"I'm sorry, Dee Dee," Theresa said. "This was all my fault. Somehow the models got the wrong time—"

"Somehow? What do you mean *somehow*?" Dee Dee asked, her voice clipped.

"Well, someone called them and told them a different time."

"Who?"

"I don't know."

"I see. So you're saying someone called all ten of the models and told them to come two hours later? Wouldn't it be more logical to assume that you made a mistake and told them the wrong time?"

She listened to Theresa struggling for an acceptable answer.

"That could be it, Dee Dee, but I'm almost positive that I didn't do it."

"Almost is never good enough, Theresa. You know better than that. They also said that you bribed the photographer, which made us go $2,000 over budget. And that's not to mention extra studio time that I had to pay for. Can you explain that to me, Theresa?"

"Dee Dee, I didn't want to further compromise the shoot, so I felt I had to do something to get the photographer to stay. I apologize for that, but as far as the models, I honestly don't know who could have called them and told them to come at a later time."

"Yeah, right," Yolanda mumbled.

"Excuse me?" Theresa said.

"Did you have anything to add, Yolanda?" Dee Dee asked, her cold brown eyes piercing through her like a laser.

"It just seems like that she's making excuses. I mean, it just looks like she isn't woman enough to admit she made a mistake," Yolanda said.

"You the last person who should be talking about anybody looking like a woman, you flat-chested—"

"That's enough," Dee Dee said. "I will not tolerate any more mistakes like this. I cannot afford it. Meeting adjourned so I can finish fixing this mess."

"Dee Dee, your husband's downstairs. He's on his way up."

She sighed.

"'Thanks, Beverly."

What is he doing here? I'm not in the mood for surprises . . .

"Come in," Dee Dee said when she heard his knock.

"Hey, baby," Jonathan said, walking in with flowers.

"Nice flowers. Are they for me?"

"Of course. A dozen white calla lilies, your favorite."

"They're beautiful," she said, taking them from him and setting them on her desk. His hand grazed hers, and she jerked away as if she had been burned.

"What's wrong?"

"Nothing."

"I disgust you that much that I can't even touch you?"

Exactly. Just looking at you makes me sick to my stomach.

"No, Jonathan," she said sighing. "What do you want?"

"I just wanted to see my wife."

"That's all? You could see me at home."

"One would think so, but you hide yourself in that room of yours—"

"Do we have to discuss this right now?"

"Just tell me this, Dee Dee. How long are we gonna sleep in separate bedrooms?"

She looked down and twisted her platinum wedding band around her finger.

Finally, she said, "It's only a temporary situation."

"Temporary? It's been going on since Michael died. I don't know about you, but that's more than temporary."

"You're the last person on earth who can give me demands. I'll move back in the bedroom when I'm good and ready and not a minute before. If I ever move back in."

He dropped his head.

When he looked back up, tears were in his eyes.

"When will you let this go? When are you gonna forgive me for Michael?"

Dee Dee looked away. *How could this man have hurt me so much? I don't know him anymore. I don't know if I want to know him anymore.*

She looked back at him. *He's so handsome. I used to feel so special to be Mrs. Jonathan Townsend.*

His skin was a deep brown, the color of melted chocolate drizzled on an ice cream sundae. His eyes were dark and mysterious and left all the ladies wanting more.

But Dee Dee knew more. Much more. And she hated him, this handsome man that was her husband. Hated him with as much passion as she had once loved him.

"I can't talk about this right now. You've picked the wrong time to bring this subject up—"

"When is the right time?"

"Jonathan . . ."

"I'm just saying that we still have a lot going for us. Don't throw all this away."

"I'll take that into consideration."

He turned to leave. "You're so cold, Dee Dee. Where's your heart?"

"It's gone. It left the day you killed Michael."

He stepped back as if he had been slapped. He walked out of her office, closing the door behind him.

CHAPTER 35

"No."

"Yes."

"When?"

"A couple of days ago."

"And you've been keeping this to yourself?" Jackie asked.

Yolanda nodded, and took a bite of her chicken sandwich. They were having a quick lunch in the salon cafe and talking about the kiss that she and Maxwell almost shared. She had tried to hold it in, but she was beginning to feel like she might explode, especially since Natalie hadn't returned any of her phone calls. Yolanda usually confided in Natalie first, but now had to settle for the next best thing.

"So why didn't he go all the way? Why didn't he kiss you?" Jackie asked, taking a sip of her iced tea.

"I don't know. I could tell he wanted to, but he just . . . stopped. Then he totally switched gears and started acting real professional, like the whole thing never happened. And now everything feels awkward," Yolanda said, remembering how he had ignored her afterward, and had kept silent the rest of the evening, talking only when she had a question about the inventory.

"Have y'all talked about it?"

"No. I told you, he's going around acting like it never happened."

"You should," Jackie said, picking at her taco salad.

"You think so?"

"Yeah, I mean what do you have to lose? You have already thrown yourself at him, so he knows you like him."

"I wouldn't say I threw myself at him—"

"Well, that's what I would call it. Look, just go talk to him. Tell him how you feel and ask him out so y'all can *talk*, and see where it goes."

"You're right, as soon as I—"

Yolanda stopped when she saw Tasha walking in her direction carrying a tray of food. She looked directly at Yolanda, rolled her eyes and sat down at a table a few feet away from them.

"Do you know her?" Jackie asked, looking at Tasha.

Tasha was sitting at a table with a few other stylists, and Yolanda could see the table becoming animated as Tasha talked.

"Yeah," Yolanda said, "but I don't know why she was rolling her eyes at me. We've always been on good terms."

"Maybe she knows your other friend, the one who tried to sit with you the other day. She quit."

"Who? Natalie quit? When?"

"I don't know. I just know I'm training a new stylist, which usually means somebody quit or got fired. I did some digging and it was that girl. . ."

"Natalie quit? Why didn't she tell me—"

She remembered. They weren't friends anymore. The thought turned her stomach upside down and she pushed her chicken sandwich away, disgusted at herself for letting things get this bad.

"What's wrong?"

"Nothing—I just, I don't know, I'm not that hungry I guess."

Jackie shrugged. "I better hurry up," she said. "I have to teach a class in fifteen minutes."

Yolanda nodded and finished her Coke.

"By the way, what was up with that comment about Theresa at the meeting the other day?"

"What comment?"

"Don't play dumb. You know what I'm talking about."

Yolanda looked down and started tearing pieces off her paper napkin.

"I don't know what got into me. It just sort of slipped out."

"Well you better *slip out* an apology. I heard Theresa is pissed at you for embarrassing her in front of Dee Dee."

"All those comments she makes about me? Please, I'm not apologizing."

"Suit yourself," Jackie said, standing up. "Don't say I didn't warn you. Theresa can be a tough one, to say the least."

"You don't like her, either?" Yolanda asked.

"I didn't say that!" Jackie said, slamming her hand down on the table. A few people glanced in their direction, no doubt wondering what Yolanda could've said to make Jackie lose her cool. "She's a sweet, talented woman who is an asset to this salon, okay? My mother would be lost without her, and we—I mean, she can't afford to lose another employee. You need to work on making Theresa feel more comfortable here. Wouldn't you agree?"

"Yeah, I guess. But—"

"There are no buts! Sure, Theresa has the personality of a bulldog ready to fight, but you can't go around saying whatever you want off the top of your head."

Jackie looked around, and then whispered, "If you just sit tight and wait, I promise you're going to get everything you want, Maxwell included. But you can't go messing things up with that mouth of yours, okay?" she said, winking at Yolanda.

"Um, okay . . ."

"My goodness, look at the time. I gotta get moving," Jackie said, leaving Yolanda at the table.

What had just happened?

"Hey, Maxwell, you got a sec?"

"Sure, come in," he said, taking off his glasses, squinting. "I need a break anyway."

Jackie walked in and sat down.

"Look, I know you're busy, so I'll get straight to the point," Jackie said, smiling that smile of hers that was always plastered on her face.

"Go right ahead."

"I had lunch with Yolanda a few minutes ago, and she gave me the impression that you tried to make a pass at her."

"What? That's crazy—"

"She said you tried to kiss her. It's none of my business, really, but I don't know the girl well, and I don't want any trouble for the salon. Mama—I mean, Dee Dee has enough on her plate to be worried about this kind of thing."

"Jackie, do you really think I would cross the line with Yolanda? She's a pretty girl, but—"

"Pretty or not, somehow she got in her head that you tried to kiss her. Did she just make all that up, or did something happen?"

Maxwell sighed.

"The other night, we almost . . . but I stopped myself! And nothing happened. I promise nothing happened."

"Well, you have to do something, or things could get out of hand. She said things have been uncomfortable, and you don't want that."

"What should I do?"

"Why don't you take her out to dinner or something and assure her that everything's all right between the two of you? You won't be at work, you can drive, and that way she can't have anything negative to say about the salon, because she chose to go out to dinner with you. In fact, if she comes in here suggesting it, make sure she thinks the whole thing is her idea. Either way, you're covered."

"You're right," Maxwell said, nodding his head in agreement. "I'll do that."

"Great," Jackie said, standing up to leave.

"Hey, Jackie, thanks for looking out, okay?"

"Maxwell, you know I always got your back," Jackie said, winking.

Yolanda waited outside Maxwell's office and tried to calm her racing heart. She agreed with Jackie's advice, but she had to admit she was a big scaredy-cat, and asking Maxwell out was a big leap for her. Before she could chicken out she knocked on his door. His deep voice beckoned her inside.

Yolanda came in and sat down in front of his desk. She tried to think of something to say.

"Yes?" Maxwell said, encouraging her to talk.

"I, um, sort of wanted to talk about the other night," she said, looking down.

"What about it?"

Yolanda looked at him.

I know I don't stand a chance with you. All signs point to no when it comes to you, and yet here I am in front of you, seriously considering asking you out. You're out of my league; if we were in leagues, I wouldn't even be able to see you because you'd be so far above me. From your Movado watch to your alligator shoes, I know I'll never have a man like you. But I can't keep living life on the sidelines. I gotta know if it could ever go anywhere between us. I gotta be bold for once. I have nothing to lose anymore, so here goes . . .

"The reason I'm here," Yolanda said, her confidence growing, "is because I've been thinking a lot about the kiss we shared—"

"We didn't kiss," Maxwell corrected.

"Did I say kiss? I meant our almost kiss. Look, I know things have been very uncomfortable . . ."

Maxwell groaned.

"I'm really sorry you feel this way, Yolanda, but it really is a conflict of interest with you here talking to me about this. Now you can make an appointment to talk to Dee Dee about anything you may have interpreted as sexual harassment."

"Sexual harassment? Oh, no, I wasn't—"

"You weren't insinuating that I was sexually harassing you?"

"No, I—"

"So, what were you trying to say?"

"I was trying to ask you on a date!" Yolanda blurted.

"Oh." Maxwell said, clearly taken aback. "I'm sorry."

"I'm sorry, too," Yolanda said, standing up. "Obviously, this was a really stupid idea, one of many of my stupid ideas. Just pretend that this never happened."

"Yolanda, wait."

"Yes?"

"There's some business stuff we need to talk about, anyway, so why don't we discuss it over dinner. We can meet someplace tonight. Would that be okay?"

The biggest smile spread over Yolanda's face. "That would be great. What time?"

"I have a late meeting with Dee Dee, so is eight-thirty okay?"

"Eight-thirty is perfect."

"Tonight then," Maxwell said, putting his glasses back on. Their conversation was over.

CHAPTER 36

"You ready?"

"Sure," Maxwell said, shutting down his computer. "Just give me a couple of minutes."

"I'll wait downstairs."

Maxwell nodded his okay and watched Yolanda walk out of his office. Looking at her body was like watching a surgery on television; it disgusted and interested you at the same time. He'd never seen a woman that skinny. Maybe on TV when one of those modeling shows was on or something, but almost all those women were white. He'd never seen a skinny black girl. Thin, but not this skinny. *Po'* was what you were called back in the neighborhood if you were too skinny. *That girl is so po' she need some meat on her bones.*

In any case, Maxwell was confident he had made the right decision by suggesting they go out to dinner. Jackie was right. He would make things right with her and get this whole thing over with. He could grant her this *one* thing. It was only dinner; it wouldn't *kill* him. Yeah, she was bony, but the girl was definitely easy on the eyes. A little plastic surgery and she'd be right up there with Theresa. *Naw, that's taking it too far.* Even with plastic surgery, she couldn't hold a candle to Theresa. *Then why am I so interested in getting to know Yolanda more?*

Yolanda couldn't believe she was sitting inside Maxwell's Hummer. *I have to be dreaming,* she kept thinking, watching him drive confidently through Houston's remaining traffic.

They'd decided to go to Blue Water, a family-owned seafood restaurant that had the best crawfish in town. The crawfish was guaranteed to make your nose run from the spices, a must for a true crawfish lover.

She felt uneasy sitting here in his car, fearing she would not be able to loosen up and be herself. His silence bothered her, but she didn't know him well enough to know if he was always this way. Or was it because she was in the car?

"You cold?" he asked suddenly, adjusting the air conditioner. "Is that too much wind in your face?"

"No, why? Do I look cold?"

"No, your hair was just blowing and I didn't want to freeze you out. It's crazy hot outside, and I normally turn the air on full force, but with you being so thin, I didn't want you to turn into a popsicle or anything."

Yolanda smiled, but hoped he could look past her weight and enjoy the evening. She decided to not spoil it with her constant blabbering, to enjoy the ride to the restaurant in silence. *Let him wonder what I'm thinking for a change.*

"So basically my pop whopped my butt for taking his truck and wrecking it while taking the test for my driver's license."

Yolanda laughed out loud, tears steaming down her cheeks. Maxwell laughed, too. He was surprised that he was actually having a good time. They'd already chowed down on enough crawfish to feed a small village and had just finished devouring the corn on the cob and potatoes that came with the meal.

Two hours later, he was still captivated by Yolanda's conversation.

"You had a very interesting childhood," Yolanda said, smiling and wiping tears from her eyes. "You must really love your dad a lot."

His face darkened.

"Yeah, I do."

"Do y'all get along well?"

"Not really," Maxwell said, taking a sip of his beer. "We're close, but everything changed after my mom died."

"I'm sorry."

"What about you?" Maxwell asked, needing to change the subject. He felt uncomfortable talking about his pop, especially to people who didn't know the dynamics of their relationship. "You get along with your folks?"

"Yeah. My family is weird. My mom calls me almost every day with a new tale of how my dad is destroying the house. He's retired, so it gives him something to do."

"Y'all close?"

"Yeah, I suppose so. We talk all the time, and I visit when I can. I have a sister, Gina. She's married with three kids. We don't talk as much as we should, but I e-mail her from time to time. You got any brothers or sisters?"

"Nope. Only child. Unless you count my frat brothers."

"Let me guess, Kappa?"

"You got it."

"Well, look at Mr. College Man! What did you major in?"

"Business."

"I bet your family was so proud of you."

"Not really. I dropped out when my mother was diagnosed with cancer. Moved back home to help my dad out."

"Sorry."

I hate thinking about that part of my life: dropping out of school, watching my mother shrivel up and die right in front of me.

He remembered looking at her sleep at night, her breathing hard and labored. Every day she seemed to be dying right in front of him, her body slowly shriveling up.

"Come here, Maxy," his mother said, beckoning him to her. She patted the chair next to the bed, motioning for him to sit. He would never, ever forget the words he spoke to her on that gray, overcast Sunday. It was the last time they talked.

She was in the bed they had moved from the guest bedroom to the family room downstairs. She was so fatigued she could barely sit up, let alone climb upstairs.

She was happiest then, her thin, frail body hidden under a mountain of covers and quilts. Friends came by in droves, sitting around her bed, regaling her with stories of her youth, knowing that these were her last days.

"What is it?" Maxwell asked, sitting by his mother's bed and holding her skeletal hand.

Her skin was dry and translucent, and blue and purple veins coursed through it. Her protruding facial bones made her appear to be wearing a mask. Her brown eyes that used to sparkle with amusement were encased in dark circles, and looked dull and lifeless.

His heart skipped a beat.

It was finally real.

Mama is dying.

"I want you to watch over your pop," she said in a strangled whisper.

He leaned in closer so he could hear.

"I'm worried about him. Try to look after him when I'm gone."

A single tear fell from Maxwell's eyes.

"I will, Mama."

"I want you to find yourself a nice girl, Maxy. Somebody you can laugh with, talk to, cry with. Somebody you can love, through thick and thin. Remember, you don't get the ones you can live with, get the ones you can't live without."

"I'll remember."

"I'm so tired, baby. So tired. Will you sit here with me 'til I fall asleep?"

He nodded, knowing if he spoke another word it wouldn't be words at all. It would be screams, angry screams that would shake the heavens, loud enough for the stars to feel his pain.

"You ready to go? I have some things to do in the morning," he said suddenly, waking up from bad memories.

"Sure," Yolanda said, grabbing her purse.

He threw ten bucks down for the tip, took another gulp of his beer, and slid off the bench, anxious to leave the restaurant and memories of his mama behind.

They walked outside to his truck. The air was still, muggy. He opened the truck door for her and then hopped in and slammed his door.

They were silent for most of the trip, but Yolanda did try to start another conversation, trying to get Maxwell to talk.

He didn't, and eventually she quieted. He could feel her uneasiness, knew she wondered what had altered his mood. Talking about his mother's death always made him quiet, introspective. He turned the radio on.

"I like that song," Yolanda said.

" 'You Are So Beautiful'? Why?"

"I don't know. I suppose every woman would love her man to sing that song to her. It's a good song."

"You want somebody to sing that to you?"

"Yeah. One day, somebody will."

"Maybe somebody will," he said, turning into the driveway of the salon. He put the truck in park and let the engine idle.

"I really had a wonderful time, Maxwell," Yolanda said.

"I did, too," Maxwell said quietly. *I know I should be the gentleman and walk her to her car, but this ain't a date.*

"Good night," he said. *She is a nice person to talk to. I'm definitely, definitely not attracted to her, but maybe we could be good friends.*

"Night," she said, turning to give him a kiss on his cheek.

He shrank away. "What are you doing?"

"I . . . um . . ."

"One second you're thinking about accusing me of sexually harassing you and the next minute you're trying to kiss me?"

"No, I . . ."

He saw the hurt in her eyes and didn't want to make matters worse. Relenting, he kissed her on her forehead.

Yolanda laughed.

"What's so funny?"

"I'm your baby sister now? Kissing me on the forehead like I'm related to you or something?"

"What's wrong with that? I like you, Yolanda, and I had a wonderful time tonight, but I think this whole thing with you is inappropriate. We can't keep playing around like this."

"But I'm not playing around. I really like you."

"That's the problem, Yolanda. I'm technically your boss. That night, I wanted to kiss you. I don't know why, but I did. But it wasn't right. And I don't feel comfortable going the way we're going."

"How do you see us going?"

"Look, I'm a grown man. I've been around the block a couple of times, and I'm really getting tired of all that mess. I don't like fooling around with a lot of women anymore—"

"Good, because I'm not interested in dating a lot of men."

"No, Yolanda, you're not getting it. I don't want to date you. I know that's blunt, but I can't seriously consider the thought of going out with you. I'm not into playing games anymore, so you might as well hear it now before I just take advantage of you, or do something worse."

She hung her head. This is just like Russell all over again, she thought. *"It's been fun, Yolanda, really it has. But in the grand scheme of things, you're not what I'm looking for in a wife. We need to part ways—"*

"You okay?"

"Yeah," she said. "It's just that I get so tired of men who decide something before anything even gets started. I don't play games, either, which is why I said I like you. It was an honest statement. But I think you're right. If you just want to put this whole thing behind us, I won't mention it again and I won't be weird at work."

"It's too late for that. Things are already kinda weird between us. But I really do want that, Yolanda. I do want to put this whole ugly thing behind us."

His use of the word *ugly* stung. Ugly, ugly . . . It wasn't the *situation* that was ugly, *she* was ugly. There was no way he would be rejecting her if she had a body like

Theresa. The hope in her heart died and she was back to square one. Skinny ole Yolanda. *Hey, Six O'Clock, you ever gonna get a man?* It was as if her father was standing right next to her, laughing. She should be laughing at herself, too. *What was I thinking? Did I honestly think I had a chance? I never did, never will.* Yolanda opened the truck door.

"Yolanda, wait."

She turned and looked at him.

"I really want us to be friends."

"Friends?"

"Yeah, I really want us to be friends."

She looked out into the parking lot, thinking.

"Would that be all right?"

"The problem with you, Maxwell, is that you don't know what you want. I don't know what this was tonight, but I'm calling it a date. You can call it whatever you want. But it wasn't just two friends hanging out. I have enough friends, and I'm not adding you to that list. I want more."

She got out of the car and slammed the door shut.

"Night," Maxwell called out, watching her painfully skinny body walk to her car. He leaned his head on the steering wheel. *What am I doing?*

CHAPTER 37

Stretched out on the sofa in the family room, Dee Dee was mindlessly flipping through the channels on the TV.

Family room. Hah. What a joke.

The room could have been ripped right out of a design magazine.

Big, overstuffed, pale green sofas were situated around the room to encourage conversation at parties. The tall, wide windows encased the room with light and provided a view of the fabulous pool outside, but today it was obscured by heavy silk draperies.

Everything was perfect. The gold-leafed picture frames were dust-free, the plants were full and green, showing no signs of neglect. The glossy magazines on the glass coffee table were new and unwrinkled. And never read. They were there purely for cosmetic effect.

It looks like no one lives here . . .

What was that song Luther used to sing?

"A House Is Not a Home."

This doesn't feel like home to me anymore. Without Michael, this is just a big empty house.

She heard a key turn in the lock and sat up, glancing at the clock on the fireplace. 6:15.

She pictured him pressing the alarm code into the keypad.

Him.

In a few minutes, he'll come in here. If he came in at all.

Years ago, he would have fixed himself a drink and would have retreated into his study until it was time for dinner.

They would sit together like a family, at least when she was home early enough, and talk. Sometimes Jackie would come by, her presence shifting their casual dinner into unsettled tension. She didn't mind, though; at least they were all together as a family.

She didn't mind smelling alcohol on Jonathan's breath when he kissed her. And she didn't mind him picking Michael up from basketball practice that day, either. *Isn't that what good fathers do? How wrong I was.*

He tried to blame it on the rain, the other driver, anything but himself.

"Where is he?" she had demanded at the hospital, taking no notice of the ugly gash on Jonathan's forehead.

"Oh my God! That car, it came out of nowhere. Didn't see it coming—"

"Where is he?"

"Tried to swerve," Jonathan was saying, eyes wild, unfocused. "Road slick . . . Oh, my God, Dee Dee. Oh, my God!"

"WHERE IS MY SON!"

"He is dead. Michael is dead."

She didn't hear him, or chose not to hear. And she didn't hear the doctors as they rattled off Michael's injuries: "Brain hemorrhage, shattered pelvis, broken ribs, a punctured lung . . ."

When she finally saw him, his body had already gone cold. He was gone. His eyes were closed, and the expression on his face was eerily calm. He looked like he was sleeping. She dreamed about him all the time. Each dream would be different. Sometimes he would wake up and everything would be okay. She would take him home and fix him macaroni and cheese from scratch, just as he liked it, with lots of cheese.

Those were the dreams she loved the most, the ones where she would wake up smiling. In most of her dreams, though, he didn't wake up, and those were the ones she hated. They were too real, too much like life. When she awakened from those dreams, she would be awash in a sense of dread that no amount of showers or baths could rinse away.

"Why are you sitting in here in the dark?" he asked, turning on the lights and causing her to squint in the sudden brightness.

Him.

All this was his fault.

Why is it drunks always kill people, but they come away with a little scratch, or nothing at all?

She looked at Jonathan's forehead, still seeing the slight scar from the accident. Plastic surgery could have prevented scarring, but he had insisted on having a scar, a reminder that his son was gone.

Hypocrite. Wasn't having an empty house and a son in the grave enough?

Not for Jonathan, though. He had to be dramatic, had to let people know he was grieving.

But sometimes, late at night, when she was in her bedroom alone, she wondered if he missed Michael. She heard him crying in his bedroom down the hall several times, but not once had she comforted him or asked him how he was dealing with losing Michael.

She pushed the thought down. *Why should she be worried about him? If he feels guilty, he should. All this was his fault.*

But a part of her, the secret part, the part she wouldn't share with anyone, felt she was responsible. She knew Jonathan liked to drink. She should have stopped him from driving after drinking too heavily. But she had gotten careless, especially with all the long hours at the salon. And with things going so well, she never imagined that Death would come knocking at her family's door. But it did. And it wanted Michael.

It was the reason she stayed with Jonathan, in this marriage, in this house. It was her prison. Her sentence for giving Death permission to take Michael.

"You're home early," Jonathan said.

"I could say the same about you."

"You feelin' okay?" You look a little tired."

Am I feeling okay? How can I feel okay when you killed my son? MURDERER!

She wanted to scream it out, so everyone would know what kind of man Jonathan was. Instead, she turned her attention to a TV program about lions and hyenas in Africa.

"Had a hard day?"

She shrugged.

"Wanna talk about it?"

"Don't be stupid, Jonathan. Why would I do anything as absurd as talk to you?"

"I thought it would make you feel better."

"Do me a favor and don't think so much. It doesn't do you much good," she said, getting up and walking past him.

"I can't keep living like this," he said.

She laughed bitterly.

"Sweetie, you call this livin'?"

CHAPTER 38

Maxwell wiped the sweat from his brow and took a long gulp of Gatorade.

"Another game, man?" Andre asked.

"Naw, gotta get to work."

"Tony, you up?" Andre asked.

"Nope, I'm heading in, too."

"No more ball? I thought you were off today?"

"I am," Tony replied, "I'm just tired of playing one-on-one."

Andre sat down on the gray metal bench and bounced the basketball from one hand to the other.

"You guys going to come to my party tomorrow?" Tony asked, pushing his thick blond hair from his eyes.

"Yep," Maxwell said.

"Yeah. I been promising to take Brenda out somewhere nice to make up for missing our anniversary," Andre said, stretching out his long legs.

"Wait a minute, you are bringing Brenda to my housewarming party? It's not going to be *that* nice. Shouldn't you take her out to dinner?" Tony asked.

"Yeah, I can get you reservations at Ray's if you want. Lyfe Jennings is supposed to be there tomorrow."

"Nope, we're coming to your party," Andre said. "That's what I want to do, so that's what we're doing. Besides, Brenda will appreciate any place I take her."

"Why can't you for once do something nice for your wife? Brenda loves you—"

"I don't need anybody telling me that my wife loves me! I know she does. But like I said before, Brenda is the kind of woman that will appreciate the little things. I don't need to make a big fuss to show her I care. That's your problem with women, you always trying to do too much for them," Andre said.

"Who you talkin' to?" Maxwell asked.

"To both of y'all. Y'all too hung up on looks to actually know what's good for you."

"Don't even go there," Tony said. "You wouldn't even be with Brenda if Rosslyn hadn't dumped your butt before prom."

Andre's face darkened. "First of all, she didn't dump me. We just grew apart. Second of all, I probably would have married Brenda anyway. I mean, she was all over me in high school. Who wouldn't love that? Besides, y'all just jealous. Y'all out here wasting y'all's time with all these women, going out partying, having fun . . ." Andre's voice trailed off. "I'm out here taking care of two boys; I mean, raising a family, that's where it's at."

Maxwell rolled his eyes.

"Oh, so you don't believe me? Well, who are you bringing to the party?"

"Nobody," Maxwell said.

"Why don't you bring that girl from the work? That new girl," Tony asked.

"Yolanda? No, that's not gonna happen. Especially, after the other night . . ."

Andre sat up. "You really starting to like this dogface, aren't you?"

"She ain't ugly!" Maxwell shouted.

"Oooh wee, ain't we getting testy? It really don't matter who you bring. As long as it's not Theresa, I really don't care."

"What do you have against Theresa? Besides the fact that she looks like a model and your wife looks like a—"

Maxwell stopped when he saw the threatening look on Andre's face.

"Look, don't get it twisted, man. Just because I make fun of Brenda don't mean you can. Don't go there. I was trying to protect you, but fine. Don't listen to me."

"Protect me from what?" Maxwell asked.

"How many times I have to tell you, pretty women can't be trusted. Especially Theresa. She's a pathological liar and you still considering taking her back because you too chicken to try it out with—God forbid—an average girl."

"Yolanda is not average. I told you she is too skinny for me. The girl is a downright bone."

"So? You like what you like," Andre said.

"Get it through your thick skull, Andre: I don't like her!"

"I'll get it through my skull when you admit you like that girl."

"I already told you, she's not all that, but there's some-thing about her . . ."

"Fine, I'll help you," Andre said. "When she walks in, I'll give you a thumbs up or thumbs down—"

"What? I'm not in high school anymore, Andre. I don't need your opinion," Maxwell objected. He hated talking about this stuff. He liked Yolanda, but not enough to call her his woman.

"Besides, she ain't even my woman."

"Yet. Dogface ain't your girl yet," Andre said, teasing.

"Shut up. I told her that we should just be friends. I mean she's nice . . ."

"Nice? That's all you can say? *She's nice?* Tony, you heard this?"

"Yeah, I heard it. I already heard that after he told me he tried to kiss her."

"What?" Andre burst out laughing, rolling all over the metal bench. "Game over man, game over! You like that chick!"

"Man, you really need to stop talking about stuff you know nothing about."

"Tony, you all quiet over there? What you think is wrong with yo boy?"

"Nothing's wrong with Maxwell; he is just being extra cautious. Something that might have done you some good."

Andre waved his hand dismissively.

"You said this girl was just gonna be your friend, right? So just bring her to the party and check out if she fits in with your scene. Right, Tony?"

"I hate to say this, but Andre's right. Just call her and see how it goes. You never know . . ."

"Never know what?" Maxwell asked.

"It's obvious that there's something you like about this girl, or you wouldn't have tried to kiss her already. All we're saying is find out more about her, to see if you want to take it further. If you don't, no harm done, no feelings hurt, you guys will still be friends."

"Okay, okay. I'll bring her to your stupid party."

CHAPTER 39

"Hello?"

"Hey, Yolanda? It's me, Maxwell."

Yolanda closed the mystery novel she was reading, not bothering to mark her page. She sat up on her sofa and smoothed her frizzy hair, as if he could see her.

"Hey, Maxwell. What's up?" she said, her voice unnaturally high.

"What are you doing this evening?"

"Um . . ."

Is this one of those times that I'm supposed to pretend that I'm busy and have lots of stuff to do? Or am I supposed to be honest and say that after I finish this book, I'm gonna watch Imitation of Life *and cry like a baby at the end as I always do?*

"Yolanda? You still there?"

"I'm here."

"Look, I know I caught you at the last minute, and it being a Sunday I know you probably have plans already—"

"It depends. Did you want to hang out or something?"

"It's no big deal, actually. My good friend Tony just bought a house in Sugarland, and he's having a little party tonight. I was hoping—"

"Sure! I'd love to," Yolanda said eagerly.

He laughed.

"I was hoping you'd say that. It starts at six, so can I pick you up in, say, forty-five minutes?"

"No problem. I'll be ready."

"You sure? Most women would need at least two hours to get ready."

"I keep tellin' you, I'm not like most women."

"Okay, I believe you. See you in a little bit?"

"Wait!"

"Yeah?"

"Does this mean you thought about what I said? Are we friends or are we . . ."

"Do you have to analyze everything, Yolanda? Why can't we be friends who are trying to learn more about each other? Nothing more, nothing less, okay?"

"Okay. I can deal with that."

"I'll see you in a little bit. Bye."

"Bye."

Yolanda threw her book down and jumped off the sofa. She did a Beyonce booty dance without the booty.

"He called me, Precious! He called me!"

Precious looked at her, yawned, and rolled over.

"And this friend of yours lives by himself?" Yolanda said, gawking at Tony's beautiful Spanish-style home.

"Yep. All by his lonesome," Maxwell said, backing up to parallel park on the street. "Let's hit it," he said, opening his door.

He got out and walked around to Yolanda's side. She was standing on the curb checking out her surroundings.

She was dressed in a white linen pantsuit. Her long-sleeve tunic was knotted at the waist with a thin gold belt. He was pleased that her outfit accented her narrow waist, one of her best features. Her hair was pinned up in a messy updo, with a few stray strands framing her face. Maxwell looked at her neck, long and graceful, like a dancer's.

"What is it?" Yolanda asked, looking up at him.

The setting summer sun cast an amber glow across her skin, making her look like an angel.

"You're stunning," Maxwell said, surprised that the words escaped his mouth, but not sorry they had.

She smiled.

"Thank you," she said, looking down.

When did she get so beautiful? Maybe it's the light . . .

"Let's go inside," he said, taking her hand and leading her across Tony's yard to his front door.

He heard the loud music and laughter even before he reached the door. Maxwell knew Tony's neighbors wouldn't mind. Tony's skin color definitely afforded him certain privileges. *Man, if this was my house I'd be sitting in the back of a patrol car for disturbing the peace.*

He rang the doorbell, suddenly nervous about what his friends might say about Yolanda. He looked at her again, making sure it wasn't just the sun in his eyes. She smiled back at him.

Yeah, she's pretty.

The wide oak door swung open.

"Hey, what's up!" Tony said, opening the massive door wider so Maxwell and Yolanda could walk through.

"I thought you said it wasn't gonna be a lot of people?" Maxwell asked, surveying the crowd. It was pretty mixed up— blacks, whites, Hispanics, a handful of Asians. Maxwell recognized a lot of them from Tony's job at the hotel.

"You know how it is, one person tells another person, and soon everybody is invited. So . . . who is this lovely young lady here?" Tony asked, a sly smirk on his face.

"This is Yolanda. Yolanda, this is my friend Tony."

"Yolanda! I've heard so much about you."

Maxwell gave him a look that said, "*Don't.*"

"Good things, I hope?" Yolanda said.

"Sure, sure. Well, you guys go make yourselves comfortable. There's plenty of food and booze in the kitchen. Oh, and Maxwell, Andre's been looking for you."

"Where is he?" Maxwell asked, looking around.

"Check in the den or dining room. He's trying to set up a domino game. Catch you guys later. I need to get back to my guests."

"See you later, man."

"Nice meeting you, Tony," Yolanda added.

"You, too, Yolanda. Hey, Maxwell, before I forget, did you see that Denzel Washington movie? You know the one with Meryl Streep?"

"No," Maxwell said, puzzled. "Why?"

"Just thought you would want to know that Ebert and Roeper give it two thumbs up. Way up!" Tony said, both of his thumbs pointing up.

Maxwell laughed.

"Well, I'll have to check it out," Maxwell said, walking into the living room, still laughing.

"What was that all about?"

"It's a guy thing. Don't worry about it. I'm gonna get a beer. You want something?"

"A beer is fine."

"Be right back."

Maxwell moved through the crowded kitchen and looked into the refrigerator.

"You lookin' for something to drink?" a voice screeched behind him.

He cringed and plastered a smile on his face.

"Hey, Brenda!" Maxwell said, turning and giving Brenda a hug. Her strong perfume filled his nostrils and he starting coughing.

"You okay?" she asked, beating his back like a runaway slave, trying to dislodge whatever had caused his coughing fit.

He waved his hand, a signal for her to stop hitting his back, and stepped away from her to catch his breath. "Beer?" he asked finally, his voice no more than a strangled whisper.

"Over there," she said, pointing to a huge ice chest in the corner, filled with different types of beer.

"Thanks," he said, grabbing two beers out the ice chest.

"So, how's everything been going?" Brenda asked.

"Great. I can't complain."

"There you are! I lost you for a minute," Andre said, sliding up to Brenda and playfully kissing her cheek.

She blushed.

How can Andre walk around with this mutant, kiss her in public, and not be ashamed of her? Her silky blonde weave, which didn't match her nappy orange hair, hung pin straight down her back. Maxwell looked away.

"Hey, man, when you get here?" Andre asked, turning his attention to Maxwell.

"Little while ago."

"Where's your friend?" Andre asked, smiling.

"She's in the other room. I'll go get her."

"Bring her in the dining room. I wanna whoop y'all's butt in dominoes."

"Let me get Yolanda and we'll meet you in the dining room."

He walked back to Yolanda in the living room and handed her a beer.

"Thanks," she said. "So what's goin' on? We gonna dance, eat, mingle—what?"

"Actually, I wanted to introduce you to one of my friends, Andre. He's in the dining room setting up a domino game. You play, right?"

"Does a dog have fleas?"

He laughed. *She always finds a way to make me laugh.*

"I'll take that as a yes. Let's go, they're already in there."

Maxwell led Yolanda by the elbow to the spacious dining room off the kitchen.

Andre and Brenda were already sitting down at the large oak table pouring dominoes out of a large metal tin.

"Y'all ready to get your butts whooped?" Maxwell asked, pulling out a chair for Yolanda.

Andre cocked an eyebrow at Maxwell. Maxwell sat down, and didn't bother to push Yolanda's seat in for her.

"I saw that," Andre said.

"Shut up. So how are Dante and Trey, Brenda? Who are they with tonight?"

"My mother. I hope they are minding their manners over there, they can get pretty wild."

"How old are they now?"

"Seven and ten. Enough about them, are you going to introduce your girlfriend?" Brenda asked.

Maxwell started coughing.

Everyone waited for Maxwell to make the introductions, but his coughing fit kept going, and going, and going.

Finally, Yolanda stuck out her hand and introduced herself to everyone around the table. When Maxwell stopped coughing, he took a swig of beer and started mixing the dominoes, not looking up to give anyone eye contact.

The game went by quickly; everyone was at the top of their game. In the end, Brenda and Andre won by a measly five points.

"That was a good game. Yolanda, you need to come by the house sometime and play with us again. That would be nice, huh, baby?" Brenda asked, nudging Andre in the arm.

"I guess. Go get me another beer," he said, sliding his empty bottle toward her. "And a plate of food; I'm starving."

She smiled and got up to see to her husband's demands.

"I'll go see if she needs some help," Yolanda said, following Brenda into the kitchen.

"Why you always talking to Brenda like that?"

"Like what?"

"Like she is your servant or something."

"She is. Besides you can't talk, you almost had an asthma attack when Brenda said Yolanda was your girl-friend. What's up with that?"

"Nothing."

"I saw the way you was looking at her, just admit you have feelings for the girl—"

"I don't!" Maxwell said sharply.

Andre laughed. "Okay, I'll leave you alone. But you was right about one thing."

"What's that?"

"She's past skinny. I think you have found the first, and only, black anorexic."

"She's not that skinny," Maxwell said.

"Uh-oh. There you go. Anytime you add *that* in front of a word you're really sayin' the opposite. You really sayin' she's *too* skinny," Andre said.

"For somebody so smart, you come up with some dumb stuff."

"For real, I'm serious. People always say stuff like that. Especially women. Oh, girl, he's not *that* fat. He's not *that* ugly. He's not *that* broke. What they really sayin' is, 'Yeah he's fat, ugly, and broke, but I love him.' So you love this girl or what?"

"Why you keep askin' me that? We not even like that."

"Then why you keep seeing her? Why you keep callin' her?"

"I dunno."

Truth was, he really didn't know. She wasn't as exciting or sexy as Theresa, but he felt a comfort with her that he had never shared with another woman. She was interesting, funny . . . He genuinely did like her, but in a totally asexual way.

But that moment they shared outside . . .

That was real. I do have some attraction to her.

"Hey, guys, you two okay?" Tony asked, sliding in a chair next to Maxwell.

"Yep. Doing great. I was just tellin' your boy about the chick he brought."

"She's really pretty," Tony said.

"She is. But have you seen her body?"

"She's a little thin—"

"A little thin? She's a bone! She makes Skeletor look like the Nutty Professor."

"You exaggerate too much, Andre. Yolanda is a nice, pretty woman. She's nowhere near as bad as you make her out to be."

"That's because you're white. Us black folks like our women bootylicious not bonylicious. I'm telling you, Maxwell, don't trust pretty women! Dump that chick before you fall in love with her and be stuck walking around with Olive Oyl."

"Don't listen to that idiot over there, Maxwell," Tony said, throwing Andre a dirty look. "It doesn't matter what we think about her. What do you think? Is she girlfriend material or what?"

"I think she's cool. We're gonna take things slow and see where it goes."

"It's okay to like her, you know. It's not a crime, Maxwell," Tony said.

"I know that. We'll see how it goes, okay?"

Yolanda walked up with Brenda close behind her.

"Here's your beer and your food. I put extra ribs on there just like you like it—"

"And the extra barbecue sauce?" Andre asked.

"Right next to your bread."

"Where's the beans?"

"Under your chicken breast."

"Go get me some more napkins. I can't eat this with only one measly napkin," Andre said, balling the napkin up and throwing it at her.

"Sorry, baby, I must have forgot," Brenda said, walking fast to the kitchen.

Andre shook his head and dug into his food, ignoring the warning glances from his friends.

CHAPTER 40

She's surrounded.
They look just like her; in fact, they are her.
They haven't moved, haven't lain a hand on her.
No beatings at all.
The little Yolandas just stare at her like she's an alien.
She tries to talk to them, but they don't listen.
One of the Yolandas pulls out a switchblade and passes it to her.
"It's your turn," she says.
Yolanda picks up the blade and begins slicing her face until blood runs down her hands and the blade is red from her blood.
The little Yolandas cheer for joy as they surround her and each of them hugs her.

Yolanda woke up and instinctively reached for the phone to call Natalie.

"Hello?"

"Nat? It's me. I had another dream again . . ."

"Who is this?"

"It's me. Yolanda. Look, I know we haven't talked in a while, but I needed . . ."

"I don't care what *you* needed, Yolanda," Natalie said harshly. "We haven't talked in over a month, and when you do call, you wanna talk about those stupid dreams? Get over yourself," Natalie said, slamming the phone down.

Now totally awake, Natalie crawled out of bed and went to the bathroom. She threw cold water on her face and began brushing her teeth.

She is so selfish! Did she even notice that I quit my job? Does she even care?

Now that she didn't have a job she had no distractions and was proud she was excelling at school. Her instructor loved her so much that he had already offered her a job at his French restaurant, Le Cardemine, an upscale bistro in downtown Houston. She would be starting at the bottom, but it was a start, and right now she had to take everything offered to her. She was greedy for knowledge and was learning fast, surprising even herself. She was up to the challenge of this new turn in her life. *It is time for me to be selfish, time for me to shine.*

"Okay, everyone listen up," Dee Dee started. "Wake Up Houston is doing a makeover show next month and wants Behave Hair Salon to do all the makeovers."

"Wow," Yolanda said.

Wake Up Houston was the number one morning TV show in Houston. With her vivacious personality and sophisticated sense of style, Claire Winnfield had attracted millions of viewers to the show. Throughout the city, the hit show was a favorite water-cooler topic of conversation. Yolanda watched the show regularly, taping every segment. She couldn't wait to tell her mother the news. She knew what a big deal it was to be featured on it.

"Now we are all going to have to work together as a team. I don't want any mistakes," Dee Dee said, glancing at Theresa, who quickly looked away.

Good! Yolanda was not mean-spirited; nonetheless, she enjoyed watching Theresa squirm.

"Theresa, you're creative director and that means you're in charge, but I don't fully trust that you can execute a project of this magnitude. So, Maxwell," Dee Dee continued, "I want you to work with Theresa."

Yolanda watched as Theresa gave Maxwell a playful wink.

"Dee Dee, are you sure about that?" Yolanda asked.

Dee Dee turned and looked at Yolanda.

"Are you questioning my authority, Yolanda?"

"No, it's just . . ."

"Perhaps you have a better idea considering your meager experience as an assistant manager. Maybe your knowledge is greater than my twenty-five years of owning a salon?"

Theresa snickered.

"I apologize, Dee Dee, I wasn't thinking." Yolanda looked down at her notepad, embarrassed. She tuned out the rest of the meeting, wishing she were invisible and could crawl out of the room unseen.

Twenty minutes later, after assigning various responsibilities for the TV show project, Dee Dee stood up and graciously dismissed them, wishing everyone a fruitful Saturday.

As Yolanda prepared to leave, Theresa confronted her, putting her hand on her shoulder.

"Hello, Theresa."

"That comment you made last week . . ."

"Yeah?"

"I didn't appreciate it. Don't ever front me like that again in front of Dee Dee," Theresa said, looking directly into Yolanda's eyes.

"What?"

"You heard me," Theresa said.

They stared at each other for a long moment.

Yolanda was the first to look away.

"I thought so," Theresa said, walking away.

"It's getting late," Maxwell said. "Let's finish this up so we can go home."

"Sure. You want me to take you to dinner? My treat."

"Cute. Real cute."

"Come off it, Max," Theresa said, using the nickname she had given him when they dated. "I've seen the way you've been looking at me."

"What way?"

"You still love me."

"Don't kid yourself."

Theresa walked over to Maxwell and stood on her tip-toes, whispering in Maxwell's ear, "After all these years, we still love each other."

"After all these years, you haven't changed one bit," Maxwell said. "Everything about you is a lie. Drop this whole act and stop pretending to be something you're not. I need more than what you can offer. Can't you see that?"

Theresa's smile faded. She stepped back and started gathering her papers.

"I think we're done here," she said.

"We will always be *done,* Theresa. Understood?"

Theresa retorted, "I don't think so, sweetheart. We've only just begun. You need to learn to relax."

"And you need to learn there's more to life than lies and deception."

"I do know that. I also know that I still have feelings for you, Max. I've thought about you every day since we broke up. You knew when I took this job . . ."

"You should have asked me first."

"Cut the crap, Max! If I had asked you, would you have said yes?"

Maxwell shook his head no.

"I came here for two reasons, Max. One, because I'm good at what I do."

"And two?"

"I want you back."

Uncomfortable silence filled the room.

"I don't want *you* back," Maxwell said flatly.

"You know, you never gave us a chance, Maxwell. You fought your feelings then, and you're fighting them now. Why?"

"I'm not fighting any feelings for you, Theresa. There are no feelings for you."

She looked at him.

"You're lying."

He turned his back to her, not wanting her to see the turmoil in his face. *What kind of stunt is she trying to pull?*

"Is there someone else?"

"No," he said turning around and facing her.

"Then why, Maxwell? Why won't you give me another chance? There is still love between us; I feel it and I know you feel it, too."

"I don't know Theresa. But what I do know is that I just can't trust you.."

"I still love you, Maxwell. Tell me you love me, too," Theresa pleaded, her eyes searching his face.

He looked down at her, his eyes dark.

"I'll admit I still care for you, Theresa, but you have to know it's not love. Not anymore. It's over," he said, with a finality to his voice.

Theresa shrugged nonchalantly, but her heart was breaking. Carol had always told her she lied so well she could have become an actress, so she smiled brightly and picked up the rest of her papers.

"You're playing hard to get. You better be glad I like a challenge," she said, walking out of Maxwell's office.

CHAPTER 41

Yolanda put on her hoop earrings and fluffed her hair. She applied a coat of lipstick then stepped back and looked at her reflection. *Not bad.* She dabbed on her favorite perfume, Ralph Lauren Romance. *Not bad at all.*

She looked happy, and she was. Maxwell had asked her out again tonight. Things were definitely looking up.

The doorbell rang and she was surprised he was early. She hurriedly cleared the bathroom counter of all her toiletries and yelled, "Just a minute." She grabbed her purse off the table in the hallway and ran to the door.

"Hi," Yolanda said.

Maxwell acknowledged her greeting with a nod; he was on his cellphone.

"Naw, man, I'm not doing that. Why? You know why."

Should I invite him in? Or just let him stand there? She waited a few uncomfortable minutes while Maxwell finished his conversation.

"Talk to 'ya later. Bye." He shook his head.

"Sorry about that. You ready?"

"Sure," Yolanda said, locking her apartment door. *No "You look wonderful" or "You smell nice." Just a cold "You ready?" He talks to me like I'm one of his homeboys, not his date.* Disappointed, she walked silently to Maxwell's truck.

"Looks like rain," he said, pulling away from the building.

"Yeah, it does."

"We better hurry then. I know you don't want to get wet."

"That is true. So where are we going?" Yolanda asked.

"How 'bout we get something to eat and maybe go dancing?"

"That sounds great," Yolanda said, excited.

"After seeing the way you were movin' at that Musiq Soulchild concert, I figured you would like that. You sure have a lot of rhythm."

"Thanks. It's the one talent I do have," she blurted.

"What? You don't think you have any talents?"

She wished she could take the comment back. She didn't want to seem like a loser, although she regularly felt like one.

"No, no, I was being sarcastic."

"Oh, okay. Cool."

Yolanda watched Maxwell drive, his eyes steadily on the road, his long, thick fingers lightly gripping the steering wheel. He looked relaxed and cool in his designer jeans and white linen shirt.

"What?"

"Excuse me?"

"You're doin' it again," Maxwell said.

"Doing what?"

"Staring."

"Oh," Yolanda said, turning and looking out at the dark, gray sky that warned of turbulent weather ahead. "I'm sorry."

Maxwell shrugged and exited the freeway, entering downtown. He eventually pulled into the parking lot of Gator's, a Cajun restaurant.

"It'll probably be better if I valet. That way you won't get wet if it rains," he said.

As if on cue, a loud crack of thunder was followed by torrential downpour.

They looked at each other and smiled.

"Let's make a run for it," he said, giving his keys to the valet. He took Yolanda's hand and they ran into the restaurant, laughing like children.

"Whew," she said, tucking her wet hair behind her ears. *So much for an hour's worth of curling.* Maxwell's white shirt was clinging to his body; she quickly looked away and checked out the scene. The place was wall-to-wall crowded. And noisy, with a live band playing zydeco music in the back. Patrons were eating at small tables or sitting at the bar having a drink while waiting to be seated. The crowd was a good mix of ages. A real cross-section—enough older people to prevent a fight from breaking out, but enough young people to keep it hip.

Still holding her hand, Maxwell led her through the crowd to seats at the bar.

"What do you wanna drink?" he asked loudly.

"Just get me a Corona."

"Good choice. Two Coronas, please," he said to the bartender.

He handed Yolanda her beer.

"Thanks," she said, looking around the room and smiling because Maxwell was still holding her hand. She felt like a queen.

That is, until she saw Theresa watching them from the other end of the bar. Her eyes were in mean tiny slits as she sat on her barstool, men buzzing around her like bees around a flower. But Theresa's eyes were strictly on Maxwell.

Yolanda coughed hard and took a swig of her beer, trying to sooth her rattled nerves.

"What's wrong?" Maxwell asked.

"Nothing," she said quickly. "You wanna go somewhere else? This place is so loud I can barely hear myself think."

"Well, well, well, it's a small world," Theresa said, coming up behind Maxwell.

First, Jackie knocked on the office door, and then put her ear to it and listened. Hearing nothing, she opened the door with her key. She walked silently across the dark room, the scent of jasmine tickling her nostrils. She sat down behind the desk and turned on a small desk lamp. She switched the computer on and took out the letter she had written. She smoothed the creases and began typing:

Dear Mrs. Hegel,

Thank you for requesting Behave Hair Salon to do the makeovers for Wake Up Houston. Due to circumstances beyond our control, we have decided to pass. Though Wake

245

SIX O'CLOCK

Up Houston is a great show, it does not fit the criteria for our salon in that it would not be seen in a positive light by many of our clients.

Perhaps you could contact Shear Happiness Salon and Spa? They have a good reputation and have been in business for many years. I have listed their contact information below.

If you have other show ideas that would fit Behave's high standards, I would be happy to see them. My apologies again.

Sincerely,
Theresa McArthur

After saving the document, Jackie e-mailed it to the show. She then printed the letter up on Theresa's personal letterhead. She found Theresa's signature stamp in a drawer and used it to sign the letter. *I've just sealed your future. My mother will fire you, and then I'll be the new creative director. It shouldn't have come down to this, Mama. You should have promoted me. I'm your daughter. You had no business promoting Theresa over me. I didn't get rid of Sheila just to have this girl come in here and upstage me. But she'll pay for your mistake. This job will be mine.*

She was tired of doing stupid work that didn't guarantee any respect. In meetings, her mother never called on her to handle anything. It was always Theresa this or

Theresa that. She remembered how she felt listening to her mother announce that Theresa was the new creative director. The pride in her voice had made Jackie's blood boil. It was the same pride-filled voice she had used to talk with Michael. *But never me. Not once me.*

This salon should stay in the family, and she let Theresa come in and break everything up. Yeah, I've made some mistakes, but my mother is a fool for not choosing her own daughter to run her salon! So I'll show her the hard way. My way.

⁂

"Theresa!" Maxwell said, turning to look at her. "I knew that was you. I would know your voice anywhere."

"So what are you guys doing here?"

Maxwell dropped Yolanda's hand.

"Nothing really. Just out talking about business stuff."

"Business stuff?" Theresa asked, looking at Yolanda. "Didn't look like business to me."

"Well, it was," Maxwell said defensively.

Theresa smiled. "Well, if y'all were just talking business you won't mind me joining you," she said, sitting on a stool next to Maxwell.

Yolanda rolled her eyes.

"When did you get here?" Maxwell asked.

"About twenty minutes ago. Thankfully, I missed the rain. Looks like you guys didn't, though," Theresa said. "You are all wet."

"I know," Maxwell said, looking down at his shirt.

"Yolanda, you look a mess. You sure you don't want to freshen up? Maybe do something with that hair?"

"No, I'm fine."

"You sure?"

Yolanda checked her reflection in the mirror behind the bar. *My hair is looking frizzy . . .*

She slid off the barstool. "I'll be right back."

She maneuvered her way through the crowd to the restroom. Or rather the line to the restroom. After fifteen frustrating minutes, she finally got into the crowded, smelly bathroom and brushed her hair into a ponytail. She freshened her lipstick and powdered her face and rushed out to get back to Maxwell. She pushed her way to where they had been sitting, but they weren't there.

"Excuse me, sir? Did you see where the couple sitting here went?" Yolanda asked the bartender.

"I dunno know, lady. Check the dance floor."

"Thanks," she said. Looking toward the back of the room, she saw a large crowd gathered around the dance floor. She bullied her way toward the front to see what was going on.

And she saw them.

They were dancing to an upbeat zydeco song, the only ones on the dance floor.

People were stomping their feet and clapping their hands, cheering them on. Yolanda watched in horror as they danced together. Theresa's blue dress twirled and moved to the beat, her body moving gracefully to the music. Maxwell was all smiles as he guided Theresa's body, his hands on her hips. They danced as if no one else was in the room. Looking at them, anyone could tell they had history a together. And possibly a future. Yolanda couldn't stand watching anymore and walked back to the bar, defeated.

Every time she was having fun with Maxwell, Theresa would show up and ruin it. *Theresa wants Maxwell back. But I like him, too. What is he doing here with me? The choice would be easy; a man that fine would never want someone like me. If I was Maxwell, I would pick Theresa. The girl had it all: beauty, brains, body. The whole package.*

Yolanda ordered another drink, a whiskey sour to match her sour mood. She sat there for several minutes nursing her drink, trying to decide whether or not she should go home.

"Whew," Theresa said, returning from the dance floor.

"That man sure can dance," she said, grabbing a cocktail napkin off the bar.

The girl even sweats pretty. I don't stand a chance.

"You're not too bad yourself," Maxwell said, standing next to Theresa.

They laughed and looked at each other, shared secrets and old memories swirling about them. Yolanda looked at them, and saw the black version of Ken and Barbie. Him, tall and protective, his dark skin shiny with perspiration; Theresa, hair bouncy as a rubber ball, looking up at Maxwell with so much love in her eyes. Yolanda felt as if she was in one of those picture puzzles that asked you to circle the object that didn't belong. She needed a big black marker to draw around herself.

I don't belong. Maybe I never did. I've been here an hour and haven't talked to Maxwell for a decent five minutes. No one knows I'm alive. I should just sneak away and go home while I still have some sort of pride left.

⟡

Maria's back was hurting. She tried stretching it, but that didn't do any good. She had finished cleaning Dee Dee's office and was on her way to Theresa's. It felt good to be the only cleaning lady Dee Dee trusted to clean the offices upstairs. The other women were jealous, but Maria knew she had earned the trust the job required.

She pushed her cart to Theresa's office. The door was slightly open. *Who have left door open?*

"Oh, excuse me Maria," Jackie said, coming out of Theresa's office. "I didn't know anyone was still here."

"I was 'bout to clean Miss Theresa's office," Maria said, peeping in. "Is okay?"

"Of course. Theresa just sent me in there to . . . to look over a few things. Go right in; it's all yours," Jackie said, walking past Maria.

"G'night," Maria said. *She such hard worker. Such sweet girl.*

⟡

"You all right?" Maxwell asked, nudging Yolanda's arm.

"You ready to eat?" Theresa interrupted, inserting herself between Maxwell and Yolanda. "I'm starving. Let's go get a table," she said, grabbing his arm and pulling him toward her.

"Okay. Yolanda, you coming?"

Yolanda nodded and smiled, not trusting her voice to speak. *I know when to fold. I could never pull a man like Maxwell. I don't have what it takes.* After they walked away and disappeared into the crowd, she finished her drink, slipped the bartender a ten and made her way out the front door.

The rain had slowed to a soft drizzle. Yolanda sat on a concrete bench outside the restaurant, away from the noise and madness, and called a cab on her cellphone. She was missing Natalie more than ever. She would have to do something to make their friendship right again.

She waited for her cab to come, at the same time wishing that Maxwell would come walking through the front door looking for her, begging her to come back inside. She knew that wouldn't happen. Maxwell had his woman by his side, so she would not be missed.

CHAPTER 42

"You mean you left and no one even knew you were gone?"

"Yep."

"I don't believe that. Not Maxwell. That doesn't sound like him."

"Well, believe it," Yolanda said. "I caught a cab home the other night. Haven't heard from him since."

"He hasn't called you?" Jackie exclaimed.

"Nope. Not once. No apology, no explanation, nothin'."

"He has your phone number right?"

"Of course he does! That's not why he isn't calling."

"I warned you about Theresa. When she has her eye on something, she usually gets it."

"Including Maxwell," Yolanda added. "I hate that girl! She really needs to mess up again so she can get fired. Man, I wish I could just box up her stuff and send her packing. I'm telling you, Jackie, that girl is on my list. If I could figure out a way to get rid of her, I would."

"I told you about saying things like that about Theresa. She's a really nice person if you take the time to get to know her—"

"Not you, too! I don't want to hear another thing about her. That girl is the devil, pure and simple. I mean, she has everybody blinded into thinking she's this really good person, but she's not."

"Listen, Yolanda, are we friends?"

Yolanda thought for minute. They talked more frequently, almost every day in fact. They ate lunch together, went out on weekends, they were definitely on the fast track to becoming friends.

"Yeah, I guess so."

"Good. And as your friend I'm telling you to leave Theresa alone. Just ignore her, and she'll calm down. I mean, after all, you are trying to take her man."

"Maxwell is not her man! They're not together any-more—"

"So are you and Maxwell together? What are y'all doing? Are you just friends? Dating? What?"

Yolanda sighed. She didn't know what they were doing. After all this time, they still hadn't kissed; had, in fact, done nothing that went beyond friends. But something was there between them, and she was sure she wasn't the only one who felt it.

"I know it looks like I'm wasting my time on him, but when we're alone we talk about things, we have stuff in common. He's a beautiful person and I really want to learn more about him."

"That's great, Yolanda, that really is. But being with Maxwell is not enough motive to want to sabotage Theresa."

"In my book it is," Yolanda said, laughing. "I'll try to ignore her, I really will. And as far as Maxwell goes . . ."

"Maybe you'll give him another chance?"

"I don't know. We'll see."

"You're such a liar! Anyway, I gotta go get some sleep. Tomorrow starts another week at work."

"Whoopee," Yolanda said sardonically.

Jackie laughed. "Night, girl."

"Good night," Yolanda said, hanging up.

Yolanda sighed and picked up Precious.

"You won't ever leave me, will you, baby?" Yolanda asked, stroking behind her ears.

Precious purred her loyalty.

"*—I hate that girl!*"

"*—if I could figure out a way to get rid of her, I would . . .*"

"*Being with Maxwell is not enough motive to want to sabotage Theresa.*"

"*In my book it is.*"

Jackie smiled and stopped the tape recorder that was hooked up to her phone.

She couldn't believe how naïve Yolanda was. How desperate she was for friends that she would just call anyone a *friend*. She couldn't care less if Yolanda got involved with Maxwell, but she needed a plan B just in case her first plan didn't go well.

She had enough evidence on Yolanda to make sure she would go down if things didn't go as planned. All their late-night conversations, all the times she had said how she hated Theresa and wished she was gone, it all

254

had been recorded. And now with Yolanda falling for Maxwell, Jackie had Yolanda's motive, too.

You better stay on my good side, Yolanda, or else you're going down, too.

CHAPTER 43

"Dee Dee you have a call on line three."

"Thank you, Beverly," Dee Dee said, picking up the phone.

"This is Dee Dee."

"Hi, Dee Dee. Patricia Hegel with Wake Up Houston?"

"Oh, yes, Patricia, how are you?"

"Better now that we've booked your replacement for the show. Listen, thanks again for recommending Shear Happiness. They've been working out beautifully."

"Excuse me?"

"Yes, we received the e-mail and the letter last week. I'm sorry our show didn't fit your parameters, but we are a hit TV show, and if we don't fit your guidelines, we'll definitely fit someone else's," Patricia said, her voice laced with arrogance.

"This must be some mistake," Dee Dee said, her heart pounding in her ears.

"Well, it can't be a mistake. When I called yesterday . . ."

"Who did you talk to?"

"Um . . . let me check . . . yes, it was Theresa. Theresa McArthur, the same person who sent the e-mail and the letter."

Dee Dee could feel her blood pressure shoot up. *Breathe, just breathe. I'm not gonna have a stroke over this.*

"Hello? Dee Dee? You still there?"

"Yes, I'm here. I'm sorry, I was off in thought. Listen, Patricia, we need to talk. I never authorized Theresa to write that letter. As far as I knew, we were still having a meeting Thursday to go over the schedule."

"I don't understand. Why would Theresa send such a letter?"

"I haven't a clue," Dee Dee said, smoothing the hair at the nape of her neck.

"Well, I'm sorry Dee Dee, truly I am," Patricia said, her tone softening. "But I've already shown the letter to the other producers, and we've booked another salon. I'm really sorry, Dee Dee."

No, you're not sorry. But I know someone who will be.

"That's quite all right, Patricia. My apologies for this misunderstanding, and please consider our salon for a future show."

"Will do."

Dee Dee hung up. She felt like all the air had been sucked out of her lungs. It was hard to breathe. *I'm going to kill Theresa. What kind of game was she playing? Did she actually think she was going to get away with trying to destroy my business?*

She closed her eyes tightly, trying to block out the light in the room. She felt a migraine coming on. She wanted to go home but knew that Jonathan was off today, and she didn't want to see him. He would just remind her of everything she'd lost and give her another migraine.

She pressed the intercom button on her phone.

"Yes?" Beverly said.

"Send Theresa to my office. Now."

"Right away, ma'am."

It was time to deal with this girl face-to-face.

❧

"Good morning, Jose," Yolanda said, walking toward the front entrance of the salon.

He stopped cleaning the tall glass window and nodded.

She paused at the front door to see if he was going to open it.

He didn't. Instead, he kept cleaning the windows, pretending not to notice her.

"Thanks for being such a *gentleman*," she said sarcastically. "I thought you were supposed to open the door for a lady?"

"When I see lady, I open door," Jose said, in his thick accent.

Jerk. She opened the door herself.

She immediately noticed Maxwell at the front desk talking to Karen, the receptionist. She had been hoping to keep busy around the salon floor all day and stay out of her office as long as necessary. She was still feeling uncomfortable about their date fiasco over the weekend. She didn't know how to act.

Should I play it cool and act like what he did didn't bother me? Or maybe give him a piece of my mind and tell him to leave me alone? Maybe he won't notice me. I could just sneak on by . . .

"Yolanda!" Maxwell called out, waving her over.

She hesitated, then walked over, a smile plastered on her face.

"Yes?"

"Dee Dee has called an emergency staff meeting in twenty minutes."

"Why?"

"She fired Theresa," Karen said.

"What?" Yolanda said, looking at Maxwell for confirmation.

"It's true. Did it this morning."

"Why?"

"I can't go into details before the meeting," Maxwell said.

"She wrote some letter to that show, Wake Up Houston," Karen said. "Wrote that Behave didn't want to be on it."

"Is she crazy?"

"Yeah, girl! People down here are sayin' . . ."

"Ladies, ladies, could we gossip some other time?"

"Oh, yeah, sure," Karen said, busying herself on the computer.

"We need to talk," Maxwell whispered.

"Really? What about?"

"About what happened this weekend."

Karen coughed, letting them know that she was there, and listening.

Maxwell pulled Yolanda to a quiet corner of the salon.

"What happened?" he asked quietly.

"What do you mean?"

"Why did you leave like that? I waited for you."

"But you didn't look for me."

"How would you know that? I looked all over for you."

"You didn't look outside."

"That's because it didn't occur to me that you had left."

"Well, what was I supposed to do? Keep watching you and your ex-girlfriend flirt? I've got better things to do."

"Who told you Theresa was my ex-girlfriend?"

"Nobody," Yolanda lied. "It's obvious by the way you two talk to each other."

"Look, I don't want to argue with you. I really want to make things right."

"How? By taking me out again and ignoring me? No thanks. If you're looking for another notch on your belt, you've got the wrong girl," Yolanda spat.

He stepped back, stung by Yolanda's words.

"I'm not like that. I'm not that type of guy."

"Really? Well, what *type* are you?"

"What do you mean?"

"What are you doing with me? One minute you're hot, then you're cold. I just don't get you sometimes."

"I'm sorry," Maxwell said, looking at Yolanda intently. "I wasn't trying to confuse you. I just need some time to figure out what I want."

"What you want, or who you want?"

"Both."

She looked down.

At least he's honest.

"Look, me and Theresa have a lot of history, but it's over. I just needed to know for sure."

"Did you sleep with her?"

"That's none of your business."

She felt stupid for even asking, but she wanted to know where she stood with him.

"I don't know what you want, Yolanda. I cannot give you a relationship. But I definitely still want to kick it with you."

Kick it? What did that mean? Are we friends or something more? I'm not gonna push the issue. I'm fortunate that he's even talking to me.

She sighed and decided to leave things as they were, and not to complain.

"All right," she said.

"I want you to come over and let me cook for you."

"You? Cook?" she said, laughing.

"What? You don't think a brotha can cook? Don't be fooled by this suit, I can throw down."

"Oh, really?" Yolanda said, intrigued.

"Yes, really. So come over tonight and let me cook something and we can talk. No distractions, no interruptions, just you and me."

"Sounds like a plan."

"Around eight?"

"I'll be there."

He smiled boyishly and walked away, leaving Yolanda on cloud nine.

She walked upstairs to her office, mentally dissecting her wardrobe at home, trying to figure out what to wear.

SIX O'CLOCK

When Yolanda reached her floor, she heard a racket coming from Theresa's office, which was across from hers. She looked over and saw Theresa slamming, tossing, throwing personal items into a large cardboard box. Even from a distance, one could see that she had been crying; her eyes were puffy and bloodshot. Yolanda felt a twinge of pity for her. But when Theresa looked up and saw her staring, she went to the door and slammed it shut.

CHAPTER 44

Theresa blew her nose again and took a long swallow of her drink.

Crown and Coke.

I don't know why I drink the same thing after all these years. Theresa was looking for another Kleenex. Finding none, she went to the bathroom to use toilet tissue. Catching a glimpse of herself in the mirror, she winced. *I'm a mess.*

Her eyes were puffy, her nose was swollen and red, and her hair was all over her head like that of a wild woman. She was still wearing the suit she had on this morning. The same suit she had gotten fired in. Fired.

I've never been fired before.

"I'm good at what I do!" Theresa said out loud, to everyone and no one.

She kept trying to forget what had happened. How Dee Dee had fired her. But the more she tried, the more vivid the memory became.

"Your inadequacy, your poor and reckless job performance are not only a threat to my business but also poison for my reputation, a reputation that I've worked too long to build."

"Dee Dee, please let me explain . . ."

"No explaining, Theresa," Dee Dee said, her tone deceptively even. "I want you out of my sight ASAP," she said, dismissing her with a wave of her hand—like she was a child, or some kind of pesky insect.

"This is a mistake, Dee Dee. I didn't write that letter . . ."

"Then who did?! Give me a name; give me something that says you didn't have anything to do with this."

"I don't know who did it, Dee Dee, but I'm telling you I had nothing to do with this! Why would I do something like that?"

"I'm still trying to figure that out, Theresa. Can you explain who wrote the letter and sent the e-mail?"

"No."

Dee Dee nodded.

"Leave, Theresa. You'll be receiving your severance package as outlined in your contract. But I advise you to leave my office right now and collect your things."

She walked out of Dee Dee's office for the last time.

She came home and crumbled into a ball, having the worst panic attack in her life. It took her over an hour to calm her nerves and that was after two pills and a stiff drink. She wasn't supposed to mix alcohol with her pills, but she didn't have anywhere to go tomorrow. With no job, she could lie in bed all day and let the medicine wear off. Theresa watched a tear roll down her puffy face and knew tonight that tear would not be lonely; it would be joined by many other tears.

On her way, to the kitchen to fix a TV dinner, she heard the phone ring; she let the machine pick up.

"Hello, Theresa, this is Carol. Give me a call at home when you get this message."

"Hello to you, too, Mama," Theresa muttered. She could never say 'mama' or 'mom'. Always Carol.

Her mother would never forgive her. To this day, Theresa still didn't know what went wrong . . .

Theresa always knew she was pretty. Everyone always told her so, even told her mother.

"That daughter of yours, Carol, sure is a looker. She could be on the cover of a magazine."

The compliments enraged her mother, and she kept Theresa childlike and innocent by keeping her hair in pigtails.

She started developing breasts at nine, and her period started later that year.

"It must be something in the water. I didn't get my cycle until I was sixteen years old. What's wrong with you, girl?" she screamed, holding her down in the bath tub, scalding hot water turning her delicate skin into raw meat. The burn festered and oozed for days until Carol took her to the emergency room, daring her to deny the lies she told the doctor. When they came home, Carol began taping her breasts down, ignoring her screams as she rubbed the tender meat on her shoulder. The tape was tight, and she could hardly breathe. But she let her mother continue to wrap her breasts flat as a mummy. Anything to make Carol happy.

"Mama, I can't breathe. Why do I have to do this every day?" she whined.

"No daughter of mine is gonna be walking these streets looking like some Jezebel! I better not ever catch you trying to take it off! You hear me?! Don't ever take that tape off unless you're bathing or going to bed. You better not leave the house without taping down. You getting too grown for yo own good, I can't have you giving people the wrong message. Shoot, you already got all my church friends thinking you gonna be some kind of café woman."

Theresa nodded, not understanding why having breasts could give people the wrong message.

She continued taping her breasts down until she got to high school and had to shower for gym class. She saw that not one of the other girls had her chest taped down. She didn't want to be different, so she asked her Aunt Mavis to take her to the mall so she could buy a bra.

"You ain't wearing one yet? What's that crazy mama of yours teaching you over there?" she asked, laughing.

After their trip to the mall, she looked at herself in the mirror and liked what she saw. She was beautiful. She decided to walk to her friend Kasandra's house and show her the new look.

"Oh, my God! You're huge! What size are you?" Kasandra shrieked.

"I don't know. The tag says I'm a 34D, whatever that means."

"You're a D-cup? You make me sick! What I would give just to get out of this training bra," she said, pointing to her chest.

She eyed Theresa up and down.

"You know, you look really stupid to still be going around school with those pigtails. Let me do something with your hair . . ."

"No way! Mama would kill me."

"Who's gonna tell? Not me. Come on, just let me play with it . . ."

An hour later, Theresa walked out of Kasandra's house, her long sandy brown hair dancing down her back and a light rosy lip gloss coloring her lips.

"Oooh weee! Baby, you looking gooood!" a boy across the street yelled.

Theresa had never received much attention from boys, and the boy's comment made her blush.

From then on, she would change clothes every morning at school before first period, and flat-iron her long sandy-brown hair until it cascaded down her back. The attention she got from the boys was just what she needed; at home, there was none. Oh, she would get slapped and kicked and punched and cursed at, while her father hid behind his newspaper, not saying a word, fearing his wife's wrath as much as his daughter did. Even the teachers noticed her newfound confidence, and her mediocre grades improved to the point of winning the Most Improved award.

"Are your parents coming?" Kasandra asked as she helped her flat-iron her hair the morning she was to receive the award at the assembly.

Theresa remembered how her mother had beat her when she told her she had won the award.

"Most improved, huh? What you doin' in school before all this to win this award, huh? Was you smokin'?"

"No, Mama—"

Slap.

"Drinkin'?"

"No—"

Slap.

"Oh, I see you . . . been foolin' around with boys, haven't you? You been lettin' them touch you and see you naked, haven't you?"

"No, Mama, please stop . . ."

"Who do you think you are, tellin' me to stop? I tell you the way things go around here, missy, not the other way around."

"No, my parents aren't coming," Theresa said, rubbing her cheek as if her mother had just slapped her.

"Good for you, I guess. Your crazy mama would beat the black off you if she saw you dressed like this. You sitting on stage in the auditorium in a skirt."

"Don't worry, they never make it to stuff like this. They definitely not coming."

Hours later when Theresa heard her name announced, walked to the podium . . . and froze.

Her mother's steely gaze pierced her skin and she literally could not move.

The principal called her name again, beckoning her to come forward.

But she still couldn't move; all she saw was her mother mouthing the words, "I'm gonna get you."

Theresa started shaking uncontrollably and dread consumed her. Then, as if trapped in a nightmare, she peed all over herself. She was that afraid of what her mother would do to her when she got home.

Screams and laughter erupted from her classmates.

When she tried to run, she slipped on her urine and fell. Covered in the ammonia-like smell she finally regained her balance and walked off the stage, running to the nearest restroom.

Her mother was waiting for her in the hall.

"You little harlot! I knew, I knew you was up here acting like some Jezebel," she hissed. "You all exposed to the world, embarrassing me like this! Showing your legs for all them boys to look at. Titties out for the world to see!"

She grabbed Theresa's long hair and pulled it so she could whisper in her ear. "You coming home right now, and I'm gonna beat you so you won't be able to show them pretty legs for a long time."

Carol always kept her promises.

Theresa was so bruised she couldn't return to school for weeks. For that, she was thankful. She didn't know how she could face anybody after that horrible day.

Once her body was healed enough, she packed some clothes and stole enough money for a taxi to her Aunt Mavis's house. Theresa left a note and told her where she was. Her mother called her one time.

"If you think my sister can raise you better than me and your daddy, then good riddance to you. You ain't been nothin' but a thorn in my flesh ever since you been born. Gone and stay with her and see how you fare. You gonna be just like her. She's a hussy, too, the same as you."

Her aunt tried all the time to tell her that her mother was the one who was crazy, that she was perfectly fine with the body she had been born with.

But she kept wondering if she'd been born different, if she'd had smaller breasts and hips, would her mother had loved her?

Maybe, if I was shaped like Yolanda, I might not have turned out just like my aunt—man after man, but still alone after all these years.

She used to be able to always count on her career, but now, with that gone, what did she have anymore?

Theresa looked around her apartment.

Nothing. She had nothing. She *was* nothing.

CHAPTER 45

Maxwell had fixed a wonderful dinner: grilled steaks, rice pilaf, and green bean almondine. And for dessert, apple pie with homemade vanilla ice cream. They ate while listening to Maxwell's favorite jazz CD and sipped on red wine and laughed and talked all evening.

He liked talking to Yolanda. She was a good listener.

Maybe it was the wine, or the good conversation, but he was slowly starting to find Yolanda beautiful. *I'll admit that she's got a pretty face. But her body . . .*

His phone rang.

"Hold that thought," he said, interrupting Yolanda's story about her father's latest remodeling job. He picked up the telephone on the end table next to the sofa.

"Hello?"

"Hey, boy! Where you been? You ain't been around the restaurant lately."

"Sorry, Pop. I've been busy."

"Busy? Too busy to see your daddy? Doing all them haircuts got you hemmed up?"

"Pop, you know that's not what I do anymore. I manage a salon . . ."

"Yeah, yeah, don't remind me. When you gonna be a real man and get you a real job and work with me at the restaurant? You know I could use you."

"Pop, I don't want to get into this with you right now," Maxwell said, mouthing *I'm sorry* to Yolanda.

She smiled and whispered, *that's okay.*

"Well, anyway, I was just calling to remind you about the family reunion this weekend . . ."

"It's this weekend?! I thought it was next month!"

"No, boy, it's this weekend. I knew you probably forgot. You gonna be able to make it?"

"Yeah," Maxwell said, mentally switching things around in his head. "Yeah, I'll be able to make it."

"Alone? Or are you bringing a special friend?"

Maxwell looked at Yolanda.

"Probably alone, Pop."

"Boy, why you having so much trouble with the ladies? I know it can't be because the way you look 'cause you get that from your old man," he said, chuckling.

"No, I don't have any problems in that department, Pop. In fact I was thinking about bringing someone," Maxwell said, looking at Yolanda again. "I was trying to surprise you."

"Well, that's good, boy. Bring her around. I'm dyin' to meet her. Come by the restaurant tomorrow so I can give you directions. Your Uncle Cecil is insisting on having it way out in the country."

"I'll see you tomorrow, Pop."

"Okay."

He hung up and looked at Yolanda. Her hair was in soft waves reaching just below her shoulders and her face was glowing from the wine.

She's beautiful, just beautiful. Why can't she be good enough? Why can't I just take her and say that she's with me. She's my woman—

Maxwell couldn't even bring himself to think it. Yolanda wasn't his woman. She wasn't his type at all. Never before would he have even seriously considered dating someone as thin as she was.

Then what is she doing here, man? You asked her over here, you could have just left her alone . . .

"You okay?" Yolanda asked.

Maxwell looked at Yolanda again.

He took a finger and slid it down her cheek. Her skin was soft and delicate. Like her. *Be careful with her.*

He liked her, plain and simple. At least with her, things were peaceful, uncomplicated. She would be a good companion on that long drive. *A companion. That is all she is to me. Nothing but a mere acquaintance. I don't like her. I can't like her.*

"You wanna meet my family this weekend?"

Yolanda smiled, her face lighting up.

He took that as a yes.

CHAPTER 46

Natalie squeezed her eyes, trying to recall what she'd just read.

"I give up. What was the answer?"

"Four hundred degrees."

"I knew that, I knew that . . ."

"Why don't you take a break?" her mother suggested, handing her back her textbook. "Dinner is almost ready."

"I can't take a break! I have my certification for sterilization test tomorrow and I'm not prepared—"

"You are prepared! You're pushing yourself too hard. Seriously, stop studying, eat some of my legendary fried catfish and relax. You're doing great at school. I wish you hadn't quit your job—"

"Oh, here we go again. I knew you had an ulterior motive for inviting me over here."

"It's just not like you to be so impulsive. You've never done anything like that before—"

"Exactly! I needed to leave that job, Mama. The way my performance was going they would have fired me anyway. It was time to leave. I have enough savings to last until I finish school."

"And then what? Working at that salon, you were making pretty good money. What are you gonna do now?"

"I told you my instructor offered me a position at his restaurant. I'm gonna start next week part-time."

"You're gonna be taking a major pay cut."

"I know that, Mama, I'm not stupid."

"I never said you were stupid, Natalie. I know you're scared. I know all this is a new experience for you. You know me and your dad will be behind you, no matter what you want to do. He has already offered you money so you can stay afloat, and you can always move back home if things get really rough," her mother offered, clearly hoping for such a scenario. "It will be just like old times."

"No thanks, Mama. I really appreciate all that you and Dad are doing for me, but this thing I gotta do on my own."

Dropping the subject, her mother began transferring the now golden-brown fish from the skillet to paper towels.

"Yolanda is really gonna miss you around that salon."

"Miss me? Believe me, mama, she probably doesn't even know that I'm gone."

"Really? Things are that bad between y'all?"

Natalie nodded.

"Well, trust an old lady. Y'all will work things out."

"And if we don't?"

Her mother shrugged. "Then you weren't real friends in the first place."

CHAPTER 47

Dee Dee pulled her black Mercedes into her long, cobblestone driveway and clicked a button on the dashboard to open one of the her three garage doors.

It had taken two years of working with one of Houston's top architects to design this house exactly as she had envisioned. She wanted the feel of living in a villa in Italy, and her goal had been achieved. The stones lining the driveway all had been shipped from Venice. The hedges and lawn had been landscaped perfectly to replicate a house in Tuscany that Dee Dee had rented on one of her many travels. The antique fountains were always on, suggesting a peace and tranquility in a home environment that was anything but.

Dee Dee sat in her car with the engine idling, wondering—not for the first time—if she should close the garage door and end it all. But finally, she turned the engine off, putting off killing herself another day. When she walked into the house, hoping not to see Jonathan, she found the lights were dimmed and heard soft music playing in the background. "Jonathan!" Dee Dee yelled, looking around and seeing red rose petals strewn around the marble floor in the foyer. *Who's gonna clean up all these flowers?* "Jonathan! Where are you?"

"In the dining room."

Dee Dee placed her purse on the antique end table in the foyer, and went into the dining room. "What the—" she blurted, shocked to see Jonathan sitting at the head of their oak and mahogany inlaid dining table, his face lit with candles.

It looks like he fixed dinner . . .

"Why don't you sit down?" Jonathan said, pointing to a chair next to him.

"I don't want to. I'm going upstairs."

Jonathan sighed heavily.

"Please, Dee Dee. I'm asking for you to please sit down."

Dee Dee reluctantly sat next to her husband, her expression questioning his motives. *I haven't sat this close to him in years. I can smell his aftershave . . .*

"What's this all about, Jonathan?"

"I wanted us to have a nice meal together."

"Why?"

"Do I have to have a reason?"

"For you? Yes," she replied.

Jonathan didn't answer; he simply took the heavy lid off her plate to reveal one of her favorite dishes: crawfish etouffee.

"I made it extra spicy, just the way you like it," he said softly, picking up his spoon to dig in.

"I'm gonna give you five seconds to get to the point or I'm leaving," Dee Dee said icily.

What does he want? Soft music? Rose petals? He can forget about sex; he blew any chance of that years ago.

"Fine, have it your way. We need to make some decisions about our marriage," he said tonelessly.

"If this is about us getting a divorce . . ." Dee Dee started.

"This isn't about getting a divorce . . . yet. It's about how after all this time you think I killed Michael."

"I don't think. I know."

"It was an accident."

"You can control how much you drink."

"I told you I only had a glass of wine with dinner!"

"You lying alcoholic!! You KNOW you had more than that!!" she screamed, her rage as hot and unforgiving as that day in the hospital, the day she learned her son was dead. At the direct hands of his father, as far as she was concerned—then and now.

"Then how come the breathalizer said I didn't?"

"I don't know. The alcohol had probably worked through your system by then."

"You know, Dee Dee, I'm hurting, too. Not once after Michael died did you ask me how I felt about losing my son."

"I don't care about *you* and *your feelings*! Feeling sorry for you won't bring him back. You need to admit that you were driving too fast . . ."

"It was raining! I tried to slow down, I didn't see that other car . . ."

"Because you were drunk! You were speeding and you lost control of that car and *you killed my son!*" Dee Dee screamed.

Jonathan sat back in his chair.

"He would have graduated high school this year," Dee Dee continued.

"I know," Jonathan said sadly.

"He was going to Georgetown. Thought he could be a big basketball star."

"I know."

"Might have made it to the NBA."

"I know."

"What do you know? You don't know anything, because you're the reason he's dead! You're the reason I can't hold him—" Dee Dee burst into tears, her sobs making her ache from pent up emotion. She held her arms around herself tightly, feeling cold and empty. Michael's laugh, his smile, his glowing eyes . . . It wasn't fair he was gone. She missed him so much. This wasn't how her story was supposed to be. No parent should bury a child, it was inhuman, an unnatural way of the life cycle. He was supposed to be here, to hold her when she got old and too sick to hold herself. She had been cheated out of the life she was supposed to have, cheated out of everything.

"I know that I still love you."

"What?"

"I love you, Dee Dee. I've never stopped loving you," he said, looking at her. "All I'm asking for is another chance."

She didn't answer, couldn't answer. For three years she had locked up her emotions, not letting herself feel anything. No pain, no joy, and especially not love. Love had cost her son's life. She felt her heart struggling to open like a flower trying to blossom with the sun's morning light. She closed it, refusing to let his words sink in, refusing to let love take over any other emotion than the rage that had filled her heart for the past three years. *I won't let him, I can't let him love me. I can't feel that again, never again.*

She lifted her head, her eyes still full with tears, and cast him a withering glance. "I have no chances in me to give."

"Then I want a divorce."

Dee Dee looked down at her crawfish etouffee. *It's probably cold by now.*

"Did you hear me?"

"I heard you. Do whatever you want."

"What about what you want?" he asked.

I want things back to the way they used to be when Michael was alive. He filled my life with so much joy and I can't figure out to how to get it back.

"I don't know what I want," Dee Dee said, her mind swirling around memories of Michael.

She missed his kiss on her cheek on his way to school. At fifteen, he never felt he was too old to give his mama some sugar. His love for her was open and free, and she never had to beg for it, he knew just when to give her a hug or a kind word. She missed his laugh and open smile. She even missed their visits to the orthodontist to get his crooked teeth straight.

"Wait till these things come out, Mama, I'm gonna be the man!"

"Boy, shut up!" Dee Dee said, laughing at her son, his awkward, lanky limbs loping beside her. But she could tell he was on the way to becoming a man, and at the time, the thought scared her because he was growing up too fast. Now she would do anything to see years added to his life. To see him graduate from high school and then college. To dance with him on his wedding day. To see his eyes fill with tears as he held his firstborn child for the first time. But no more, her son was dead. His life was frozen and barren, locked in a place that wouldn't let him live again.

Her son. Her dead son.

"I know what I want," Jonathan said, putting his hand over Dee Dee's. She didn't pull away.

"I want you back, baby . . ."

"I'm not your baby," Dee Dee said curtly.

"Still, I want you back. The old Dee Dee. The one who used to cry at those stupid long-distance commercials and would laugh herself silly watching old movies."

Was that me? Did I ever live so carefree, with so much life? No, that couldn't be . . . "That part of me is gone. It's dead. I'm dead."

"No! You're not dead. You're alive and we can work this out. It's gonna be tough, but I know we can get through this."

"I don't know," Dee Dee said, pulling her hand away.

"When did you become so cold? It's like you won't allow yourself to feel anything."

Jonathan grabbed Dee Dee's hand and placed it over his heart. He began to cry.

"Can you feel this?" he asked, his voice choking on his sobs. "Can you feel how much I love you, and how sorry I am?"

He dropped down to his knees and put his head in Dee Dee's lap.

"I'm sorry. I'm sorry. I'm so *sorry!*" he said, over and over again, his deep sobs tearing through his body. She could feel his warm tears on her black slacks.

Dee Dee sat still for a minute. And then she placed her hand on his head and began rubbing softly.

Remembering Michael's favorite lullaby, *Summertime*, she found her voice and began singing it.

Summertime . . .
and the livin'
is eeeeasy
fish are jumpin'
and the cotton is hiiiigh
oh, your daddy's riiiich
and your mama's good looookin'
so hush little baby
don't you cryyyyy . . ..

Jonathan shifted and looked up at Dee Dee, his eyes red with tears.

"You still remember that song?" he asked.

Dee Dee nodded.

"I wanna, try Dee Dee. Please let's try again."

"Okay."

Tentatively, Jonathan reached up and kissed her.

Dee Dee had forgotten the taste of his lips. They were so warm and tender. She closed her eyes and, for the first time in three years, she let her husband make her feel alive.

CHAPTER 48

"How have you been holding up?"

"Okay, I guess." Theresa said, using the remote control to turn the TV volume down. "You wouldn't believe how much you can learn by watching daytime television. It's so fascinating!" Theresa said sarcastically.

"Well, you just sit tight; I'm looking into who really sent those letters. I know you could never do a thing like that."

"It's good to know that somebody believes me, that somebody is on my side."

"I'm always on your side. I told you that. I really have a strong hunch on who was setting you up, but—"

"Really? Who do you think it was?"

"I can't say right now—"

"I lost my job, remember? If you think you know who did it . . ."

"I have a hunch, but that's it for now. But don't worry, I'm on the right track, we'll have the culprit soon and you'll have your job back. I promise."

Theresa sighed. "I guess that's better than nothing. Thanks for all your help, Jackie, you've been a lifesaver."

"Girl, you know I got your back."

CHAPTER 49

"Tony, you workin' out this morning?"

"No, I'm busy."

"What about tonight, then? I could switch some things around . . ."

"No, tonight is not good, either."

"Tony, what's goin' on? Lately when I call, you're either busy or not at home. You seeing somebody?" Maxwell asked.

"No," Tony said quickly. "I mean, it's this new promotion. I'm so busy I can't even think straight. I'm always tired, and the last thing on my mind is going to the gym."

"Okay man, but don't start missing too many workout sessions. You're gonna start turning all flabby and mushy," Maxwell joked.

Tony was silent.

"It was a joke, man."

"Well, that wasn't funny. What if I did get all big and fat? We wouldn't be friends anymore or something?"

"Tony, lighten up . . ."

"Society puts too much emphasis on weight nowadays. It shouldn't matter if I was fat or bony—"

"Tony, it doesn't matter! What's gotten into you? It was a joke, man. That's it. Since when you start getting so sensitive about weight, anyway?"

"I don't know, but weight is a sensitive issue with a lot of people. You can't play like that."

"Okay."

Tony's voice dropped to a whisper. "This isn't a good time; I'll call you later," he said, hanging up.

Maxwell looked at the phone in his hand, puzzled. *What was wrong with him?*

❧

"What you doin' today? Lifting weights or running?"

"My arms are still sore from yesterday. Let's just jump on the treadmill," Andre said.

"Fine by me," Maxwell said, walking to the cardio machines.

He stepped up on a treadmill and started on a low setting to warm up.

"So Tony was too busy to come?" Andre asked, setting his treadmill.

"Yeah. Called him this morning, but he had an attitude."

"I know. I called him last week and he was getting all defensive, like a Brenda having a PMS fit."

"What did you say?"

"Nothin' really. Talked about how Brenda's thighs were getting too big—they make a swish-swish sound when she walks. And they're covered in cellulite. It's pretty gross."

"Let me guess; he jumped down your throat because you talked about her weight?" Maxwell asked.

"Yep. Got all pissed off. Called me shallow, vain, and a whole lot of nonsense and hung the phone up in my face."

"That's how he acted with me this morning!"

"I'm not tripping, though," Andre added. "I know being around all that food at work must drive him crazy. He is probably worried about getting big or something. You know most chefs are overweight."

"I know, especially the good ones."

They finished the rest of their workout in silence.

CHAPTER 50

Yolanda lay her head back in the tub, letting the warm, rose-scented water soothe her tired muscles. With Theresa gone, Maxwell had dumped more work on her. She didn't complain; more work meant more responsibility, but she hadn't expected to be so tired.

She closed her eyes and replayed the night at Maxwell's apartment.

He wants me to meet his family.

Yolanda smiled, nervous and excited at the same time.

This is getting serious. Am I his girlfriend? Is he trying to ask me to be his one and only?

But what if he'd only asked because he didn't have anyone else to bring?

Shut up, girl, you're as good as gold. A man as fine as Maxwell could bring anybody he wanted. But he's bringing me! Out of all the women he could take, he wants me.

Her musings came to a halt when the phone rang. She picked up the cordless phone from the floor.

"Hello?"

"Yolanda? It's me, Maxwell. What you doin' tonight?"

Calm down. Be cool. Don't tell him you planned on sitting in the house and organizing your closet . . .

"Nothin' much."

"You wanna go to the movies? That new Martin Lawrence movie is playing; we could check it out."

"Sure." *Oh yeah, we're dating! He asked me out again! Yolanda Peterson, you have a boyfriend!*

"What time does it start?" she asked.

"Eight-thirty. Is that too late?"

Are you kiddin' me? I'd fly to Egypt at three in the morning for a date with you.

"No, that's fine by me."

"Cool. Let's meet at that new theater they built downtown. You know the one?"

"Yeah, I know where that is. I'll meet you there."

"Great. See ya soon."

"Yesss!" Yolanda screamed.

We're dating!

Seconds later, the phone rang again. *He must have forgotten to tell me something.*

She purred, "Did you forget something, baby?"

"Baby? It's me, Gina. Who did you think it was?"

"Nobody, Gina," Yolanda said, embarrassed. *You only call when you want something, or you have something else to gloat about. What is it this time? Did your husband buy you another new car? Or is that fat baby of yours walking, talking, or doing something babies do that grabs everyone's attention?* "What do you want, Gina?"

"I was just calling to see if you've decided about what you wanna do this year for Mama and Daddy's anniversary? It's their fortieth, so we have to make this one big."

Yolanda sighed.

Every year she and Gina split the cost of their parents' anniversary gifts. It started small at first: gift certificates, dinners to five-star restaurants, tickets to a new Tyler Perry play. But lately, Gina had been hatching more elaborate plans. For their twenty-fifth, a trip to Hawaii; two years ago, matching Movado watches. Last year, Gina tried to hire a contractor to remodel their master bathroom, but their father had refused, saying he didn't want another man touching his *throne*. They bought them a plasma TV instead.

"What is it you wanna do this year, Gina?"

She was already annoyed, because no matter how much she helped and contributed, her father always gave all the credit to Gina. It was as if he was blind when he read the zillion cards they gave him; 'From Gina' was the only name he saw. She didn't know why she kept doing it. Maybe she thought her father would eventually give her the validation she desperately needed.

"I'm thinking that we should throw them a huge party at my house!"

Yolanda let out the huge breath she had been holding, relieved that it wasn't too elaborate or expensive.

"I'll do all the cooking, 'cause we both know you suck in that area, and you can do the decorating."

"Thanks," Yolanda said sourly.

"I'm looking on the Internet for different recipes . . . Oooh, by the way, how should I get them to the house? You know it's a long drive."

Gina loved to brag about the new house they had built in the Woodlands, a small suburb on the outskirts of Houston. It was a huge six-bedroom custom-made house, and Gina would use any excuse to have company over so she could brag about something new she'd bought: a new oil painting by some struggling unknown black artist, a new oriental rug, new silk curtains.

"I don't know . . . why don't you—"

"I could have Trevor pick 'em up and tell them we're gonna take them out to dinner, then say he forgot something at the house! Then they come in and *Surprise!* They see the party."

"That'll work."

"How should I tell people to dress?" Gina asked.

"Probably—"

"I know! Cocktail! You know, like after five? That would be so cute! Mama never gets a chance to dress up; she'll love that, huh?"

"I guess," Yolanda said. *Why is she asking me all the questions if she's just gonna answer them herself?*

"I hope Mama likes it. I'm gonna make those stuffed peppers she likes so much, and that Southwest chicken dish she loves . . ."

"It sounds good, Gina."

"Yeah, so anyway, we're gonna throw it Sunday."

"Sunday! This Sunday?"

"Yeah. What's the problem?"

"I have a . . . I have something to do on Saturday."

She didn't want to say that she had a date. She didn't want Gina in her business, asking her stupid questions. *I mean, sure we're dating, but until I'm positive, I'm not talking about this with her.*

"What has Saturday got to do with Sunday?"

"I won't be able to help prepare."

"I told you, you don't have to cook. All you have to do is put up some decorations and decorate the tables. What's the big deal?"

"Gina, I'll be there."

"Good. What's so important on Saturday, anyway? You got a date or somethin'?" Gina asked, laughing.

Yes! And he's ten times better looking than Trevor.

"I have to work late," Yolanda lied.

"That's *sounds* like something *you* would be doing on a Saturday night. Well, I'll call you tomorrow with more details. Bye."

"Bye."

Yolanda sat back in the tub, the water now cool and clammy. She put the cordless phone back on the floor and dipped her head under the water, trying to drown out the bad thoughts about her sister that were crowding her head.

They were in the parking lot outside the movie theater. It was filled with hyperactive pubescent teenagers waiting for their parents to pick them up.

"That movie was hilarious! Martin Lawrence is crazy!"

"Yeah, he's a trip."

"So what are we gonna do now?" Yolanda asked, eagerly anticipating a long evening with Maxwell.

He was quiet for a moment.

"You feel up for a nightcap?"

Yes! I'm in!

"Yeah, sure. I don't mind," Yolanda said, keeping her voice controlled and even to disguise her excitement.

"All right," he said, heading for his truck. "It's not that far from here; just follow me."

She nodded and walked to her car parked three spots down from him. She got in her car, buckled her seatbelt and followed Maxwell out of the parking lot.

They were in front of his building in no time.

Yolanda hadn't looked around that much the last time she was at Maxwell's place, having been enthralled that he had actually invited her over for dinner. *This time I'm gonna look around more, make myself more at home. I mean, that's what a girlfriend does, isn't it?*

In Texas, bigger was always better, so Yolanda wasn't surprised that Maxwell's apartment was in a skyscraper. Skyscrapers were the crowning jewels in Houston's urban revitalization program. His building was twenty-three stories high, and its residents loved its powerful location, romantic views, and unequaled access to the city's urban pulse points. Downtown Houston, once neglected and left to rot, was now an invigorating place to call home.

Maxwell got out of his truck and handed the keys to the valet.

"Good evening, Mr. Alexander. Will you be needing your vehicle again this evening?"

"Nah. Not tonight. Thanks, Herman."

Another valet, a tall white man, opened the door for Yolanda and asked her the same: "Good evening, ma'am. Will you be needing your vehicle again tonight?"

Yolanda looked at Maxwell, not sure how to answer.

He burst out laughing.

"Yeah, John. She's gonna need her car tonight," Maxwell said, shaking his head.

They walked toward the entrance, with Maxwell walking slightly ahead of her.

"Good evening, Mr. Alexander. Ma'am," the doorman said, holding the door open for them.

The lobby was modern, yet traditional with shiny, marble-tiled floors and dark mahogany-stained walls. The concierge looked up from his desk and smiled pleasantly.

"Good evening, Mr. Alexander."

"Evenin', Peter."

"Have a nice evening, sir. You, too, ma'am," he said to Yolanda as they headed to the elevator.

Once inside, she asked, "Are you always this nice to everyone?"

"What do you mean?"

"You know everyone's names, and you actually talk to them. . .."

"They know my name. Why wouldn't I know theirs?"

"I don't know. Most guys don't, though."

"I'm not most guys," he said, looking down at her and giving her a small wink.

They stepped out of the elevator and walked down the long hallway to his apartment. He unlocked his door and Yolanda stepped in.

"Make yourself at home," he said, as he went to the kitchen to answer his ringing phone. She followed him to kitchen and took a seat on a barstool behind his kitchen counter.

"Hello? Oh, hey . . . Nah, I'm not doing nothin' . . ."

Not doing nothing? Hanging out with me is doing nothing?

"Yeah, listen man, let me call you back. I got company. What? I told you, Andre, it's not like that. We work together, that's it."

Maxwell turned his back on her and whispered something into the phone.

Yolanda ignored the conversation.

Things are still going well. At least you got invited back to his place. How many have done that?

She walked around, taking in the contemporary leather sofa and sleek, modern club chairs. Floor-to-ceiling windows extended the length of the living and dining rooms, offering a breathtaking view of downtown Houston. The eggshell-colored walls were covered with vivid art. One of the oil paintings caught Yolanda's eye and drew her toward it. The kaleidoscope of colors—deep marine blues and dark forest greens—rendered the painting dark and moody, yet inviting.

"That's one of my favorites," Maxwell said, handing her a glass of wine.

"Thanks," Yolanda said, taking the white wine. "How did you know—"

"I love black art. It's a hobby of mine."

Ian Bellman started off as a local Houston black artist. His broad, bold use of color soon caught the attention of the art world. His work hung in galleries all over the world, including New York, London, and Tokyo.

"This must have cost you a lot. I've rarely seen one in someone's private collection."

"It was my mother's. She had quite an eye for talent."

"You must really miss her," she said.

He nodded and took a sip of his drink.

"This is a nice place," Yolanda said, looking around.

"You acting as if you haven't been here before . . ."

"Yeah, but the first time I was so nervous, I didn't really look around much."

"You were nervous?" Maxwell asked, surprised.

"Don't act like you couldn't tell; I was fumbling and stuttering all over the place."

"You nervous now?" he asked, gazing down at her.

She looked down afraid to meet his eyes.

He placed his hand under her chin, and lifted it. "Look at me," he said, his deep voice smooth and reassuring.

Yolanda looked up at him.

"Are you nervous now?" he asked again.

"No," she said. But her lie was exposed when she took a sip of her wine and some of it dribbled it down her chin and onto the front of her shirt.

Nice going. Why don't you just start drooling and put a handicapped sticker on your car? Any woman can drink without spilling it on herself.

She swiped at her chin.

"Gotcha," he said, smiling. Taking her hand, he led her to the kitchen and handed her a paper towel to wipe her shirt.

"I'm just teasing you."

"I made a mess," Yolanda said, dabbing at her black shirt.

"No, you didn't. You're still cute."

Cute? You think I'm cute . . .

"Seriously though, I was thinking about buying this place."

Who cares? You just said I was cute. I'm cute!

"Why wouldn't you buy this place? It's wonderful. You're close to all the hottest clubs and restaurants . . ."

"Yeah, but I'm getting older, and downtown is not exactly the kind of place you want to raise a family, you know?"

You bet I know.

"You wanna sit down?" Maxwell asked.

"Sure."

She followed him to his sofa and sat down.

He picked up a remote on the oak coffee table, pressed a button, and the room filled with soft jazz music.

"You're the first person who knew who did that oil painting."

"Really?"

"Most women just comment on how pretty the colors are."

"I keep telling you, I'm not like most women," Yolanda said, winking at him.

Maxwell smiled and took another sip of his drink.

"What are you drinking?"

"Crown and Coke. Why?"

"I don't know. Just asking."

He's awfully quiet. Maybe I should say something. But what do I say? I shouldn't say anything. In a lot of cultures, silence is a good thing. But we live in America, stupid, I need to say something. Maybe he's so quiet because he's comfortable with me. It means our relationship has progressed to the point where we don't have to entertain each other. Or it could mean he's bored. For goodness sake, say something!

"So," Yolanda said, toward him, "It's been pretty hot lately, huh?"

Oh, no, girl. You're drowning. Not the weather. Any other topic besides the weather . . .

"Yep. Pretty hot."

"If you could pick anywhere else to live, just for the weather, where would it be?"

"California. I lived there for almost a year when I was in junior high because of my dad's job. In Sacramento. Everything was just so balanced. Not too hot, not too cold, just right."

"Like Goldilocks."

"Huh?"

"You know, when she was eating the porridge? One was too hot, one was too cold, but baby bear's porridge was just right."

He gave her a weird look and shrugged.

"I guess you could look at it like that."

Stupid, stupid . . .

"Why did y'all move back?"

"Because of my mom's first bout with cancer. All our family is here, and my mom wanted to be close to her family."

"Is that her?" Yolanda asked, noticing a picture of a smiling woman on the end table next to the sofa.

"Yeah."

"May I?"

"Sure."

Yolanda studied the picture of his mother. It was a sunny day. She was smiling, and her thin, shoulder-length black hair was blowing across her face. Her wide, expressive eyes were distracted, as if her mind was on something else. *She must have known already. Must have had some kind of foreboding.*

"She's pretty."

"Was," he said, reaching over and taking the picture, looking at it intently. He set his drink on the coffee table, and then placed his hand over his mother's face, as if he could feel her flesh pulse with life. He then placed the black-framed picture on the coffee table next to his drink.

"I'm really sorry," Yolanda said.

"You know what I miss the most about her?"

"What?"

"Our conversations. Mama always told the truth. No matter how much it hurt, she spoke the truth."

"You loved that about her, huh?"

"Loved and hated that about her," he said, with a wry smile. "I remember when I was in college and was stayin' with this chick in her apartment, driving her car, and eating her food. Somehow, she found out and called me right up and told me I was a punk. I mean she told me *off*. I almost hung the phone up in her face 'til I remembered who I was talking to. Here I was, twenty years old, thinking I'm grown. But she was right. I had no business in that girl's house like that. So I up and moved out the next day. Been on my own ever since," he said, his voice tinged with pride.

"I bet she was proud of you."

"Yeah. Yeah, I think she was."

"I've been to your father's restaurant that one time, but I don't really know him. What's he like?" Yolanda asked, greedy for more information about his personal life.

"Pop is . . . Pop is just . . . I don't know. He's a hard man to describe. You'll see this weekend."

"So let me guess, you're more of a mama's boy?"

He smiled. "I'll be the first to admit it. Yes, I'm a mama's boy. Me and Pop just don't click."

"Why is that?"

"I don't know. It just seems like we're always going in different directions. We just don't see eye to eye on a lot of things."

"That shouldn't be a reason to not get along."

"For us it is," he said.

Yolanda looked at her watch.

"It's getting late; I should be going."

She thought she saw a flicker of disappointment cross his face, but he quickly recovered and yawned.

"Yeah, you're right. I gotta get an early start tomorrow."

She stood and got her purse. Maxwell led her out of the apartment to the elevators.

"Well, I guess I'll see you at work. Thanks for having me over. I liked your place."

"I liked talkin' to you."

"Well, I just plain ol' like you," she said.

He looked down.

"I'm sorry—"

He looked up. "You have nothing to be sorry about. I really enjoyed your company tonight. I, I . . ."

She touched his hand. "I understand," she whispered.

He sighed. "You don't. But thank you for trying."

"I'm your girl, that's what I'm here for—" she stopped, when she realized her mistake.

"You are my girl, Yolanda."

She heard the *ding*, and knew her elevator had arrived.

But she couldn't move, couldn't breathe, afraid she would say something to mess everything up.

"Good night, Maxwell," she said finally, stepping onto the elevator.

CHAPTER 51

"Man, I got some news about yo boy Tony."

"Can this wait, Andre? I gotta a lot of work to do," Maxwell said, looking over a new inventory form for their new product line.

"Believe me, man, you'll want to hear this."

"Okay," Maxwell said, putting the form down. "What is it?"

"I saw him last night at that new Mexican restaurant downtown, Salsa? He was on a date."

"So? What's new about that?"

"She was black."

"Really? Tony's got a little jungle fever? Well, what can you expect? He's been hanging around us black folks for so long . . ."

"That ain't all man. She was fat."

"What?"

"Fat," Andre said. "Real fat. Hippo fat. She was . . ."

"Obese?" Maxwell offered.

"Yeah. That chick was obese."

"Man. So Tony got him a fat black girl. So that's why he's been actin' so funny. What's her name?"

"I dunno. I didn't say anything to him."

"You didn't introduce yourself to her?"

"Nope. I left them alone. He was obviously ashamed of her, they were sitting in the darkest corner of the restaurant."

"Is she pretty at least?" Maxwell asked.

"Well, if you can get past all that weight, she gotta a little Star Jones essence about her. The old Star Jones, though, not the new and improved one."

"Say, let's mess with him a little bit this evening. We supposed to meet him and play a little ball. We oughta figure out what's really goin' on with him and that fat girl."

"Man, I was thinkin' the same thing," Andre said. "I can't wait to see his face when he finds out we know about his little—nah, wait, let me take that back— his *big* secret."

"You crazy man. See you later," Maxwell said, hanging up.

"I'm tired," Tony said, taking a long sip of Gatorade. "That's it for me; I need to take a shower."

"So soon? You got plans tonight?" Maxwell asked, a wicked smirk on his face.

"No, not really."

"Man, you sure?" Andre asked.

"Dude, I think I would know if I had plans. What's up with all the questions?"

Maxwell shrugged.

"I dunno . . . Thought maybe you had a date tonight or something."

"What gave you that idea?"

Maxwell gave Andre a knowing look.

"Say, Tony, how many times you seen Jurassic Park? About twenty times?" Andre asked.

"So? It's my favorite movie. What does that have to with—"

"And which dinosaur did you like the best? The brontosaurus?"

"I guess . . ."

"Is that the same one you took out the other night?"

Tony's face darkened. "What are you talking about?"

"The dinosaur you were out with at Salsa. Although I really couldn't see you behind her fat head, but I'm guessin' that was you behind Mrs. Brontosaurus."

Maxwell burst out laughing and gave Andre a high five.

"I mean, I'm not hatin' though," Andre added. "Hungry Hungry Hippo was my favorite game growing up."

Without warning, Tony rushed Andre, slamming him against the wall and putting him in a chokehold.

"Don't you ever talk about Sharon like that! YOU HEAR ME? NEVER!"

Maxwell ran to Andre's aid and dragged Tony off him.

"What's wrong with you?" Maxwell yelled, trying to hold Tony back from attacking Andre again.

"Yeah, man," Andre sputtered, his voice raw. "We were just playin'!"

"Playing? That wasn't funny!" Tony yelled, his face red.

"Get off me!" Tony screamed at Maxwell.

Maxwell let go of Tony, trying to remember the last time he had seen Tony so upset.

"Both of you guys make me SICK! So what if Sharon's got a weight problem? So what? That's why I didn't tell you, because I knew you guys would freak out. None of you can say anything to me about my woman. Nothing. Andre," Tony said, looking at Andre, his eyes cold and deadly. "Your raggedy butt can't talk about nobody's woman. The whole world can see what Brenda's problem is."

"Say man—" Andre started.

"SHUT UP!" Tony yelled, his eyes blazing. "You should have been the main person on my side, walking around with Brenda should make you respect any man that ventures past his comfort zone and actually falls in love. Especially with somebody you didn't think you could ever be with. But you wouldn't know anything about love, 'cause the way you talk to Brenda, its clear to everyone around you that don't love or respect her."

"I love her," Andre said in small voice.

"No, you don't. You can't even pretend to love her. You too hung up on a girl that doesn't even exist, a girl who don't love you—"

"Rosslyn did love me!" Andre exploded.

"Even if she did, Andre, that was fourteen years ago! Let it go!"

Maxwell chuckled.

"And you," Tony said, turning his attention to Maxwell, "I expected this kind of mess from Andre, but not you. But, hey, I guess your daddy is right about you. You are a coward."

"What?"

"Did I stutter? Don't act so surprised. You're a coward. You so worried about what other people think, you can't even stand up and admit you love that girl—"

"Yolanda?"

"Yeah, idiot, Yolanda! I saw the way you were looking at her at my party. You love her. You just too much of a coward to show it. But you know what? I'm not listening to you guys anymore. Especially when it comes to women. With Sharon, I've found everything I want and more. I'm gonna make her my wife."

"Man, you crazy," Andre said.

"You're probably right. I'm crazy enough to find something in my life and go for it. That's more than I can say for you two," Tony said, storming off the court.

"Man, he was pissed," Andre said, rubbing his throat.

"No joke?" Maxwell said, his voice dripping with sarcasm as he watched Tony walk away.

CHAPTER 52

"I'm kind of glad she's gone."

"Really?" Yolanda asked, surprised by Jackie's honesty. "I thought I was the only one who felt that way."

"Of course you feel that way. You're in luuurve!" Jackie said in a syrupy voice.

"I'm not in love!" Yolanda said, looking around the salon cafe to make sure no one had heard Jackie. "I just like him a lot."

"Whatever. All I'm saying is that things will be a lot easier for you now that Theresa is gone. You have to admit, the girl was giving you the blues."

"I know." Yolanda said, taking a sip of Coke. "That's why I don't understand how she got fired. I didn't like her, but I thought she was doing a pretty good job."

"Well, obviously she wasn't if my mom—I mean, Dee Dee—fired her."

"Still, Theresa wasn't a stupid woman. She is too smart to make such dumb mistakes."

"What if I told you that she wasn't the one making the mistakes?"

"What do you mean?"

"That maybe someone was making those mistakes on purpose."

"And saying Theresa did it? No way. Who would do something like that?"

Jackie raised her eyebrow.

"You didn't . . ."

"Let's just say I helped the both of us."

"That was pretty low . . ."

"And stealing her man wasn't?"

"I didn't steal her man!" Yolanda shot back.

"Look, don't get all serious on me, I was just talking in the hypothetical. We both know I never did anything, right?"

Yolanda looked down at her half-finished tuna melt. Suddenly, she wasn't hungry anymore. *I don't like Theresa, but this is going too far. It shouldn't cost her job.*

"Right?" Jackie asked, more firmly this time, her voice low.

"Right."

"So after that he's gonna put in new kitchen cabinets, and then, baby, he's gonna buy me a new refrigerator!"

"That's great, Mama," Yolanda said, her long legs stretched out on her couch. She mentally blocked out the surprise anniversary party she and Gina were throwing them, not wanting to spill the secret.

"What's wrong, baby? Ain't you excited about my new refrigerator?"

"Of course, Mama, I'm really happy for you. It's just that I have a lot on my mind."

"Well, that's what I'm here for, baby. Talk to mama."

"I miss Natalie," Yolanda blurted.

"Y'all still haven't patched things up? You need to call her, baby, right now."

Yolanda sighed.

"I wish things were that simple."

"They are. In life, things are always that simple. Don't waste another day wishing to talk to that girl. Call her right now; she probably misses you, too."

"What do I say? It's been so long, Mama. She probably hates me."

"Start off with 'I'm sorry I've been such an idiot.' It always works with your daddy."

Yolanda burst out laughing.

"Good night, Mama."

"You gonna call her?"

"Yeah, Mama. I'll call her as soon as we hang up."

"Okay, baby. I love ya. 'Night."

Yolanda hung up, and stared at the ceiling. In one quick motion, she dialed Natalie's number before she lost her nerve.

Natalie answered on the third ring.

"Hello?" she said, her voice groggy.

"Hey, Nat, it's me, Yolanda."

"Oh."

Yolanda could hear the disappointment in Natalie's voice.

"I know this isn't a social call, Miss Big Time Manager, so what do you want?"

"Nothing really. I—I just . . . I just wanted to talk."

"Talk? For what?"

"I want us to be friends again."

"Tough tittie."

"I'm sorry, Natalie. I know I haven't been a good friend to you, but I really miss you. I was completely wrong and should have been there for you, but I wasn't. I've been so selfish lately, and never considered your feelings at all throughout this whole mess. So I'm asking, no, begging, for us to be friends again."

Silence.

"Natalie? You there?"

"I'm here."

"What are you thinking?"

"I'm thinking how I should hang this phone up in your face. I'm thinking how bad things got that it motivated me to quit my job so I wouldn't see you at work and cuss you out. I'm thinking how I should trash that office of yours. But then I think about how hard it is to be going through something new in my life and for you to not be part of it. I think about you calling me and telling me about those stupid dreams," Natalie said, her voice thick with tears. "You really hurt me, Yolanda. Out of all the people in my life, I never would have guessed you would've treated me like that."

"I'm sorry," Yolanda said. She was ashamed of herself. With all the teasing she had gone through, she had sworn she wouldn't treat anybody as she had been treated most of her life. But she didn't do it to just anybody; she did it to Natalie, her best friend. She ignored her and pushed her aside, not giving one brief thought to how Natalie felt. *She's never gonna forgive me . . .*

"I can't promise anything, but I would like to try to be friends again."

"Thank you!" Yolanda shrieked, wiping fresh tears off her cheeks.

"Besides, right now with me starting my new job—"

"New job? That was quick! Which salon are you going to work for?"

"It's not a salon, Yolanda. When I quit doing hair, I did just that—I quit doing hair. I'm working at a restaurant now."

"A restaurant? What? Since when?"

"I've always wanted to cook, Yolanda, you know that."

"Yeah, but you always said that was just a hobby, nothing really serious. Are you sure this is something you really want to do?"

"I couldn't be more sure of anything in my entire life. This is what I want to do."

"I'm really sorry I wasn't there supporting you. I know I've messed up . . ."

"Yeah, yeah . . ."

"No, Natalie, I'm really sorry."

"I forgive you already! So how's work been goin'? You been keeping busy?" Natalie said, changing the subject.

"Yeah, it's been pretty hectic. Me and Maxwell were on the phone the other night—"

"You and Maxwell? So y'all a couple now?"

"I'm meeting his family this weekend."

"Oooooh!!!" Natalie squealed. "That sounds serious."

"Maybe," Yolanda said, smiling. "You heard Dee Dee fired Theresa last week?"

"Tasha called me and told me about it. I heard the whole salon's been gossiping about it. She said Jackie might be the new creative director."

Yolanda thought about their conversation today at lunch and wondered if she should tell Natalie about it. She decided against it, giving Jackie the benefit of the doubt. Maybe she *was* talking hypothetically.

"I don't, know girl. Dee Dee hasn't mentioned anything yet."

"Enough about work, tell me more about Maxwell. Have y'all gone out on a date? What are you gonna wear this weekend?"

They talked all night, two friends catching up. Natalie, with her future as a chef, and Yolanda, with her hopeful future with Maxwell. Their voices intertwined until it was just one voice, never missing a beat.

CHAPTER 53

That was stupid.

Jackie took another sip of her drink and tried to keep her mind on her favorite television program, but couldn't. Her mind kept going back to her lunchtime conversation with Yolanda.

That was a mistake.

She finished her drink and went to the kitchen to fix another. She added more vodka this time, because the alcohol made her think better. Made her mind clearer.

I've gotta think this one out.

She sat down on her sleek stainless steel bar stool. It wasn't comfortable, but comfort wasn't her issue right now.

I have to get myself out of this mess. Everything was going so perfectly. Theresa was gone, and her mother had no choice but to pick her as the new creative director.

Maybe Yolanda won't say anything. I mean, how can she? She doesn't have any proof; it would be her word against mine. If she does blab to Maxwell, I'll just tell mother that they're sleeping together and were trying to sabotage me, because they know I'm next in line for the position. It really doesn't matter what I say; she don't got nothing on me.

Still, she could not convince herself Yolanda was not a problem. She gulped her drink down and poured yet another, adding more vodka than before, plotting a way to get Yolanda fired. *Yolanda, baby, you're going down.*

CHAPTER 54

"So you'll be ready around one o'clock? It's a long drive to Beaumont, and Pop wants me there early."

"I'll be ready."

"I'm not gonna hold you. I have to do some things before I pick you up. See you later," Maxwell said.

"Good-bye," Yolanda said quickly, but he'd already hung up.

Too late.

He always hangs up before I can say good-bye.

She hung up and looked over at Precious, who was sitting on the bed licking her paw.

"Today is gonna be a great day, Precious!"

Precious looked up, meowed, and went back to licking her paws.

She grabbed her robe and went to the bathroom and turned on the shower. She stripped off her pajamas and got under the water, jumping when the scalding hot stream hit her. She was so nervous and excited she hadn't even checked it.

I'm meeting Maxwell's family today. And not just his immediate family— his whole family! This definitely means we're dating. If I'm meeting his family, that means 'relationship.' He could have asked anyone, but he asked me. He's falling for me. Yes, ma'am, Maxwell has got the hots for yours truly!

She and toweled off and decided to go pick up her dress at the tailor's. After much careful deliberation, she and Natalie finally had decided she should push herself out her comfort zone and wear a dress. It was a pretty cornflower blue sundress with a matching cardigan. Normally she hated showing her legs, but for this special occasion she decided she should dress up. *It's not every day that I meet my man's family.*

"Hi, Anna. I'm here to pick up my dress," Yolanda said, holding her ticket.

Anna was a petite middle-aged Vietnamese lady. Her straight blue-black hair was cut in a blunt bob, too severe for her long face. Yolanda had been going to her for years.

"Yes, Mrs. Peterson, it ready. You want to try on?"

"No, that's okay. I'm in a hurry."

"Pretty, pretty dress," Anna said, passing Yolanda her dress over the beige laminate counter.

"Thanks. How much?"

"Twelve-fifty."

Yolanda handed her a twenty.

"Mrs. Peterson, how long you come here?" Anna asked, handing Yolanda her change.

"Oh, I don't know, five, six years maybe? Why?"

"You get lot of things altered."

"Yeah, I guess I do," Yolanda said, picking up her dress.

"I tell you something?"

"Sure."

"You skinny. String bean. Hard to alter. You need to eat, fill out as woman. Maybe get surgery. Breasts 'plants. Do you good."

"Excuse me?"

"You flat everywhere. Spend too much money on alteration. Need bigger breasts, save money on clothes. Then find nice man. Marry and have kids."

Yolanda just stood there, stunned by the woman's audacity. Finally, she walked out, trying not to cry in front of her.

"You come back, okay?" Anna sang out.

Yolanda got into her car and burst into tears. *Why can't I be okay just the way I am? Am I really that bad to look at?* Yolanda looked at herself in the rearview mirror and did something she never did. She got angry. *Who was she to tell her to gain weight? Who does she think she is? Who made her the judge of what's beautiful? She actually thought she was giving me good advice by telling me to get implants! I'm sick of it. I'm tired of people telling me I'm not good enough.* Yolanda wiped her tears, blew her nose and walked back into Anna's shop.

She was helping another customer.

"Hello, friend! You forget something?" Anna asked.

"Yeah, I did. I would think that if a person came in and was loyal that you would appreciate her patronage, not give her a lecture about her body. Who made you God? Stick to your job of fixing clothes and keep your comments to yourself. I'm beautiful, with breasts or not. And I'll have you know I have a boyfriend who thinks

I'm beautiful, smart, and funny. I'm perfect no matter what you think," Yolanda said, breathing hard.

"Yeah," the other customer said, turning to Yolanda. "You told her."

Anna looked small and pitiful.

"I so sorry, Mrs. Peterson."

"You are sorry. Sorry for thinking you could tell somebody who's giving you money every week that she is ugly. Not good enough. But you know what, Anna? Me and my flat chest are gonna take my flat money somewhere else!"

Yolanda stormed out. With every step she felt lighter. It felt good to tell someone off. *I should do this more often.*

CHAPTER 55

Beaumont was a small, quiet, country community about an hour's drive from Houston. Yolanda and Maxwell talked all the way there. He eventually turned into a small dirt road and drove into a huge field filled with hundreds of people milling about eating, drinking beers, dancing or just sitting around playing cards and dominoes.

"You have a big family," Yolanda said, nervous. She felt overdressed when she noticed everyone wearing jeans with red shirts that said 'Alexander Family Reunion' on the front. *Stupid Natalie. I knew I shouldn't have worn this dress.*

"It's pretty big. They're good people; you'll fit right in. Come on," Maxwell said, getting out of his Hummer.

Yolanda opened her door and stood by the truck. *I don't feel right about this. I don't belong . . .*

"Come on. You can't stand there all day," he said, grabbing her hand.

"Let me introduce you to everybody . . ."

"Hey, Max! Max, that's you?" a voice boomed from behind them.

Maxwell turned.

"Hey, Uncle Leroy! What's up!" he said, dropping Yolanda's hand to give him a big bear hug.

"Boy, you lookin' grown. Lookin' just like your daddy. What you been up to? Still cutting hair?"

"Naw, I'm manager now."

"What you say! You doing really good. Who is this with you?" Uncle Leroy asked, pointing to Yolanda.

"Oh, she's my . . . friend. My co-worker. This is Yolanda," he said awkwardly.

Uncle Leroy shook Yolanda's hand.

"Nice to meet you," he said, grinning widely.

"This is my dad's brother," Maxwell said.

"I can see the resemblance."

"Hey, baby, where you want this ice to go?" a short, plump woman asked. Yolanda could only assume she was Leroy's wife.

"Put that down a minute and come over here and see your nephew."

"Max! That's you? Boy, come over here and give me some sugar!" she screeched.

Maxwell walked over like a shy schoolboy and gave her a hug and kiss on both cheeks.

"It's good to see you! You just get here?"

"Yeah, a couple of minutes ago."

"Loretta, quit manhandling the boy and come over here. He brought somebody with him. What you say your name was?"

"Yolanda."

"Her name's Veranda."

"Well, hello, Veranda!" Loretta said, giving Yolanda a hug.

"It's Yolanda," she said, barely able to breathe as Loretta hugged her tightly. Her make-up was tacky and overdone. Her thin eyebrows were dark and artificial, and her red blush was stenciled in two perfect round circles on her cheeks. Her pink lipstick was lined with a black lip liner and her lipstick was thick as buttermilk biscuits. Yolanda could scrape off one coat of that lipstick and it would be enough for all the women at the reunion to have pink shiny lips.

"Girl, you ain't nothin' but skin and bones! I feel like I could just break you in half! But you sure do have a pretty face. Don't, she Leroy? Don't she have a pretty face?"

"Sure do."

"Thank you," Yolanda said. *I hate when people say I have a pretty face. Why can't they just say I'm pretty?*

"Why are y'all talking in this circle acting all antisocial? Y'all need to mingle or something."

"Hey, Pop," Maxwell said, giving his father a hug.

"Well, where is she? Where is this girl of yours?" his father asked.

Is that how Maxwell described me? As his girl?

"She's right here!" Loretta said smiling. "Ain't she got a pretty face, Ray?"

Ray turned and looked at Yolanda.

"Her face is all right, but where's the rest of her? She ain't got—"

"Oh, hush!" Loretta said, coming to Yolanda's aid. "Let's go over here to this pit, Yancey, and get you something to eat."

"It's Yolanda. And I'm fine."

"Please get something to eat, girl. You look so hungry you makin' me hungry," Maxwell's father said.

"Pop . . ." Maxwell warned.

"What?"

"That's enough."

I'm so sick and tired of all the comments about my weight! I want to go home. Why didn't Maxwell prepare me for this? I wish I had some jeans on. . ..

"Come on, lemme introduce you to the women side of the family."

"Um, I don't know. I should probably stay with Maxwell . . ."

"Girl, gone and go! Maxwell don't want to be around you!" Ray said. "Go with Loretta."

She looked at Maxwell. He nodded his consent, and she let Loretta lead her to the other side of the field.

"What'cha want on your plate?" Loretta asked.

"I don't know. A little bit of everything, I guess."

"Now don't you worry one bit about what Ray said. He always saying something negative about somebody. He didn't used to be like that. He changed after Clarice died. Tore him up to watch his wife die like that. Yes, indeedy, when Clarice died she took the best of him with her. Now, go sit in one of those chairs over there. I'm gonna fix your plate for ya."

Yolanda looked over to where Loretta was pointing. It was a huge group of women sitting around talking and laughing, balancing huge plates of food on their laps.

"Go on now, chile. They ain't gonna do nothin'. I'll be right over there."

She walked over to the group of women. They were all beautiful in different ways and all had the body Yolanda dreamed about: thick and curvy in all the right places. She sat down in a green plastic chair.

"Hello."

"Hey," some of them said, looking at her curiously.

"Who did you come with?" one of them asked.

"Maxwell."

She burst out laughing.

"No, really. Who did you come with?"

Yolanda shifted in her seat.

"Maxwell."

"He brought you?" another asked, looking disgusting.

"Yeah, you got a problem with that?" Yolanda countered, defensively.

"No, but he probably does," the girl said viciously, taking a swig of her beer. They all cackled.

Loretta arrived with Yolanda's plate of food and a cold beer.

"So I see y'all getting along over here. What's so funny?"

"Nothing," the women said, still giggling.

"Did y'all introduce yourselves?"

"Not really," one of the women answered.

"Well, this here is Yorna, Maxwell's friend . . ."

"Yolanda," she corrected.

"Sorry. These are all my cousins and nieces."

Yolanda barely listened as Loretta rattled off names. She didn't really care either.

"Excuse me, Loretta? Where's the bathroom?" Yolanda asked, needing an excuse to get away from these truly awful women.

"Further down, in that house down there."

"Thanks," Yolanda said, taking her food and her beer. She looked for a quiet place to sit and found one by a tree. A huge knot had formed in her throat, but she ate her food anyway, trying to appear too busy eating to need or want conversation.

Where is Maxwell? Why isn't he looking for me? He should know that I would feel awkward in a situation like this. He's always leaving me alone . . .

"You want another beer?"

"No thanks," she said, looking up as Maxwell's father pulled up a chair and sat next to her.

"Nice day," he said, looking up at the sky.

"Yes, it is," Yolanda agreed.

"Why you sitting over here by yourself?"

She shrugged.

"I'll tell you why. It's because you don't fit in here, especially with my son. I mean, look at you! You weigh a hundred pounds soaking wet, Yannie."

"It's Yolanda," she said, close to tears.

"It don't really matter. I ain't gonna see you again. I don't know why my son brought you here. I can't figure out what he sees in you. Maybe you helping him get his mind off Theresa. But looking at you," he said, giving Yolanda a disapproving glance, "I wouldn't think so. But I'm gonna save you a lot of heartache right now. Leave my son alone. Y'all don't look right together; you just ain't his type. You ain't good enough. Man like that needs a real looker, a trophy, and frankly you don't cut the mustard. I was hoping he was bringing his old girlfriend, Theresa. Now she was fine."

Yolanda swiped at a tear.

"Now don't get your feelings hurt; I'm doing you a world of good. I know for a fact he's not interested in you, not like that, anyway. He couldn't be," he said, rolling a toothpick around in his mouth.

"You don't know what you're talking about," Yolanda said, her voice shaking.

"Oh, I don't, huh? Well, if he likes you so much, where is he? Why ain't he here with you?"

Yolanda put her head down.

"He ain't with you because he's 'shamed of you. Don't want nobody to know he with you. He's a smart man. If I was with you, which I wouldn't be, I wouldn't want to be seen with you, either."

He got up and walked away, leaving Yolanda reeling from his casually spoken cruel words.

"I wanna go home."

"What? Now? We've only been here a little over an hour."

"Please, Maxwell, I want to go home. I'm not feeling well," Yolanda said, clutching her stomach. It took her almost thirty minutes to find him. *I'm sick of this place, all these people, all these comments. I just want to crawl into my bed and cry.*

"Okay," Maxwell said, " but let me say good-bye to a few people first."

"No, Maxwell, now. I want to go home *right now.*"

He stood up, gave her a look, and grabbed his truck keys off the card table.

She practically ran to his truck, not caring if he was behind her. *I have to get away . . .*

"What's wrong with you?" he asked, catching up and grabbing Yolanda's arm.

"Nothing," she said, snatching her arm away and getting into the truck.

He got in and backed the truck out of the family reunion. Soon they were back on the freeway, heading back to Houston.

"I'm gonna ask you again, Yolanda, what's wrong?"

Yolanda said nothing. She stared blankly out the window, not trusting herself to speak.

"Did you eat something bad? What is it?"

"What am I doing here? What are you doing with me? Why do you keep asking me out? What do you want?"

"Whoa, slow down. I told you I want to get to know you better."

"Bull. What's the real reason?"

"I enjoy your company."

"How can you enjoy my company when you're never with me?"

"I am with you."

"No you're not. You're always somewhere else. You act like you're ashamed of me or something."

324

Maxwell was silent.

"Is that it? Are you ashamed to be seen with me?"

He kept driving.

"No," he said finally, "I'm not ashamed of you."

"Then what is it?"

"I haven't figured out what to do with you yet."

"What to do with me? Be a man and tell me the truth! You are ashamed of me!"

"No! Maybe . . . sometimes . . ."

"Well, I'll do both of us a favor. Stop calling me. Find somebody else to mess with."

She turned on the radio and moved as far away from him as possible, leaving no space between her and the truck door.

"Please, Yolanda, I still want to talk . . ."

"Shut up, Maxwell," Yolanda said, looking out the window. "Just shut up."

CHAPTER 56

Jackie stopped the tape recorder, satisfied. She'd done enough editing for today. She was beginning to be so good at this, she almost felt as if she could work for the FBI.

She had to follow Behave protocol, though, and that meant talking to Maxwell first. She wondered how he would react to learn that poor sweet Yolanda was the one who had betrayed Theresa. Jackie was surprised he had actually taken a liking to her. She wasn't supposed to last this long, but it looked as if he might have feelings for the girl.

Oh, well, you lost one girlfriend before, now you'll have to lose another one.

Her sole reason for not turning in the tapes earlier was that it would bring Theresa back to her old position. *And where would that leave me? In the cold, as usual. Can I really trust that Yolanda hasn't told anyone? No, it's too late for that, too late to trust anyone now.*

She didn't have much time left. She had to take Yolanda down; she didn't look like the type who would go along with her plan. As much as Yolanda hated Theresa, she wouldn't dare cross that line.

Well, that's the difference between you and me, Yolanda. You're weak, and I'm strong. You cower; I fight back. When things aren't going my way, I make them go my way. You're never gonna get ahead in life if you insist on going on like this, retreating and being totally submissive.

Jackie liked the fact that she was a surprise. No one ever suspected that her smile was deadly, a weapon in the guise of friendliness. Her bubbly persona made people feel comfortable around her and made them drop their guards and *bam!*— she was in. She couldn't believe how many people fell for it.

Except her mother.

Her mother could always see straight through her, and Jackie never even tried the fake act with her. Dad had called and said they had patched things up and that she should come over so they could have a family talk.

Family? Ha.

Now that her parents were okay, they instantly thought that she should be resilient and be okay, too. Well, she wasn't.

They had been so wrapped up in their own pain since Michael's death, no one had ever asked her how she felt about losing her brother. No one had ever asked her how she felt about anything.

If they had asked her, they would have learned that she had hated Michael with as much passion as they had loved him. Learn how for years she prayed he would die so she could live. But in death, he had become more perfect, more worshipped than he had been alive. If he had lived he would've made mistakes and become flawed and tarnished, just as she was in their eyes. Instead, he had been put on an even higher pedestal, and nothing Jackie did could erase the spotless record he'd left behind; nothing could erase the good memories they clung to.

She had come to understand the saying, *Be careful what you wish for.* Wishing Michael dead still gave him all the glory. She should have wished for her own death, then maybe she could have had all the adoration from her parents that he was still getting from beyond the grave.

CHAPTER 57

"Who is it?"

"It's me, Yolanda. Let me in."

Natalie unlocked the front door and looked at her friend—a crying mess on her doorstep.

"Oh, no. What happened?"

Yolanda flopped down on the couch and bawled, burrowing into the soft cushions.

Natalie sat beside her and rubbed her back. After several minutes, she heard her mumble something.

"What?"

"He's ashamed of me!" Yolanda cried, sitting up and wiping her eyes.

Natalie handed her a tissue and listened to her vent her frustrations.

"The whole thing was a disaster. He left me alone with all his rude family, who let me know every chance they got how I wasn't pretty enough for Maxwell. Then, to make matters worse, his own father told me I wasn't good enough for his son and to take a hike."

"His daddy?"

"Yep. Told me I wasn't pretty like Theresa and that I should stop seeing him."

"Aww, man, what did Maxwell do?"

"Get this, I ask him if he's ashamed of me and he says yes!" Yolanda said. "How could he say something like that? I feel so stupid for not seeing this sooner."

"How would you have guessed something like this? You've met his friends, you guys talk on the phone all the time, he takes you out . . . I mean, a guy doesn't take you to meet his family if he is ashamed of you. Guys just don't do that."

"Well, he did! Now that I think about it, of course he is ashamed of me. As soon as we got there he palmed me off on one of his aunts and disappeared. I didn't see him the whole time. He should've walked me around and introduced me to everybody, not left me there standing like an idiot," Yolanda said, blowing her nose hard.

Yolanda's cellphone went off and she grimaced when she saw the caller ID. She let it ring. "That's Maxwell. Probably trying to tell me how he's only ashamed of me in public and loves me as long as he can hide me from the rest of the world. What was I thinking, anyway? Things would never have worked out between us. We never kissed and went on maybe four or five dates? That clearly doesn't mean we're official. I mean, I'm better off knowing now, right? Right?"

"I don't know, Yolanda. I love you and I was worried that something like this was going to happen. Not like how you think, though; I never thought Maxwell was out of your league. I thought that you were way out of his league."

"What? Come on, Natalie, I really don't want to hear a bunch of mess right now—"

"No, seriously, Yolanda. Think. You are a beautiful woman."

"Natalie, stop—"

"No, Yolanda." Natalie took her hands and held them. "Look at me. You need to stop making excuses and apologizing to everybody for the way you look. You are thin. Like Tyra Banks says, So what? Who really cares about all that? You project to the world that you are unhappy with how you look, and people see it and dog you out. You don't think that I have moments when I look in the mirror and see this fat pig staring back? But I push those thoughts down, toss my weave, and tell myself I'm beautiful. Because I am beautiful. And so are you. And because I believe, so does everybody else. People are gonna think how they wanna think, Yolanda, you can't control that. All you can control is this," Natalie said, tapping Yolanda's forehead. "How you think has to change, Yolanda."

Yolanda cried heavy tears on Natalie's shoulder.

"It's okay," Natalie said, not caring that Yolanda's tears were staining her shirt. "Now stop all this crying and do what I do in situations like this."

"What's that?" Yolanda asked, wiping her face.

"Eat!"

CHAPTER 58

"Where do you think I should hang the banners?" Gina asked, holding a six-foot-long banner reading, "Happy Fortieth Anniversary!" in big, bold red letters.

"I don't care."

"I think it should go over the fireplace, but then it might clash with the balloons. Maybe I should put it by the stairs? What'cha think?"

"It's just a stupid banner, Gina! Hang it anywhere, it doesn't manner."

"What's wrong with you, Yolanda? You've been in a pissy mood all day! I just asked you a simple question. Mama and Daddy will be here any minute, so where should I hang this?"

Yolanda snatched the banner from Gina, tore off a piece of double-stick tape, and stuck the banner on her sister's forehead.

"There! You happy? You're always the first thing everybody has to see so . . . SURPRISE!" she yelled, storming out of the family room into the kitchen, ignoring the strange glances coming from their guests.

Gripping the edge of the oyster-grey granite countertop, she watched drops of water fall into the stainless-steel sink. *An $800,000 house with a leaky faucet? How ironic.*

Drip . . .
Maxwell is ashamed of me.
Drop . . .
His father hates me.
Drip . . .
Maxwell doesn't want to be seen with me.
Drop . . .
I'm a fool.

"Hey, Six!" her Uncle Jeff said loudly, barging into the kitchen, his bear-like frame swaggering from the brandy he had been sipping all evening.

"Why you treatin' yo sister like that? We all tryin' to get along here," he said. His dark skin shone like freshly polished mahogany; his voice boomed with humor-laced authority.

"I'm not in the mood for your stupid jokes, Jeff," Yolanda said, busying herself by getting a vegetable tray out of the refrigerator.

"Hey, Six, remember this?" he asked, placing his wide, thick-fingered hand against the wall, and making an up-and-down motion. He laughed long and hard when he saw Yolanda's face and realized she knew exactly what he was talking about.

It was an old joke that her father and her uncle dreamed up years ago. They would put their hands on a wall, or table, and rub on it, insinuating that Yolanda was just like whatever surface they were rubbing: flat. Normally, she would tolerate the jokes and would shrug them off. But today was different. After all the ridicule she had suffered yesterday at Maxwell's family reunion, she had no more tolerance for bad jokes at her expense. She was full.

"How's Vivian doing?" Yolanda asked, knowing that questions about his ex-wife set him on edge.

In a flash, his smile was gone.

"Um, I don't know. Haven't seen her in a while."

"I heard she is dating a younger man," Yolanda lied, loving the effect her words were having on him. "Mama showed me a picture of them from a trip they took together. To Hawaii," she added. His eyes glistened; he'd always wanted to go to Hawaii, but could never afford it.

"They make such a cute couple! He's so handsome! Did I forget to mention that he's white?"

Yolanda watched his hand tremble. His brandy glass fell and shattered, the pieces flying all over Gina's kitchen floor.

"Oh, no! Did you hurt yourself?" Yolanda asked, smiling, and walking over to check his hand. *I knew pulling out the race card would get you. You racist pig . . .*

"Vivian done got herself a white man?" he asked, his hands still shaking.

"Yep. Although he could hardly qualify as a man, considering he's more like twenty-two."

"Girl, why you tell me some stuff like that? You used to be my favorite niece, but now I don't know . . ." he said, his eyes glossy from unshed tears.

Yolanda knew that in bringing up Vivian she might have gone too far, but why did she have to be the one who took all the jokes? *What's wrong, Uncle Jeff? Can't take a little teasing?*

"If you can't take the heat, Uncle Jeff, then stay out of the kitchen," Yolanda said, watching a tear finally escape and roll down his cheek.

"Come on everybody! They're walking up the driveway!" Gina called from the family room.

Yolanda brushed past her pitiful uncle and went into the family room. Over fifty of her parents' family and friends were gathered in the dark, waiting.

Yolanda went to stand next to Gina, but she moved toward the front of the room, closer to the door.

Well, forget you, too, Gina.

Her mother's high-pitched laughter signaled everyone to stay quiet.

Her parents opened the door, Trevor flicked the lights on, and everyone yelled, "Surprise!"

Her mother clutched her chest, her mouth agape, while her father just looked around the room beaming.

"Oh, no! I don't believe this!" her mother said, her face lit by the flashing cameras all around her.

Don't mention blood pressure. Don't mention blood pressure. . . .

"Y'all got my blood pressure all up!" she said, laughing as she went around the room giving everyone hugs.

"Gina? Baby girl, I knew you were planning something! Come here and give yo daddy a hug!" her father said, walking over to Gina.

"Y'all give it up for my daughter Gina! She planned this party all by herself!"

They hugged and everyone clapped.

Furious, Yolanda pushed through to where Gina and her father were standing and started clapping insanely.

Soon she was the only one clapping.

"Well, isn't this just *peachy!*" she said, her voice heavy with sarcasm.

"A father and daughter embracing with so much love . . . When you look at them, you almost forget he has another daughter. Hello, Daddy! My name is Yolanda, in case you've forgotten!" she said, waving to him as though meeting him for the first time.

"Six, what is wrong with you?"

"My name is *not* Six O'Clock! It's *Yolanda!* Not Yoranda or Veranda, but *YOLANDA!*"

"Yolanda, stop all this!" her mother hissed. "You've had too much too drink . . ."

"I haven't had anything to drink. Not one *drop* of alcohol! I am totally sober. Sober enough to tell my father that I'm *sick* and *tired* of you giving Gina all the credit. I helped with this party, too, but noooo, all you see is Gina. Gina, Gina, Gina! You have *two* daughters! *Twoooo!*" She pushed Gina's cake to the floor.

"Noooo!" Gina cried instinctively, running to catch the cake before it hit the floor, but it was too late. She ended up slipping in cream cheese icing and falling in a heap atop the cake.

"Six hours! It took me six hours! Amaretto cream is mama's favorite, and now it is *ruined!*" Gina sat on the floor, her body wracked by deep, heavy sobs.

Without a word, Trevor took his wife's hand and led her upstairs to change her clothes. You could hear Gina's sobs throughout the house.

Yolanda looked around and saw a roomful of disapproving stares and shocked expressions.

Mortified, horrified, and emotionally spent, she lowered her head and walked out the front door.

CHAPTER 59

"Open up, Maxwell, I know you're in there!!" Andre yelled, banging on Maxwell's front door. "Open up!"

"Man, are you crazy!" Maxwell asked, yanking his door open. "This ain't the ghetto, man. You can't just knock on the door like you the police!"

Andre brushed him aside and walked into the apartment.

"Come on in," Maxwell said sarcastically as Andre walked over to the bar and fixed himself a stiff drink.

"Man, it's eleven in the morning! What's your problem?"

"My kids. They acted berserk this morning. I caught them packing some clothes up, trying to run away. Can you believe that? Like they in a battered home or something. Then they told me I need to stop making *their* mama cry. Told me they were going to find their mama a new husband. They said—and get this—I was *verbally abusing her*. Verbally abusing her? Since when these kids start picking up such mess? At school? Or is it the TV?"

He finished his drink and poured himself another.

"Man, you know how kids are—"

"No! They were serious. They were so angry . . ."

Maxwell watched as Andre walked over to his sofa and cried.

What is wrong with my friends? One is pissed, not taking my calls, and dating a fat black girl, and the other one is reaping what he sowed, sitting on my sofa crying like a baby.

Maxwell sat down on the sofa and gave Andre a minute to compose himself.

"You know, Tony was right. All this time, I have been holding out a piece of my heart to Rosslyn. Fourteen years and I can still remember her smile," Andre said, wiping tears from his eyes.

"But it wasn't real, man. It was a fantasy—"

"I used to resent marrying Brenda. Back then, I wasn't in love with her. But she was, she was loyal, man. I could count on her, you know? Looking back, Rosslyn always made me feel unsure of myself, like if I made a mistake she was outta there. And in the end she did leave me. That's why I chose Brenda. I knew she would never leave me, never make me feel like I wasn't good enough."

"Did you ever think that you made her feel like that? Made her feel—" He stopped and thought about Yolanda. He shook his head. "Made her feel inadequate?"

"I know this whole time y'all saw how I was treating Brenda and knew it was wrong. Deep down, even I knew it was wrong. But I thought," he sighed. "I don't know what I thought. But I didn't know I was making her cry. I never meant to make her cry," Andre said, in a small voice.

"Do you love her?" Maxwell asked.

"Yeah. I've always loved Brenda. I know she isn't the most attractive woman. But her heart? It's the most beautiful thing in the world. Yeah, I love her."

"Well, Chrisette Michele is gonna perform at Ray's tomorrow night. Maybe it's time you showed her a nice time. Get her mama to watch the kids, you know, a nice romantic evening. And don't worry about the kids, they're resilient. Just give them some time. Be there for Brenda and they will be okay."

"Yeah, I know. It's the worst feeling in the world seeing your life and knowing you could have done better."

Maxwell nodded. Looking at his friend like this made him think about Tony and what he had said. *I am a coward. I do love Yolanda. And I've blown it.*

"Hello?"

"Tony?"

"Maxwell, dude, stop calling me. I don't want to talk to you."

"Look, we gotta talk."

"About what? Do you know how many times I wanted to tell you about Sharon? How many times I wanted to call you and tell you I've found the love of my life? But I knew you would be immature about the situation . . ."

"Immature?"

"Did I stutter? All you care about is what other people think. It's like all you do is rate women all the time on how they look. That was cool in college, but we're grown men now. That's not what it's all about."

"I know man, I know. And I'm sorry. From the heart, brother, I didn't know it was that serious."

"Well, it is. I proposed to her last night. We're getting married this spring."

"Congratulations! Man, that's great—"

"Cut the crap, Maxwell. You don't have to pretend that you're excited. I already know how you really feel."

Tony sighed.

"It really doesn't matter anymore. What's done is done. I know what Sharon looks like. And maybe when she's ready, she'll lose the weight. Or she won't. Either way, she's beautiful."

"That's wonderful, man. And regardless of what you think, I am happy for you. So when do I meet the girl?" Maxwell asked.

"Soon. We're going out of town this weekend so I can meet her parents. Maybe when we get back from Chicago, you and Yolanda—"

"Gotta stop you right there, man. Things not going too well with us."

"What did you do?"

"Why it gotta be me all the time? Maybe she—"

"I'm gonna ask you one more time, what did you do?"

"It was at the family reunion. I don't know what went wrong, but I guess some of my family were dogging her because of her weight, and you know . . ."

"No, I don't know."

"She asked me if I was ashamed of her."

"And? What did you say?" Tony asked.

"I sorta told her I was," Maxwell answered.

"Sorta told her, or plain out said it?"

"Man, it doesn't matter. All I know is she's not taking any of my calls, and at work she's all cold."

"Can you blame her?"

"No. So what do I do?"

"Get on your knees and beg," Tony said.

"I ain't doing all that."

"Is she worth it?"

Maxwell thought about all their long conversations, the way she laughed, the way she looked when the sun touched her soft skin. He loved the way she made him feel, as if he could do anything. It was funny, he only thought about the way she looked when his friends were around. But he thought Yolanda was beautiful, inside and out. He couldn't believe how blind he'd been, how had devalued her good qualities because she didn't have a J. Lo butt or big breasts. She was a good woman. The kind of woman you want to bring home to mama. The kind of woman *his* mama would have been proud to call her daughter. Maxwell was ashamed, not of Yolanda, but of his shabby treatment of her. *Why was I such a coward with her? Why didn't I walk that girl into my family reunion, announce she was my girlfriend, and not care what anybody thought?* He didn't want to be like Andre, messing over a good thing, or his father. He wanted to be what his mother raised him to be: a good man.

He sighed. "I miss that girl, Tony. Miss her a lot. Yeah, she's worth it."

"Well, little doggy, time to get on them knees and get to begging."

CHAPTER 60

"I made a fool of myself last night," Yolanda screeched into the phone.

"What did you do?"

"What didn't I do? I went to my parents' anniversary party and lost my mind. I just exploded," Yolanda said, sighing deeply.

"What did your dad do this time?" Natalie asked.

"The sad part is, he didn't do anything out of the ordinary. Just the same old thing—constantly praising Gina."

"While ignoring you?"

"Exactly. For some reason, this time I couldn't take it. No, I refused to take it. I made a huge scene and . . ." Yolanda stopped, too embarrassed to tell Natalie what else she had done.

"And what? What else did you do?"

"I threw my parents' anniversary cake on the floor."

"Are you crazy?"

"Yes. I confess. I need to be locked up in some mental ward."

"Did Gina make it?"

"Yeah . . ."

"Oh, no! You know how sensitive that girl is! Especially when it comes to her special desserts."

"I know. She spent about six hours making this four-tiered creation, and I pushed it onto the floor. I've tried to call them to apologize, but no one is picking up the phone. It's as if they've banned me from the family."

"Can you blame them? You ruined their anniversary party!"

"I know, I know. I probably could've handled it differently if I hadn't had such a crappy weekend."

"You can't let what happened at the reunion ruin everything. As much as you don't get along with Gina, pushing that cake was a big no-no. You can't take all your frustrations out on them. Who you need to be taking it out on is Maxwell. Has he called again?"

"I don't want to talk about it."

"Yeah, you can. I'll pick you up, and we'll go get lunch and you can tell me more about it."

"Fine."

"Be there in an hour."

"What made you pick this place?" Yolanda asked, pulling out a chair at Romano's Macaroni Grill.

"I don't know. I guess I wanted to switch things up a bit," Natalie said, sitting down.

"You hate Italian food."

"Not all the time," Natalie said, picking up her menu. "Okay, tell me, has Maxwell been calling you?"

"Yeah, he's been calling like crazy. We talked briefly."

"And? Come on, what else?"

"Nothing happened. He said he was sorry and that he wanted to see me to explain a few things."

Yolanda thought back to the desperation in his voice.

"Please, Yolanda, we really need to talk."

"We don't have anything to talk about. I think you said all you wanted to say."

He sighed. "Look, can I come over?"

"In daylight? Whoa, that's a bold move for you considering how ashamed you are of being with me. You don't want to risk somebody seeing you leave ol' skinny girl's apartment, do you? Yeah, I think the phone fits your personality better. No one can see us talking, no one will even know I exist, which is what you prefer, right?"

"No, that's not right at all. You're taking this whole thing too far. I really like you—"

"Oh, now you like me all of a sudden? Hmm, let's see— you reject kissing me twice. You see your ex-girlfriend at a restaurant and leave me to get home by a taxi. Then you leave me all by myself at your family reunion to be seriously dissed by your family. Yeah, you sure do like me, Maxwell. Promise me you won't fall in love with me; you may just kill me."

"Is that why you wanted to leave? Somebody said something to you?"

"It doesn't matter. None of it matters. The point is that you've made it quite clear that you don't want me. So I'm doing us both a favor . . ."

"And then what?" Natalie asked, taking a bite out of her fried calamari.

"I hung up the phone in his face."

"Really?"

"Yep."

"Felt good, didn't it?"

"It felt great."

"Uh-oh, speak of the devil," Natalie said, looking beyond Yolanda.

Yolanda turned and saw Maxwell and Theresa entering the restaurant.

"Great. I really can't handle this," she said, picking up her purse to leave.

"No! You're not going anywhere. You're in control, remember?" Natalie reminded her.

"Right, right. Maybe he won't even come over here."

"Fat chance. They're walking this way."

"What do I say?"

"Just relax," Natalie said, as Maxwell and Theresa approached their table.

"Hi, Maxwell, Theresa. Small world," Natalie said, rubbing her belly.

Yolanda kept her head down, pretending that something on the menu was keeping her attention glued to it.

"It sure is," Maxwell said, looking at Yolanda.

"How are you doing?" Maxwell asked softly, his brown eyes boring into her.

"Just fine," Yolanda answered, looking up and giving him a warm smile.

"So, Theresa, you found a job yet?" Natalie asked.

"No, not yet. But it won't be long," she answered coldly.

346

"We're out to lunch just talking," he said, still looking at Yolanda. "We're just friends; I'm just giving her moral support. That's it."

"You don't have to explain anything to me, Maxwell. I'm not your woman. You've made that perfectly clear," Yolanda said, taking a sip of her iced tea.

Theresa yawned loudly.

"I'm ready to eat, Maxwell," she said, putting her arm through his possessively.

He shook her off, his eyes still on Yolanda.

"You've been doing okay?" he asked again.

"You already asked her that. She's fine, Maxwell. I'm the one who lost her job, remember?" Theresa said, irritably.

"How can we forget, Theresa? The whole salon knows how you lost you're job," Yolanda said.

"Excuse me?"

"Who else has been giving you moral support?" Natalie asked Theresa, trying to ease the tension.

"Nobody else, really. Although Jackie calls me just about every day."

"Really?" Yolanda interjected. "Jackie calls you?"

"Yes," Theresa said, rolling her eyes.

"What do y'all talk about?" Natalie asked.

"She keeps my spirits up. She's trying to talk to her mother, see about getting my job back. Jackie's the only one who believes me. She knows I never wrote those letters. She thinks she is on to something. She told me she had some evidence about who really did it."

"Really?" Yolanda asked.

"Yes, *really*. She knows I'm innocent. Anyway, I'm hungry," Theresa said, tugging at Maxwell's sleeve. "Let's go to our table."

"In a minute. I need to speak to Yolanda."

Theresa gave Yolanda a hard look, then turned sharply on her heels and walked toward their table.

"Don't keep me waiting long," she called out.

"We really need to finish our conversation."

"We are finished."

"You hung up the phone; I never got a chance to explain to you my side—"

"I know your side, Maxwell. You're ashamed, remember?"

He sighed.

"Listen, can we talk?"

"We are talking."

"I mean privately."

"Why? I'm just gonna tell Natalie everything you said, anyway, so let's just cut out the middle man. What do you want?"

"I want to apologize."

Yolanda sat back in her chair and looked at Maxwell.

"Go ahead."

"I'm sorry," he said, his voice low and sincere.

"You are sorry, Maxwell. I already know that. Anything else?"

He opened his mouth as if to speak and then closed it, shocked by Yolanda's blunt and unyielding response.

He nodded and walked away like a defeated puppy dog with his tail between his legs.

Yolanda looked at Natalie and they burst out laughing.

"You learn fast! That was good!"

"It felt good, too," Yolanda said. And it did. It felt good to be in control.

Their lunch arrived and they were still laughing.

"Man, I haven't laughed this hard in months," Natalie said. "I feel kinda bad for Theresa, though. That's nice of Jackie, trying to get her job back."

"Yeah that's real *nice* of her," Yolanda said nastily, disgusted by Jackie's behavior.

"What, you don't like her? I thought y'all were starting to be friends."

"What if I told you Jackie wasn't all she seemed to be? That she was one way one minute, another the next?"

"I wouldn't be surprised. Remember that day at the salon cafe when she told me off?"

"Yeah, I remember. Sorry about that," Yolanda said sheepishly.

"All in the past," Natalie said, waving her hand.

"I think that Jackie is the one who wrote those letters."

"What? Are you sure? How do you know?"

"She told me."

"She just flat out told you? That was stupid."

"Well, it was more like she hinted. But still, I know she did it."

"Why would she do something like that?"

"Simple. She wants Theresa's job."

"That greedy dog! She already has a good job. If she just waited, her mom probably would have given her the whole salon," Natalie said, chewing on a piece of lasagna.

"Homeboy keeps looking at you, by the way," she added.

Yolanda turned around and saw Maxwell watching her. He winked at her, and Theresa turned to see what had him so distracted. Her eyes became cold, hard slits when she saw it was Yolanda.

Yolanda smiled, and turned back to Natalie.

"So what are you gonna do?"

"He can look all he wants, I don't care. It doesn't mean anything . . ."

"Girl, I wasn't even talking about him! You really like him, don't you?"

"I haven't felt this way about anybody since Russell . . ."

"It's that serious? Well, don't worry, the way he keeps looking at you, you ain't the only one."

"You think so?" Yolanda asked, allowing a bit of excitement to creep into her voice.

"I know so. He likes you, Yolanda. Dog him out a little longer, and he'll be in the palm of your hand. But *anyway,* back to what I was saying earlier, what are you gonna do about Theresa?"

"What do you mean, 'what am I gonna do?' Nothing!" Yolanda said.

"You can't just sit around and do nothing! It's your moral responsibility to tell someone."

"I'm not helping that woman; I can't stand her. When we worked together, she did everything in her power to make my life miserable. I'm not saying anything. Dee

Dee's not gonna believe me over her own daughter. Forget it."

"Look, I know you don't like Theresa . . ."

"You got that right."

"But that still has nothing to do with her losing her job, and it doesn't justify your withholding information that could clear her name. That isn't right. You have to tell."

"Jackie is gonna kick my butt! She'll deny the whole thing."

"So? You're in control, remember? It's better than her lying and saying you did it."

"You think she would do something like that?"

"Oh, wake up, Yolanda. Stop being so naive. She probably realized she made a mistake by telling you and is figuring out a way to get rid of you even as we speak. Why do you think she's telling Theresa she's gonna find the person who wrote those letters? You better tell someone, Yolanda, and quick. It's your job or hers."

Yolanda nodded reluctantly, but she had to admit that Natalie was probably right about Jackie. She remembered how Jackie had talked to those women in that club. The girl was psycho.

"But I still need to get proof. Nobody is gonna believe me without proof."

"Behave is a big salon, Yolanda. I'm sure somebody saw something. Just ask around. You'll get the answers you're looking for."

"Okay," Yolanda said, sighing heavily to show her reluctance, "I'll start looking into it."

"Good. I'm thirsty," Natalie said, draining the last of her Coke. "Where's the waiter?"

CHAPTER 61

"You are about to call her, right?"

"Yeah."

"You're doing the right thing, you know."

"I know," Yolanda said, sighing. "It's just that, I know if the situation was reversed, she wouldn't do the same for me."

"It's not about her," Natalie said. "You wouldn't be able to live with yourself if you let Jackie get away with it. I know you don't like Theresa, but she doesn't deserve to lose her job. You neither, remember?"

"I know, I know. I'm calling her right now."

"Good. Call me later and tell me everything."

"Okay," Yolanda said, hanging up.

She'd never had a real conversation with Theresa. She never thought she had to.

She looked at the number she had scribbled down from her Rolodex this morning. Theresa McArthur. 281-555-2817. She picked up the phone and dialed it.

"Hello?"

"Hi, is this Theresa?"

"Yes, who's this?"

"It's Yolanda."

"Who?"

"Yolanda Peterson? We work together. Well, at least we used to, anyway."

"Oh."

Silence.

"What do you want?" Theresa asked.

"I just wanted to know how you've been holding up."

"No, you didn't. You didn't call to ask how I'm doing. We don't like each other and never will. So again I ask, why did you call me?"

Yolanda hesitated. *Why am I trying to help this woman? I should hang up and let her butt stand in an unemployment line . . .*

"Look, I think somebody was setting you up."

"Duh. I've been saying that for weeks."

"I know who it is."

"I'm listening," Theresa said.

"It's Jackie," Yolanda blurted.

"What? No way, sistuh, try again. I know it's not her."

"How?"

"Because she's the only one who's been calling *genuinely* concerned about my welfare. Besides, it wouldn't make any sense. Jackie is Dee Dee's daughter. All she has to do is just wait, and she'll probably get the whole salon."

"Maybe so, but I still know it's her."

"Okay, Sherlock, how do you know?"

"For one, you need to drop the attitude," Yolanda said. "You're the one who doesn't have a job . . ."

"Sweetie, if you were fired, you'd have an attitude, too, okay? You come skating in here, becoming assistant manager, trying to steal my man—"

"Maxwell? Is that what this is all about? I'm tryin' to help you get your job back, and you trippin' about Maxwell? Baby, if you can get him, take him."

353

"*If I can get him*? Please, I already got him. This body gets me any man I want, which is more than I can say for yours."

"If that was true, why is he all up in my face all the time trying to go out with me?"

Silence.

After a long moment, Theresa said, "Either tell me what you know or hang up. Your choice."

Yolanda chewed on her lip, irritated by Theresa's tone. *Do the right thing*, she chanted in her head, letting Natalie's words calm her down.

"Believe whatever you want to believe, Theresa. You can sit on your couch and be bitter and blame everybody else or you can do something about it and get your job back. Your choice," Yolanda said, throwing Theresa's words back at her.

"You have my attention. Go on. I'll lose the attitude."

"I know it's Jackie because she told me over lunch a couple of weeks ago."

"A couple of weeks ago? Why didn't you say anything?"

"Because I don't like you."

"So what changed? You still don't like me; why all of a sudden this change of heart?"

"It wasn't right. And just because I don't like you, doesn't mean that you deserve to be fired, especially if it wasn't your fault."

"So now what? All this is just hearsay. We can't tell Dee Dee without proof."

"I know, that's why I called you. Maxwell mentioned that you got fired because of some letters and e-mails?"

"Yeah. She must have gone in my office and forged my signature."

"Forged, huh?" Yolanda said, thinking. "Maybe I could get your signature and her signature and show that she forged it."

"No, that won't work. I had a stamp made with my signature on it. Anyone could have gotten a hold of it. This is Dee Dee's daughter, remember? This isn't just some random employee. We need rock-solid evidence, like an eyewitness or an alibi or something."

"Right. First thing tomorrow I'll ask around. Maybe somebody saw something. Meanwhile, give me a copy of those e-mails and letters. You do have 'em, right?"

"You bet your butt I do."

"Fax them to me tomorrow. Maybe I can figure something out."

"Sure."

"I'll call you tomorrow and let you know what I came up with."

"Hey, Yolanda?"

"Yeah?"

"Thank you," Theresa said.

"You're welcome."

CHAPTER 62

Jackie has done this kind of thing before. Yolanda was in her office studying the e-mails and letters Theresa had faxed her that morning. She was looking for a clue, *anything,* that would point to Jackie. The strongest evidence that could potentially nail her conniving friend was right there in front of her, but so far it had yielded nothing. She also had spent much of the morning asking people if they had seen anything suspicious, anybody going into someone's office after hours. No one had seen anything.

Yolanda's sleuthing was at a standstill. And she was beginning to regret having clued Theresa in on her suspicions. She had already called twice asking if there had been any progress. She was understandably worked up about clearing her name and getting her job back. But unless something breaks soon, Yolanda was thinking, Theresa might have to get on that unemployment line after all.

"Excuse, can I come in? I leaving early and need all trash."

"Sure, Maria, come in," Yolanda said, pulling her wastebasket from under her desk and handing it to her. "Maria, have you seen anything weird going on? Like somebody coming out of someone's office? Maybe late at night?"

"No, no, Miss Yolanda, I haven't seen that," Maria said, removing the plastic trashcan liner and replacing it with another. She handed the wastebasket back to Yolanda.

"Thanks, anyway," Yolanda said.

"Unless you talk about when I see Miss Jackie come out of Miss Theresa office."

Yolanda wasn't sure she had heard right. "Say again?"

"Miss Jackie, she such sweet lady. I see her coming out Miss Theresa office. I think nothing of it," Maria said.

"When?"

"Oh, maybe month? Two month ago? I can't remember. That sort of thing happen when you get my age."

"Your certain it was Theresa?"

"Oh, yes. Yes, I sure. She spoke to me; such a sweet lady. Yes, that was her. Anything else?"

"No, Maria. You've been all the help in the world."

After Maria left, Yolanda took another look at the letters and e-mails. *Wait a minute . . .*

August twenty-fifth. 9:00 P.M. The date. The time and date.

How could I have missed that?

She picked up the phone and dialed Theresa's number.

"I just got an eyewitness and your alibi," Yolanda said, smiling.

Maxwell took the long way to work and dialed Yolanda's cellphone.

He knew she wouldn't answer; she hadn't picked up all week, but he still left a message.

"Hey, Yolanda. This is Maxwell again. Listen, I know I messed up, but I really want to make things up to you. I drove by your apartment last night and knocked on your door, but I guess you weren't home. I know things are awkward at work, especially 'cause you're not talking to me, but again, I just want to let you know how sorry I am, and I promise if you give me another chance, I'll make it up to you."

He hung up the phone, hoping that she was at least listening to the messages and wasn't erasing them. At work she gave no indication as to whether she'd heard them or not, but he kept hoping that she was listening.

His cellphone rang, and he almost hit another car in his rush to answer it, hoping it was Yolanda calling him back.

He put it on speakerphone.

"Hello?"

"Hey, son. You know you got a lot of people mad at you. What were you thinkin' leaving the family reunion so early? And without saying good-bye?"

His disappointment was sharp and immediate when he realized it wasn't Yolanda.

"Sorry, Pop. I had to take Yolanda home. She wasn't feeling well."

"Good. I'm glad you got rid of her," his father remarked.

"Wait a minute. Who said anything about getting rid of her?"

"Well, I figured after our talk—"

"What talk?"

"When I told your little friend to go home, that you couldn't possibly be interested in her."

"You did what?" Maxwell yelled, furious.

"Yeah. I helped you out, son. Told her the truth."

"And what truth is that?"

"That you 'shamed of her, can't stand to be around her."

"You told her that?"

"Yep."

"Why?"

"Was I lying, son? You know you can do better than that."

"So that's why Yolanda was so angry at me! You told her I was ashamed of her. You're wrong, Pop. You had no business . . ."

"Wrong? Man, I was doing you a favor. Don't lie and tell me you actually like that girl?"

Yeah, I do. I do like that girl.

"Yeah, Pop, I do. I more than like her. I'm in love with her. And it wasn't any of your business . . ."

"Watch your tone boy. I'm still your father."

"Since when? You haven't acted like a real father since Mama died. Now you're a bitter old man who is scared to be alone."

"Oh, so now you're my shrink? You think you know me?"

"Yeah, I know you. Do you honestly think those young girls you messing around with care about you? They just want your money, Pop, that's it. Let something happen to you and the money run out. They won't stick around long."

"You just jealous 'cause I got all the pretty women and all you got is some broomstick . . ."

"Maybe so, Pop. You probably do get all the women. But that's not me, and never will be. I'm not like you, this new you, anyway. I'm into something genuine, somebody real. Somebody like Mama. All this game playin', lyin', and cheatin'? I'll leave that to you, Pop. 'Cause that mess you doing? It's old. Played out. Just like you."

Maxwell hung up.

CHAPTER 63

Everything looks different.

Smaller.

Yolanda looks down at her hands and realizes she's different. She's all grown up.

She's an adult.

She sees the other Yolandas across the playground.

They're still little girls.

As they approach, they're laughing at her.

"MONSTER FACE! MONSTER FACE! MONSTER FACE!" they chant.

Yolanda reaches up and touches her face.

She feels the angry cuts she had inflicted on herself.

Angry, she charges the group of Yolandas, and single-handedly strikes them all down dead.

The playground is filled with dead little Yolandas.

She walks toward the swings, stepping over dead bodies along the way.

She gets on the swing, and pushes herself hard and fast, pumping her long legs furiously to go higher.

The wind blows through her hair, and she looks up at the sky.

The sun is shining.

Yolanda turned over in her sleep, a smile on her face.

CHAPTER 64

"Guess who just aced her last exam?"

"Natalie . . ."

"Yep, and I'll be starting my new job next week!"

"Congratulations! I'm so happy for you. I know you're excited."

"I'm busting, girl, I'm busting! Who knew that in this short time I'd be on the road to opening up my own restaurant? I'm gonna stay with the restaurant for a couple of years, get some experience, then I'm gonna strike out on my own. Dad said he would help get me started."

"That's great! Wow, my girl with her own restaurant! I'm so proud of you!"

"Thanks, girl. So what's up? I know you have news, too."

"Let's just say Theresa will have her job back soon."

"Really? You got proof?"

"Yep. An eyewitness and an alibi."

"Really? Who?"

"Maria."

"The cleaning lady?"

"Yeah. She saw Jackie coming out of Theresa's office."

"Good. What else?"

"Well, when I looked back at that e-mail Jackie sent, it said August twenty-fifth, 9:00 P.M."

"And?" Natalie asked impatiently.

"That was the night Maxwell took me out and she showed up. She couldn't have sent that e-mail because she was too busy making my life miserable at that restaurant."

"You're like a little detective."

"I know. Maybe I should open up my own detective agency."

"Yeah, call it Yolanda's House of Pain. If you do the crime, she'll make you do the time."

"You're sick, but you knew that, right?"

"So I've been told," Natalie said, laughing.

"So what do you have to do now?"

"I have to talk to Maxwell tomorrow, and then with Dee Dee."

"You ready?" Natalie asked.

"I better be."

"Hi, Maxwell. Can we talk?" Yolanda asked, standing outside his door.

"Sure."

I knew she would come back to her senses.

"First off, this isn't a social call. This is about work. Period."

"Oh," he said, his pride deflated. "Well, have a seat then," he said, motioning to a chair in front of his desk.

Yolanda sat down.

"I think someone set Theresa up."

"What do you mean?"

"I mean, that I think Theresa is telling the truth. She never wrote those letters."

"Then who did?"

"Jackie."

"Jackie? No way."

"She told me about two weeks ago . . ."

"Wait a minute, slow down. You're telling me Jackie wrote those letters? That doesn't make any sense."

"Think about it, Maxwell," Yolanda said, leaning forward. "If your mom owned this salon and didn't promote you, you'd be pissed, right?"

"I guess," he said slowly, letting the information sink in.

"She has wanted Theresa's job all along."

"But Jackie? She's the sweetest person I know . . ."

"That's all an act. She's a wolf in sheep's clothing."

"These are some pretty strong accusations, Yolanda. Do you have any proof?"

"Yes. One, she told me. Two, Maria saw Jackie coming out of Theresa's office, and three, the night that last e-mail was sent, Theresa was with us."

"With us?"

"At Gator's. She interrupted us, remember?"

"I remember," Maxwell said, sitting back in his chair.

"You said she told you all this about two weeks ago?" he asked.

"That's right."

"Why did you wait so long to tell someone?"

She shrugged her.

"Is it because you don't like Theresa?"

"Maybe . . ."

"What if I told you that there's nothing going on between me and Theresa . . ."

"Maxwell, could you stop thinking about yourself all the time? I don't like Theresa because she's a stuck-up witch who'll find any reason to put me down. It has nothing to do with your relationship with her, past or otherwise. I could care less," she lied.

Maxwell looked at Yolanda for a long moment.

"Did you get any of my messages?" he asked softly, knowing it wasn't the right thing to ask, but also knowing he had to ask.

She looked down.

"Yes," she said.

"Well?"

"I don't know anymore. I've had a crush on you for years—"

"Really?"

"Yeah. And it's like when I got to know you, I was . . ." She paused, trying to find the right word.

"Was what?"

"Disappointed," she said.

He sat back in his chair.

"Fine," Maxwell said abruptly. "I'll report your findings to Dee Dee first thing tomorrow morning."

"Tomorrow? Can't you do it today?"

"I have to write the report today, but she won't see it until tomorrow. Don't worry, it'll get my first priority. Anything else?"

"Do you believe me?" Yolanda asked.

"It doesn't really matter, but yes, I believe you."

"Why?"

"You've never lied to me before," he said, looking deeply into her eyes.

She looked away.

"By the way, what time do you want me to set the meeting for?" Maxwell asked.

"What meeting?"

"When an employee accuses an employee of doing something, Dee Dee summons everyone to her office to straighten things out. It makes it easier to get the truth. Me and you will go in first, tell your side, and then she'll bring Jackie in. You're not afraid, are you?"

"Of course not," Yolanda said stoutly.

She stood, and was leaving his office when he called her name.

"Yolanda?"

"Yes?" she asked, turning around.

"When I first met you, I wasn't disappointed by you. I was pleasantly surprised that I had finally found a woman that I could see being with for years to come and never being bored, never running out of things to say, never running out of laughter. That's what I found out when I got to know you. I know you're disappointed now, I'm even a disappointment to myself, but I promise you, if you give me another chance, I'll never disappoint you again."

Yolanda stood there speechless, not trusting her voice to speak.

366

This is all I've wanted, a man to say that he wants me. But I need more than that now. And I don't know if you can give that to me. . . .

The sound of her pager going off broke the silence.

She looked at the number, and didn't recognize it.

"Can I use your phone?"

"Sure," he said, irritated that she was still blowing him off.

"Hello? Did someone call me?"

"Yolanda? It's me, Gina."

"Oh."

She hadn't talked to her sister since the fit she had thrown at the anniversary party.

"Dad is in the hospital."

"What?"

"He had a heart attack."

"Oh, my God! What hospital?"

"He's at Herman Hospital in the Medical Center Downtown. He's in ICU. You have to come and get me, because the BMW is getting serviced and Trevor has the Range Rover. . . ." She broke down crying.

"I'll be right there," Yolanda said, hanging up the phone, her hand shaking.

"What's wrong?" Maxwell asked, walking over to Yolanda and putting his arms around her.

"My father is in the hospital! It's all my fault . . . what I said at the party . . . I put pressure on him."

She held onto him, and cried in his arms, afraid she would never be able to tell her father she loved him.

She broke from his embrace and wiped her tears.

"I have to go."

"Let me take you; you're in no condition to drive."

"I have to pick my sister up—"

"That's okay, just give me directions—"

"No!" she said forcefully. "When are you gonna get it, Maxwell? I don't want you anymore. I'm tired of you wanting me just so your ego gets puffed up because another stupid woman at work wants to date you."

"You're not stupid, Yolanda! You're one of the smartest, most intelligent women I know—"

"And it's time I start acting like it," Yolanda said. "Goodbye, Maxwell."

"But I—"

"But what? But you're ashamed of me? You wish I looked different? That's never gonna happen, Maxwell, and I'm tired of people trying to turn me into somebody I'll never be. So I'm gonna find a man who loves me, just for who I am," she said, walking out of his office.

"But I love you," he said to an empty room.

CHAPTER 65

Yolanda and Gina rode to the hospital in silence, both feeling numb at the possibility they might lose their father.

Yolanda cleared her throat.

"Look, Gina, about the anniversary party—"

"Forget it. Don't worry about it," Gina said flatly, concentrating on the radio, and mindlessly flipping from station to station.

"Look, I really need to apologize . . ."

"What's wrong with us, Yolanda? Why aren't we closer?" Gina asked.

"I—I don't know," Yolanda stammered, thrown off guard by the question.

"I've been thinking about that a lot lately, but especially when I heard Daddy was sick. I think I know why now."

"Why?"

"I'm jealous of you."

"What?"

"Well, not exactly. Of the relationship you and Mama have. I've always been envious of that. Always wished me and Mama could talk like you guys talk. Hard as I try, we just don't have that connection. I guess it's just not meant to be."

"This is crazy. For years I've been jealous of you because of *your* relationship with Pop. Y'all are so close . . ."

"Y'all are close, too! He's always teasing you and making you laugh."

"I hate it when he does that!" Yolanda said.

"I wish Daddy would talk to me like that—What are you doing?" Gina asked, looking at Yolanda like she was crazy.

"Looking outside to see if any pigs are flying. They have to be, the day Gina says she's jealous of me."

"You have a lot going for you, Yolanda. You're not stuck at home all day with spoiled, whiny kids. You have the freedom to come and go as you please. You're blessed."

Yolanda turned and looked at her sister, saddened that she had wasted so many years. *I should know you so much better . . .*

"Maybe after we leave the hospital, you could come over for a little while? We could rent some movies, order pizza, you know, have a girl's night?"

"I'd like that," Gina said, swiping at a falling tear.

"Crybaby."

"Shut up."

"Hey, Mama," Yolanda said, giving her mother a big hug. "I'm so sorry."

"Girl, don't worry 'bout that. We all human," her mother said, hugging her back.

"Gina, get over here and give Mama a hug."

Gina walked over, and embraced her mother.

"How is he?" Yolanda asked, looking at her father across the room. His skin was dry and had a grey tinge to it, as if he had been rolling around in ashes. He was surrounded by tubes and machines. Yolanda turned away. It was difficult to look at him.

"He's in stable condition. The doctor's say he's gonna pull through. This attack really damaged his heart. Just think if I wasn't home to call 911 . . ." Her mother closed her eyes, trying to chase away the thought that she had almost lost her husband.

"He's gonna be weak as a kitten, but at least he's alive. He's been asking for you."

"For me?" Gina asked.

"You, too, baby, but he really asked to speak to Yolanda. Alone. Come on, baby, come walk with me to the cafeteria to get some coffee. I could use the exercise."

"Sure," Gina said, following her mother out of the hospital room.

Yolanda walked slowly to her father's bed.

"Hey, Daddy."

His eyes flickered, then opened. He looked up at her and smiled.

"Hey, Six," he said slowly, breathing hard.

"Daddy, I'm so sorry! I don't know what got into me . . ."

"Hush, girl . . . Got things to tell you. Not much energy," he said, pointing to the chair beside his bed and gesturing for Yolanda to sit down.

"Ever since you were nine years old I knew you were smarter than me. Your vocabulary—whew—it blew me away. The way your little mind would work, it was something to see. I have to admit, I didn't like it. I was never smart. Things you take for granted, things that come to you so easy, for me, it was tough. So I teased you."

He paused, a single tear falling down his ashen cheek.

"I knew it was wrong. Every time I saw your face fall, I wanted to go in and give you a hug, but I couldn't. Your drive, your determination; those are things I wanted. And I didn't like it," he said, his voice barely above a whisper.

"It was easier to talk to Gina. She is on the same level as me. But you, you're going places. It's not easy for me to say this, but after your behavior at the party—"

"Daddy, I'm sorry about that—"

"Hush, and let me finish. After that party, I saw how I let the teasing get out of hand. It's hard to see a child to become smarter than you, even if that is what you dreamed for them. You excel at everything you do, and it is difficult for your old man to watch that and not feel a twinge of jealousy. It's not right and it never was, but I'm sorry. I had to tell you how sorry I am. I didn't want to leave this earth with you thinking that I don't love you."

"I never knew you cared," Yolanda said quietly.

"I care. I always have. You are special, Yolanda. Always was something to look at." He gestured at the side table. "Look at my pocket watch over there and open it."

Yolanda found the gold pocket watch laying inside the drawer. She pulled it out and opened it. Inside was a picture of both his daughters from when they were two years old. Gina was on the left smiling widely into the camera, her features striking even then. Yolanda was on the right. She was smiling, too, but she didn't have the same sparkle that Gina had.

"I've never seen this picture before. Why haven't you showed this to me before?"

He shrugged. "See how Gina on the right looking—"

"Wait a minute. Gina's on the right? Then who is on the left?"

He smiled. "Who do you think?"

Yolanda burst into tears. "This is me?"

He nodded.

Yolanda studied the picture again through her tears. "I was so beautiful."

"Correction. You *are* beautiful. I love *both* my daughters. I do. I'm just sorry I didn't tell you more often."

Yolanda looked at the picture closer. *I am beautiful. All these years . . . I've been beautiful all along.*

"I love you, too, Daddy. Thank you."

"Now. Come closer. This important."

Yolanda leaned over trying to hear what he had to say.

"Go. Get. Doughnut."

"Daddy! No!" she said laughing, giving him a cheek.

"Had to try."

CHAPTER 66

Maxwell sat at his desk, trying to concentrate on his work, but was distracted, his mind taking him back to Yolanda's father.

He took his glasses off and decided to take a break and do his daily walk around the salon. Maybe get a coffee to clear his head. He opened his office door and saw his father standing there, hand raised, preparing to knock.

"Pop? What are you doing here?"

"Can I come in?"

"Yeah, sure." Maxwell sat back at his desk, and his father took a seat in front of him.

"So this is your office . . ." Ray said, his eyes looking around the room, taking everything in. "It's nice."

"Funny how this is the first time you've been in it."

"Yeah, well, that's one of the reasons I'm here. This isn't easy for me to do, but I'm here to apologize."

Maxwell leaned forward. "You, apologizing? Pop is actually saying he's sorry?"

"Well, that's what I'm trying to do if you'll let me."

Maxwell nodded and let his father continue.

"I know I was wrong for what I did. But I was only trying to protect you . . . I honestly felt y'all weren't a good match."

"It wasn't any of your business, Pop. That's always been your problem, always trying to interfere in my life—"

"You are my life," his father said softly. "Before Clarice died, she made me promise to look after you. That's all I was doing, son, trying to make sure you were happy."

"I am happy. With Yolanda, not Theresa."

His father sighed.

"If you so happy with her, why did you dump her at the reunion? When I found her, she was sitting under a tree all by herself. Looked like she'd already been crying. It didn't look like you were happy with her. I really thought I was doing you a favor."

"Look, I'll be the first to admit that I'm wrong, too. I've treated Yolanda badly, all because I cared too much about what everybody thought. I know she's kinda thin—"

"Kinda thin? That girl is—"

Maxwell gave his father a look.

"Sorry, sorry. Continue."

"Look, Yolanda is thin; bony, in fact. But so what? I love her."

"Love her?"

"That's right. I love that girl."

His father looked stunned. "I didn't even know you were on that level with her."

"I tried to fight my feelings for her, because I didn't want to fall in love with her. But it happened anyway."

"I know I was picking on you to find a woman, but why this girl? What happened to working out things with Theresa? She's on your level—"

"And what level would that be, Pop?"

"Theresa's beautiful, son. She can walk into a crowd and turn heads. That is what every man needs—"

"Oh, really? Arm candy? You think that is all I need in a woman? You think having a showpiece, a trophy, is gonna make a good wife? Do you think Theresa's beauty is reason enough to marry her?" Maxwell shook his head. "Mama would be ashamed of you," he said, quietly.

"Don't you bring Clarice into this!" Ray warned, his lips trembling with anger. "Your mama was a beautiful, sweet, caring—"

"I know. And the list stops after beautiful with Theresa. She had a lot of stuff happen to her in her past, stuff she won't even share with me. And it's changed her, and not for the better. She's not for me, Pop."

"And this other girl—"

"Her name is Yolanda, Pop."

"Yolanda, Yolanda. Gotta remember that. So did I mess things up with y'all?"

"Yeah, you did. It's not your fault, though. She was bound to say something soon after the way I had been treating her. Her father is in the hospital, so I sent her some flowers . . ."

"That's smooth, boy. Women love flowers."

"I'm not trying to be smooth, Pop. I'm trying to show her that I'm concerned."

"Well, don't worry, she got the goo-goo eyes for you. Keep this up and she'll be back."

"You think so?"

"Is a Seven Up?"

Maxwell laughed.

"This Yolanda girl, you think she's the one?" Ray asked.

"Maybe. But I would like to find out."

His father shrugged. "If you think this girl, I mean, Yolanda, is good for you then give it a shot. I'll stay out of your business. You're grown, whatever you decide is fine by me."

"Wow, my father is finally letting me grow up." Maxwell wiped imaginary tears from his face and said in a mocking tone, "I'm so proud of you!"

"Boy, shut up! Now what about you giving me a tour of this place?"

CHAPTER 67

Dear Yolanda,
Just a little something to show I care. Hope everything is going well with your father. Do you think things will ever be good between us again?
Maxwell

Yolanda smelled the beautiful red roses on her desk again.

"You ready?" Maxwell asked, entering her office.

"As ready as I'll ever be," Yolanda said. She stood and smoothed her suit. She wanted to look professional, trustworthy, especially when she was about to tell her boss that her daughter was betraying her.

"You look nice," Maxwell said.

"Thanks."

She walked out of her office, following Maxwell down the hallway to Dee Dee's office.

"The flowers are beautiful," she said. "Thanks."

"It's the least I could do. Is your dad gonna be okay?"

"Yeah, he's gonna pull through. He's tough. Thanks for asking."

"How come you still aren't returning my phone calls?" he asked.

"I don't want to talk to you. Our relationship is strictly business from now on, okay?"

"Yolanda, I'm sorry. . .."

"Whatever," she said, waving her hand. "I don't want to talk about this right now. I have better things to do than to satisfy your overweening ego by accepting your apology. Now are you gonna open the door or what?"

He stiffened. He opened the door and Yolanda strode into Dee Dee's office, file in hand with the evidence she had gathered about Jackie: a copy of the e-mails and letters and a signed eyewitness statement from Maria saying she saw Jackie coming out of Theresa's office. She was ready.

"Please have a seat," Dee Dee said, without looking up from her desk. Maxwell looked at Yolanda, then they walked over and sat down.

Dee Dee looked up.

"I understand you have some information that proves Theresa was innocent. You think someone was setting her up?" she asked.

"I don't think, Dee Dee, I know," Yolanda said.

"Well? Who is it?"

Yolanda cleared her throat. She looked at Maxwell. He nodded his head and she continued.

"It's your daughter. It's Jackie."

"What? That's absurd! Jackie would never do such a thing!"

"I have proof."

"Show it to me."

Yolanda passed her the file.

"I've already seen these letters. And this letter from Maria? She's an old woman. She sees and hears a lot of things that don't happen. Besides, it's not uncommon for Jackie to go into someone's office."

"But after hours?" Yolanda asked.

"It may be a little unorthodox, but yes, even after hours."

"Did you see the time at the bottom of that e-mail? Dated August twenty-fifth?"

"Yes, I see it. What's your point?"

"My point is that Theresa couldn't have sent that e-mail."

"And why not?"

"Because she was with me," Maxwell interjected. "With both of us, actually," he added. "We all went to dinner that night . . ."

"What time?"

"I picked Yolanda up around eight. We got there about eight-thirty."

"When did you leave?"

"Yolanda left early; she wasn't feeling well. Theresa and I stayed."

"'Til after nine?" Dee Dee asked.

"Yes, we left there and then went dancing somewhere else," he said. He looked at Yolanda, but she refused to look back.

Dee Dee sat back in her chair, silent.

She pressed a button on her phone and asked Jackie to come into her office.

"I'm about to teach a class. Can it wait?"

"No, it can't, Jacquilyn. My office. Right now."

She picked up her cup of coffee and took a long sip. Her hands were shaking.

"All right, Mama, what is so important . . ." Jackie said, bursting into Dee Dee's office, stopping short when she saw Yolanda and Maxwell. She gave Yolanda a long, hard look.

"What's going on?" she asked, still looking at Yolanda.

Yolanda refused to look at her, keeping her eyes on a black figurine on Dee Dee's desk.

"Sit down, Jackie," Dee Dee said.

"I'm not sitting down until someone tells me what's going on here."

"Fine. Stand. What were you doing on August twenty-fifth at 9 P.M.?"

Jackie looked at her mother.

"Why?"

"I'm curious."

"You're not curious. You want to know something."

"I want to know what you were doing that evening."

Jackie looked at Yolanda.

"It's a simple question, Jackie, answer it," Dee Dee demanded.

"Sure. Me and Yolanda went out for drinks. She was upset because Maxwell wasn't interested in her, but she kept throwing herself at him. She felt like a fool so I—"

"That's a lie!" Yolanda blurted.

"—so I took her out to cheer her up," Jackie continued, ignoring Yolanda's outburst. "I tried to make the poor girl feel better about herself."

"Have you ever seen these letters? Or e-mails?" Dee Dee asked, showing Jackie the papers.

Jackie looked through them.

"Nope," she said, passing them back to her mother.

"They don't look familiar?"

"Never seen them before."

"You don't remember me showing these to you after I fired Theresa?"

"Oh, yeah. Yeah, I remember that now," Jackie said, shifting from one foot to the other.

"Did you write these, Jackie?" Dee Dee asked calmly, looking into her daughter's eyes with wrenching intensity.

"No! How could you even ask me that?"

"You had nothing to do with this?"

"That's what I'm saying! I don't know what Yolanda said to you, but I swear—"

"Maria saw you coming out of Theresa's office that night."

"So? That doesn't mean I wrote—"

"And I know you couldn't have gone out with Yolanda, because she and Maxwell went out that same night. I would love to believe that Yolanda and Maxwell are lying, but so far all signs are pointing to you," Dee Dee said, her voice trembling.

"You skinny crackhead," Jackie said glaring at Yolanda. "I helped you."

Yolanda looked up then and saw that Jackie's eyes were shiny as glass with unshed tears.

"You were nobody without me . . . I helped you get Maxwell . . ."

"Jackie! Did you do it?" Dee Dee shouted.

"YESSSSSS!" Jackie screamed at the top of her lungs. "I DID IT!"

Her face was twisted, ugly. She looked like an animal, except animals don't cry. Slow, painful tears crept down her cheeks.

"Oh, Jackie," Dee Dee said, deflated. "Why?"

"Why? You want to know why? First it was Sheila! It took me ten years to get rid of her, but finally I did."

"You framed Sheila?"

"YESSS!" Jackie screamed, spittle flying. "Sheila *and* Theresa! Two *whores* who tried to ride on your coattails. Look around you, mother! You have this huge empire, and all I want is just a small slice, just a little piece of the pie. But you gave it away, to some stranger no less. So I set out to take it, 'cause I knew my own mother wouldn't give it to me."

"You're so young, Jackie . . ."

"Michael was young! He was only fifteen when he died, and you would've let him rule the world if you could. Why not me, Mama? Why couldn't you let me rule, too?" she cried.

"Oh, Jackie, why did you do this? You would've had everything you ever wanted and more. But you couldn't wait. You never could wait. That's why I would've given Michael the world. Because he would have realized he wasn't ready and would have given it right back. That's what you never understood. You're not ready. And you never will be."

"You are always breaking my heart," Jackie said quietly.

Jackie walked over to Dee Dee's desk and angrily knocked Michael's picture off, breaking the antique silver frame and shattering the glass into countless little pieces.

"Now your heart is broken, too," Jackie said.

She walked out and slammed the door, the walls reverberating behind her.

Dee Dee looked down at Michael's picture on the floor. A piece of glass was on Michael's smiling face and glinted in the fluorescent light.

"Maxwell, make sure Jackie has all her stuff gone by the end of the hour."

CHAPTER 68

"Girl, this is one great party."

"I know. Dee Dee really did it up for Theresa and Sheila. And can you believe she made Sheila partner? I think she probably feels guilty for firing her."

"She probably doesn't want a lawsuit. But if she threw me this kind of welcome-back party, I wouldn't sue either," Natalie said.

"How's your dad doing?"

"Better. He's still in the hospital, and he's going to need to really be careful from now on. Mama already hired somebody to finish the rest of the house, so when he comes home he doesn't have to worry about all that."

"I'm glad y'all patched things up. Is he still going to call you Six O'Clock?"

"I think it would be pretty hard for him not to call me that; he's been calling me that for years. But it's okay now. The name doesn't bother me anymore."

"What? Doesn't bother you? It's been driving you crazy for years—"

"I know, I know, but it's just a name, right? And it doesn't mean the same thing it used to. I really am Six O'Clock, straight up and down—"

"Flat as a board, skinny as a—"

"Okay, I don't need help talking about myself," Yolanda said, laughing. "The point is, I am Six. That's just who I am. And I'm skinny. So what? I'm still a great person, and I don't need a different nickname to prove that. So he can call me that forever; it's who I am. And I like it."

"Who knew that watching hours of Tyra was going to sink in and you were finally going to get some self esteem? Good for you!" Natalie said, laughing.

Yolanda shrugged. "Sue me; she's my favorite talk show."

"I can't stay long; I gotta get back to work."

"Aw, come on, at least stay a couple more minutes?" Yolanda gave her a big puppy-dog expression.

"Okay. Just a few more minutes."

∼◊∼

"What are you doing up here? You better not be working and missing my big party downstairs," Theresa said, walking into Maxwell's office.

"I'm just finishing up," he said, turning off his computer.

"Don't rush. I got us a little champagne so we could celebrate."

"I really shouldn't . . ."

"Aww, come on," Theresa cajoled, pouring champagne into two flutes. "I never did thank you for helping me get my job back."

"Thank Yolanda. She did all the work," he said, taking the champagne.

386

"I did. I've been calling her every day thanking her."

He took a sip of champagne.

"It's weird how everything worked out, huh?"

"What do you mean?"

"I mean, it feels like everybody is getting a second chance—Sheila, me, us."

"No, Theresa." His voice was firm and steady, so there was no misunderstanding. "I love Yolanda."

"What! Her! You couldn't possibly have feelings for that, that bone!"

Maxwell stiffened. "That *bone*, as you call her, just got you your job back, so I think you should treat her with a little more respect."

Theresa ran her hands through her long hair. "Maxwell, be reasonable. Yolanda's a sweet girl and all, but you can't be serious about starting a relationship with her. You both have nothing in common—"

"Funny, I was thinking the same about you."

Theresa's hand trembled and she sat her champagne down on Maxwell's desk.

"I love you."

"No, you don't. You love the idea of us together. Not the real thing." He caught her hand, trying to stop her from trembling. "Face it, Theresa. It's over. It's been over."

She snatched her hand away. "You're gonna be sorry," she seethed.

He left the room, and Theresa closed her eyes. She didn't want to watch the love of her life leave for the second time.

"Can we talk?"

Yolanda rolled her eyes.

"Sure. Talk."

"I haven't been honest with you," Maxwell said. "This whole time I've been lyin' to myself, to you, trying to pretend I didn't feel anything for you. But I do, Yolanda. I care for you a lot."

"Is that it?" Yolanda asked impatiently.

"No, there's more . . ."

"Let me give you *more,* Maxwell. I'm tired of you. I'm tired of you not knowing what you want, so I'm gonna tell you what I want. I know I'm not the most beautiful thing out here, and I'm far from bootylicious. I'm bony. But I'm human. I have feelings. And you may think you're all that, Mr.GQ, with your Armani suits and alligator shoes, but I deserve better than you, Maxwell. I don't need a man to second-guess whether or not he wants to be with me or be ashamed to be out in public with me!" Yolanda said, trying not to cry.

"You can believe whatever your father thinks or everybody else thinks, Maxwell. I may not ever gain a single pound, but I'm beautiful. And if you don't believe that, we never had a chance," she said walking away.

"I LOVE YOU!" he yelled. Over the noise of the crowd. Over the sound of the music. The party quieted as Yolanda turned around, thinking she needed her hearing checked.

"Excuse me?"

"I love you," Maxwell said, walking up to Yolanda.

"You don't love me. You're just saying that."

"I'm saying it because I feel it. My mother once told me not to get the woman I can live with, get the woman I can't live without. That's you, Yolanda. I can't live, no, I can't breathe without you. Give me another chance. I want you to be my woman. My one and only. You bring out the best in me, baby. Make me a better man."

"I can't," Yolanda said, turning away.

Maxwell grabbed her in a tight embrace and hugged her, rocking her back and forth in a slow two-step.

"You are so beautiful, to me . . ." he sang in Yolanda's ear.

She began to cry.

"You're everything I've ever hoped for, you're everything I neeeed . . ." he sang, his voice cracking.

Oblivious to the watching partygoers, he got down on his knees.

Yolanda could barely see, her eyes blinded by tears.

"Yolanda, you are so beautiful to meeeee," he ended, his voice screeching.

Everyone applauded and Yolanda turned and saw that Natalie was crying, too. She gave her a thumbs-up sign.

"Maxwell?"

"Yes?" he said, standing up, and leaning close to Yolanda.

"Keep your day job," she said, kissing him on the lips.

THE END

ABOUT THE AUTHOR

Katrina Spencer lives in Texas with her husband and daughter. And yes, most of the teasing and insults found in this book were drawn from her real life. Find out more about her at *www.katrinaspencer.com.*

2009 Reprint Mass Market Titles
January

I'm Gonna Make You Love Me
Gwyneth Bolton
ISBN-13: 978-1-58571-294-6
$6.99

Shades of Desire
Monica White
ISBN-13: 978-1-58571-292-2
$6.99

February

A Love of Her Own
Cheris Hodges
ISBN-13: 978-1-58571-293-9
$6.99

Color of Trouble
Dyanne Davis
ISBN-13: 978-1-58571-294-6
$6.99

March

Twist of Fate
Beverly Clark
ISBN-13: 978-1-58571-295-3
$6.99

Chances
Pamela Leigh Starr
ISBN-13: 978-1-58571-296-0
$6.99

April

Sinful Intentions
Crystal Rhodes
ISBN-13: 978-1-585712-297-7
$6.99

Rock Star
Roslyn Hardy Holcomb
ISBN-13: 978-1-58571-298-4
$6.99

May

Paths of Fire
T.T. Henderson
ISBN-13: 978-1-58571-343-1
$6.99

Caught Up in the Rapture
Lisa Riley
ISBN-13: 978-1-58571-344-8
$6.99

June

Reckless Surrender
Rochelle Alers
ISBN-13: 978-1-58571-345-5
$6.99

No Ordinary Love
Angela Weaver
ISBN-13: 978-1-58571-346-2
$6.99

2009 Reprint Mass Market Titles (continued)

July

Intentional Mistakes
Michele Sudler
ISBN-13: 978-1-58571-347-9
$6.99

It's In His Kiss
Reon Carter
ISBN-13: 978-1-58571-348-6
$6.99

August

Unfinished Love Affair
Barbara Keaton
ISBN-13: 978-1-58571-349-3
$6.99

A Perfect Place to Pray
I.L Goodwin
ISBN-13: 978-1-58571-299-1
$6.99

September

Love in High Gear
Charlotte Roy
ISBN-13: 978-1-58571-355-4
$6.99

Ebony Eyes
Kei Swanson
ISBN-13: 978-1-58571-356-1
$6.99

October

Midnight Clear, Part I
Leslie Esdale/Carmen Green
ISBN-13: 978-1-58571-357-8
$6.99

Midnight Clear, Part II
Gwynne Forster/Monica
    Jackson
ISBN-13: 978-1-58571-358-5
$6.99

November

Midnight Peril
Vicki Andrews
ISBN-13: 978-1-58571-359-2
$6.99

One Day At A Time
Bella McFarland
ISBN-13: 978-1-58571-360-8
$6.99

December

Just An Affair
Eugenia O'Neal
ISBN-13: 978-1-58571-361-5
$6.99

Shades of Brown
Denise Becker
ISBN-13: 978-1-58571-362-2
$6.99

2009 New Mass Market Titles

January

Singing A Song...
Crystal Rhodes
ISBN-13: 978-1-58571-283-0
$6.99

Look Both Ways
Joan Early
ISBN-13: 978-1-58571-284-7
$6.99

February

Six O'Clock
Katrina Spencer
ISBN-13: 978-1-58571-285-4
$6.99

Red Sky
Renee Alexis
ISBN-13: 978-1-58571-286-1
$6.99

March

Anything But Love
Celya Bowers
ISBN-13: 978-1-58571-287-8
$6.99

Tempting Faith
Crystal Hubbard
ISBN-13: 978-1-58571-288-5
$6.99

April

If I Were Your Woman
La Connie Taylor-Jones
ISBN-13: 978-1-58571-289-2
$6.99

Best Of Luck Elsewhere
Trisha Haddad
ISBN-13: 978-1-58571-290-8
$6.99

May

All I'll Ever Need
Mildred Riley
ISBN-13: 978-1-58571-335-6
$6.99

A Place Like Home
Alicia Wiggins
ISBN-13: 978-1-58571-336-3
$6.99

June

Best Foot Forward
Michele Sudler
ISBN-13: 978-1-58571-337-0
$6.99

It's In the Rhythm
Sammie Ward
ISBN-13: 978-1-58571-338-7
$6.99

2009 New Mass Market Titles (continued)

July

Checks and Balances
Elaine Sims
ISBN-13: 978-1-58571-339-4
$6.99

Save Me
Africa Fine
ISBN-13: 978-1-58571-340-0
$6.99

August

When Lightening Strikes
Michele Cameron
ISBN-13: 978-1-58571-369-1
$6.99

Blindsided
Tammy Williams
ISBN-13: 978-1-58571-342-4
$6.99

September

2 Good
Celya Bowers
ISBN-13: 978-1-58571-350-9
$6.99

Waiting for Mr. Darcy
Chamein Canton
ISBN-13: 978-1-58571-351-6
$6.99

October

Fireflies
Joan Early
ISBN-13: 978-1-58571-352-3
$6.99

Frost On My Window
Angela Weaver
ISBN-13: 978-1-58571-353-0
$6.99

November

Waiting in the Shadows
Michele Sudler
ISBN-13: 978-1-58571-364-6
$6.99

Fixin' Tyrone
Keith Walker
ISBN-13: 978-1-58571-365-3
$6.99

December

Dream Keeper
Gail McFarland
ISBN-13: 978-1-58571-366-0
$6.99

Another Memory
Pamela Ridley
ISBN-13: 978-1-58571-367-7
$6.99

Other Genesis Press, Inc. Titles

Other Genesis Press, Inc. Titles (continued)

Bodyguard	Andrea Jackson	$9.95
Boss of Me	Diana Nyad	$8.95
Bound by Love	Beverly Clark	$8.95
Breeze	Robin Hampton Allen	$10.95
Broken	Dar Tomlinson	$24.95
By Design	Barbara Keaton	$8.95
Cajun Heat	Charlene Berry	$8.95
Careless Whispers	Rochelle Alers	$8.95
Cats & Other Tales	Marilyn Wagner	$8.95
Caught in a Trap	Andre Michelle	$8.95
Caught Up In the Rapture	Lisa G. Riley	$9.95
Cautious Heart	Cheris F Hodges	$8.95
Chances	Pamela Leigh Starr	$8.95
Cherish the Flame	Beverly Clark	$8.95
Choices	Tammy Williams	$6.99
Class Reunion	Irma Jenkins/ John Brown	$12.95
Code Name: Diva	J.M. Jeffries	$9.95
Conquering Dr. Wexler's Heart	Kimberley White	$9.95
Corporate Seduction	A.C. Arthur	$9.95
Crossing Paths, Tempting Memories	Dorothy Elizabeth Love	$9.95
Crush	Crystal Hubbard	$9.95
Cypress Whisperings	Phyllis Hamilton	$8.95
Dark Embrace	Crystal Wilson Harris	$8.95
Dark Storm Rising	Chinelu Moore	$10.95
Daughter of the Wind	Joan Xian	$8.95
Dawn's Harbor	Kymberly Hunt	$6.99
Deadly Sacrifice	Jack Kean	$22.95
Designer Passion	Dar Tomlinson Diana Richeaux	$8.95
Do Over	Celya Bowers	$9.95
Dream Runner	Gail McFarland	$6.99
Dreamtective	Liz Swados	$5.95

Other Genesis Press, Inc. Titles (continued)

Ebony Angel	Deatri King-Bey	$9.95
Ebony Butterfly II	Delilah Dawson	$14.95
Echoes of Yesterday	Beverly Clark	$9.95
Eden's Garden	Elizabeth Rose	$8.95
Eve's Prescription	Edwina Martin Arnold	$8.95
Everlastin' Love	Gay G. Gunn	$8.95
Everlasting Moments	Dorothy Elizabeth Love	$8.95
Everything and More	Sinclair Lebeau	$8.95
Everything but Love	Natalie Dunbar	$8.95
Falling	Natalie Dunbar	$9.95
Fate	Pamela Leigh Starr	$8.95
Finding Isabella	A.J. Garrotto	$8.95
Forbidden Quest	Dar Tomlinson	$10.95
Forever Love	Wanda Y. Thomas	$8.95
From the Ashes	Kathleen Suzanne	$8.95
	Jeanne Sumerix	
Gentle Yearning	Rochelle Alers	$10.95
Glory of Love	Sinclair LeBeau	$10.95
Go Gentle into that Good Night	Malcom Boyd	$12.95
Goldengroove	Mary Beth Craft	$16.95
Groove, Bang, and Jive	Steve Cannon	$8.99
Hand in Glove	Andrea Jackson	$9.95
Hard to Love	Kimberley White	$9.95
Hart & Soul	Angie Daniels	$8.95
Heart of the Phoenix	A.C. Arthur	$9.95
Heartbeat	Stephanie Bedwell-Grime	$8.95
Hearts Remember	M. Loui Quezada	$8.95
Hidden Memories	Robin Allen	$10.95
Higher Ground	Leah Latimer	$19.95
Hitler, the War, and the Pope	Ronald Rychiak	$26.95
How to Write a Romance	Kathryn Falk	$18.95
I Married a Reclining Chair	Lisa M. Fuhs	$8.95
I'll Be Your Shelter	Giselle Carmichael	$8.95
I'll Paint a Sun	A.J. Garrotto	$9.95

Other Genesis Press, Inc. Titles (continued)

Icie	Pamela Leigh Starr	$8.95
Illusions	Pamela Leigh Starr	$8.95
Indigo After Dark Vol. I	Nia Dixon/Angelique	$10.95
Indigo After Dark Vol. II	Dolores Bundy/ Cole Riley	$10.95
Indigo After Dark Vol. III	Montana Blue/ Coco Morena	$10.95
Indigo After Dark Vol. IV	Cassandra Colt/	$14.95
Indigo After Dark Vol. V	Delilah Dawson	$14.95
Indiscretions	Donna Hill	$8.95
Intentional Mistakes	Michele Sudler	$9.95
Interlude	Donna Hill	$8.95
Intimate Intentions	Angie Daniels	$8.95
It's Not Over Yet	J.J. Michael	$9.95
Jolie's Surrender	Edwina Martin-Arnold	$8.95
Kiss or Keep	Debra Phillips	$8.95
Lace	Giselle Carmichael	$9.95
Lady Preacher	K.T. Richey	$6.99
Last Train to Memphis	Elsa Cook	$12.95
Lasting Valor	Ken Olsen	$24.95
Let Us Prey	Hunter Lundy	$25.95
Lies Too Long	Pamela Ridley	$13.95
Life Is Never As It Seems	J.J. Michael	$12.95
Lighter Shade of Brown	Vicki Andrews	$8.95
Looking for Lily	Africa Fine	$6.99
Love Always	Mildred E. Riley	$10.95
Love Doesn't Come Easy	Charlyne Dickerson	$8.95
Love Unveiled	Gloria Greene	$10.95
Love's Deception	Charlene Berry	$10.95
Love's Destiny	M. Loui Quezada	$8.95
Love's Secrets	Yolanda McVey	$6.99
Mae's Promise	Melody Walcott	$8.95
Magnolia Sunset	Giselle Carmichael	$8.95
Many Shades of Gray	Dyanne Davis	$6.99
Matters of Life and Death	Lesego Malepe, Ph.D.	$15.95

Other Genesis Press, Inc. Titles (continued)

Other Genesis Press, Inc. Titles (continued)

Peace Be Still	Colette Haywood	$12.95
Picture Perfect	Reon Carter	$8.95
Playing for Keeps	Stephanie Salinas	$8.95
Pride & Joi	Gay G. Gunn	$8.95
Promises Made	Bernice Layton	$6.99
Promises to Keep	Alicia Wiggins	$8.95
Quiet Storm	Donna Hill	$10.95
Reckless Surrender	Rochelle Alers	$6.95
Red Polka Dot in a World of Plaid	Varian Johnson	$12.95
Reluctant Captive	Joyce Jackson	$8.95
Rendezvous with Fate	Jeanne Sumerix	$8.95
Revelations	Cheris F. Hodges	$8.95
Rivers of the Soul	Leslie Esdaile	$8.95
Rocky Mountain Romance	Kathleen Suzanne	$8.95
Rooms of the Heart	Donna Hill	$8.95
Rough on Rats and Tough on Cats	Chris Parker	$12.95
Secret Library Vol. 1	Nina Sheridan	$18.95
Secret Library Vol. 2	Cassandra Colt	$8.95
Secret Thunder	Annetta P. Lee	$9.95
Shades of Brown	Denise Becker	$8.95
Shades of Desire	Monica White	$8.95
Shadows in the Moonlight	Jeanne Sumerix	$8.95
Sin	Crystal Rhodes	$8.95
Small Whispers	Annetta P. Lee	$6.99
So Amazing	Sinclair LeBeau	$8.95
Somebody's Someone	Sinclair LeBeau	$8.95
Someone to Love	Alicia Wiggins	$8.95
Song in the Park	Martin Brant	$15.95
Soul Eyes	Wayne L. Wilson	$12.95
Soul to Soul	Donna Hill	$8.95
Southern Comfort	J.M. Jeffries	$8.95
Southern Fried Standards	S.R. Maddox	$6.99
Still the Storm	Sharon Robinson	$8.95

Other Genesis Press, Inc. Titles (continued)

Still Waters Run Deep	Leslie Esdaile	$8.95
Stolen Kisses	Dominiqua Douglas	$9.95
Stolen Memories	Michele Sudler	$6.99
Stories to Excite You	Anna Forrest/Divine	$14.95
Storm	Pamela Leigh Starr	$6.99
Subtle Secrets	Wanda Y. Thomas	$8.95
Suddenly You	Crystal Hubbard	$9.95
Sweet Repercussions	Kimberley White	$9.95
Sweet Sensations	Gwyneth Bolton	$9.95
Sweet Tomorrows	Kimberly White	$8.95
Taken by You	Dorothy Elizabeth Love	$9.95
Tattooed Tears	T. T. Henderson	$8.95
The Color Line	Lizzette Grayson Carter	$9.95
The Color of Trouble	Dyanne Davis	$8.95
The Disappearance of Allison Jones	Kayla Perrin	$5.95
The Fires Within	Beverly Clark	$9.95
The Foursome	Celya Bowers	$6.99
The Honey Dipper's Legacy	Pannell-Allen	$14.95
The Joker's Love Tune	Sidney Rickman	$15.95
The Little Pretender	Barbara Cartland	$10.95
The Love We Had	Natalie Dunbar	$8.95
The Man Who Could Fly	Bob & Milana Beamon	$18.95
The Missing Link	Charlyne Dickerson	$8.95
The Mission	Pamela Leigh Starr	$6.99
The More Things Change	Chamein Canton	$6.99
The Perfect Frame	Beverly Clark	$9.95
The Price of Love	Sinclair LeBeau	$8.95
The Smoking Life	Ilene Barth	$29.95
The Words of the Pitcher	Kei Swanson	$8.95
Things Forbidden	Maryam Diaab	$6.99
This Life Isn't Perfect Holla	Sandra Foy	$6.99
Three Doors Down	Michele Sudler	$6.99
Three Wishes	Seressia Glass	$8.95
Ties That Bind	Kathleen Suzanne	$8.95

Other Genesis Press, Inc. Titles (continued)

Tiger Woods	Libby Hughes	$5.95
Time is of the Essence	Angie Daniels	$9.95
Timeless Devotion	Bella McFarland	$9.95
Tomorrow's Promise	Leslie Esdaile	$8.95
Truly Inseparable	Wanda Y. Thomas	$8.95
Two Sides to Every Story	Dyanne Davis	$9.95
Unbreak My Heart	Dar Tomlinson	$8.95
Uncommon Prayer	Kenneth Swanson	$9.95
Unconditional Love	Alicia Wiggins	$8.95
Unconditional	A.C. Arthur	$9.95
Undying Love	Renee Alexis	$6.99
Until Death Do Us Part	Susan Paul	$8.95
Vows of Passion	Bella McFarland	$9.95
Wedding Gown	Dyanne Davis	$8.95
What's Under Benjamin's Bed	Sandra Schaffer	$8.95
When A Man Loves A Woman	La Connie Taylor-Jones	$6.99
When Dreams Float	Dorothy Elizabeth Love	$8.95
When I'm With You	LaConnie Taylor-Jones	$6.99
Where I Want To Be	Maryam Diaab	$6.99
Whispers in the Night	Dorothy Elizabeth Love	$8.95
Whispers in the Sand	LaFlorya Gauthier	$10.95
Who's That Lady?	Andrea Jackson	$9.95
Wild Ravens	Altonya Washington	$9.95
Yesterday Is Gone	Beverly Clark	$10.95
Yesterday's Dreams, Tomorrow's Promises	Reon Laudat	$8.95
Your Precious Love	Sinclair LeBeau	$8.95

Order Form

Mail to: Genesis Press, Inc.
P.O. Box 101
Columbus, MS 39703

Name _____
Address _____
City/State _____ Zip _____
Telephone _____

Ship to (if different from above)
Name _____
Address _____
City/State _____ Zip _____
Telephone _____

Credit Card Information
Credit Card # _____ ☐ Visa ☐ Mastercard
Expiration Date (mm/yy) _____ ☐ AmEx ☐ Discover

Qty.	Author	Title	Price	Total

Use this order

form, or call

1-888-INDIGO-1

Total for books	_____
Shipping and handling: $5 first two books, $1 each additional book	_____
Total S & H	_____
Total amount enclosed	_____

Mississippi residents add 7% sales tax